D0263202

'Diamond is the master of g___

___ng Standard

'All hail the new Queen of Crime!'   *Heat*

'A web of a plot that twists and turns and keeps
the reader on their seat . . . don't read it before bed
if you're easily spooked!'   *Sun*

'A page-turner with a keep-you-guessing plot'
                                Sunday Times Crime Club

'Packed with twists until the last page'   *Closer*

'Deliciously dark, keeps her readers guessing throughout as she leads us on a very secretive, VERY twisted
journey'   Lisa Hall, bestselling author
                              of *Between You and Me*

Also by Katerina Diamond

KATERINA DIAMOND burst onto the crime scene with her debut *The Teacher*, which became a *Sunday Times* bestseller and a number one Kindle bestseller. It was longlisted for the CWA John Creasey Debut Dagger Award and the Hotel Chocolat Award for 'darkest moment'. *The Teacher* was followed by sequels *The Secret*, *The Angel*, *The Promise*, *Truth or Die* and *Woman in the Water*, all of which featured detectives Adrian Miles and Imogen Grey. *The Heatwave* was her first standalone thriller and became a *Sunday Times* bestseller.

Katerina has lived in various glamorous locations such as Weston-Super-Mare, Thessaloniki, Larnaca, Exeter, Derby and Forest Gate. Katerina now resides in East Kent with her husband and children. She was born on Friday 13th.

Trick or Treat

Katerina Diamond

avon.

Published by AVON
A division of HarperCollins*Publishers* Ltd
1 London Bridge Street
London SE1 9GF

www.harpercollins.co.uk

HarperCollins*Publishers*
1st Floor, Watermarque Building, Ringsend Road
Dublin 4, Ireland

A Paperback Original 2021

First published in Great Britain by HarperCollins*Publishers* 2021

ISBN: 978-0-00-848408-8

Typeset in Sabon LT Std by Palimpsest Book Production Limited,
Falkirk, Stirlingshire
Printed and Bound in the UK using
100% Renewable Electricity at CPI Group (UK) Ltd

MIX
Paper from
responsible sources
FSC® C007454

FSC
www.fsc.org

This book is produced from independently certified FSC™ paper to ensure
responsible forest management.

For more information visit: www.harpercollins.co.uk/green

To Anna-Marie – My oldest and shortest sister.

Chapter One

Jason Hitchin walked towards the street Amanda's parents lived on. He was going to make her pay for what she had done to him; how dare she think she could embarrass him in front of everyone that way and just get away with it. No. He was no mug.

Her dad's car wasn't parked on the drive, as they had gone away to spend some time on their yacht in Spain for the half-term holidays. She needed the break, apparently, or at least that's what her Instagram post had said, along with a little sad face emoji, as if somehow *she* had been hurt. Wouldn't it be nice to just pick up and fuck off to Spain whenever you felt like it? Jason had only ever been abroad once, to France, on a booze run with his older brother, Luke.

Every house apart from Amanda's had embraced the Halloween spirit, with webs, skeletons and animatronic witches. None of that pound-shop tat either – really pricey stuff ready for all the kids to descend on the area later in the day. The street was quiet apart from a tiny maskless Spider-Man cycling up and down the same stretch of pavement. He had a bright orange bike – a nice one, nicer than anything Jason had ever owned. It wasn't like he begrudged the kid the bike, but it did remind him of all the broken hand-me-downs he'd had to put up with over the years. Never anything shiny and new like this bike, never anything that was just his. Even the coat Jason was wearing had belonged to his brother first. The best thing about Luke being in prison was that Jason could nick all of his clothes, now he had grown into them.

The kid on the bike tried to cycle around Jason but swerved too hard and ran into a newly planted baby tree, his tyre getting caught in the wire cage around it. He tugged at the handlebars in frustration. Jason looked around, worried the sound of the kid wrestling with the bike might bring his parents outside. Instinctively, he rushed over to assist the boy, who must have been around seven years old.

'Here. Spidey, Stop, you'll damage the tyre. I'll help you.'

'Not supposed to talk to strangers,' the boy said.

'Well, I'm Jason, so I'm not a stranger anymore. I'm not going to hurt you, just stand over there while I get this bike free, if it makes you feel safer.'

'You won't steal it?'

'It's a bit small for me, mate.'

'If you try to I will scream, my mum will come out and tell you off,' the boy said, pointing at the house directly opposite Amanda's.

'Looking forward to tonight?' Jason smiled. He missed having a brother around. His brother probably would have nicked the bike and flogged it – it was a BMX and worth a few hundred quid.

'I've got a bucket we made at school.'

'Bucket. Solid choice.'

Jason managed to free the bike from the steel trap and tapped the tyre to make sure there was no lasting damage. He presented it to the boy, who suspiciously snatched it out of his hands before hopping back on and cycling off.

'Thanks, Jason,' he called out without looking back.

Jason turned his mind back to the task at hand. Amanda's house.

Five months they had been together, and he'd thought she really cared about him. Then he'd found out about her and Rich Carlton, some posh kid they vaguely knew from the Westbrook Academy. An anonymous email from 'a friend' showed a TikTok of Amanda and Rich kissing in the background. The video taken at a party she had talked him out of going to. After seeing the video he couldn't help feeling she had dissuaded him from coming because he wasn't good enough, didn't wear the right trainers or shop in the right places.

Jason had showed Amanda the video and she'd tried to deny it for all of ten seconds before begging for forgiveness. He'd considered forgiving her, too, but he couldn't erase the image of her and Rich. It was all he saw when he closed his eyes. So, no, he couldn't forgive. Plus, Amanda had never really liked him; Jason knew it in his heart. She was only going out with him to annoy her dad, or something.

Jason knew where the spare key to the house was, but if he used it they would know it was him and he couldn't risk that. It didn't matter, he knew the house well enough to know the back door was regular glass and easily breakable. He just hoped none of the neighbours heard him and reported it. With his hood up, he slipped down the side of the house, where they kept the bins, and through to the back. He yanked his sleeve over his fist and punched through the glass before reaching in and pulling the bolt. It was a nice neighbourhood, and nothing bad ever happened here, so he knew there was no reason for any kind of security alarm.

Jason had been to this house many times before, back

when he was welcome. Somehow, Amanda had managed to spin the story and make it his fault she had cheated on him, and so her parents – even some of their mutual friends – had rallied around her to make sure she was OK. No one seemed to care that he was the wronged party in all this.

Looking around the room, he wondered what he should break first. He planned to steal some of Amanda and her mum's jewellery to make it look like a robbery, and so he could retrieve the gold Elizabeth Duke bracelet he had bought her, which she'd refused to return when he broke up with her. At eighty quid, it had cost him most of his savings – there was no way she was keeping it.

Pulling on the disposable gloves he'd brought with him, he grabbed the cricket bat Amanda's father kept pride of place above one of the fireplaces in the living room. It was signed by Graham Gooch and was in pristine condition . . . until now.

Jason swung the bat at the framed pictures on the mantel, making sure to not just shatter the ones with Amanda's photo in them. He considered smashing the figurines on the sideboard that Amanda's mother had obviously spent years collecting, but thought better of it because he quite liked Amanda's mum. Photo frames could be replaced, after all. He could feel his anger mounting as he heard the glass exploding when the smooth willow of the bat made contact with it. When he stopped and looked at his handiwork he felt better, as though this purge of his emotions was just what he needed to get over her, to move on.

He left a few things intact as he moved upstairs to the bedrooms. He felt out of place in this house, not just now, but always. He knew that Amanda was roughing it with him – he was her experimental bit of working class before she moved on to university and found someone a little more within her league. Someone with prospects and a future; someone who probably wasn't destined for prison like every other male member of his family; someone like Rich Carlton. In her parents' bedroom Jason pulled some clothes out of the cupboard and threw them around the place, then put the contents of the jewellery box in his pocket and zipped it closed. He had no idea what he was going to do with it but it wouldn't make sense for the place to get robbed and the jewellery not be taken. Especially not these days, when it was so easy to sell gold.

Finally, he got to Amanda's room. He had lost his virginity in that bed, a month before they got together properly. She threw a house party one night and it had just happened. She hadn't even looked at him before that evening, then suddenly, before he knew it, they were professing their love for each other. She was the kind of girl Jason never thought he would get his hands on. It would never have even occurred to him to try. She was the one that came onto him, she was the one that made all the moves. Then she'd just thrown him away when she was done. Well no, wasn't how this was going to go down. She wasn't getting the last word.

An engine rumbled outside the window and he rushed to look; he would have to make a run for it if it was them back from their holiday. A white van had turned into the street and was pulling into Amanda's drive – looked like a couple of builders. He couldn't carry on trashing the place while they were parked there. He studied the two men in the front seat for a moment before noticing the gun on the dashboard. The hairs on the back of Jason's neck stood on end when he realised they were watching the boy who was still cycling up and down the street on his own. Jason pulled out his phone and quickly took a few photos of the men. What he had assumed were beanies revealed themselves to be balaclavas as the men pulled them down over their faces.

Should he call the police? That would land him in a whole heap of shit. He couldn't just let this happen though. He picked up a sweater off the floor and dialled triple nine before wrapping the sweater around the mouthpiece in an attempt to conceal his voice. He knew his phone was untraceable. It was something his brother made him promise: always use pay-as-you-go phones with disposable SIMs; don't let anyone trace where you are. That's how they'd got Luke on his GBH charge – by finding his location through his phone.

As Jason spoke to dispatch, refusing to answer the questions that might give him away, the engine on the van started again, one man exiting the passenger side and sliding open the back door. Jason felt powerless as the boy cycled towards the van. He knew what was going to happen next, but it still made him sick to his stomach to watch as the scene played out before his eyes.

'Please, you have to hurry. They've taken him, the little boy across the road. They grabbed him and put him in the back of a white van. Forty-six Golding Road.'

He had to get out of there. He knew the police would be all over the place within a matter of minutes.

He remembered there was a shortcut back to the main road and so he dropped the cricket bat and ran out of the house. The boy's bike lay on the pavement, the wheels still spinning as Jason looked on in horror. What had he just seen? One thing was for sure, he was in more trouble than he'd ever been in before.

Chapter Two

Sara Carlyle picked the half-eaten plate of toast up off the living room floor. Marcus had barely touched it, but it was stone-cold and rock-hard now so she would just have to make him something else when he came back inside. She looked at the clock. He had been out at the crack of dawn every day since getting that bike. Still, it was better than every other school holiday when he was glued to Minecraft until his eyes went square.

The phone rang and she looked at the clock; it was just before nine. Who the hell phoned before nine? She picked up the receiver.

She heard the sound of a click before a voice started – deep, clinical, inhuman.

'THIS IS A RECORDED MESSAGE. LISTEN CAREFULLY. WE HAVE YOUR SON. DO NOT CALL THE POLICE OR WE WILL KILL HIM. WE WILL CONTACT YOU AT SIX WITH FURTHER INSTRUCTIONS.'

The line went dead and she dropped the phone, rushing outside. Marcus's bike was abandoned on the pavement in front of the drive where her neighbour usually parked his car. She felt her throat closing and her heartbeat spiking. Where the hell was Marcus? She looked up and down the street but it was completely isolated. There was no one there.

'Marcus!' she screamed at the top of her lungs into the

street. There was no reaction, not even a rustle from the trees. Everything remained completely still. She had to call Peter, he would have to come back from work. She desperately wanted to call the police, but the voice had said not to. She didn't know if someone was watching and so she went back inside and rang her husband at work, frantically pacing as she waited for him to answer the phone.

'Sara? What is it? I've got a viewing in ten minutes.'

'Someone's taken Marcus. They've taken him! What do we do? They said not to call the police and that they would call back tonight,' she said, gasping for air between words.

'I'll be home in a minute. Best do what they say. Don't tell anyone and let's see what they have to say when they call back.'

'I can't just do nothing!'

'I'm on my way right now.' Peter hung up.

Sara stood in her kitchen, the plate of stiff toast on the counter waiting to be thrown in the bin. She could see the teeth marks where Marcus had taken a couple of bites before rushing outside. She didn't know what to do so she went to the living room and stared out at the street. At the bike still lying on the ground. She went outside and picked it up, sobbing as she put it in the garage, safe for when he came home. If he came home.

Chapter Three

The sound of Imogen's breathing soothed Adrian when he woke up from his ever-fitful sleep. He was always relieved when she was next to him in those moments after waking, when he wasn't sure where he was. Heart thumping as his eyes snapped open with a start – this was his new normal morning routine, a moment of sheer panic. But then he would see Imogen and know he was safe. It was peaceful with her there, at least when she was asleep and he didn't have to pretend to be OK or happy.

He reached across and touched her face, but she didn't stir. He didn't know why he couldn't be affectionate like this when she was awake, but in truth it terrified him to get too close. Since *that* night, any intimacy between them had been merely a performance, a part of the act to appear normal. He was sure she felt it too, even if she didn't know why he was distant, why he was absent from everything. He wanted to be able to reclaim that part of himself – he had to, if this relationship had any chance of survival. Maybe this time he could.

He leaned over and kissed her, sliding his hand under the covers, brushing his fingers against her stomach, hoping he would be able to go through with it. She stirred, at first pulling away and then reaching up to draw him closer, her hand on the back of his head, gently balling his hair into a fist. That ever-present churning in his stomach started to grow and, as her fingers wrapped around and tugged the hair tighter, his throat started to close. He had to get away from her. Everything overshadowed by the feeling that he shouldn't be doing this, the feeling that this was bad, that he was wrong for wanting to be close to her. Would he ever be able to feel close to her again without the sensation of that man's hands on him? Imogen's grip loosened and he pulled back.

'Sorry, I didn't mean to disturb you,' he said, desperate to get away. He wished he had just slipped out of bed without waking her. Every time he thought he could go through with it, and every time the panic set in as soon as she touched him. His skin recoiled at the touch of her hands. *Stop. Please stop.*

'You can wake me up like that any time you want,' she said, running her finger along his lips.

Suddenly, he was in the van again, trousers round his ankles, the man pushing his fingers deep inside his throat, making him vomit . . .

'I've got to get in to work soon,' he said, making his excuses so he could escape.

'How soon?'

He kissed her again, his hand firmly around her waist, and she ground into him. Powerless to stop his body from responding to the friction, he inched back before there was only one way out of this. It had taken him days to recover after the handful of times they had made love over the last year. How she was still with him, he didn't know. She must think he hated her, but that couldn't be further from the truth. She wasn't the person in this relationship he hated.

'We'll pick this up again later,' he said, smiling and kissing her on the nose. A full stop to the current course of action.

He got up and went in the bathroom before she had time to protest and try to convince him otherwise. He pressed his back against the closed bathroom door and

10

tried to compose himself. He had gotten good at hiding his disgust and self-loathing from her. It wasn't that he didn't want to make love to her, it was that he couldn't do it without being thrust back into that van. The few times he and Imogen had had sex since the attack, he'd felt so dirty afterwards. Guilty for wanting it, guilty for using another person's body for his own gratification, even though he knew that wasn't what he was doing. It was as though he'd become the faceless man that pinned him down and taken everything from him, and the idea he could be anything like that had made him sick. His mind was playing tricks on him again. He knew that, and yet logic could not prevail, it was out-manoeuvred by his burgeoning shame.

The shower was almost the only place he felt comfortable these days. Enclosed in a cocoon of steam where no one could speak to him or look at him, he felt free to be sad, or angry, or whatever other bullshit negative emotion was plaguing him at the time. With the water too hot to bear, it was the only way he could at least temporarily feel clean. He'd managed to cut it down to two showers a day, but in the days and weeks after the attack he'd been in there half a dozen times a day, scrubbing himself to shed the skin he'd inhabited on that night.

When he got out of the bathroom, Imogen was already dressed for work and pulling her hair into a ponytail. He felt bad for being relieved that she was leaving.

'I just got a call to a possible crime scene, so I have to shoot off. I'll see you tonight.'

As she walked past him to the door, she kissed him on the cheek and left without even giving him a second look. They had moved from the honeymoon period of their relationship to uncomfortable indifference with surprising ease. He heard the front door shut and then

11

sat on the edge of the bed. He couldn't live like this for much longer. His phone was on the bedside table, and he picked it up and dialled the number of the only person he had told about the rape, besides his priest.

Adrian saw Zoe Hadley waiting for him at the bus stop outside the hospital. Zoe was the duty doctor for the station sometimes and their point of contact on domestic and sexual violence cases at the hospital. After the rape he'd needed a medical note to get time off work and he knew from working with her before that she could be trusted. They had been on a date once, before Imogen, but it went nowhere.

He didn't want to go inside this time – in truth, the place made him nervous. Zoe offered him a cigarette, but he refused.

'Adrian, how are you? Let's walk, I've got some time.'

They proceeded to walk up the road that ran away from the hospital, and he shook his head in defeat. 'I just don't think I'm getting any better. It's been well over a year – why can't I move past this?'

'You've been through a major trauma. Don't be too hard on yourself, there is no set timeframe for getting over a serious sexual assault. I can put you in touch with a therapist, if you want. It might help you process things if you have someone impartial to talk to.'

'I'm not ready for that yet. I'm not ready to talk about it.'

'I understand, but maybe that's how you move forward.'

'I haven't even told Imogen yet.'

'What do you think she'll say? Do you not think she will support you?' Zoe asked.

'I feel like I've left it too long now. How do I tell her I've been lying to her for over a year?'

'I don't know Imogen that well, but she strikes me as a good woman. I don't think you should be afraid to talk to her about what happened to you. It's completely reasonable that it would take time to be able to say anything, she will understand that,' Zoe said.

'I don't even know how to say the words. And every time she touches me I just want to crawl into a hole and bury myself.'

'Are you feeling suicidal?'

'Sometimes the idea randomly pops into my head, but it leaves just as quickly. I wouldn't do that. It's just so hard dealing with all of this. I'm exhausted. I feel like I'm constantly pretending to be someone I'm not – well, someone I used to be, and I'm not even sure I'm doing that good a job of it.'

'You are doing so well. Really. The next step is for you to talk about it with someone, though – I mean, properly talk about it. There's a men's sexual assault group that meets weekly in one of the churches in town. I'll send you a picture of the leaflet with the details and maybe you could pop along there and speak to one of those guys. They won't judge you at all.'

'I just don't know how to talk about it.'

'Could you talk to me about it?'

'You've already done so much for me. I couldn't.'

'There's nothing you can tell me I haven't heard before. Nothing. So don't think I can't handle anything you might have to say. I can. Do you want to try?'

'Now?'

'Sure. You don't have to say much. It might be a good way to practise.'

Adrian opened his mouth to speak. *What words do you use? How do you put them together? How do you say something like that?* The words wouldn't come.

'Every time Imogen comes home, I think today is the day I should tell her. Every single day. But every day my throat closes as I try to speak and I just chicken out. I don't know how to say it to her, any of it,' he said, hating to admit to his weakness.

'I understand. No one said this would be easy.'

'I've just been in this limbo ever since that night. I don't know what it is I'm waiting for but I need to accept that it's never going to happen. It's like I think life's just going to snap back into place to how it was, and I know now it never will. This is who I am. But Imogen deserves better than that.'

'She deserves the truth so that you can figure out – together – how to move forward. You can't do this alone. It's like rowing with one oar: it's exhausting and you just go round in circles.'

'I have to get to work now,' Adrian said, suddenly desperate to get out of the conversation. 'Thanks for taking the time to talk to me. Again. I'm sorry to be such a burden.'

'You really aren't a burden. You need to stop talking like that, Adrian. You have people around you that love you and will want to help you through this. Think about how you would feel if this had happened to someone you loved. Would you think of them as a burden? Would you want them to suffer alone?'

He sighed. She was right, of course, but that didn't make it any easier.

'No, of course not. I better go. Thanks, Zoe.'

'Absolutely any time, Adrian. I mean that.'

He smiled and crossed the road. He had indulged that part of himself for long enough for one day.

He had to go back to pretending for now. It was safer that way.

Chapter Four

Imogen arrived on Golding Road to find DI Matt Walsh parked and waiting for her. Most of the houses were double-fronted and pristine, but each had a slightly different aesthetic, even though they looked as if they had all been built at the same time. They were colonial in style, with lots of whites and greys, almost as though there was a uniform colour scheme that had been agreed. It was a modern development playing at old-school charm. Shutters flanked the windows and small sculpted hedges covered in fake cobwebs trimmed the uniform front gardens. Even though the developers had gone to great pains to diversify the property designs, there was something very Stepford about the small cul-de-sac.

Imogen had been to estates like this before. A faux-eclectic mix of houses, all under strict rules about what colours they could paint their exteriors and how high their hedges were allowed to be. There were alleys that cut off into almost identical streets. It was an overpriced part of town and anyone who lived here most likely had a few quid in the bank. This was echoed in the tasteful Halloween decorations, nothing overtly scary and only the best organic pumpkins on display, some professionally carved as though entered into some imaginary competition. Imogen imagined the sweet treats on offer tonight from these houses wouldn't be from your supermarket variety packs.

This possible kidnapping was Imogen's first solo posting in her Family Liaison Officer capacity. She had trained last year to become a FLO and recently finished her probation period. It was just an extension of her Detective Sergeant duties and she had jumped at the opportunity when it arose, desperate to spend as much time at work as possible.

'Have you been waiting long?' Imogen asked, eyeing up the surroundings.

'Literally just got here,' Walsh said, squinting into the low autumn sun, his hair showing silver in the light.

'So, what's the story?' Imogen said.

'Anonymous phone call suggesting possible kidnapping. The caller said a boy was taken across the street from forty-six Golding Road, but a uniform tried forty-six and there was no one home. Looking through to the lounge it all seems a bit smashed up, but there is no young boy listed as living at that house. Just a family with a teenage girl.'

Imogen walked up to the house the call had supposedly come from. It was the only one that didn't appear to have any Halloween decorations. It was set back from the road and had shutters on the inside of the windows. The angle of the slats on the shutters meant she could look inside and, sure enough, there was debris and a mess on the floor. She walked to the front door and peered through the letterbox, spotting a pile of mail left on the mat. She could see a cat bed in the hall, so it was entirely possible a cat had knocked the stuff from the mantel onto the floor. Imogen's mother had had cats and pushing stuff off things was their second favourite thing to do, after eating.

'Any idea where the occupants are?'

'Was waiting for you. What are your instincts on this one? I've got a bad feeling.'

'Did the call say across the street? Do you think they meant the house opposite?' Imogen said.

She looked back across the driveway onto the street. The way the low hedges were arranged it was most likely that the neighbours opposite would have seen something if anything had indeed happened. Imogen walked across the road, DI Walsh following her, and knocked on the door of number forty-seven. She looked around the yard and saw an abandoned Nerf gun on the front lawn, along with several neon-orange Nerf bullets in the grass and a clumsily carved jack-o'-lantern on the front step.

A few moments later, the door opened. The woman who answered was breathless and looked confused when she saw them; it was clear she had been crying. Seconds later, a man opened the door further and ushered her back into the house, but the woman just took a step backwards and looked at Imogen expectantly.

Matt Walsh pulled out his warrant card. 'I'm DI Walsh, this is my colleague DS Grey. We had a call about a disturbance. I don't suppose you know anything about that, do you? Did you hear or see anything unusual this morning?'

'No, I'm sorry,' the man said. 'We don't know anything about that.'

'Do you have a son?' Imogen asked.

'Why would you need to know that?' he asked.

Imogen could see the wife holding her breath and wringing her hands together.

'Could I speak to your son? Maybe he saw something.'

'I'm afraid he's not here right now. He stayed at a friend's house last night.'

'What are your names, please?' DI Walsh said, pulling out his notepad, which, Imogen observed, made the husband tense up immediately.

The wife's face contorted with anxiety, telling Imogen she desperately wanted to speak.

'My name is Peter Carlyle and my wife here is Sara Carlyle. Now, if you don't mind, we don't have time for this. I have to get to work.'

'What's your son's name?' Imogen asked.

'Marcus,' Sara Carlyle whispered, her voice fragmenting as she said it.

'Are you OK, Mrs Carlyle?' Imogen asked.

'Yes, sorry. I just have a migraine.'

'She gets them quite often – don't you, love? She just needs a lie-down,' Peter Carlyle said, rubbing his wife's hand, which seemed only to irritate her.

'OK. Well, let us know if you hear anything,' DI Walsh said before shutting his notepad and stepping back from the door.

Imogen kept her eyes on Sara Carlyle's face as the door closed and, as they walked back towards the car, she became increasingly convinced that something wasn't right. She had heard the 999 call and the caller had sounded genuinely panicked, something that was hard to fake.

'Why would someone call in a fake kidnap?' she asked as Walsh put his hand on the car door.

'I don't know. To mess us around?'

'The wife. . . did she seem OK to you?'

'No, but they said she had a migraine.'

'I say a lot of things, doesn't make them true.'

'I'll bear that in mind,' Walsh said with a half-smile.

'I think they're hiding something. I've had my fair share of migraines and the wife looked bereft to me, not in physical pain.'

'You want to go back and ask more questions?'

'I think we should, yeah. It doesn't feel right to just leave.'

'Your call. Let's do it.'

Imogen marched back up to the house and knocked on the door again. Through it she could hear Peter Carlyle speaking to his wife in a terse manner, clearly trying to calm. Seconds later, the door opened and Peter Carlyle's strained smile greeted them.

'Could you tell us about your neighbours across the way?' Imogen said, her eyes trained on Sara Carlyle, who seemed to be urging Imogen to ask something specific.

'They are away, as far as I know. Why?'

'Sorry, can I just clarify something? You said your son was staying at a friend's house. Is he somewhere local?' Imogen said, still looking at Sara who was rubbing her knuckles nervously.

'Look, this is silly. We told you we don't know anything, now leave us alone,' Peter Carlyle implored with a hint of a laugh, but Imogen could hear the tension in his voice.

'Where's your son, Mrs Carlyle?' Imogen directed the question at Sara.

Seconds later Sara Carlyle clasped her face in her hands and sank to the floor. Peter Carlyle rushed to her side and pulled her up.

'I think we had better come in, don't you?' Imogen said and Sara nodded immediately. Peter Carlyle seemed more reserved about the situation – whatever the situation was – but he acquiesced and nodded for them to come inside. The Carlyles led them through to the kitchen and Sara steadied herself as she sat at the table.

'My son Marcus has gone missing,' Peter Carlyle said eventually.

'When? How long ago?' Imogen pulled out her own notebook and started writing.

'About an hour ago. He was outside cycling. He got

a new bike for his birthday and he's been riding it up and down the street relentlessly for the last couple of weeks. He's probably just wandered off to a friend's house.'

'How old is he?'

'He's only six. He was just outside the house. I only stopped watching him to put the washing in,' Sara added.

'And where were you at this time, Mr Carlyle?'

'I was at work, my wife called me and I came straight home.'

'And is his bike missing, too? What colour is it?' Imogen asked.

'No. I found that on the drive. It's an orange BMX,' Sara said.

'A stunt bike? What type? They can be pretty pricey,' Imogen said.

'It was a Fit 2021 Misfit. It cost about four hundred,' Peter Carlyle said, clearly agitated that they were still there and asking them questions.

'So, he definitely wouldn't just abandon it,' Walsh said.

'No, he wouldn't have just left it on the street. He was so careful with it. He's been after one for months – his friend got one for his birthday, you see, so he wanted one, too,' Sara said, a numbness creeping into her voice.

'Is there something you aren't telling us here?' Imogen asked. 'Has anyone contacted you about your son's whereabouts?'

Both relief and fear passed over Sara's face. She was definitely holding something back. She looked to her husband for permission to speak but his face remained blank and tense. Imogen simply stared until he finally exhaled and put his hand on his wife's shoulder. Permission granted.

'A man called. Told me not to contact the police, told

me they had Marcus. Can I ask, how did you know to come here?' Sara said.

'Someone reported seeing a boy being taken off the street and put into a vehicle. Is your neighbour across the road away for long, do you know?' Imogen asked, noting down everything the Carlyles were telling them.

'They are on holiday – in Spain, I think. They went as soon as the schools broke up. I don't have any contact details for them though, I'm sorry,' Sara added. 'They have a boat so they're usually out of contact for a couple of weeks when they go away.'

If the neighbours weren't there, someone else must have reported the kidnapping from inside the house. A burglar with a conscience? It was entirely possible, but it was also entirely possible that something innocent had happened: maybe that's just how the neighbours kept their lounge. As there had been no reports of a break-in, Imogen and Walsh would just have to contact the owners and see if anyone they knew had been inside earlier in the morning.

'Do they have a cat?' Imogen asked, looking to prove her earlier theory that a cat might be responsible for the mess she had seen through the window across the road.

'Yes, Misty. Horrible thing. What's that got to do with anything?' Peter Carlyle said.

'Did the man on the phone sound familiar to you?' Imogen said to Sara, ignoring the remark from her husband.

'No. His voice was disguised, I think. It sounded a bit robotic.'

Imogen thought it could well be a text to talk feature using an AI voice. Hopefully they could get a sample of the voice if the man phoned back. Presumably he wanted money if he had already called once.

'And what time did you notice Marcus was missing?'

'I didn't. I thought he was outside riding his bike when I got the phone call at about ten to nine.'

'What was he wearing?'

'Um, a Spider-Man costume and black and white Vans trainers. He might have been wearing a baseball cap, a snapback – I can check if it's still in his room – it's got a picture of the Hulk on it.' Sara reeled off the list as though she had been waiting for the question.

'What is your relationship with your son like?' Imogen asked, readying herself for the inevitable fury at the suggestion the Carlyles had anything to do with his disappearance.

'What do you mean?' Sara said, completely blindsided by the question. 'We love him.'

'He's six years old, he gets everything he wants. He's a happy child,' Peter Carlyle said pointedly.

'That's really helpful, thank you,' Imogen said. They could pick this up later on.

'Right. We're going to have to call this in to our DCI. The general protocol with cases like this is to control as much of the situation as we can so, for now, you need to not tell anyone else. No one, is that understood? We will also need to keep a log of any phone calls, anyone coming in or out of the house – any contact at all. Until we know where this is coming from, we can't risk upsetting whoever has your son,' Walsh said, nodding to Imogen.

'You aren't going to look for him?' Sara asked, distress evident in her tone.

'Yes, but we have to do it without alerting the media. At this point in time, we have to assume that these are professional kidnappers, in which case it's best to make them think we are sticking to their script for now,' Walsh said.

'What can we do?' Peter Carlyle asked.

Imogen stepped forward. 'Lots of things. You can get some things together for us. You'll need a pen and paper. Speed is of the essence. What I need from you is an up-to-date photograph. And all of his personal details: full name, date and place of birth, along with a detailed physical description, height, eye colour, hair colour and length, whether or not he wears glasses, if he has any birthmarks or scars, if he has a hearing aid, et cetera. We also need details of any medical conditions, like asthma or diabetes, and any regular medications that he can't be without. Information on his school – especially his classmates and his close friends – and anyone your son might get in a car with such as relatives, close family friends, your colleagues, neighbours, et cetera. Also, I know he's only six, but if he has any social media or internet accounts and you know the passwords for them that would be great. We need you to write down a list of questions only you can answer, things we can ask him when the kidnappers inevitably contact you again and ask for money. We are also going to need a DNA sample, so a hairbrush of his or something, and an officer will take your son's passport, too, assuming he has one.

'Finally, we'll need your individual personal details, such as your full names, ages and address, any telephone numbers, languages spoken, your family bank details and any vehicles registered to this address. Do you own any other properties? We need to know about them. Do you have any pets? The more information we have, the quicker we can cover our bases,' Imogen said, trying to think if she had forgotten anything.

'Why do you need his DNA? Do you think they are going to hurt him?' Sara said.

'At the moment, Ms Carlyle, we are flying blind,' Walsh

23

said, 'but the good thing is that we're coming in at the start. Kidnap cases with police involvement turn out a lot better than those without. While you get all of the requested information together, we'll get a tech team to come in to connect to your phones and make sure that when they phone back, we can record them. But remember, you absolutely cannot tell them we are here.'

'We're going to do everything we can to find your son,' Imogen said.

'Thank you. Sorry, I've forgotten your name,' Sara said.

'I'm DS Imogen Grey. Can I use your garden to make a quick call? I'll be back momentarily.' She tried to give a comforting smile before leaving the house and calling the kidnapping in. She dialled DCI Kapoor.

The call was answered quickly; evidently it had been expected. 'Grey?'

'Yep, a boy has been taken. Marcus Carlyle, six years old. The parents have been contacted already and told not to involve the police, so we need to tread carefully in case someone is watching. Walsh is inside now getting any pertinent information about the boy and the family. The couple – Peter and Sara Carlyle – have no idea who might have called the police. Should we quietly canvas the neighbourhood?'

'No. As we don't know yet if this a straight-up abduction or a kidnap with ransom, we need to do things differently. I've already called the Anti Kidnap and Extortion Unit for advice and they said they can have someone with us in a couple of hours. My contact has sent through a list of things we can do until he gets here, but the overall advice is to keep this as small as possible for as long as we can. If word gets out, we'll be inundated with false sightings and information. Remember, this is not the same as a child rescue alert situation – we have to assume the kidnappers are organised and for now our best play is not to spook them.'

'OK, ma'am. I feel like I've already made a connection with the mother,' Imogen said.

'OK, I will speak to the FLO coordinator and get someone over to assist.'

'Gary will be with you soon to set up the phones and some surveillance equipment,' Kapoor added, referring to Gary Tunney, their forensic tech specialist. 'When he arrives, stay in one room, if you can, so Gary can sweep for anything that shouldn't be in the house. The kidnappers may have set up something to monitor what the family does. Also, check out the kid's room and see if there is any evidence that he's run away, just to be sure.'

'OK.'

'Let's make the best use of the time we have and let's just hope the kidnappers don't yet know we're involved. I'll get someone on this end to go through the traffic cams and see if there have been any sightings of the white van the triple-nine caller mentioned. In the meantime, keep me updated on any developments at your end and I'll let you know when the AKEU support is here.'

The phone rang off and Imogen looked back into the house. The next few hours were crucial – the golden hours, they called them – because, the more time went on, the further away Marcus Carlyle could be taken by his kidnappers. It had been over an hour since the mother had realised the child was gone, and about fifteen minutes longer since the phone call to the police – which had taken place while the kidnap was in progress. This definitely gave them an edge when it came to gathering

CCTV evidence: that fifteen-minute window could hold a wealth of information. Imogen took a breath before heading back into the house.

'Mrs Carlyle, could you show me Marcus's room please?' Imogen said.

'Of course, follow me.' Sara got up without looking at her and started towards the stairs, Imogen following.

The staircase was lined with family photos and Imogen could see the Carlyles doted on Marcus – there were so many pictures of him, lots of them posed and by professional photographers, all housed in the same white-painted frames to match the aesthetic of the house. At the top of the stairs, they entered a large room that was brightly coloured and spotlessly clean. On the largest wall, there was a hand-painted mural of outer space, the planets in their correctly proportioned sizes and colours, along with all the moons, each with the name of the celestial body written in white next to it. The ceiling was painted with constellations and nebulae and the bed was in the shape of a rocket – a dream bedroom for a child. On the bed was a silver astronaut stuffed toy.

'Is there anything out of place or missing, do you know?'

'He didn't run away,' Sara said quickly, opening a wardrobe that was pristinely packed, everything ironed and folded meticulously.

Imogen looked around the room and saw there was an iPad charging on the desk. She pulled out a latex glove and put it on.

'We will have to take the tablet, if that's OK. See if Marcus has been communicating with anyone on it.'

'Of course. He's only allowed to use it for an hour a day – Peter rigged the modem so it only supplies Wi-Fi for a limited time every day. Marcus usually just watches Minecraft videos.'

'Well, the techs will still want to take a look. Kids are clever, you never know what they are getting up to online.'

'Whatever you need. I just want him home.'

Imogen took a clear bag from her pocket and slid the iPad inside. Looking at the shelves, she imagined it would have been obvious if anything was missing or out of place, because everything was so carefully positioned.

'Is the hat you mentioned here? Or do you think he's wearing it?'

'He is wearing it; it's not on its peg,' Sara said. Her expression changed quickly as she remembered something. She reached into her pocket and pulled out her phone, clicking on the photos icon. 'I took this photo this morning, actually. It's the first time he's worn that costume and he looked so cute in it when he got dressed.' In the picture, Marcus was pulling a big smile, his front tooth missing and his cap on, tilted slightly to the side, both thumbs up. He was a happy-looking kid.

'He looks very sweet. I'll get a copy of that from you, if you don't mind,' Imogen said with a sympathetic smile. Having a photo taken on the same day someone went missing was a rare gift, even in this day and age when people literally took snaps of every meal they ate.

As they left the room, Imogen could feel a knot building inside her. Cases with a ticking clock like this – with a living victim – were always harder, knowing they had to find someone before they got hurt. She was already feeling personally responsible for Marcus and she had only just got there. *Please let us find him, please let him be all right.*

Chapter Five

Imogen sat in the briefing room with a stack of information Gary Tunney had sent through from the Carlyle house. He'd included all the material they had asked for from the family as well as anything else he thought might be pertinent, such as maps of the neighbourhood, any known predators in the area, and any hits on the family via a search engine. Denise, the Duty Sergeant, had printed everything out for Imogen at Gary's request, and as much of a techie that Gary was, Imogen appreciated his penchant for printing everything off: sometimes nothing beat staring at a piece of paper. DCI Kapoor bustled into the briefing room at that moment with a man Imogen hadn't seen before; she assumed he was the AKEU support officer. DC Ben Jarvis followed shortly afterwards and Imogen resisted rolling her eyes at the sight of him. She didn't trust him and hoped the rumours of him moving to CID were greatly exaggerated. Finally, another young man joined them. There was something incredibly familiar about him, but she certainly didn't recognise him in uniform. He was from somewhere else; it was on the tip of her tongue but she just couldn't quite place him. It would come to her.

'Everyone, this is an old friend of mine, Investigator James Ridgewell from the Anti Kidnap and Extortion Unit in the National Crime Agency. He will be assisting us in this case,' DCI Kapoor announced.

'Thank you, DCI Kapoor. My role here is purely to advise and support you with my expertise gained working in the AKEU for twelve years. Dealing almost exclusively with cases like this gives me insight that you may find invaluable,' Ridgewell said, leaning forward and offering his hand to Imogen, which she took and shook.

DCI Kapoor stepped forward and introduced everyone else.

'After passing his National Investigators exam and completing his advanced detective training and his FLO training, Trainee Family Liaison Officer DC Ben Jarvis is coming to CID with the hopes of working in the serious crime division. Also, this is Family Liaison Officer DC Gabriel Webb, who I know you have also met before. Gabriel served as a PC in the Medway area of Kent for two years before applying for CID. Another possible candidate to join our team. Both DC Webb and DC Jarvis are at your disposal during this case, Imogen. They need to learn, so make sure you use them,' DCI Kapoor said.

Imogen glanced at DC Webb and felt her cheeks flush a little with embarrassment. He looked different to how she remembered him. She had arrested him three years ago, charged him with murder and he had gone to prison, only to be released three months later, after she had unequivocally proven his innocence and found the real culprit. Back then he had long hair and wore eyeliner; he wasn't the kind of person you imagined joining the police, certainly not in the family liaison department. Now his black hair was neat, long at the top but swept away from his face, shaved at the sides and the back. Still on the edgy side, but definitely more practical. According to the rules, there was nothing stopping him joining the police as he hadn't ever actually committed any crimes. The real question was why *would* he join the police after such an ordeal? She hoped he didn't still hold a grudge against her.

DC Jarvis, on the other hand, was an unpleasant man and she didn't relish the idea of working with him on a daily basis. He had asked her out more than once and it had taken longer than it should have to get through to him that she wasn't interested. She didn't particularly like his work ethic, either; from what she had seen in the past he had a habit of cutting corners and passing judgements that weren't his to pass. Plus, he'd punched Adrian in the face one time. There was a sense of entitlement about Jarvis that made her uncomfortable.

She nodded at the DCs.

'What can you tell me?' Ridgewell asked.

'The kid was outside playing when he was taken. Six years old. The mother, Sara Carlyle, was the only parent at home when it happened but didn't see or hear anything. It's a pretty nice neighbourhood and it sounds like the boy regularly spent plenty of time out on the street on his bike, which was brand new and left behind. The husband was already at work when the call from the kidnappers came through and alerted the mother that her son was missing. We think it's possible there was an unconnected break-in at the house opposite around the same time, as that's where the triple-nine call originated from. The Carlyles say the family that live there are on holiday but the front room is full of debris, which is why we suspect a break-in. We're trying to contact the homeowners, but it appears they are on a boat with limited contact.'

'So, we may well have an eyewitness to the crime itself,' DCI Kapoor said. 'Unfortunately, we can't get into the neighbours' house until we have spoken to the occupants but, in the meantime, have the senior tech officer go through the audio of the emergency call and see if he can figure anything out about our mystery caller.'

Imogen slid the folder of information Gary had given her across the table to Ridgewell. 'This is what we have so far. I wasn't sure what information we needed but I just got everything I could think of. Luckily, the mother took a photo of the boy that morning in the exact outfit he was wearing. That's in there, too,' she said.

Ridgewell took it and started to thumb through the pages, occasionally nodding approval at the contents.

'What was the demeanour of the parents when you spoke to them?' he said without looking up from the file.

'The mother was a mess, the father seemed to be trying to hold it together. I don't know though. . .' Imogen started.

'Be honest with me. First instincts are important on this one.'

'Well, the father, Peter Carlyle, he just seems a bit. . . cold, maybe? Or controlling. I don't know. Why does that matter?'

'It might not matter at all, but I am a big believer in trusting your gut,' James said. 'Where money is involved, people do crazy things. Aside from what you have – which I can see is really comprehensive and beyond thorough, well done – we need to look into the family in depth. People lie and conceal any skeletons in their closets, so we need to uncover those and make sure they aren't being exploited here.'

'I will get right on that,' Imogen said.

The mood in the room was sombre. They were all waiting for this James Ridgewell guy to fix everything, but it seemed this was going to be another tedious and meticulous search for a chink in the plan the kidnappers had made. They knew what was going to happen next; the police were playing catch-up.

'Assuming these guys are professionals, they may well have done this before, possibly even several times. The emotional cost is so high that it's much easier to control the people you are stealing from without police involvement. So, they know things we don't. Assuming this is a straightforward ransom situation, they may have a cut-off point where they no longer want to wait for the money and so we can't dick them around if we want to get Marcus Carlyle back alive. Our absolute best course of action is to try to catch them at or straight after the ransom drop. That's the riskiest time for them. The problem there, though, is that they currently know where that is going to happen and we don't, and we can't put any contingencies in place until we know more. The only source of information we have access to right now is the Carlyles. Why were they targeted? Was this opportunistic or personal? Have the kidnappers been watching the house? We need to find all of those things out,' James said.

DC Webb stepped forward. 'What can we do right now?'

'Can you get some officers to pose as cold callers in the neighbourhood? We don't know if anyone is watching the property, and looking at a map there are plenty of vantage points, so go in as meter readers or whatever. Ask the neighbours if they've seen anything, and note any shifty behaviour or responses they get from the neighbours, too. Could use the possible break-in at forty-six to ask about suspicious characters in the area. We don't want to tip anyone off about the missing boy yet. The last thing we need is for the press to get hold of it until we know what's going on.'

'We can sort that out. Anything else?' Imogen said.

'Someone needs to keep an eye on what the parents are doing. One of you needs to keep a constant log of comings and goings.'

'DI Walsh is with them right now and a couple of non-uniformed officers are nearby and waiting for confirmation to go in – we were waiting for your instruction as we don't get a lot of child kidnapping cases here. Didn't want to mess it up. Out of curiosity, why do we need to keep an eye on them?'

'They're understandably emotionally invested and might do something that blows the whole thing and they will blame us for it. I know this sounds callous, but we really need to make sure they follow the plan, as any deviations could get their kid killed. We all want the same thing: for Marcus Carlyle to get home safely.'

'Have you ever lost anyone?' Webb asked.

'Yes. It's not a nice feeling. I don't want to go through that again. Especially not with a child. So, let's get this right. I'm going to look through all of this and get it back to you. If the kidnappers have set a time for their next call, they're unlikely to get in contact before then. The plan is everything.'

'Anything else we should specifically be doing at this stage?' Imogen said.

'The usual. Look through the CCTV, not just for today though, go back over the last few days, weeks even. Whatever the nearest camera points to the house are, check them for a white van, and look for patterns in behaviour. Also, you need to get the boy's schedule for the last week – who he has seen, when he was outside alone, every movement you can find. Ask anyone he interacted with if they can remember him saying anything that might give a clue to who has taken him. Speak to his close friends and find out if he was being groomed online or anything like that. You said the parents own a business?'

'They run a property management company. Well, he does, she's a housewife.'

'Find out who his co-workers are, who she hangs out with, and if either of them are having an affair. Do they owe money? We need to turn them inside out. Someone knew when and where to take the boy from, someone knew how much money to ask them for. Someone knew their home phone number. A professional kidnap is not planned in one afternoon. The chances are one or both of the parents have run into one of the kidnappers at some point in the past.'

'OK, sir,' Imogen said, slightly in awe at the thoroughness of Ridgewell's instruction.

'Do you have a desk I can work from?' he asked.

'You can use the desk opposite mine. DC Jarvis, would you show Mr Ridgewell where to go?' Imogen said. She had only recently stopped referring to it as 'Adrian's desk'.

Jarvis stood up and opened the door, and Ridgewell picked the folder off the table and followed the DC out.

'Is there anything you need me to do?' DC Webb asked the DCI.

'Stick with DS Grey for now. You can go back to the house. I'll coordinate from here and put some officers to use looking through CCTV. We'll also check for any known sex offenders in the area. While you're there, see if the mother will let you go through the kid's room again. There's a chance you might notice something DS Grey didn't. Also, have another look at that house opposite and keep trying to contact the family that lives there. Someone made that phone call. We have a witness; we just need to find him.'

Chapter Six

Jason lay on his bed flicking through the channels on the TV, occasionally checking the news on his phone. There was no report of a kid being taken but he couldn't risk getting in trouble with the police by contacting them. Maybe he was confused about what he'd seen. Surely if it was really something it would be all over the news by now?

Jason's mother was at work and he was alone in the house. Part of him wanted to go back to Amanda's place and see if he could find out anything else, maybe even finish what he had started. He couldn't stop himself from checking her Instagram account obsessively, but she had obviously blocked him from viewing her profile as it was now set to private. She made him so cross. He wasn't sure what he had expected to happen between them, but this felt like a massive punch in the guts.

Feeling like a loser wasn't even second nature to Jason, it was first nature. He could see his life mapped out before his eyes – his older brother was in prison and it seemed almost inevitable that he would follow in his footsteps. He wasn't old enough to be put in the big-boy prison yet and, as he'd heard some horrific stories from his brother about the young offenders' place, he thought it best to keep his nose clean for now. He was angry though, all the time. Angry at his mum, angry at his brother and, probably most of all, he was angry at himself. At least it was school holidays so he didn't have to go and sit in class and be made to feel like a total dimwit as well. Unfortunately, most of the teachers had made up their minds about Jason as soon as they'd heard his surname and realised he was related to Luke, who had previously been expelled for being extremely disruptive and chinning the deputy head.

Jason looked at the photos of the two men he'd taken a picture of that morning. One was slightly obscured and therefore useless, but the other face was clear. It felt real, what he had seen. So why was no one saying anything about it? Why was there nothing on the news? As he stared at the face of the man he could make out, he tried to think if he recognised him in any way. Why hadn't he got the reg number of the van?

The doorbell rang, interrupting him. Jason went and pulled the door open and was confronted with the very unfamiliar sight of his father. He recognised him, of course, but to say it was a shock to see him there after all this time – at the house – would be an understatement.

'Jason? Look at you! You've shot up,' Doug said, as though it were an overnight thing and not something that might occur naturally over the seven years he had been absent.

'What are you doing here?' Jason asked.

'Give your old man a hug,' Doug said, grabbing Jason by the shoulders and pulling him in for an embrace. It had been a long time since anyone had embraced Jason in this way and it was uncomfortable, to say the least. This day was shaping up to be a strange one.

Doug pushed his way inside the house as though he had never left. Jason noticed him eyeing the place on his way through to the kitchen before opening the fridge and grabbing the bowl of leftover spaghetti from last night that Jason's mum had left him for his dinner.

'I should call Mum,' Jason said, unsure what to do. His father was essentially a stranger and it felt wrong for him just to be inside the house like this.

'How about we go out for the afternoon? Are you still into go-karting? We could find a track somewhere.'

'I haven't done that in a long time,' Jason said.

'Well, how about the cinema then? I'd like to hang out with you a bit before your mum comes home and puts the kibosh on it. Where's your brother?'

'On remand up at Exeter Prison. I'm seeing him tomorrow,' Jason said.

'The apple didn't fall far from the tree on that one, did it? How long is he in for?' Doug chuckled , as though Luke being in prison was a laughing matter. Jason was confused.

Doug put the bowl down and opened the fridge again, grabbing the can of mojito Luke had bought for his mother's birthday just before going inside. The longer Doug stayed in the house, the more Jason felt like he was overreacting for wanting him to leave. He was his dad, after all. He couldn't ask him to go, could he?

'Last time I spoke to him he reckoned he would be out soon. He's got a hearing sometime next week and thinks the judge will throw the case out,' Jason said.

'Good lad. They never could keep hold of me either,' Doug said, draining the can and leaving it next to the half-finished bowl of spaghetti on the side. He grabbed an apple from the fruit bowl on top of the fridge before making his way into the lounge and flopping on the sofa. Jason followed slowly behind him.

'What are you doing here?' he asked again. It was the only real question he had but, in truth he didn't much care where his father had been. From what he had gathered from the very few-and-far-between conversations he had heard his mother and brother have about his father, Doug always had some ulterior motive. He was here for a reason and Jason had the feeling it wasn't just to see him.

He thumbed at his phone in the palm of his hands, feeling disloyal for not alerting his mother immediately, but also curious to spend this time bonding with his father. They never talked about him much and Jason always did remember him as being quite a fun dad. Not like some of his mates' dads, who sometimes knocked them around. He should find out for himself what his father was like, shouldn't he? Maybe his mum and brother had vilified him just because he wasn't around and was therefore easy to blame for things. Jason was going to give Doug one chance; first sign of trouble and he was calling his mother. He put his phone in his pocket and sat on the sofa with his father, something he never expected he would ever do again.

'Christ, it's like a time capsule in here. It's like I never left. I remember putting this wallpaper up when you were just a nipper.'

Doug started flicking through the channels on the TV like it was something he did every day. Just like that, he felt comfortable enough to be in this room with Jason.

Meanwhile Jason was completely discombobulated by the whole experience. Why was Doug back? What did he want? He tried to ignore the feeling of dread that was creeping over him as his father laughed too hard at jokes that weren't even that funny. What could he do, though? It was his dad. So many times when he'd been arguing with his mother he wished he had a father he could call and go and stay with. Maybe he was being too pessimistic about this whole thing. It might be fine. It might be good.

Chapter Seven

Working for a private security service was different to how Adrian had imagined it would be; there was a lot more sitting in cars than he had anticipated. Today, Mick Roper was in the driver's seat next to him eating his third bacon sandwich of the day, and the inside of the car stank of it. Adrian and Mick had joined the police at the same time, back when Adrian was still technically a teenager and Mick a couple of years older; the age difference had seemed so much more significant back then. The last police case Mick had worked on had been one in which he'd found the bodies of a father and his children. The man had murdered them before killing himself, just to spite the mother, who'd been awarded full custody. The experience had messed with Mick's head, especially as he'd become a father himself not long after, and so he'd taken some leave he'd never come back from. At the time, Adrian had thought Mick was making a huge mistake, but after the last case Adrian had worked, he could appreciate why. Some cases just got to you in a way you couldn't come back from.

Mick had heard that Adrian had left the police and contacted him before he'd even started looking for a job. At the time, Adrian wasn't sure how he was going to reclaim a place in society after being sexually assaulted in the back of a white van for over five hours. Like a guardian angel, Mick Roper had offered him a position with the private security firm Shieldwall Security, and it seemed too great an opportunity to pass up. Especially when Mick had explained the nature of the work. It all sounded quite boring and uneventful, which was exactly what Adrian needed.

They had been contracted by a client who suspected one of their employees of corporate espionage. It was written into each of their contracts that the confidentiality of company projects was to be protected at all costs – and buried within that clause was the fact that monitoring and surveillance on top-secret assignments was a possibility. Mick and Adrian's current assignment was to watch this one guy and take photos of every person he had an interaction with outside the office while the company worked on a particularly ground-breaking project that was set to go live in three weeks' time. There were two teams working on this task to ensure the man was watched around the clock. Adrian was grateful that he and Mick got the day shift as he didn't fancy being out all night. Things were hard enough at home without adding a night shift to the mix.

So far, the man they were following – Ethan Garvey – had barely met up with anyone. He went for his lunch in the same spot every day, ordered the same thing, stayed for exactly the same amount of time before heading back to work, and then after work headed to the gym to swim exactly fifty lengths in exactly thirty minutes. Garvey never deviated from the routine and, aside from a couple of minor interactions in the gym, he left, went home, ate dinner and then watched TV with his wife. At that point the night shift took over and Adrian and Mick headed home. The main takeaway Adrian had from this whole case was that people were all creatures of habit and he wondered how dull anyone who was following him might find his life. He barely left the house anymore, except to come to work, or maybe go for a run with Imogen, an activity he regretted every single time he did it as she was a much more experienced runner than he was.

'Do you know what the project is?' Adrian asked, breaking the silence.

'What project?'

'The one this guy is working on.'

'Haven't got a clue. They don't usually tell us that part. I've done jobs for this company before. It's usually just information-gathering. Sometimes there's more to it, but more often than not it's just observing the subject,' Mick said with a shrug.

'What happens to the information?'

'Above my pay grade, I'm afraid. Definitely above yours.'

'Do we ever interact with the subjects?'

'Sometimes; depends on the job. For now – for this case – we just take notes and photos and send them on at the end of the day. Tomorrow we might have new instructions.'

Ethan Garvey had spoken to exactly three people outside of work today. Adrian didn't remember stakeouts being as boring as this when he'd been in the police, although he knew he was romanticising the job since he had left. If he really thought about the hundreds of hours he'd spent looking through CCTV footage he'd realise he was lucky to be out of it, for that reason alone.

'Where am I dropping you?' Mick said, starting the engine as the second team arrived for the night shift. Shieldwall was a strange company. Adrian had only briefly nodded at the other team from across the road a couple of times. They'd never been formally introduced, and he had no idea how many people even worked for the company, having met only a handful himself. Mick had explained that, because of the nature of the work, it was important there was very little staff overlap, which was why they liked to keep the employees separate.

It didn't particularly make sense to Adrian, but he was happy to accept the explanation. He'd resolved to be better at blindly following orders in his new life, noting that deviating from the allowed parameters had always been what had got him into trouble in the past. It was all very clandestine and there were a couple of times when he'd felt uncomfortable with what he was doing, but only momentarily. When it wasn't under the umbrella of police surveillance, it seemed seedier somehow.

'The top of Polsloe Road, if you don't mind,' Adrian replied.

'That's a bit out of your way. Where you off to today?'

'I just need to rent a sander from the tool hire place by there. I'm redecorating my son's room. Going to sand back the floors.'

'I hate that shit and I usually mess it right up. Just get someone in. I would.'

'I'm enjoying it. Keeps me out of trouble,' Adrian said, smiling.

They pulled up on the corner of Polsloe Road and he jumped out of the car and crossed the road towards the tool hire place. He slowed his pace until Mick's car was out of sight, then walked straight past the shop and through the streets until he reached Priory Road. It was a nice road with neat red-brick terraced houses and fairly expensive cars in the drives. Everything looked very normal, very neat. Very *nice*.

He kept walking until he reached the house he was

looking for. He had searched the address online and found an image of the outside showcasing a red door and the words 'Elms House' spelled out in the stained-glass panel above the entrance.

Adrian slunk back to the house across the street and hid to the side of it, watching to see who came out. The sound of his heart beating got louder in his ears as he waited, his breath quickening. What if this was the one?

This was the home of a man from the list of names Adrian kept in his pocket at all times for over a year now, usually crushed inside his clenched fist. He had memorised all of them and was gradually visiting them one by one. So far, he hadn't recognised any as the men who had taken him off the street that night in August last year. Before leaving the police, he had printed off a list of possible suspects from the case he had been working on. Mostly men with a criminal record who had done some work for Reece Corrigan, the man they were investigating at the time of Adrian's attack. The events of that night hung in his mind like a sword, always there, the presence of the memory felt with every decision he made, every face he had seen since that night, every voice he had heard. He was starting to doubt himself, wondering if he would even know what his attackers looked like, what they sounded like.

Within twenty minutes, a car pulled up outside the house and a man got out. Adrian knew as soon as he saw him that he wasn't one of the two men he was looking for. One of the only things Adrian was positive about was that the men from the van were both white. This man was not. A mixture of emotions came over him. He felt himself relax, happy he wouldn't have to confront his rapist tonight.

There weren't many names left on his list and he was

afraid neither of the men would be on there at all. He might have felt relief now, but he wanted to succeed nonetheless. What if he never did? Could he live with that? As much as he was afraid of ever seeing the man again, Adrian had to know who he was, and wouldn't stop until he did. He couldn't go through the rest of his life wondering what that man was doing now.

In the weeks after the rape, Adrian didnt think he would ever be able to deal with looking for the men, but as time had gone on he felt compelled to find them. The idea that they were living without retribution became an unacceptable thought. Tentatively, he'd started to familiarise himself with the names on the list, eventually memorising them.

It had been Christmas with his nineteen-year-old son, Tom, that made him confront the reality that these men were still out there, and they could do it again. Tom could just as easily have been their victim, and maybe one day he would be if no one stopped them. So, for the last ten months, Adrian had been investigating when he could, trying to find the men that threw him into the back of that white van and ruined his life.

As Adrian's breathing returned to normal, he realised he had been leaning against the wall for support, his mind blurring out the present again, disconnecting him from reality as he was pulled back to that night.

Not here. Not now.

He couldn't help feeling so alone in this. Composing himself, he started to walk back towards his house via the town centre. For today, at least, he got to go home and play at normal again for a while. Until next time.

Three more names to go. It had to be one of them, it just had to.

Chapter Eight

Imogen held Sara Carlyle's trembling hand as they both stared at the phone, waiting for it to ring. Gary had put software on the landline and both the Carlyles' mobiles to record any incoming calls, along with a location tracker app that connected to his own rig. He had swept the house for any transmitters or cameras and found nothing, so it was likely the kidnappers didn't have eyes on the inside of the house, at least. Outside, there was a connecting fence at the back of the house that the police could enter the property through without being seen from the street. They just had to hope the kidnappers didn't know about that.

The bucket Marcus had made to collect his Halloween sweets sat empty on the kitchen counter. The pumpkin from the front step had been brought inside to stop any would-be trick-or-treaters from ringing their doorbell. Imogen saw Sara visibly wince at the laughter of children passing through Golding Road to knock on doors and ask for chocolate treats on this mild October evening. Life went on.

They sat patiently, time moving slower than usual as everyone grew restless. Imogen felt like they should be out looking, and of course the DCI had people back at the station combing through CCTV, to see if any footage had been captured of a van anywhere in the city between the hours of seven and nine thirty a.m. Unsurprisingly, there'd been no shortage of Transit vans at that time in the morning but they'd been able to rule a few of them out quite quickly. Imogen wanted to be asking the neighbours questions, looking for eyewitnesses, the usual things they did when someone went missing but they'd been expressly told not to do that by the Anti Kidnap and Extortion Unit officer. A few tentative enquiries had been made by officers dressed as tradespeople. She didn't want anything she did to make things worse and so she waited.

She was grateful the DCI had put DC Webb with her. She'd had a connection with him the first time they met; in a way, he reminded her of herself. That was why she'd worked so hard to find the culprit and clear his name after they had charged him with a crime he didn't commit. She looked over at him standing in the corner of the room against the wall, statuesque and unflinching as he stared straight ahead. He had a natural pout, a 'don't mess with me' face, and if she hadn't known him she might have been intimidated. It was good to have some new faces around. They had been operating on minimal support for a few years now but finally they now had the budget to get some new officers in.

Gabriel Webb was quite different to Matt Walsh, who had been her partner since Adrian left. Walsh was a man of few words, and what he did say felt very measured. He and Imogen didn't chat, they didn't banter – it was always work, always business, and any personal information she did know about Walsh had been extricated under duress. Part of her liked that, but she also acknowledged it was hard to get the same level of trust with someone you don't exchange anecdotes with. That's where you find the similarities, how you learn to relate to each other. She certainly didn't feel close to Walsh in any way. She didn't even know where he lived. She trusted him, but not in the way she had trusted Adrian. She missed that close working relationship.

No one was talking, everyone in the room too afraid to speak.

The landline phone rang.

Imogen pushed a piece of paper in front of Sara Carlyle. On it were a list of questions the Carlyles were to try and ask while on the phone. They'd already been briefed that the longer they could keep the voice on the phone, the better, but instructed not to push the kidnapper too hard.

Imogen picked up the headphones so she could listen in on the call and nodded at Sara.

Sara answered the phone. 'Hello?'

'DO NOT SPEAK AGAIN UNTIL I SAY YOU CAN. YOU WILL PAY SIX HUNDRED THOUSAND POUNDS IF YOU WISH TO SEE YOUR SON AGAIN. I WILL CONTACT YOU AT NINE A.M. TOMORROW MORNING AND TELL YOU WHERE TO DELIVER THE MONEY. DO YOU UNDERSTAND?'

Imogen could hear easily enough that the voice was synthetic. It was a little familiar, but American and clearly some kind of AI voice generator. Hopefully Gary would be able to give them more information on it once he had a chance to dissect the recording.

'I don't think I can get that money, not in that time,' Sara said.

'YOU HAD BETTER THINK OF SOMETHING,' the voice said after a short pause.

'Wait! How do I know Marcus is OK?' Sara said, looking at the written instructions on the paper in front of her.

There was a slight shuffling on the other end of the line and then . . .

'Mummy! Mum—'

'Marcus baby, Mummy's here.' Sara clutched the phone, as though if she just held on tight enough he wouldn't hang up.

'REMEMBER WHAT I SAID – NO POLICE. I'LL CALL AGAIN TOMORROW,' the voice demanded before the phone went dead.

Sara was frozen so her husband came and gently took the phone out of her hands and put his arms around her as she began to sob.

'He can't spend the night there. What if there's no bed? What if he's cold? You know he gets scared in the dark,' Sara cried.

'It's one night. We will get the money and then we *will* get him back. Let's try and stay positive,' Peter said, gently rubbing her shoulder.

Imogen looked over at Gary, who shook his head almost imperceptibly. The trace was no good. Imogen gestured for DC Webb to follow her over to where Gary was sitting at the counter. Sara and Peter Carlyle were hugging by the dining table and hopefully out of earshot.

'I couldn't get a trace. It said the call came from Budapest, which is unlikely. Whoever it is knows what they are doing.'

'Is that a complicated thing to do then?' Webb said.

'Not if you know how. You have to wonder how many of these things happen under the radar. It's only by pure dumb luck that we are even involved in this at all,' Gary said.

'My God, that's a terrifying thought,' Webb said.

'Gary, will you be all right here while Webb and I go back to the station to speak to the DCI? You can monitor the phones in case anything else comes through and if you have any issues just call; we can be back in no time. Jarvis will be here, too,' Imogen said, almost apologetically.

'No problem,' Gary said.

'Don't worry. There's nothing to do here for now. Just keep an eye on the parents, that would be great, and we will be back as soon as. I know it's Jarvis's job to do that, but I would appreciate it if you could also note if anything odd happens,' Imogen reassured Gary, who she could tell was concerned.

'So, what happens now?' Peter Carlyle said from the other side of the room.

Imogen walked towards him and folded her arms. He hadn't shed a single tear yet and there was something about him she didn't like. Maybe it was how he comforted his wife; it felt controlling in some way. Or maybe there was a simpler explanation. Either way, she felt compelled to keep an eye on him.

'For now, nothing. We just wait. I'm going back to the station with DC Webb to see if any of our avenues of investigation have come to anything. DC Jarvis will stay here with you and be your point of contact for now. He can reach me at any time and I will come straight back if you need me.'

'What about the money?' Peter said.

'Do you have that amount of money?' Imogen asked.

'Not really. And definitely not by tomorrow morning. If we sold our share of the business, then maybe, but we couldn't do it in that short space of time. Not a chance.'

'My dad . . . we could ask my dad,' Sara said.

'Do you think he would?' Peter said.

'For Marcus, of course he would.'

'Our best chance of recovering Marcus is to pay the ransom,' Imogen said.

'What if we can't get the money in time? Can you catch these men?'

'We will do our absolute best. Kidnapping is high-risk

for the criminals too because it's not a crime they carry out and walk away from – the crime happens in at least two parts. Our best opportunity to find these men is through a handover where they have to make themselves vulnerable in order to get the money. We have very limited information and limited evidence of the original crime. This ransom is our best shot,' Imogen said.

'Have you worked on a kidnapping before?'

'Not me specifically, but we have a specialist in to advise us on the best course of action.' Imogen tried to reassure Sara.

'What if it all goes wrong? What happens to Marcus then?' Sara said.

'Can I speak?' Gary said from his station at the breakfast counter.

'Of course,' Imogen said.

'I *have* worked on a couple of cases like this before and I was told there are three possibilities in a kidnap case. The first is that Marcus was taken by experienced kidnappers and all they will want is a pay day – it's a business to them and so they will want to be in and out as fast as possible. Second possibility is that your son was taken by amateurs who are also just looking for money – in which case there is a higher chance of something going wrong because they are stressed out and don't really know what they are doing. And the third possibility is that they have no intention of giving you your son back after getting the ransom. If that's the case, they might try and get money for him some other way if things don't go the way they want. The best thing you can do is get the money together and let DI Walsh and DS Grey find these people.'

'Oh my God!' Sara sobbed.

'For what it's worth, I think you are dealing with

50

professionals, which is good news. If you pay the ransom, then they will give your son back. They might be able to hide a kidnapping, but they can't hide a body because that means the police would get involved. For now, they don't know we are involved and clearly do not want us to be so it's in their best interests for all of this to go smoothly and for them to return your son. The money really is your best bet,' Gary said gently.

'I agree,' Imogen said, Marcus Carlyle's scared voice still reverberating in her mind. 'We're going to go now and leave you for a little while and check on how we are getting on with the search. OK? Mr Tunney and DC Jarvis here will stay with you. We won't be long,' she promised. She needed to get out of there in order to feel like she was actually doing something.

She nodded to Webb to follow her before exiting via the back door and walking through the garden, a little of the tension leaving her body as she moved. What a horrific situation for that poor family. She would never forgive herself if anything happened to Marcus Carlyle. She had to find him.

She found herself breaking into a sprint back to the car as soon as she was out of view. There was no time to waste.

Chapter Nine

Back at the station, Imogen was putting together a profile of the parents and their families, as well as of Marcus and his network of friends. Sara Carlyle had an extensive family in the Cornwall area but very limited contact with them. After looking through her social media they'd put together a list of people who regularly 'liked' photos of Marcus on Sara's social media accounts. She was most friendly with her father online; they came across as very close.

Peter Carlyle had no discernible social media presence, or family, and the only photograph they could find of him online was in the background of one of Sara's. There was no law against that. Imogen herself wasn't that big on posting online; she had created a Facebook account ages ago, but hadn't logged into it in a couple of years.

At only six, Marcus was too young for all that and there was no indication he had anything other than a Minecraft account. There were a few photos of him on the school website, but he wasn't named anywhere.

So far, the investigation team was completely in the dark as to who might have taken him and why. And until the kidnappers gave them a location for the ransom drop, it was difficult to prepare for whatever would happen next. All they could do was make sure they had as much information as possible. Typically speaking, every hour that passed, the likelihood of them finding

Marcus alive decreased significantly. If the kidnappers got fed up of waiting, if things didn't go the way they wanted, if they thought the police were involved . . . anything could set them off. They were a variable the police just couldn't account for.

Imogen listened to the 999 call for what felt like the fiftieth time. It was muffled, clumsily disguised. It sounded like a teenager, or a younger boy maybe. He was panicked, upset. The phone's SIM was a pay-as-you-go that you didn't even need to register so she had no idea who the caller was or even if he was from the neighbourhood. If only he had told them more. He had said 'they', which meant there were at least two kidnappers. He had also said 'white van', which was a useful starting point. But there was nothing else of any use on that call. It was so frustrating. Imogen pressed play and listened to the tape again, desperate to find something, anything.

'DS Grey?' DC Webb said.

'Did you find something?'

'I was looking through the list of staff and parents at the school and going through social media stuff, seeing if there was anything to go on, and I noticed that some of the parents have public photos or are tagged in other photos with their kids – mostly from the nativity or the school sports day. Some of the kids in the pictures have been named by the people commenting, and others have school badges and the like.'

'Why don't they make that stuff private?' Imogen said.

'Right? I looked through all the likes and comments on the photos where Marcus appears and there is one name that is common on all of them, and doesn't neces-sarily appear elsewhere,' Gabriel said.

'Who?'

'A bloke called Nigel Twyford. Apparently he's an

assistant at the school. He's not on the staff list but volunteers at the library and at sports events. The school still run clubs throughout half-term so I gave the headmistress a ring to ask about him. She said he starts at eleven every day, which means he was free at nine this morning, when the first call from the kidnappers came through.'

'What else do we know about him?'

'I looked on his own social media but it's locked down, completely private and very secure, so there's not much to see about him there. But then I searched his name and saw it appear on one of those forum sites – an unofficial one for the school – for kids who left years ago, like an alum site,' Gabriel said ominously, with a raised eyebrow.

'What are they saying about him?'

'Apparently, he has been there for nearly thirty years. Always volunteered at the library.'

'And?' Imogen urged him to continue.

'And there have been rumours about him over the years, though nothing has been proven. A few of the people on the forum – men – said he tried to touch them up. I checked over on the school website and it says he does a reading group for boys. Marcus was in it.'

'Shit. You think he had a special interest in Marcus?'

'Maybe. It's got to be worth checking out.'

'I'll check that Jarvis is all right to stay at the Carlyle house for a couple more hours while we go pay this Twyford bloke a visit,' Imogen said.

'If it is him, what do you think he's done with Marcus? And what's with the ransom?'

'Maybe the ransom is just a red herring, to keep us off the scent for a while. Are you OK? This is tough for a first big case. No one likes it when kids are involved.'

'I'll be fine when we get Marcus back,' Gabriel said.

'Let DI Walsh know where we're going then meet me in the car park.'

Was this worse than a straight kidnapping? Imogen didn't know. If this man had taken Marcus, then at least there was a chance he was caring for him and treating him well. There were, of course, other possibilities that she refused to entertain until she spoke to Twyford. There had been rumours about teachers at her own primary school, she remembered. Maybe every school had rumours. There was always that one teacher you were advised to stay away from. In Imogen's case, it had been Mr Carol, the art teacher. She had never noticed him being inappropriate, but she knew full well that didn't mean a damn thing, and certainly didn't mean other people didn't have cause to be wary of him.

In this case, however, they had to keep an open mind until they'd spoken to Nigel Twyford. She grabbed her keys and headed for the car, not looking forward to the questions they were going to have to ask.

Chapter Ten

Jason looked at the clock, anxiously awaiting his mother's return from her shift at work. The kitchen was a mess, and Doug was lying on the sofa. He'd had a nap after going through most of the cupboards looking for food, and was generally acting like it was his house. Maybe it technically kind of was his home, even though Jason's mother had paid the rent on her own for the last seven years. Still, Jason couldn't help feeling upset by his father's presence.

'I don't suppose you can get served at the offie, can you?' Doug asked.

'Cigarettes, yes; alcohol, no.'

'Well, that's no good, I want both.' Doug chuckled.

Jason braced himself as the key turned in the lock. His mother was home. She walked into the lounge and barely looked at Doug before turning to Jason with a concerned face. She didn't seem surprised though, which he found strange.

'Would you give us a minute, love? I brought some shopping home – put it away for me?'

Jason jumped up and rushed to the hallway to grab the bags, relieved he wouldn't have to bear witness to his parents' reunion.

In the kitchen he cleared down the sides; anything to stay out of the lounge. He could hear them shouting at each other, his father's voice trying to placate and comfort

56

his mother. His timing was impeccable; Jean hadn't been seeing anyone for a few weeks so there was no man in the house to fight his mother's battles – not that she needed help. She was fierce when she needed to be and, although she had been in many relationships, she never depended on the men to take care of her or the boys. She always said they had Doug to thank for that. Eventually, the rowing stopped and Jason left the kitchen to go back to check no one had accidentally glassed anyone else. He saw his parents kissing and quickly rushed upstairs to his room, shutting the door before he saw anything else.

Lying on the bed, he pulled his phone out of his pocket and looked at the pictures he had taken earlier that morning. It seemed like so long ago now. He wondered if it was all some Halloween prank – maybe that's why it wasn't on TV or anything. Jason looked online and no mention there either. He must have been mistaken, but then what were these pictures? There was a knock on the door and it opened immediately, Doug poking his head inside the room without waiting for Jason to invite him in.

'I'm going to get us all a Chinese for dinner tonight. Celebrate us being back together.'

'You're staying?'

'Your mum's said I can stay here a few days, but I'm not going anywhere. I'm back, son. I'm never leaving again. Now, what do you fancy?'

Jason smiled, hoping it looked more convincing than it felt. What he dreaded most of all was telling Luke when he visited him at Exeter Prison tomorrow. Maybe he could just keep it to himself and by the time Luke got out his father would have done a runner again. Except, what if he didn't? What if he really did stick around this time? Luke could barely stand to talk about him, and Jason was terrified of what Luke might do if he actually saw their father in the flesh again. His brother's temper was what had put him in prison in the first place.

'Can I get sweet and sour chicken balls with fried rice?' Jason asked.

'Only if you promise to give me a real smile. You look like you just found your dog dead. Don't look so worried. It's all going to be great, I promise. I thought you would be happy to have me back.'

'It's not that, honest. I've just got some stuff on my mind.'

'Tell me, that's what I am here for. I won't tell your mother.'

Jason got his phone out and opened the photo gallery. He showed Doug the pictures he had taken that morning. He handed the phone to Doug.

'I went to my ex-girlfriend's house this morning to, like . . . trash it – she cheated on me. And anyway, while I was there these two blokes grabbed this kid that was riding a bike outside the house opposite and shoved him into this white van.'

'Jesus,' Doug said, with a bit of a smirk on his face, as though he was excited in some way, which made Jason feel uncomfortable.

'They drove off with him. I called the police and stuff but it's not in the news or anything, which is really odd, right?'

'That's pretty weird. Nothing on the news?' Doug said. Jason could see the cogs in his mind working overtime as he tried to think of something.

'What is it?' Jason asked hesitantly.

'Maybe we should go and have a look and see what's going on down there. Maybe we can find something out.'

'Why do you care?' Jason asked.

'No reason. Just feels good to help sometimes, you know?' Doug smiled.

Jason had to admit he would quite like to have his dad around, feel a bit more normal for a while. Taking his dad to have a look couldn't hurt, it might bring them closer together. With Luke coming out, too, maybe they could be a real family again. Jason only had the vaguest recollections of what it had been like the first time around. He knew it wasn't going to be that simple though, especially not if Luke had anything to do with it. His brother hated Doug with a vengeance, although Jason had never really understood why.

Chapter Eleven

DC Gabriel Webb was still getting used to everything. Though he'd left prison over three years ago, at the time the whole world felt like it had been turned upside down. Friends he thought he had were no longer of interest to him, and he'd broken up with his girlfriend a few months after getting out, even though thinking about her had been the only thing that kept him going when he was inside. His parents wanted nothing more to do with him and, by the time his name had been cleared, he'd decided he was better off without them. In his tiny bedsit in the shitty part of town, he'd taken stock of his life and thought hard about who he really wanted to be. Knowing how it felt to have your life snatched out from under you in an instant, he wanted to make his count.

He'd thought about the people he admired in life and it all came back to the only person who had ever really given a crap about him. DS Imogen Grey. Once he had made that realisation everything slotted into place. Now here he was, sitting beside her in a car. He had always mistrusted and feared the police but then he'd met her and she'd changed his life, quite literally. That was when he'd decided to join the police.

He'd been worried it wouldn't be allowed because of his prison sentence, but the fact that he had been proven innocent and cleared of all charges meant his record was clean. It was as though he had never been inside at all. He wished that were true. To say the experience had changed him was an understatement. Not wanting to cross paths with anyone from his life before his sentence, he'd moved to Kent and applied to join the police there. As soon as he was qualified, he wanted to come back to Exeter, to show the people who thought he was a lost cause that he had made something of himself. He was here to put things right; he had a lot of atoning to do.

They pulled up outside the cottage Nigel Twyford lived in, which looked like something out of a fairy story. The windows were illuminated with spooky candles and cobwebs, pumpkins and ghost bunting. Everything about it gave Gabriel the creeps, but only because of the rumours surrounding the man living there. To Gabriel this felt like an obvious lure for children. There was a white picket fence and blooms of every conceivable colour everywhere they looked. The gate squealed as they approached the front door, which was flanked by two hydrangea bushes in powder blue.

They knocked and the door opened to reveal a woman. Immaculate from head to toe, she was not what Webb had been expecting. She was wearing a pinafore apron with frills, pockets, and a bow at the back. Her hair was silky silver with a curl in a Monroe bob. In her hand she held a large bowl full of sweets. It was as if they had stepped back in time to the fifties.

'Mrs Twyford?' DS Grey said as she walked forward.

'Hello, dear, you look a bit old to trick-or-treat,' the woman said, smiling. It was like walking in on Snow White sixty years later; Gabriel half expected a bird to come and land on her shoulder.

'I'm DS Grey; this is my colleague, DC Webb. Does a Nigel Twyford live here?'

'Yes. My son. Come inside,' she said without asking

for any further information. Webb felt bad, like they were entering under false pretences. He needed to get rid of that Boy Scout streak he had running through him if he was going to do well at this job.

The house inside was like a museum exhibit, an almost perfectly preserved snapshot of the past, everything well looked after but worn. Gabriel remembered his grandmother having the same wallpaper in her house; he hadn't been in there for over fifteen years and it wasn't new when he last saw it. He hadn't thought about that house for a long time. In his mind he had cut all memories of any family, both alive and dead, it was less painful that way.

The woman led them through a long corridor to the back of the house, and Gabriel had to duck to get into the dark kitchen where a grey-haired man was sitting, his face illuminated by the screen of his laptop. The light flicked on overhead.

'Nigel, these police officers are here to talk to you,' Mrs Twyford said.

'Police?' the man said, looking more worried than any innocent person should as he slowly closed his computer.

'Mr Twyford, could we talk to you about a pupil you work with? Marcus Carlyle.'

'Marcus, yes. Is he all right?'

'Where were you this morning at around eight thirty?'

'I was here.'

'No, I had my bloods appointment this morning, remember?' Mrs Twyford gestured to her arm. 'You took me to the hospital to get my INR levels checked.'

'This morning? Are you sure?' Gabriel said.

'I may be old but I am not senile. Would you like some tea?' she said, smiling to Imogen and Gabriel.

'I'm sorry. No, thank you,' Gabriel said.

'That's right, I was with Mother. Is Marcus all right?' Twyford repeated.

'The school said you have a close relationship with him,' Imogen said.

Gabriel thought he saw Twyford's cheeks redden at the suggestion he had a special relationship with Marcus and, just like that, Gabriel could tell those whispers about Nigel Twyford were a little more than rumours. He wondered if DS Grey had said that deliberately to get a reaction from him. Smart.

'They're a nice family, and he's always been a happy child, as far as I know,' Twyford said. 'I don't see his father at the school very often but his mother dotes on him. What is it they call them? Helicopter parents? She's one of those. Never leaves him alone for a second.' He smiled, never once breaking eye contact with DS Grey.

Gabriel noted the irony of the words spoken by an unmarried fifty-seven-year-old man who still lived with his mother.

The kettle whistled on the stove and snapped the connection between Twyford and DS Grey. Gabriel looked down at his hands. Noticing they were clenched into fists on the table, he splayed his fingers out flat before lifting his head again and smiling, putting the mask back on.

'Right, then. Thanks for your help. We'll get out of your hair,' DS Grey said as she backed out of the kitchen.

'Thank you. Sorry to disturb you,' Gabriel said before following DS Grey outside. She was already beyond the gate and opening the car door so he rushed over and jumped in next to her.

'Well, that guy's hiding something,' DS Grey said.

'He has an alibi though,' Gabriel pointed out.

'We'll see about that. It's probably too late now, but

when we get back to the station put in a call to the hospital and see if you can find anyone who was on shift when Mrs Twyford went in for her bloods this morning. Maybe there will be someone who can help us there tonight.'

'You think the old lady was lying?'

'Look at that house. Did you see all the photos of Nigel Twyford dating back the last fifty-odd years? It was like a shrine. She worships him and if she thought he was in trouble I don't think she would even hesitate to cover for him. Besides, old ladies lie, too. Everyone does if they think they have a good enough reason.'

'And if their alibi doesn't hold up?'

'Then we get a warrant and get that laptop.'

Chapter Twelve

Adrian was alone in the house again. It always felt uncomfortable being here on his own. Being anywhere on his own. This wasn't necessarily a new thing, although his feelings had all been amplified since the rape. Before the attack, he would have gone to the pub to blow off steam after work, but he hadn't touched a drop since that night. He blamed his drunken state in part for the fact those men had been able to manhandle him into that van, though he wasn't actually sure if he would have been able to fight them off even if he had been sober. The whole night had been a harsh lesson in why he needed to sort himself out.

In his modest back yard he had installed a punching bag to try to get fighting fit – or fitter at least. He grabbed the bandages Imogen insisted he wear and wrapped his hands as he headed out into the darkness of the yard. She generally had more experience with anything sport-related; she was driven like that and just seemed to enjoy it. Adrian, however, was not that way inclined. He had always been lucky physically, but time was catching up with him and his lazy ways were catching up to him as well. He had to change, he had to be better, he had to keep himself safe.

He took a deep breath and started to hit the bag. The first few times, his hand smashed on the side and slipped across the plastic covering. Adjusting his stance, he focused before throwing another punch. Moving around as he hit out, not really thinking about anything but thrashing the bag, over and over again. Expelling tension this way was preferable to the nervous energy he gathered when he was on his own doing nothing. It wasn't even about the aggression, it was just the mindless repetition he enjoyed. Not really caring much about his form, all he wanted to do was punch the bag until it hurt to punch it anymore.

After his workout, he got in the shower, still uneasy being naked, still afraid to look at his body in the mirror, thankful he had no nasty visible scars from his ordeal to obsess over. Washing quickly, he got out, got dressed and lay on the bed, just staring at the ceiling. Waiting for something, though he didn't know what.

The front door opened – Imogen was home. Instinctively, he shut his eyes, keeping them closed while he listened to her clatter around downstairs. He smiled as he heard her swearing to herself when she knocked the broom over in the kitchen, something she always did. The thump of her feet on the stairs was followed a couple of minutes later by the sound of the toilet flushing, then the tap running as she washed her hands.

She walked into the room and undressed to her vest and pants before coming to lie next to him, nuzzling into him. His eyes remained tightly closed, despite the fact he was desperate to turn to her, to kiss her, to pull her into him, to make love to her. The feeling that it was wrong superseded any desire he had to be with her, that it was bad somehow to want to be with someone in that way. Logically, he knew that wasn't true, but the message wasn't getting through to his body, which was tense beyond reason.

'Are you awake?' she said.

He couldn't lie, he knew she was only asking because she knew he was in fact awake.

'Hey,' he said, sleepily turning towards her. 'You're late. You catch a big case?'

'A kid's been kidnapped. They just grabbed him off the street in broad daylight, chucked him in a white van and drove off. Can you believe that?'

The words reverberated in his mind; he should say something else before she did.

'That's awful.'

'Can you imagine how scared he was? To just be pulled into that van with those strangers like that? Not knowing where he was going or what was going to happen to him.'

Yes. I can imagine that. I wish I could stop imagining that.

'Did you eat anything? You missed dinner,' Adrian said, desperate to change the subject before he said something he regretted. Like the truth. He couldn't do that to her. He wasn't ready.

'Lost my appetite, really. I spent most of the day trawling through a lot of useless information. I can't shake the bad feeling I have about the dad. That's crazy though, right? A dad wouldn't be involved in kidnapping his own kid.'

'I mean, he could be. Not all fathers are good fathers,' Adrian said.

'We've certainly seen a few bad ones. Like Corrigan,' Imogen said solemnly, putting her hand around his waist and pulling herself closer to him.

Hearing Corrigan's name made Adrian pull away and get up off the bed. She seemed startled by his sudden movement, maybe even wondering what she had done wrong. They had been working the Corrigan case when he was raped. Adrian had got too close to the truth and Corrigan had known exactly how to stop him, how to stop anyone. He'd hired two men to follow him and then sexually assault him. Even with Corrigan now dead, it wasn't enough, Adrian still needed to know who the men who actually took him were, the name of the man who assaulted him. It was over a year ago now but sometimes it felt like yesterday. The anniversary had been and gone, and he'd gone through the motions, just like any other day this year. He had held his breath and waited for the worst to happen, neglecting the fact it already had.

So many of these little cues had been lined up for him in conversations over the last year, as if the universe was trying to force him to tell Imogen the truth before he was ready. The opportunity presenting itself in almost every conversation they had. *Say it now . . . Or now . . . How about now?* Like a constant voice in the back of his mind, it thrummed away. Adrian knew though . . . he knew once he told her he couldn't un-tell her. He couldn't have her look at him like that. It would destroy them.

'Let me make you something to eat,' he said, leaving the room before she had a chance to respond. Pounding down the stairs like someone was chasing him, he rushed over to the sink and splashed cold water onto his face in a bid to snap himself out of the place he felt himself going. Sometimes it was so much closer than others, that abyss. Hearing about the boy in the van, Corrigan's name again . . . It was so near to the surface and he felt those feelings rise again. Fear, shame, disgust and the deepest loneliness he had ever experienced.

'You OK?' Imogen said, standing in the doorway, clearly concerned.

'Yeah. Just a bit warm.'

'You're not coming down with something, are you? You look really pale.' She reached towards him, hand extended to touch his forehead and check his temperature. He moved out of the way; he couldn't stand the thought of being touched right now. He really hated himself for the way he was behaving.

'I'm fine,' he said, trying not to snap, trying to plaster on a smile and look normal. It wasn't easy. Certainly not convincing.

Imogen backed away from him, folding her hands across herself and leaning against the counter, rejection written all over her face, even as she tried not to look hurt. He reached past her and pulled a bowl of food he had saved for her from the fridge.

Why did you do that to her? You absolute shit.

She was so close, but they couldn't have been further apart.

Chapter Thirteen

ONE DAY MISSING

Even though they knew the kidnappers were going to get in contact, there was still a feeling of surprise in the room the next morning when the phone finally rang, three minutes later than they had said they would call. Imogen could see those had been some of the longest three minutes of Sara Carlyle's life. What if they never called again? What if that was it? What if Marcus was gone? Imogen couldn't even begin to imagine the torment that poor woman was going through.

On the third ring, Peter Carlyle answered. He had insisted on it and James Ridgewell had said there was no reason why he couldn't. Imogen was still unsure of Peter Carlyle, but still couldn't figure out why. There was no particular reason, just a feeling.

'DO YOU HAVE THE MONEY?' the voice asked.

'I can have it by two this afternoon at the earliest.'

'WE WILL CALL YOU AGAIN TOMORROW MORNING AT NINE A.M. MAKE SURE YOU HAVE THE MONEY.'

'Wait!' Peter said, but it was too late. They had hung up.

'What just happened? What the hell did you do?' Sara Carlyle said, standing quickly, her voice panicked as she stared at the phone in horror.

'I just told them we couldn't get the money until later. You were here, you heard what happened. They must know it's not that easy to get hold of that kind of money in such a short space of time.'

'Did you speak to my dad?' Sara said.

'I told you I did. He's getting the money for us, but he couldn't get it until two today,' Peter Carlyle explained to his wife, clearly agitated.

'He can't spend another night with those people. We don't even know if they're feeding him!' Sara said.

'Listen, I know it's hard, but they are going to call again. If you haven't got the money by then we may have to attempt a fake drop,' Imogen said.

'No way. You are not putting my son's life at risk like that. Don't the police have funds for this sort of thing?' Peter Carlyle said, moving towards Imogen and pointing his finger, not something she was a fan of at the best of times. She inched backwards, feeling intimidated, but, before Carlyle reached Imogen, DC Webb stepped in between them and placed his hand on Peter Carlyle's chest.

'You don't want to do that,' Webb said, looking Carlyle square in the eyes. He was almost a foot taller than the other man and, although there was nothing threatening about the way he had intervened, the sheer size of him made Carlyle think better of it.

'I'm sorry, it's just . . .' Carlyle said, unable to finish the sentence.

'We completely understand how upsetting this must be for you,' Gabriel said calmly, but still with a hint of warning to back off. 'We all want the same thing – to get Marcus home safely.'

Peter Carlyle pulled back and went up the stairs. He was stressed and it was understandable, but still, there

71

was something about him that was bothering Imogen. Did he know more than he was letting on?

'Thank you,' Imogen said to DC Webb and nodded towards the garden. They went outside and Webb pulled the door closed behind them.

'Did I do something wrong?' he asked.

'No. God, no. Not at all, great job de-escalating that situation in there.'

'Oh. Thanks. I just thought he was out of order.'

'Tempers are frayed, it must be difficult for him,' Imogen said, even though she wasn't convinced by Carlyle's concerned father act.

'The way he's acting though . . . I don't know, he doesn't seem as worried about his son as he could be – he barely even mentions his name. I guess we all deal with things differently,' Webb said.

'I'm with you, I don't like the way he's behaving. There's an underlying aggressiveness about him I don't like. Now you mention the name thing though, you're right. He does seem focused more on the money than the fact his son is missing. I don't know. Maybe I am reading too much into it.'

'For what it's worth, I think you could have taken him,' Gabriel said, the smallest of smiles creeping into the corner of his mouth as their eyes connected for a moment. Imogen felt a slight flush in her cheek, trying to ignore the fact Gabriel Webb was, physically speaking, exactly her type. He was very sweet, too – a gentle giant.

She led them back through the garden, opening the door again, and, as they both went inside, she walked across the room and tried hard not to look at him after he'd returned to his corner. There had been a connection between Imogen and Gabriel back when she had first arrested him – an attraction. Maybe she was just looking for some kind of affirmation that she wasn't invisible or undesirable. Things had been tough with Adrian lately, and it was getting harder to ignore the fact that he just didn't feel the same way about her anymore. Unsure why she was even still trying to cling onto something that felt so dysfunctional and broken. There was a difficult conversation coming, she knew that much. She just wanted him to fight for them, even just a little bit, but at the moment it felt like he had all but given up.

Gabriel's phone beeped and he went back outside to answer it. Imogen watched him pace as he spoke and she caught her eyes drifting involuntarily over his shoulders and down his back. Instantly, she chastised herself for being such a creep.

He hung up and came back inside, leaning in close to her and speaking in a whisper: 'That was the hospital – the nurses that were in yesterday morning are back in today. I just spoke to one of them and they said Twyford dropped his mum off at eight a.m. but then left. She remembers because she had to call Mrs Twyford a cab when she was done.'

'I'll call Walsh. Hopefully, they can pick him up before he starts work.'

Imogen looked over at Peter Carlyle, who was now sitting on the sofa anxiously watching the news. She had no concrete reason not to trust him but, on the few occasions she had trusted the wrong person, it had been because she'd ignored the warning feeling in the pit of her stomach, dismissing it as paranoia. Trying to give herself the benefit of the doubt didn't come easy to Imogen. This time though, she couldn't shake the suspicion that Peter Carlyle was actually the big bad wolf.

Chapter Fourteen

Imogen arrived at the Twyfords' with Gabriel Webb as the search warrant was being carried out. Sweet wrappers still strewn in the gutter from the night of trick-or-treating before. The dogs had been given Marcus's pyjamas but found no trace of him at the house, and Nigel Twyford himself was missing. His mother said he was at work but, when they'd checked with the school, they'd been told he hadn't shown up today. His car was still parked in the driveway so, wherever he was, he'd either gone by foot or public transport.

Imogen approached the forensic team leader, Karen Bell.

'Find anything?'

'We found Twyford's laptop in the toilet cistern. It's already back at the station.'

'Is that ruined then?'

'It would be more ruined if he had set fire to it. There are things that can be done with it. Gary will know how to deal with it. Other than that, everything was very particular in his room. I don't think he was in charge of his own laundry or cleaning – I suspect his mother did most of it – and the room was cleaned this morning with bleach. It's spotless. Go up and look for yourself though. It doesn't look like the room of a man in his fifties – he has collections of children's books and toys, quite immature tastes, but that's not incriminating in itself, and I don't think it's been decorated or changed since he was a teenager. He still sleeps in a single bed. Not that there's anything wrong with that either, of course, but it's very unusual.'

'Thanks, Karen,' Imogen said, heading towards the staircase. As she and DC Webb passed the window, she saw that Mrs Twyford, who was standing in the front garden, had a scowl that sent shivers down Imogen's spine. Whatever was going on, she had lied to the police just yesterday to protect her son. Imogen suspected there were very few aspects of Nigel Twyford's life that his mother didn't control.

The bedroom was as Karen had described it. Without meeting Nigel Twyford, one would assume it was the bedroom of a boy in his teens. Pictures from kids' shows on his walls, toy cars, games spefically aimed at younger children. Conversation starters maybe? It wasn't until you opened the wardrobe and saw the clothing, which consisted of maybe five complete outfits pressed and folded and one solitary dark suit that swung at the disruption of the open door, that it became apparent an adult man lived here. Of course, none of that was illegal, but dumping his laptop in a toilet cistern after a visit from the police was suspicious as hell.

Imogen went back downstairs into the lounge and studied the photos of Nigel that seemed to be everywhere. There had to be a clue somewhere as to where he was. In several of the pictures he was holding some kind of marrow or pumpkin. Imogen looked into the garden, seeing only flowers. Returning her attention to the pictures, she could see the separation of the various plots in the background and realised that Nigel Twyford must have an allotment. Her gut told her that was where they'd find him.

There weren't many in town, but maybe she could save time by getting through to the mother. She picked up the photograph of Nigel Twyford and took it out to the front yard where Mrs Twyford was still standing.

'Can you tell me where this this?'

'How am I supposed to know?'

'Look, if we can speak to your son then we can clear this up. The more police time he wastes the less inclined we are going to be to go easy on him when we finally find him – and believe me, we will.'

'I don't know where he is.'

'Mrs Twyford, I don't believe that for a second. Do we need to take you to the station for questioning or are you going to tell us where Nigel is? I cannot stress this enough: we will find him.'

Mrs Twyford's pursed her lips and sighed as she seemed to consider Imogen's words before finally offering, 'Barringdon Road allotments. You better not hurt him,' she hissed.

Imogen signalled to Gabriel it was time to go and they rushed to her car. The hope was that when they located Twyford, they found Marcus with him. The dogs not picking up even the slightest trace of the boy at the Twyfords' gave Imogen pause, but they couldn't ignore his false alibi and the destroyed laptop. She daren't hope that it could be this easy. Was it ever?

Chapter Fifteen

Jason went through the doors into the visitors' room and sat at one of the empty tables. He hated being in this building – it smelled strange and he couldn't bear to think of his big brother not being able to leave – but his mother wouldn't visit and so Jason felt he had to. Plus, Luke thought it was good for Jason to see how crap prison was so he couldn't glamorise it in his head, the way Luke had when he was younger.

Doug was waiting outside on the street for Jason. Having his father back was strange enough as it was, and Doug was barely giving him any breathing room to acclimatise himself to being in his company. He was just . . . there. All the time. Jason guessed he was trying to make up for lost time but wasn't sure if this was the right way to go about it. When he'd woken up this morning he'd seen his father coming out of his mother's bedroom, something that made him more uncomfortable than he'd thought it would. Happy families was an idea Jason had given up on a long time ago.

The side door opened and the inmates entered. Jason nervously looked for his brother, who appeared almost immediately. On a few previous occasions Luke hadn't been able to attend for one reason or another, and sometimes you didn't find out till you were already there, so it was always a relief when he saw Luke finally walk through that door.

Luke sat down with a smirk on his face, excited about his imminent release. It was by no means guaranteed, but who was Jason to deny him some hope?

'Look at you, your hair is getting long. You need to buzz it off again,' Luke said.

Jason instinctively rubbed his head. 'I'm growing it out a bit. I want to bleach it.'

'Old-school Eminem. Will look great. How's Mum?'

'She's OK. Looking forward to you getting out.'

'Me too, mate.'

Jason knew he had to tell him; he felt so bad that it hadn't been the first thing that came out of his mouth. 'Dad turned up yesterday.'

'What?' Luke said, his smile instantly disappearing. 'Turned up where?'

'At home.'

'Listen to me, mate.' Luke leaned forward and lowered his voice. 'You need to stay away from him. He's not your friend. You don't know him, not really. I know what he's like. He will make you feel really special then make you feel like shit. Just don't let him get inside your head. He's nothing to us; he's not family, he's just a sperm donor. Remember that.'

'He seems all right. I don't know, maybe he's changed.'

'You will think that every single time he comes crawling back, and every time you will be wrong. No doubt Mum was all over him like a rash,' Luke said as he started chewing on his nails, clearly already fed up with talking about it.

'She was pissed off at first but he stayed over.'

'Of course he fucking did. She never learns. Just make sure she doesn't give him any money. He clears us out every single time,' Luke said.

'Like you said, I don't really know him and maybe this is my chance.'

'Don't let him talk you into anything stupid. It's what he does. How do you think I ended up with this?' Luke pointed at his hearing aid.

'Mum said you were born deaf in one ear.'

'No, I was in the car with that bellend and he was drunk and he let me drive. At eight years old. I smacked into another car – you won't remember because you were only about three. The doc said I was lucky I survived. Still, I get it. You need to find out for yourself. Just watch your back. He will get in your head. Don't let him. There's only one person Doug cares about, and that's himself. Don't get sucked in.'

'How's it going in here?' Jason said, changing the subject. His brother was clearly getting agitated.

'It's shit. What can I tell you? I won't be in here much longer though so whatever. I'll just keep my head down for a few more days.'

'I better get going. He's waiting for me outside.'

'OK. Next time I see you will be on the outside and we can have a proper hug. Love you, bro.' Luke stood and signalled to the guard that he was ready to leave.

'Love you, too.' Jason smiled and watched as Luke left the room. He respected him more than anyone else in the world and so he wouldn't just dismiss what he was saying. There was a chance he was wrong though; there was a chance Doug was for real this time and they could be a family again. His big brother didn't know everything. If he did, he wouldn't have ended up inside.

Outside the prison, Jason walked down the ramp towards his father, who offered him a cigarette.

'I want you to show me where you took them photos yesterday. Like, the exact spot you took them from,' Doug said, a look on his face that said he had been thinking about it for a while. Jason noted he didn't ask how Luke was, and wondered why Doug would need to see where the photo was taken. What could he possibly gain from seeing where it happened? Was this what Luke had warned him about?

Jason kept walking, through town and down the other side, without speaking to his father. It was like he was on autopilot, going to see Amanda again. He did kind of miss her. He had checked her Insta this morning and in the profile picture she was on a boat somewhere in the Mediterranean. He couldn't even imagine that. Maybe she was right to have moved on. He ducked down the footpath that ran along the back of her road – there was an alley you could cut through to her back garden, he had sneaked out that way before. He jumped the wall and then opened the back gate for Doug to walk through.

Jason felt guilty when he saw the smashed glass he had left the day before. He also felt guilty for bringing his father – a man who was essentially a stranger – to Amanda's house. He could hear Luke's words of warning rattling around in his head and could tell he was going to regret this. Still, he led Doug inside, ignoring the mess he had left in the lounge and walking straight up to the bedroom that overlooked the drive.

'Wait,' Doug said as Jason made his way towards the window.

'What is it?' Jason stopped and Doug grabbed his jeans, pulling him to the ground.

'Stay down. We need to be careful no one on the street sees us in here.'

'What are we doing here? Did you see something in the pictures?'

'I saw exactly the same thing you did.'

'So why are we here?'

'I reckon this is a kidnap and ransom situation. The reason it's not in the news is because they are keeping it on the downlow.' Doug pulled a small pair of binoculars from his pocket, which Jason recognised from the cupboard in his bedroom. His dad must have gone through his room. He turned and looked at the house opposite, saw there was a car in the driveway. It seemed odd for a weekday morning, especially as all the other drives on the street were empty.

'That doesn't really answer my question. Why are *we* here?'

'We are here to help.' Doug smiled and winked at him, which made Jason feel very apprehensive about what they were doing. He had the feeling the only person Doug was there to help was himself.

Chapter Sixteen

Imogen watched as Nigel Twyford dug his nails into his forearm and rocked gently on his chair in the interrogation room at the station. He was not the same man she had met yesterday. Clearly, he was holding something inside that was eating away at him.

'Do you know where Marcus is?' she asked.

'I swear I have no idea. If I knew, I would tell you.'

'Why did you try and destroy your laptop?'

'It was an accident,' he said desperately.

Imogen raised one eyebrow. 'It's hard to drop something that size in a cistern accidentally.'

'I was looking up YouTube videos on how to fix the flush. I was balancing it and it fell in.'

'So you left it there and went and hid at your allotment?'

'I'm sorry. I wasn't thinking clearly.'

'Well, our computer guy has taken your laptop to pieces and is drying it out as we speak. It's only a matter of time before we can get to the data on that hard drive.'

'What do you mean? You can fix it?'

'We can get hold of the information on there as soon as it dries out, which will take an absolute maximum of forty-eight hours, although my guy thinks it will be a fraction of that time.'

'But it was completely submerged.'

'Yeah, you would think that would do it, wouldn't you? But no, apparently not. We might lose a few things, but the bulk of it will probably still be on there. Is there something on there you don't want us to see?'

Sobbing, Twyford buried his face in his hands and muttered unintelligible words to himself. He was as close to cracking as anyone she had ever interviewed before.

'I'm sorry, I don't know what's wrong with me,' he whimpered.

'Did you take Marcus Carlyle?' Imogen asked, aware time was slipping away from them. Marcus could be anywhere by now and they didn't know what his food or air situation was. She had hoped they would find him at the allotment and have reunited him with his parents by now. Twyford had been there but no sign of Marcus. She didn't want to admit to herself that they had wasted valuable time going after the wrong man.

'I swear. I don't know where he is. I had nothing to do with that. I didn't know he was gone until you came to my house last night.'

'So why did you run?'

'I panicked. I thought you knew something about me.'

'What is there to know about you, Nigel? Did you do something bad? Are we going to find stuff about Marcus on your computer?'

'No, I swear. I mean, I take the school photos on sports day, so I do have pictures of Marcus. But I swear, if he is missing, I had nothing to do with it.'

'What other pictures do you have on there?' Imogen said.

'What do you mean?'

'I mean, sports day pictures are not a reason to try and destroy your laptop. You said you thought we knew something about you. Something about what you do online, you mean?'

'Please. I didn't do anything wrong.'

'We will find out soon enough.'

'I just look, I don't do anything else. I don't even watch videos, just look at pictures.'

'Pictures of what, Nigel?' Imogen pressed.

'I've never touched any of them, I swear. I just look, that's all.'

'Do you have illicit images on your computer? Pictures of child abuse? Is that why you put it in the cistern?'

'I try . . . I don't want to be this way. I never act on anything, I just try to mind my own business and get on with my life. I look at those pictures because they stop me from doing anything bad. I don't do anything. I never touched anyone. I'm not a danger to anyone,' Twyford repeated, to himself as much as anyone else.

'But you volunteer at a school and surround yourself with young children. Do you think that's wise?'

'I haven't done anything, I swear. Please just let me go home.'

'What are we going to find on the laptop, Nigel?'

'Nothing about Marcus, I promise. I have nothing to do with him.'

'Where did you go after you dropped your mother off at the hospital yesterday morning? Do you have an alibi?'

'I was at the Quay. There was a Bear Cub excursion down there. I went down to watch.'

'What do you get from that, if you don't mind me asking?'

'I don't know. I try not to do things like that but I can't stop. I promise I never hurt anyone though. I can't help how I feel.'

'No, but you can help your actions. Looking at images of child abuse – because, make no mistake, that's what it is – is very damaging to the victims in those photographs. How do you think they feel knowing they are out there being shared and looked at by people like you? Don't you think that hurts them?'

'I'm sorry, I'm so sorry.'

'Did anyone see you at the Quay? Can anyone corroborate your story?'

'I spoke to the Cub leader. I know him. We're friends on social media, that's how I knew they would be there. He posted about it online in the local group. His name is John Wendon. His wife was there too; she will have seen us talking. I made out I was just walking past by accident.'

'You can stay in the holding cell until we have verified your alibi. By then, the images will probably be lifted from your hard drive and we can charge you for that. Either way, you aren't going home today.'

'Can I call my mum?'

'Not just yet,' Imogen said, nodding to the uniformed officer to take Twyford away and shove him into a holding cell until they got confirmation of his alibi. She didn't envy Gary's job of obtaining those images.

She'd believed Twyford when he said he didn't have anything to do with the abduction of Marcus Carlyle. Which meant they were back at square one. All she could think about was that poor kid, alone somewhere, waiting for someone to come and save him. And in the back of her mind she couldn't ignore the sense that they should be looking even more closely at Marcus's father. Adrian was always so much better at following his gut instinct than she was. *Be more Adrian*, she thought to herself. He would listen to that voice in the back of his mind and he wouldn't give up until they found that kid.

Be more Adrian.

Chapter Seventeen

The piece of paper felt like fabric in Adrian's hand – it had been folded and unfolded, crumpled and straightened out so many times that it had lost its form altogether. The ink on the names had faded to a faint pencil grey, although he had memorised them all by now. This sheet of paper had become his comfort blanket in this last year, had given him a purpose to get out of bed every day. He wished Imogen was enough but no, her presence had stopped him from ending it all but now he wanted to get back to a life he could be proud of again.

He thought back to 'before' and how much he had taken for granted then. It felt like a million miles away, unreachable. Even something as simple as walking to the corner shop for a pint of milk was an agonising battle between himself and his fear. Staying like this just wasn't an option. He had to feel like he was *doing* something. He wasn't sure if he was suited to revenge, but he would cross that bridge when he got to it. For now, he just needed to know.

The tears came less and less these days, but they still came. He had finished work over an hour ago but instead of going home he drove to the coast and parked where he could see the sea. He found it calming being here; it felt more isolated than the city and somehow safer because no one knew where he was. Tonight the sea was still, a surprisingly warm November evening. A young couple strolled past his car and onto the beach, cuddling into each other, barely a whisker of air between them as they walked along the sand to watch the sunset.

Being in the car felt better than being at home, than being at work, than being anywhere. Maybe it was the state of moving that was comforting. As he drove, he wondered what route the van had taken that night. If he was traversing those same roads. It made the scene of the crime feel so much bigger than that van. Would he ever be able to shake the feeling of that night as long as he lived around here? There were so many thoughts, so much anger still inside him. Every morning he woke up and looked at Imogen, wondering whether it would be kinder to set her loose, but knowing that if he did there was no guarantee he would be able to stay afloat.

Over the last year, he had tried to remember anything that might lead him to the perpetrators. He was thankful there was so much he didn't know. In some ways he wished he still had a physical reminder of what happened because there were times when he thought he had just imagined it. He didn't know what possible reason he would have for doing that, but it felt so intangible right now, that he wasn't sure it was even real. More than anything he needed a voice, a face, a name. *Something* that would make him feel less out of control. The same handful of moments played in his mind, as though reliving them over and over might change the outcome in some way. But nothing ever changed. He never made any different decisions, he never managed to fight them off, he never managed to escape. Rewind. Start again.

The phone on the seat next to him vibrated. It was Imogen.

'Hey,' Adrian answered, grateful she had pulled him out of the eternal loop of events in his mind. He hated himself for it, but he didn't know how to stop.

'Are you home? I've got a couple of hours off. Should I come over?'

'I'm in the car. I'll be home in twenty minutes. I'll pick up a curry or something on the way, if you want?'

'You sure? If you're tired we could just leave it till tomorrow?' Imogen said.

'Whatever you want, Imogen,' he said. Why couldn't he just tell her to come over? Why couldn't he say he needed her? She was his best friend, not just now but always; the best friend he had ever had and he didn't know how to reach her. They had worked together for four years, been in a relationship for close to two years, and for over half of that time he had been like this. Maybe she was wising up to the fact that he wasn't worth the effort.

'I've probably got a late one tonight actually so maybe I will leave it. Do you mind?' she asked.

'Whatever's best for you. I'll see you tomorrow.'

Before he had a chance to say anything else she hung up. He should have asked her about her day, he knew that, but every interaction caught him like a rabbit in headlights. Being a human being felt like the most elusive thing in the world right now – as much as he tried, he just couldn't remember how. He would sleep in the lounge tonight, in front of the television to distract him from the fact he was alone. Sometimes he needed the pretence of a relationship to remind himself to eat, or drink, or sleep. When he was alone all those regular things he used to do didn't seem so important, if they even crossed his mind at all. At the far end of the beach, he saw the black silhouette of the couple holding hands, their footprints in the sand snatched away by the lace foam that decorated the edges of the rising tide.

Chapter Eighteen

Jason and Doug had been sitting in that bedroom for what seemed like hours. Jason was relieved that Amanda's parents hadn't changed the Wi-Fi password and his phone was still connected; he had run out of data a week ago. The light was dimming outside and Doug kept getting his binoculars out and fixed on the house opposite.

'What are you looking for?' Jason finally asked.

'I've got a sixth sense for stuff like this. Something ain't right. The curtains have been closed all day but there's definitely people in there. It just doesn't feel like a normal house. I reckon there's police in there.'

'You think I really did see a kid getting taken?'

'Yes, I do. And I reckon if it's not in the news it's because they want some money to return him.'

'I should give those pictures I took to the police.'

'No way. You can't get involved. With our family history, you'll probably get put inside or something. Maybe we can find the kid ourselves.'

'How are we going to do what the police can't?' Jason said.

'Kidnappers are looking out for the police. They don't know about us though.'

'I want to go home. Mum's going to be wondering where I am.'

'Jase, we could make a lot of money.'

'What are you talking about? How?'

'For now, we just have to be patient and watch that house.'

'What about the kid?' Jason said into dead space, his father was no longer paying attention to him. Instead, he was looking across the road to the other house like it was a burger or something. Jason could see the cogs turning in Doug's mind, even though he couldn't work out what he was planning to do. How had he ended up in this situation with him?

'I need a piss,' Jason said, standing up, thinking he could make his exit.

'Can I borrow your phone to call your mum and ask what she wants for dinner? We can pick it up on the way home.'

Knowing his father didn't have a phone, Jason unlocked his and handed it over. 'Here,' he said.

Doug took the phone and slipped it straight into his pocket. 'Now sit the fuck down.'

Jason wished he had never brought his father here. He leaned against the wall and closed his eyes; he didn't know what to do.

It started to get dark.

Chapter Nineteen

TWO DAYS MISSING

Imogen stared at the clock in the Carlyles' kitchen. Gary was sitting underneath it, poised and ready for the call. Everyone was ready for the call. Peter Carlyle had got the cash to pay the ransom from his father-in-law Gregory Dunn. The bank were reluctant to hand over such a large sum in one go, and usually a written application had to be tendered with notice for a withdrawal of such a significant amount, but DCI Kapoor had put a call in to the bank manager to get things moving swiftly. The plain-clothed officers were in place at both exits of the street as well as at various other points, including the major transport links at both train stations, ready to follow at a moment's notice.

The phone rang.

Imogen nodded at Sara, who was a woman clearly at the end of her proverbial rope.

She picked up the phone.

'DO YOU HAVE THE MONEY?'

'Yes.'

'WALK TO THE PHONE BOX BY THE BUS STATION ON PARIS STREET WITH THE MONEY IN A MEDIUM SUITCASE AND AWAIT FURTHER INSTRUCTION. YOU HAVE TWENTY MINUTES. DO NOT WEAR A COAT. WE KNOW WHAT YOU LOOK LIKE, MRS CARLYLE, SO DO NOT TRY AND SEND

ANYONE ELSE IN YOUR PLACE. IF WE SUSPECT YOU HAVE ANYTHING CONCEALED ON YOUR PERSON, WE WILL KILL YOUR SON AND YOU WILL NEVER FIND HIS BODY.'

The line went dead.

Gary jumped up and handed a small black plastic object to Sara.

'This device is on open transmit and has a GPS locator. Keep this on you and we won't lose you. We will be able to hear everything you say as well.'

'Keep it on me how? You heard what he said.'

'If you don't mind, either myself, or DS Grey, can tape it just underneath your chest. It will be practically flush to your skin and almost invisible.'

'I'll do it,' Imogen said. Taking the tape from Gary and nodding for Sara to lift her shirt as everyone else in the room respectfully averted their gazes, Imogen taped the device in place. She could feel how nervous Sara was as she smoothed the tape down; she was trembling.

'Mr Carlyle, could you get a medium-sized suitcase, please?' Webb said and Mr Carlyle swiftly disappeared up the stairs.

Imogen placed her hand on Sara's shoulder. 'You will be safe; we won't let anything happen to you.'

'I don't care about me, all I want is my Marcus back,' Sara said as she took hold of the locket around her neck and opened it, showing the pictures inside to Imogen. One was of a baby, whom Imogen assumed to be Marcus, and one was a more recent photo of the six-year-old.

'We will be right behind you,' Imogen reassured her.

'What if you don't find him?' Sara started to cry. 'What if they kill my baby?'

'There are a lot of people working to make sure that doesn't happen,' Imogen tried to reassure her.

'Do you have any children, DS Grey?'

'No, I don't,' Imogen said. She usually hated answering that particular question as she always felt it was loaded with judgement. She had never really considered having children in the past and now, due to an injury she had sustained in the line of duty, she probably couldn't have them anyway.

'The thing no one tells you about having children is how much you love them, how much it consumes you. It's like there's no room for anything else. I am so full of love for Marcus that it physically hurts to be away from him. I wanted a child for so long and never thought I would have the chance. Then I met Peter and Marcus came along. If anything happens to him, I don't know what I will do.'

'Let's focus on the things we can control for now.'

Sara closed the locket and kissed it. 'Please be safe,' she whispered.

'That's a beautiful locket,' Imogen said, unsure what else to say to a mother who was clinging desperately onto hope. It was gold and oval shaped with a thistle engraved on the front and a sapphire embedded in it. 'It's really unusual.'

'Peter gave it to me as a wedding present; it was his mother's. She passed just before we met so she never got to meet Marcus.' Sara put the locket inside her top and took a deep breath.

'We're going to do everything we can to get Marcus back, and the best way to do that right now is to follow their instructions to the letter. Are you ready?'

Sara nodded.

Gary and Peter Carlyle had finished putting the money in the suitcase. Imogen couldn't help wondering if the kidnappers knew about Sara's connection to the millionaire Dunn – he was in the local newspapers often enough – and if they did, why hadn't they asked for more? She walked Sara to the door and watched her leave, pulling the suitcase behind her. She had fifteen minutes to get to the bus station.

As soon as the call had come through, plainclothes officers had been notified to go straight to the bus station so they could hide among the crowds and watch the phone box. Imogen went out the back of the house and through the garden to her car, which was parked nearby. She wanted to stay close to Sara Carlyle. She had a bad feeling about this.

Chapter Twenty

Jason woke up shivering on the floor of Amanda's bedroom. His father was shaking his shoulder.

'We got to go, something's happening,' Doug said urgently.

'What do you mean?'

'A woman just came out the house across the road and is walking up the road. We need to follow her.'

Jason jumped to his feet, his head spinning a little as his father pulled on the sleeve of his hoodie to get him out of the house faster. As he was leaving, Jason noticed Doug had been through the fridge and left a huge mess on the side. Maybe Luke was right about him. Maybe he was just a taker who only looked after himself. The one thing Jason knew for sure was he couldn't back out now, whatever his father was up to. He was stuck in it, too.

They cut through the back garden and into the alley that ran parallel to the street out front, reaching the end just in time to see the woman turn towards the town centre.

'If you're right about this then won't there be police following her?' Jason asked his dad.

'You're right, just keep your eyes open. Let me know if you see anyone sus.'

'Apart from us.'

Doug chuckled but his eyes stayed focused on the woman up ahead. Jason kept checking behind them but couldn't see anyone else following her or them. Maybe his dad was wrong about this. He wasn't entirely sure why he was letting Doug drag him into this nonsense. Was he that desperate for his attention or approval? He had managed pretty well this far without a dad. Maybe Jason could leave now. Get away before things went pear-shaped.

But Doug still had his phone.

'Can I get my phone so I can call Mum? She's probably doing her nut and we don't want her on our case. At this rate she'll be calling out the police – I've been out all night.'

'Good thinking,' Doug said, still focused on the woman, who was almost at the bus station now. He handed over the phone and Jason took a picture of the woman to keep up the pretence for a moment.

'Where's she going?' Jason asked.

'It's smart, sending her to the bus station. Loads of people there, hard for the police to follow her if she gets on a bus or something. That's how I would do it.'

'How you would do what? Have you done this sort of thing before?' Jason asked, a little horrified at the cavalier way in which his father spoke about the kidnapping of a child.

'Of course not.'

They reached the bus station and saw the woman rush towards a phone box. A man was just about to answer the ringing phone when she shouted, 'That's for me' and grabbed the receiver, pulling the suitcase into the box with her.

Jason and Doug watched as she seemed to take some instructions, nodding and appearing to say yes. She then walked over and got in the queue for a bus to Okehampton, which was pulling up. Jason could see the expression on her face; it was the same one he had seen on his own mother's face a million times before when she had been worried about him. There was a certain look your mother had that hit you right in the heart. Doug scanned the bus station nervously, obviously aware the police would be following and watching her from somewhere, and trying to work out where they were. He pulled Jason towards the bus queue and they waited behind the woman.

Jason couldn't help notice that his father's gaze was fixed on the suitcase. He must have been thinking there was money in there. The bus arrived and Jason watched as the people in front got on the bus one by one, followed by the woman. Again, his brother's voice rang out in his head. *Don't get sucked in.* Doug stepped on the bus and reached into his pocket for money. He didn't have enough so he turned to Jason.

'Sorry, Dad,' he said as he handed him the cash he had in his pocket and then backed away. He knew Doug wouldn't get off that bus now, he was committed to whatever it was he was doing, and Jason wanted no part of it. He ran to the edge of the station just in time to see the bus pulling out, his father's glare boring into him as it went past and out of the station. The crushing weight of stress left him as he saw the bus disappear, along with his father. Whatever Doug was planning to do wasn't going to end well, Jason knew that much.

He would go back to Amanda's house and clean up now. Feeling guilty for ever going there in the first place and though he had known it was a bad idea at the time, he couldn't stop himself. Meeting his father was like staring in a mirror he didn't want to look into. That rash and impulsive behaviour, that notion that he was somehow smarter than everyone else. He wouldn't

Chapter Twenty-One

Sara Carlyle got off the train at Exeter Central Station. As instructed, she had left the suitcase on the bus, wedged under the back seat, and got off at Exeter St David's. From there she'd been told to get on a train to Exeter Central and walk the rest of the way home.

She tried not to look around too much because she didn't want to make eye contact with anyone she shouldn't. She wondered if the transmitter thing had worked as she hadn't spotted anyone following her or noticed any of the officers who had been in her house. All she wanted was for Marcus to be returned safely.

The voice on the pay phone had instructed her on the route to walk home and so she turned into Gandy Street before taking a left at the end to walk past the library. She used to spend a lot of time in the library before she met Peter, and she had the strangest pang of nostalgia as she caught sight of the building. As she passed it, the street got narrower and the anxiety began to creep up. She hadn't realised it was possible to feel any more anxious than she had been. Something was wrong. She could feel it. There was someone behind her.

The second it occurred to her she felt an arm around her neck, pulling her backwards into an open doorway. She clawed at the arm, trying to pull it far enough from her throat so she could take a gulp of air. Wherever she was, it was dark and smelled of beer and urine. Was this where they were keeping Marcus?

'Where's the fucking money?'

'I did what you asked! I left it on the bus.'

'Don't fucking lie to me.'

'I swear to God, I swear on Marcus's life that I left it where you said. The Okehampton bus. I got off at St David's and got on a train to Exeter Central. I wouldn't lie. Please.'

'It wasn't there.'

Oh my God, was he lying? She left the money there, she was certain of it. She had made sure she followed their directions to the letter.

'I swear I left it there,' she said, sobbing now, wondering what they would do to Marcus.

'I want that money. You will have to get more,' the man said, his hot breath in her ear. He brought a knife in front of her eyes, its sharp bevelled edge catching the light.

'I can't, we don't have more. You promised you would let Marcus go.'

'Do you know what I'm going to do to that kid now?' he whispered.

She could feel him smiling.

Then she felt him thump her in the stomach, except the only hand he had free was the one with the knife in it. Was the knife inside her now? He hit her again. She could feel wet as it ran down her leg and she knew what he was doing: he was stabbing her. She counted four times before everything started to go white and she couldn't hold her own weight anymore. She slumped to the ground and could see the bright light of the doorway in front of her from where her cheek rested on the cold, dirty floor. Daylight, so near and yet so far. She saw the man's feet as he stepped over her and left her there. He was wearing desert boots. Even with her last breath, all she could think about was Marcus.

Please don't hurt him. Please don't hurt him. Please don't hurt him.

Chapter Twenty-Two

Jason had been staring into space and biting his nails for the last half an hour. After returning to Amanda's and wiping everything down, he had gone home and put the television on, but not the sound. He would apologise to Amanda when she got back from Spain, if she would listen. Turned out, she was right about him, he could see that now. Meeting his father again had cemented the feeling that she was just too good for him.

There was a knock at the door.

Doug had a big grin on his face when Jason opened it and he walked into the kitchen and started emptying his pockets onto the dining table. There were several bundles of bank notes, thousands of pounds.

'What have you done?' Jason asked timidly.

'We're rich. Let's go and celebrate.'

'Where did you get that money?'

'Don't you worry about that – what matters is that it's ours now. Come on, I want to buy you some trainers and a new phone or something. You don't have to slum it anymore.'

Doug grabbed Jason and pulled him into a hug, obviously elated with himself. Jason had never seen so much money and it was hard not to feel excited about what it could mean for him. His father pressed a bundle of twenties into Jason's hand and Jason couldn't help but smile.

'How much is there?'

'This is just a little bit of it. I put the rest in a safe place where no one will ever find it, and no one will even think to look at us for it. It's ours. Now, let's go and have a few bevvies.'

'I'm not even seventeen yet.'

'I know a pub we can go to, don't worry. Let's call a cab.'

Just like that, Jason was swept back into his father's shenanigans. There was something magnetic about him, but also dangerous. Jason knew as they got into the cab that he should have said no. He didn't even want to go but there was no way to refuse.

It was strange – almost like he was in his father's thrall. Jason longed for Luke to get out of prison. In two days' time, if Luke's case got thrown out, it would be easier. He knew Luke wouldn't stand for his shit. But for now, Jason didn't have the energy to stand up to Doug, and so he followed.

Chapter Twenty-Three

Imogen pulled up in the adjacent street and then walked through the back way to the garden gate. She knocked on the French doors and DC Webb nodded for her to come in. She went straight over to him.

'What does he know?' she asked quietly.

'Just that there has been a complication and Sara was taken to hospital, nothing else. I told him you would be back soon to fill us in.'

'How is he?'

'Understandably quite stressed.'

'Where is he?'

'He just went to the bathroom,' Gabriel said, but Peter Carlyle had already appeared in the doorway.

'DS Grey. What's happened? Is there any news? I've been going out of my mind,' Carlyle said as he bounded towards her.

'We were following your wife, when she was asked to board a bus. We followed the bus but then she had to get off and get on a train, at which point we lost her momentarily.'

'What about that thing you put on her to track where she was?'

'We aren't sure what happened there; someone will check the device.'

'Where is she now?'

'I'm afraid, when we lost her, she was attacked.'

'Attacked? What do you mean? Weren't you watching her?'

'Like I said, we lost her for a moment and I'm afraid she was stabbed.'

'Oh my God. Not my Sara!' Peter Carlyle buried his face in his hands and started to sob, but Imogen found herself wondering if it was partly to hide his eyes, which were barely reacting to anything. Did he even care?

'Mr Carlyle, the doctors think she is in with a good chance of recovery as miraculously the knife missed everything important. She's in theatre right now.'

He pulled his hands away from his face, his eyes completely dry and his pupils fixed, as Imogen had suspected they would be. 'She's still alive?'

'Yes, she's still alive, Mr Carlyle.'

'Thank God,' he said, half laughing.

She wasn't sure but, for the tiniest of seconds, she thought she saw something other than relief on Carlyle's face – was it surprise? But why would he be surprised that his wife was alive – he'd only just learned she'd been hurt? As she stared at him, she felt a chill go through her, as though she was seeing past the veneer to something else. Peter Carlyle had expected her to say that his wife was dead. In fact, he almost seemed disappointed that she wasn't. Whatever was going on here, this man was at the heart of it. Imogen had never been more certain about anything in her life.

'Don't worry, Mr Carlyle, I promise I will make it my personal mission to find out who is responsible for this and make them pay.'

'What about Marcus?'

'I'm afraid, until your wife wakes up, we won't know exactly what happened.'

Imogen studied his face for any kind of tell. He knew more than he was letting on, that was for sure.

The phone rang. It was almost certainly the kidnappers again. Imogen went and grabbed the headphones and Gary nodded that it was OK to answer the phone. Carlyle reached for the receiver.

'Hello.'

'WHERE IS THE MONEY?' The familiar sound of the artificial voice came over the line.

'What did you do to my wife?' Carlyle said, sounding annoyed.

'THE MONEY, WHERE IS IT?'

'What do you mean, where is it? Don't you have it?'

'THE MONEY WAS NOT LEFT IN THE AGREED LOCATION. YOU HAVE ONE MORE CHANCE. YOUR WIFE BROKE THE RULES SO SHE PAID THE PRICE. NEXT TIME WE COME FOR YOU. WE'LL BE IN TOUCH.'

'My wife did exactly what you said. Did you lose the money?' Carlyle said, the pitch of his voice getting higher as he spoke.

The line went dead.

'She *must* have followed their instructions. She wouldn't have jeopardised Marcus's life in any way, so what the hell happened to the money?' Carlyle said to Imogen.

'We don't know what her instructions were, so we are going to have to find that out. There are people combing through video footage of the station to see if we can nail down what happened after she took the call in the phone booth. Hopefully, that can tell us what went wrong and why Sara was attacked. I am going to go back to the station and oversee the operation myself. We'll get to the bottom of this.'

'I can take you to the hospital if you want to be with your wife,' Walsh said to Carlyle.

'Right. Shouldn't I stay here in case they call back though?'

'It's entirely up to you. We can connect you to your landline remotely if need be.'

'It doesn't feel right to leave the house. Sara wouldn't want me to. Marcus has to be my priority right now.'

'I fully understand. DC Jarvis will stay with you. He can call us if you have any issues,' Walsh said.

'Mr Tunney, would you meet us back at the station as soon as humanly possible?' Imogen said, trying to impart how urgent this was to Gary.

'I'll get Danika from the tech team to come and take charge of this,' he said, texting someone as he spoke to Imogen.

'We'll see you soon, Mr Carlyle,' Imogen said.

She was in a rush to get back to the station. She hadn't lied to Peter Carlyle but she also hadn't told him the truth. The thing that had been bothering her since they met seemed to have solidified in the last half an hour. He had something to do with this kidnap. Things that weren't adding up before were making more sense now, but she needed to know more about him to understand what was going on. They would follow the video footage of Sara Carlyle to trace her steps, but Imogen knew in the back of her mind that the key to finding Marcus was closer to home.

Chapter Twenty-Four

In The Black Lamb, a couple of the regulars seemed – bizarrely – genuinely pleased to see Doug. Jason had never seen this place before. It was down a back alley somewhere in the St Thomas area, as he hadn't really been paying attention when the cab dropped them off. He was more concerned about where the money had come from and what it meant now that his father had it rather than whoever it was supposed to be going to. Doug had rationalised his actions by telling Jason the money they used was probably police money and therefore taxpayers' money and so it was theirs anyway. Jason wasn't sure that was how these things worked. Still, he stayed and let his father buy him drink after drink as the proprietor of the bar didn't seem to have a problem with serving Jason, who would be the first to admit he couldn't pass for eighteen.

He watched as his father told the patrons stories of his time away and how well things had been going for him. As Doug got drunker, his tongue got looser, and he started to tell his audience about how he had found a suitcase on the bus and when he looked inside to look for the owner's ID – to return it like the good Samaritan he was, of course – he saw all the cash. A few people told him he should hand it in; others just seemed generally impressed with his good fortune as he bought round after round for everyone.

Jason was drunker than he ever remembered being as his father poured him another glass of champagne, which Jason didn't even like, but Doug had insisted on buying as it was the most expensive thing the pub sold. Jason didn't know how much was in that suitcase but he knew at this rate it wouldn't last his father long. Things started to blur as the barmaid sat on Doug's lap and whispered into Doug's ear. Jason felt like he was in a movie montage of hell as he watched people slip further into debauchery, himself included. What he did know was he was going to have one hell of a headache in the morning.

Chapter Twenty-Five

Another name checked off Adrian's list. Another dead end. With every name he pursued he grew more and more stressed that he would never find the men who had attacked him. That he would be stuck in this purgatory forever. Worse than that, he worried he had seen them already and not recognised them at all. He always thought he would *know* when he found them, but what if he couldn't trust his own memory? These questions replayed in his head like a scratched and broken record.

He was alone in the house, Imogen having made her excuses not to come over. Again. He knew it was all his fault. He couldn't stop thinking. Not thinking about anything in particular, just a constant jumble of what-ifs and imagined scenarios. The TV at least gave him a chance to block that out.

The biggest problem with being alone at home was the way his mind would just switch to a place where he didn't want to be alive anymore, the idea popping into his mind with such ease it was as though he was simply suggesting a cup of tea to himself. For the most part, he managed to squash it, put the thought away and focus on something else, but tonight he was struggling – too wired to stay awake, too wired to fall asleep.

He put something on that he had seen a million times, something he knew wouldn't thrust him into a black hole he couldn't get out of. Whatever the plot was, though, it wasn't going in. Instead, the same movie played over and over in Adrian's mind: the acrid smell of the van, the feeling of the man's rough hands on his bare legs. The rage built inside Adrian and he wished he could go back and do things differently, try for a different outcome. But there was no possible way to do that, and so he was stuck.

Chapter Twenty-Six

Jason was awoken by the sound of glass breaking. He sat up in his bed and looked out of the window into the garden to see a fox running across the paving slabs and cutting into the neighbours' yard through a hole in the fence. Feeling uneasy, he pulled shorts on and slipped out of his room into the hallway.

There was a noise coming from downstairs, like someone sneaking around, trying not to be heard. Jason crossed the hall silently and tried to get a better view down the stairs by leaning over the bannister. He saw the flickering of a torch as it passed across the walls in the lounge and quickly moved to open the door to his parents' room as quietly as he could. He crept towards the bed and tapped on his father's shoulder.

'What's the matter?' Doug whispered hoarsely.

'There's someone downstairs,' Jason said.

'Who?'

As Doug spoke, they both heard the creak of someone ascending the stairs. Jason looked at his mother who was still asleep.

'We need to call the cops.'

'No cops. I'll sort this.' Doug swung his legs out of bed and grabbed his tracksuit bottoms. It jarred Jason to see that this man, who was almost a stranger to him, was naked in his mother's bed. He couldn't even think about that now though. He moved to the other side of the bed and shook his mother awake.

'Jason?'

'Mum, there's someone in the house, you need to hide.'

'What do you mean?'

'Someone's broken in. They're coming upstairs now. You need to hide.'

'Get under the bed,' she said urgently. 'I'll call the police. Just stay there, please. I couldn't bear it if anything happened to you.' She kissed him on the head and grabbed her phone from the bedside table. 'Go on. Please! I'll get in the wardrobe.'

There wasn't a lot of room under the bed, but he managed to pull out an old floral holdall of his mother's and shimmied in behind it, pulling it back after him. He could see part of the floor through a small gap.

His heart was thumping and all he kept thinking was how he wished Luke was here. Luke wouldn't be as scared as him. Luke would know what to do.

'You better fuck off out of here before I mess you up!' Doug called out.

The door swung open and the light turned on. Two sets of boots entered the room and Jason heard his mother shriek in terror, followed by a thump as she dropped her phone. Jason could see the phone but couldn't reach it. His own was still in his room, and he cursed himself for leaving it in there. There was no way he could get it without alerting the men in the room to his presence, so he stayed completely still.

Whoever the hell these men were, there was one thing Jason knew for sure and that was that this was his father's fault.

'What do you want?' Jean screamed. 'Leave us alone!'

'Where's the money?' a voice Jason didn't recognise

shouted. The voice was muffled, and he wondered if they had face coverings on.

'The money! Where the fuck is it?'

Jason heard the sound of his father being thrown up against the wall and watched as his feet dangled a few inches above the carpet.

'I don't know what you're talking about,' Doug wheezed.

'Doug. What's happening?' Jean sobbed.

'Shut up!' one of the men said, before Jason heard the sound of his fist connecting with his mother's face. She fell to the ground next to the bed, face to face with Jason, and he realised now that he was crying.

'*Don't*,' she mouthed as she looked into Jason's eyes. Maybe she thought he was going to jump out and save her, but the truth was he was too terrified to move. This was unreal. He wished he knew where the money was so he could tell them and they would leave, but he had no idea. He watched helplessly as his mother's hair was grabbed by a large fist and she was pulled to her feet.

Jason could hear Doug gurgling and choking as the masked intruders tried to ascertain the location of the money. He heard his mother get hit two more times, but still Doug wasn't saying a word. Maybe he was right not to say anything – maybe he knew the men would kill them anyway. Or maybe he just cared more about money than he cared about either Jean or Jason.

'If you don't give us the fucking money we're going to cut your wife open.'

'I swear, fellas, I have no idea what you're on about.'

'Did you think it wouldn't get back to us? Flashing your money around at The Lamb and telling people about the suitcase you supposedly found. You're not too smart, are you?'

Jason heard fabric tearing as his mother's sobs got louder, a scream that pierced through him, all he could see were the blood droplets hitting the floor . . . He crossed his arms over his head and buried his face in the musty carpet, blocking out the sound of his mother's cries.

'I can't tell you what I don't know,' Doug said.

Jason wanted to punch him, or worse. His father knew exactly where that money was and he wasn't saying a thing. He hated him with every fibre.

He knew he really couldn't help, he wouldn't do anything but make the situation worse, and so he stayed where he was. He felt a thump as someone landed on the bed and closed his eyes, trying to close his ears, too.

He was clutching his head so tightly he didn't even notice when the noise stopped.

When Jason finally looked up, the light had changed in the room. It was both dark and bright at the same time, that period between night and day. The silence was alarming and unbearable, but he waited to make sure the men were gone before pushing his way out from under the bed, gasping for air as though he had been underwater. He lay on the floor for a moment, breathing greedily as he stared up at the ceiling, listening for any noise at all, afraid of what the lack of noise might mean. He sat up and saw the red splattered up the wall before he saw his mother. Jean was laid out on the bed, her clothes torn and cuts all over her skin. She looked dead. He quickly looked away. Doug was on the floor, his face now unrecognisable. The carpet beneath him was a deep chocolate colour, the blood having saturated it so much. There was no way he was alive and Jason found himself almost relieved that he wouldn't have to listen to him anymore.

He turned back to his mother, moving to place his hand on her forehead and quickly pulling the covers over her. As he did her eyes fluttered open and she looked at him.

'Mum?'

'Jason,' she whispered.

'I'll call for help, Mum, just wait there.'

He rushed to his room and grabbed his phone, clumsily unlocking it and dialling triple nine. He asked for an ambulance and ran back to his mother's side, telling them the address then tossing the phone on the floor. He stroked her forehead and whispered apologies in her ear as he listened to her jagged breath fade. He couldn't lose his mother, he just couldn't.

Chapter Twenty-Seven

THREE DAYS MISSING

Imogen charged into the reception at A&E, holding up her warrant card, and the nurse behind the counter pressed the button to open the doors into the main emergency area as soon as she spotted it. A doctor saw her and waved her towards him. Introducing himself as Dr Howell, he rushed towards one of the theatres where there were already two uniformed officers waiting outside.

'How is she, doctor? Any change overnight?'

'Still touch and go. She was stabbed at least five times – although the good news is it's all in the stomach area and her attacker seems to have missed all of her major organs. There is a wee chance she will pull through. The bad news is we believe the knife may have nicked her spine, and so she could be left with significant mobility issues even if she does make it.'

'Big knife then?'

'Yes, it seems to have been. Plus, she is quite a small woman.'

'What's the prognosis?'

'I don't think we can know just yet. She lost a lot of blood, DS Grey. We'll be going into surgery shortly and I'll get you an update as soon as I know more.'

'Thank you, doctor,' she called after him as he left.

Imogen should have stayed closer to Sara during the

drop. The difficulty was always that you never knew who was watching and where they might be, so you had to hang back enough to make sure they didn't spot you.

There was nothing she could do at the hospital for now, so she decided to head back to the Carlyles' house and let Peter Carlyle what was going on. She wanted to do it in person. Instead of walking straight back to her car though, she pulled out her phone and called Adrian. She wasn't sure he would even answer – he seemed so distant and he never rang her anymore, it was always her reaching out, always her trying to make contact. She just couldn't understand what had gone wrong between them.

'Hey,' he said.

She could hear the smile in his voice, which was nice. Reassuring.

'Hi there, I've had a tough couple of days. Needed to hear a friendly voice.'

'Wrong number?' Adrian said.

'Hush. How's your work going?'

'Mick's just gone to get some hot coffee so your timing is impeccable. It smells a bit funky in the car and I would kill for a cheeseburger, but it's fine. I miss you, though.'

Did he? When they were together, she felt like he would rather be anywhere else. She wondered if it was weird to have a better relationship over the phone than in person. He was always so much more relaxed, so much more Adrian, than when they were actually in the same room together.

'I miss you, too,' she said. She did miss him, and not just now, while she was at work – she felt like she was missing him all the time. There was a part of her that ached for her Adrian back, a part of her that couldn't quite remember who her Adrian used to be. He hadn't always been like this. Maybe it was her that had changed.

'I should be finished around five tonight. Can I come to yours?' she asked.

'You never need to ask. I'd like that. I'll cook something nice.'

'Don't worry, I wasn't going to offer.'

'Thank fuck for that,' he said teasingly.

'I better go,' she said as she spotted Dr Howell making his way back to her.

'Me, too,' Adrian said and rung off.

And that was that. She did feel lifted after speaking to him. Even though she knew it would be short-lived, she cherished that feeling of normalcy she had when she spoke to him on the phone.

'Doctor Howell?' Imogen said.

'I just spoke to one of the surgeons in the room. He said Mrs Carlyle's stable for now but has been put in a medically induced coma. She lost a lot of blood and although it sounds awful it's her best chance of survival at the moment. Her body will have an uninterrupted chance to heal.'

'Thank you so much.'

'What happened? Do you know?'

'Not yet, but I'm going to find out,' she said.

Until they spoke to Sara they couldn't know for sure what had gone wrong. Then there was Carlyle's reaction. He knew she had been stabbed before Imogen had told him: he had prepared himself for it. What he obviously hadn't expected was that she would survive. What else hadn't he accounted for? And where the hell was Marcus?

Chapter Twenty-Eight

Imogen knew when she was being lied to. God knew she had had enough practice, what with whatever was eating Adrian these days and a childhood spent with her unreliable mother who was a terrible liar, but a liar nonetheless. And, right now, the one thing she was certain of in this case was that Peter Carlyle was a liar. He had remembered himself quickly but there had still been that smallest of moments when he was surprised his wife had lived, quickly shifting his expression with the hopes that no one had noticed. Unlucky. Imogen had noticed.

Imogen decided against going to the Carlyles' from the hospital, instead heading to the station for an update. When she arrived, she went straight to the briefing room and sat patiently waiting for the others. She had called through to the team, so she could run through a couple of things. What possible motivations could Peter Carlyle have for wanting to kidnap his own child? Of course, the easy answer was money, but on the surface the Carlyles weren't struggling, from what the police had found. They were comfortable, had savings, assets, all of that, and so far there was no evidence of poor money management or debts. A deeper dig into their accounts would show any discrepancies. Maybe Imogen was being unfair to Carlyle, but she just couldn't shake the bad feeling he gave her.

She wondered what Adrian would do in these circumstances. She knew that his answer would be to go in all guns blazing and almost get fired, so she would have to try a more measured approach. Still, she found herself smiling a little just thinking about Adrian's unorthodox approach to police work. She hadn't really appreciated how loose he was with the rules until she'd started working with Walsh full time. She missed it.

Gary rushed in and sat down, nodding a hello to Imogen.

'What do you need?' he asked.

'Carlyle's financials. Has he made any large payments lately? Got any hidden debts? There's something not right about him, do you feel it?' Imogen said.

'That's not really my job . . .' Gary said.

'Come on, it's me. I value your intuition.'

'The guy is weird. I don't know how I would react in his situation, but I know if Franka got hurt I wouldn't have behaved like that. I can dig deeper. You think he's in on it?'

Before Imogen could answer, DCI Kapoor and the AKEU liaison James Ridgewell stepped into the briefing room, looking for an update.

'Nigel Twyford's alibi checks out, he was down on the Quay perving on the Bear Cubs at the time of the abduction,' Imogen said, no time to waste.

'What about his computer? Did we get anything off it?'

Gary sat forward. 'Yes, we got a lot – too much, if you ask me. There were a few images of Marcus but no more than any of the other boys in his class, and nothing other than sports day shots. But considering it's a mixed-gender school, you wouldn't know it to look at his pictures. There was other stuff, really awful stuff. I couldn't go through all of it, but I saw enough to know he's facing a stretch in prison. There's more than sufficient evidence to charge him.'

'And Sara Carlyle?' DCI Kapoor said.

'She was put into a medical coma this morning, so we can't ask her anything right now. There's something that isn't adding up though. Hear me out. What if Sara Carlyle was always supposed to die at the drop? I felt like when I told Peter Carlyle she was still alive he was surprised, rather than relieved,' Imogen said.

'I got that impression, too,' Gary added.

Imogen turned to Gary. 'Can you find out if he has any kind of life insurance policy out on her, or vice versa?'

'I'll see what we can get. The ransom money came from the father-in-law, didn't it? So I'm guessing Carlyle's not liquid rich.'

'Good thinking. Imogen, you speak to Gregory Dunn about the money and see if you can get a sense of his feelings for his son-in-law,' DCI Kapoor said.

'Anything else?' Gary said, tapping away on his keyboard.

'I want to get hold of his phone records as soon as possible,' Imogen said.

'I've got something,' Gary said. James Ridgewell was visibly impressed at the speed that Gary worked, which made Imogen feel bad for not being more appreciative of him. She was just used to him being brilliant at his job.

'What do you have?' DCI Kapoor said.

'I've found payments going back almost a year to a couple of separate life insurance companies. He paid for them out of their joint account, which Mrs Carlyle gave us access to. Looks like he was in control financially, even though the bulk of their money was hers.'

'Life insurance on the wife? Taken out less than a year ago? If you're right about Peter Carlyle, then you are right to be concerned about Marcus. It would change things completely because if Sara Carlyle was always supposed to die after the ransom had been handed over, who knows what they have planned for Marcus,' James Ridgewell said.

'Why would anyone do that? Aren't there easier ways of doing it?' Imogen said.

'Depending on his motivations. Maybe he doesn't like the life he ended up in and feels like this is the only way to get out. People do fucked-up things for money. A lot of the kidnappings I have seen have been orchestrated from inside the family units,' James Ridgewell said.

'He was weird from the start. We were never supposed to be involved at this point, and I'm guessing our involvement has made things a lot harder for him,' Imogen said.

'I expect he thought he could just pull the wool over his wife's eyes for long enough to get money out of her father and then we would come in after the fact. It's now even more imperative that we figure out where Marcus Carlyle is, in case he doesn't factor into his father's plans for the future either. The clock is ticking. Let's hustle,' DCI Kapoor said.

'If he is behind this, then the kidnappers have known from the start we were involved. So maybe we don't need to be keeping this as low-key as we have been.' Imogen said.

'We can't just assume that. We need some kind of proof.' DCI Kapoor said.

'I'll go speak to Gregory Dunn, see if we can get new insight into Peter from him,' Imogen said.

'Take Webb with you. I trust you to handle the interview and show him how it's done,' DCI Kapoor said.

'OK,' Imogen said, conflicted about the possibility of another day in close quarters with Webb. Her conversation with Adrian earlier aside, she was still feeling very neglected and sometimes she caught Webb looking at her in a way that made her feel there was potential for something more to happen between them. She couldn't let herself get confused over this though. As lost as she was right now, as alone as she felt, the answer wasn't there.

So why did she keep thinking about Webb? It wasn't deliberate and it wasn't welcome but there was no denying the chemistry between them.

Chapter Twenty-Nine

Jason walked into the hospital with a bunch of pink carnations for his mother. He had been avoiding this all morning, and when he saw her his guilt ballooned inside him. Her face was swollen and one of her eyes was completely sealed closed as she watched daytime television on the TV on the wall. If only he had slammed the door in his father's face when Doug had first appeared on their doorstep . . . If only he had listened to his brother . . . He couldn't help but feel responsible for this.

There were two other beds in the room. One was empty but the one nearest the window had another woman in it, much older than his mother, lying silently with tubes and wires poking out of her. Jason felt grateful that his mother had escaped with just a few nasty cuts and bruises.

'Baby boy,' Jean said, genuinely happy to see Jason.

'Mum,' he said, trying to hold it together. She was such a mess. He saw a giant bunch of luxurious flowers on the table next to her bed and she noticed him looking at them.

'Oh, they're hers,' Jean said, pointing to the lady in the other bed. 'Her name is Barbara. Her son, Christopher, brought them in for her but she can't see them so he said I should look after them. I don't think she's going to be waking up. There but for the grace of God.'

'What happened to her?'

'Some kind of aneurysm. According to the nurses, Christopher comes in to sit with her every visiting time and she just lies there while he reads to her. It's so sad.'

'Sorry I didn't come in earlier,' Jason said, feeling guilty that someone else's son was spending more time with her than he was.

'It's fine. It's been a tough few days for you,' she said, looking down at her hands with her one good eye, a tear rolling down her cheek.

'I'm sorry about Dad.'

'That's not your fault. He did what he always does, upset the wrong people. He thought he could talk his way out of any situation and, you know what, he usually could. Look where it got him. The sad thing is I am not even surprised. It was always going to end with him dying this way. I think even he knew it.'

'I'm sorry I even let him in. I shouldn't have.'

'You did nothing wrong; he was your dad. I am the one who should have known better and turned him away,' Jean said, her voice thick with emotion. 'I knew what he was like and you didn't. I'm supposed to be the one looking after you. You never should have had to see him like that, all beat up and bloody.'

'I always thought Luke was exaggerating about him.'

'Let's not talk about him anymore. He's gone,' she said with a sense of finality.

Maybe this was the only way to be free of someone like Doug, for him to simply not exist anymore. Multiple head injuries, they said. He had charmed his way back into their lives with minimum resistance from Jason and Jean and, from the stories Jason had heard, it wasn't the first, second, or even third time he had done that. Some people just got their hooks in you like that.

Jason had to be different. Watching his forty-year-old

father behave in a way that might be considered acceptable for a messed-up teenager had been an eye-opener. Given all of the bad decisions Jason had made – from breaking into Amanda's house in the first place to absolutely every choice he'd made since then – he wondered if he was genetically predisposed to being a fuck-up like his father.

Jason wouldn't take that path. Having spent time with his father, he understood himself so much more, and he understood his mother's frustration with everything he did.

'Do you want me to read to you?' Jason said. Jean smiled and reached out her hand to him.

'Just sit with me, that's enough.'

He settled into the seat next to her and leaned his head on the side of the bed. She stroked his hair and he cried as he tried to think of a way to repair the mess he had made.

Chapter Thirty

The phone screen went to black, a half-typed message disappearing with it, as Adrian thought better of contacting Imogen and slipped the phone back in his pocket. Mick was sitting next to him, watching old episodes of *Porridge* on his phone. They had been monitoring Garvey's front door for the last forty minutes. Finally it opened, and he emerged with his wife and young daughter, who was wearing a ballet costume. They got in the car and drove away.

'Aren't we following them?' Adrian said as they remained parked.

'Not today. Today we have a different mission. Put these on,' Mick said, handing Adrian a pair of disposable gloves.

'Why do we need these?'

'We've got to get into his office. We can slip round the back; there's a spare house key under the blue pot, according to the night team.'

'What? We can't do that.'

'I warned you there would need to be some flexibility on your part, and you're not the Adrian I remember if you're going to let the law get in the way of doing your job. Your loose interpretation of the rules is one of the reasons I recommended you for this job.'

'I didn't think you meant breaking and entering. I'm not the same guy I was ten years ago.'

'We won't be breaking anything. I just need to get a copy of something. In and out.'

'This feels wrong,' Adrian said, even though he knew he wasn't going to do anything to stop it. Powerlessness seemed to be his natural state these days.

'Let's argue after. Time is slipping away. Sit in the car if you want but I've got my orders and I'm going in. Technically, he's the one who broke the law as he stole something from his company and I need to retrieve it.'

'Then why don't they call the cops? And why aren't the other team doing this?' Adrian protested.

'You know the answer as well as I do. Too much on the police's plate to make this a priority and this is a time-sensitive issue. I volunteered us for this op. Are you coming or not?'

Mick jumped out of the car and walked across the fairly deserted road, looking to see if anyone was watching him. Adrian was torn about what he should be doing and could hear Imogen's voice in his mind telling him to get the hell out of there. He knew this wasn't legal but at least if he went with Mick he would be able to make sure no other laws were broken. He was here now. After this job he would have to make it clear to Mick that he couldn't be involved in any further law breaking.

The house was not what Adrian was expecting. He thought they had been following a ruthless thief all this time but, looking around, it was just a home. Hand-drawn pictures and school attendance certificates hung on the kitchen walls. Magnetic letters on the fridge spelled out the words 'Miss Maisie is clever'. There were unwashed dishes in the sink, and leftover food in bowls on the table. They had obviously left the house in a hurry. This guy was clearly a family man and Adrian questioned what they were even doing there. He guessed he didn't have the whole story, and though he'd like to believe that Mick didn't either, he wasn't so sure. Adrian didn't trust his own instincts these days; he'd just assumed his partner was steering him right, but this really didn't feel OK. Mick started pulling out drawers and rifling through them.

'We shouldn't be in here. I didn't sign up for this,' Adrian repeated.

'We'll only be a minute. We have to get back what he stole,' Mick said.

'What are we looking for?'

'A USB stick – red, apparently – with a company logo on it.'

Adrian opened a drawer and saw kids' vitamins, an inhaler and some Peppa Pig plasters. This was all wrong.

'What does this guy do again?'

'I told you, he's a lab technician for Quartec Pharmaceuticals.'

'And they think he's trying to leak some top-secret information?'

'Exactly. It's only kept on those USBs and one of them is missing. He seems like he could use the money. Doesn't look like he's making much. I always thought a job like that would be coining it in.'

Mick was making no effort to hide the fact he had been looking through the drawers. If anything, he seemed determined to make a mess, leaving them open, throwing stuff on the floor so he could see better.

They heard a key in the front door. Adrian hid beside the fridge and Mick ducked behind the counter just before Ethan Garvey walked into the kitchen and stopped. He immediately realised something was up, thanks to Mick's carelessness.

'Who's there?' Garvey said, his question followed by the unmistakeable noise of a knife being pulled from a knife rack at speed.

Mick stood and put his hands up.

'Calm down, sunshine. We are here on behalf of your bosses.'

'Who is we?'

Adrian stepped out from beside the fridge and nodded apologetically. To say this was awkward was an understatement.

'You better put that down before you hurt yourself,' Mick said, gesturing towards the knife.

'You're too late if you're here for the data. I already passed it on.'

'We've been told to get it back no matter what. Who did you pass it on to?'

'I'm not telling you that. Quartec are going to get in deep shit when this information hits the news. They're putting people's lives in danger.'

'You're a whistle-blower?' Adrian said.

'Quartec are about to release a contraceptive drug that they skipped several stages of testing to meet the release date deadline, even though there have been reported side effects of infertility and sometimes even malignant growths in the test subjects. The finalised test data that was released was fabricated to get the drug passed.'

'That's none of our business, we just need the stick,' Mick said impatiently.

'It's gone. It's probably already been uploaded. You're too late.'

Adrian hadn't noticed Mick pick up the broom until he swung it and hit Garvey in the side of the head. The knife fell out of Garvey's hand as he dropped to the floor and Mick jumped the counter in one clean movement – which

Adrian had to admit was pretty impressive, if terrifying – and pressed his knee to the back of Garvey's neck.

This was now several uncomfortable steps past surveillance.

'Who did you give the files to?' Mick asked.

'What are you doing?' Adrian said, his adrenaline spiking. Seeing Garvey lying pinned down like that, his face down and bloody, he felt sick. He had to get out of there. Without warning he was back in that van, the taste of his own blood in his mouth more than a memory, the smell of grease and chemicals, the crushing weight of the man moving against him. He was frozen again, unable to move, unable to do anything but watch. Locked in.

'We need to get that file, that's the objective of this assignment.'

'It's gone,' Garvey said through bloodied teeth, the hint of a chuckle in his words.

'Let's go, now! This is over,' Adrian said, snapping back into the present for at least long enough to get out of there. He tugged at Mick's collar until he stood up, and then Adrian rushed out of the front door and over to the car, Mick following a few moments later.

'You can't pull shit like that on a job, Ade.'

'We were breaking the law, Mick. Going inside was one thing, but that was aggravated assault. What the fuck did you think you were doing? You could have fucking killed him!'

'OK, maybe I got a bit carried away. I apologise.'

'Apology accepted. This time. Next time I will call the cops on you myself. Now take me home,' Adrian said, more shaken than he had been in months. Was this how it would be for the rest of his life? It was like all the progress he had made over the last year was gone and he was back in that van. He wanted to get inside his house where he felt safe. He hoped Imogen would be there, he didn't want to be alone, even though there hadn't been a moment since the rape that he hadn't felt alone.

They got in the car and Mick started to drive as they sat in silence, Adrian trying to hold it together until he was alone and could freak out in private.

'We good?' Mick said.

'Of course. Just wish you had given me a heads-up, that's all.'

'Maybe. I think I just got carried away. Thought it might be like the old days.'

'Is beating the shit out of people part of our job description? Because if so, I missed that memo.'

'Not at all. I took some artistic licence.'

'How do you know Garvey won't go to the police?'

'I'm not worried about Garvey,' Mick said as he stopped the car outside Adrian's house.

'See you tomorrow,' Adrian said, his voice clipped. Hopefully Mick knew how annoyed he was.

He went inside and closed the door behind him before rushing up to the bathroom and leaning over the toilet, half expecting to throw up. Feeling that dirt on him again, the dirt he had tried to wash off a million times since the night of the attack, the dirt that never went away. He got in the shower and went through his cleaning ritual – soap, rinse, repeat – until the water started to go cold.

In bed alone, he closed his eyes as tight as he could muster, even though it was still light outside, desperate for sleep to take him before he had the chance to start the exhaustive overthinking bedtime loop. In the night he would pray for morning to come quickly and in the day he would pray for the night to come without incident. He was wishing his life away instead of living it. How much longer could he exist like this, he wondered.

Where was Imogen? He hadn't heard anything more from her after their call earlier. Maybe she was finally giving up on them. It wasn't like he could blame her.

Chapter Thirty-One

Despite her initial reservations, Imogen had decided she really liked working with DC Webb. They just clicked. He was one of those people who had an aura about them. She hated herself for even thinking like that, but after all those years with her mother's crystals and tarot cards, something was bound to stick. She tried not to think about her mother too much these days because she still felt guilty. It had been two years since she had passed away and Imogen had still barely acknowledged it; she just couldn't face it yet. She pushed the thoughts of her mother away and glanced across to DC Webb, who was just staring out the passenger-side window in a bit of a daze, clenching and releasing his jaw. She didn't want to be drawn to him, but she could be a professional about this; he needed guidance and she was going to give it to him.

'You OK?' she asked.

'Yes, sorry. Just thinking.'

'I often wondered what happened to you, you know. After we got you out of prison,' Imogen said.

'After I got out, I couldn't go back to my parents' house, that wasn't my home anymore. My parents washed their hands of me as soon as I went inside and they didn't seem to care much that the charges were dropped. I haven't seen them since. I decided I just wanted to do something good with my life, you know?

I'm not smart enough to be a doctor or anything like that so I thought—'

'So, you thought you'd be a detective?' Imogen said with a smile and a raised eyebrow.

'That came out a little more insulting than I intended,' he said, blushing.

'I knew what you meant. Just taking the mick.'

'I didn't say anything before because it's a bit embarrassing, but it's a real honour to get to work with you. You don't even realise this, but you saved my life. You're the reason I joined the police.'

Now Imogen was the one blushing. Luckily, they had arrived at their destination and she didn't have to think of a response to his compliment.

It was obvious that Gregory Dunn had money. She drove through the open iron gates of his estate and parked up outside a large converted barn, the kind you saw on those TV shows where people hunt for their dream homes. A large man poked his head round the front door at the sound of the car and waved them towards the house. If this was Gregory Dunn, he obviously hadn't heard the news about his daughter.

'Hello!' he bellowed, beckoning them towards the house like they were old friends. Imogen wondered who he thought they were. They got out of the car and wandered over, Imogen holding up her warrant card as they approached.

'Mr Dunn? I'm DS Grey and this is my colleague, DC Webb.'

'How can I help you?' he said, smiling.

'We would like to speak to you about a police matter.'

'I heard things went a bit wrong yesterday but Peter said you had it all under control and not to worry. I take it you didn't get Marcus back?'

Imogen gently shook her head and the smile disappeared from Gregory Dunn's face.

'Why not? I gave Peter the money. What happened? I've been calling him, but he doesn't answer – just left a message on my machine . . . Come inside, sorry, how rude of me.' He pushed the door open and went into the house, suddenly seeming shaken.

Dunn steadied himself as he sat on a kitchen chair, his face pale. He looked a completely different man to the one who had greeted them outside just a moment ago.

'Can I get you a water or something?' Gabriel offered, his hand on Dunn's shoulder. Dunn nodded and Gabriel went over to the sink, took a glass off the draining board, and filled it with fresh water.

'There was a complication at the drop. We're still unsure of what exactly went wrong but we're looking into it,' Imogen said.

'I had better try and call Sara again,' Dunn said, searching for his phone. 'They told me not to call, not to clog up the lines until this was all over. I've been trying to keep myself busy but all this clandestine business is driving me a bit potty.'

'I'm afraid Sara was injured after she dropped the money off. She's going to be OK though. She's come out of surgery and is in a medically induced coma at the moment. I promise it sounds worse than it is. Her prognosis is good.'

'Surgery? What the hell happened?' Dunn asked, clutching at his side.

'The drop went badly but until we hear what Sara has to say we won't know what went wrong. Sara was stabbed and—'

'Stabbed? How? Weren't you watching her? What are you people playing at?'

'I'm sorry, Mr Dunn. We were following Sara but a kidnapping is a complicated and delicate situation,' Imogen said.

'So Marcus is still missing?' Dunn snapped at her.

'We still don't know where he is. Rest assured, our people are working around the clock.'

'So why have you come to see me? To ask for more money? Is that what they want?' he said.

'We just wanted to ask you some questions about your daughter and her family.'

'Peter, you mean,' Dunn said, shaking his head.

'What can you tell us about him?'

'Is he involved in this?'

'We just want to understand the financial situation. We wondered why they came to you for the money?'

'The house is Sara's. She bought it before she even met Peter eight years ago. As for the business, that's all Sara, too. Peter just runs it. I own twenty per cent of the business and under our agreement they aren't allowed to sell any of their share without my approval. Their money is all tied up, there was no way they could raise that kind of capital in such a short space of time. I can.'

'Have they ever asked to sell it?'

'About a year ago, but I said no.'

'Did they give a reason for that?'

'They were going through some marital problems and thought moving away and getting a new start would make things better. You can't run away from your problems though, especially not when you are married to them. It's no secret that me and Peter have never really got on very well. He's a bit of a snake. I've never trusted him and I've told Sara as much.'

'That must have made things tense between you,' Imogen said.

'It's always been just us two – her mother died when she was very young – and so it's my job to make sure she doesn't get hurt. She trusts me and I trust her. Sara convinced me he wasn't a bad guy.'

'How did she do that?'

'He signed a pre-nup. If they divorce, he gets nothing. Everything remains in her name and he is on the books of the business as an employee only, not a proprietor. He did have some money of his own when they met, of course – owned a yacht and Maserati – so it wasn't like he was a bum who was just in it for the money.'

Imogen shot a glance at Gabriel, who had clearly noticed the same thing she had.

'And what happens to the house and business in the event of Sara's death?'

'He gets half, Marcus gets the other half.'

That was considerable motive in Imogen's eyes. It was all just speculation at this point, but at least it made her feel justified in looking further into Peter Carlyle. He had everything to gain by the death of his wife and son, but they needed to find out the details of the insurance policies before they could go after him. So far all of this was stemming from a hint of a look on Peter Carlyle's face and that would hardly stand up in court – she needed to get to the bottom of this and find hard evidence.

'Thank you for answering our questions, Mr Dunn.'

'Please find Marcus. Sara absolutely worships him, and I don't know if she would get over it if anything happened to him. I think Peter has always been jealous of the way she dotes on that boy.'

'If you could keep our conversation between us that would be great,' Imogen said.

'Don't worry, I won't say a thing. If you think he was involved doesn't that mean the kidnappers have always known that the police have been involved from the start?'

'We would assume so, but we need evidence before we can proceed with that assumption.'

'If they do know then we have wasted so much time. I could do one of those things on TV – you know, a plea? I could offer a reward for any information.'

'Rewards tend to bring with them a lot of misinformation. For now, before we know for sure whether Peter is involved, we have to act as we have been,' Imogen said.

'Of course,' he said.

'Thank you, Mr Dunn,' Gabriel said. He made his way towards the door, followed by Imogen.

Outside, they got back in the car.

'Well, that was enlightening,' Imogen said.

'I guess Peter Carlyle just became our prime suspect,' Gabriel replied.

'You're damn right he did.'

Chapter Thirty-Two

Back at the station, Imogen was sifting through everything they had so far on the Carlyles to see if there was anything there she had missed. The information from the father-in-law, Gregory Dunn, had certainly cemented her suspicions about Peter Carlyle. He was no good and she was convinced that, on some level, he was involved in the disappearance of his own son and the attempted murder of his wife. Speculation was fine, evidence was better.

As she worked she found herself occasionally glancing at DC Webb who was sitting opposite her reading through the property portfolio of Dunn and Co. A long shard of his jet-black hair had fallen out of place and was hanging in front of his face. He glanced up from under his eyelashes and caught her looking, holding her gaze for a moment.

'Find something?' he said.

'No. You?' she said, instantly flicking her eyes back down at the page, embarrassed to be caught.

'Maybe. I'll tell you when I'm sure.'

She had texted Gary to ask if he had any more information on the insurance company payments, and she saw him bounding towards her with that look on his face that said he had found something. He didn't wait for an invitation to sit and – thankfully – hadn't seemed to notice the slightly awkward moment between her and Webb.

'So, the insurance payments on his account were indeed for life insurance. There were four payments in total. Each payment we saw on his account was for two policies.'

'You're confusing me. What do you mean?' Imogen said.

'The insurance was for both Sara and Marcus. Who takes out life insurance on their kid?'

'That's not a normal thing to do,' Imogen said.

'Right?'

'Anything else?' she asked, knowing there was something else.

'This is weird. So, there was another regular payment – this time going out of the Dunn and Co. business account, rather than the Carlyles' personal joint account – and, according to the paperwork I've found, it was set up by Peter Carlyle. We didn't notice it before because it came through the business, but since Gregory Dunn gave us full access to everything . . .'

'What is it?' Imogen said, not sure she could stand Gary's build-up any longer. He clearly had something exciting to tell her.

'I called Gregory Dunn to ask about it but he had no idea what it was. There is no evidence that Sara even knew about it—'

'Jesus, Gary, will you get to the point!'

'Peter set up regular payment going out to Shieldwall Security.'

'What?' Imogen said, jarred to hear the name of Adrian's employer.

'If only you knew someone who worked at Shieldwall . . . Maybe you could find out what exactly it is that Peter Carlyle was paying for? Dunn said they don't normally use private security.'

'Shieldwall do loads of stuff. It could be anything.'

'But you're going to ask Adrian, right?' Gary seemed excited to have an excuse to involve Adrian. She knew he missed having him around.

'I'll have to tell him, but I think I should probably go through proper channels before I do anything underhanded.'

'Where's the fun in that?' Gary said.

'If you have a way of finding out what Peter Carlyle was using Shieldwall for without alerting him to the fact that we're looking into his affairs it might be safer for Marcus,' Gabriel said, obviously listening to their conversation.

'I'll see what the Anti Kidnap guy thinks. I guess he is the best person to ask about this,' Imogen said.

'Is it all right if I keep looking into these properties in the meantime? There are loads of empty ones, and a few commercial and unfinished ones, so I wonder if we might get some pertinent information from them. Maybe I could go and check them out?' Gabriel said.

'First of all, contact the person who owns the building where Sara Carlyle was found, see if they have any connections to Dunn and Co. After that, go home and get some sleep. Then I reckon in the morning take Jarvis and do a quick recce of the properties. Let me know what you find.'

'What are you going to do?' Gary said.

'I'll speak to the DCI and Walsh, see what the next steps should be. Walsh said he would call if the kidnappers got in touch. Then I'll call the hospital and check on Sara Carlyle's condition. Then, I guess I go home,' Imogen said.

'I'll keep digging into Carlyle, see if I can find any social media connections for him, or anything online,' Gary said.

'I don't know what I would do without you, Gary,'

Imogen said before heading to DCI Kapoor's office to relay what the team had found. It finally felt like she had something, like she was a step ahead of the game. There was nothing worse than feeling you were five moves behind the criminal. She wished she had trusted her instinct from the beginning, and filed this under lessons learned. Self-flagellation wouldn't help anyone right now, least of all Marcus Carlyle. There was no time to waste.

As Imogen walked across the bullpen to DCI Kapoor's office, the phones started to ring. DCI Kapoor opened the door and ushered her over.

'We've got a problem,' Kapoor said as Imogen entered the DCI's office and saw the TV was paused on the image of Gregory Dunn talking at a press conference with the caption: 'CHILD KIDNAPPED, REWARD OFFERED FOR INFORMATION THAT LEADS TO RECOVERY'. Imogen blew her cheeks out in frustration.

'I told him not to do that,' she said.

'This is a logistical nightmare,' Kapoor said. 'This should never have happened.'

'I explained to him this wasn't a good idea. He asked me about it directly. I said rewards lead to misinformation.'

'Well, I think we can all understand his frustration. I just hope it doesn't cost Marcus his life. You better buckle up, detective, we are about to be inundated with false leads.'

'Maybe we'll get lucky,' Imogen said unconvincingly.

'I'll sort out some extra bodies to take on the phone lines. Brace yourself, Grey.'

Although this was far from ideal, Imogen could only hope they would get some pertinent information from at least one of the tips. Rewards did bring the crazies and the liars out, but all they could do was make the best of the hand they had been dealt. What's done was done and maybe this would lead to the break they needed to find Marcus.

Chapter Thirty-Three

It was unusual for Imogen to get back to Adrian's house and find it completely dark this early in the evening, Adrian was usually cooking or watching some pseudo-documentary on TV. She ventured upstairs and saw Adrian was asleep. Not wanting to disturb him, she got in the shower – just a quick in and out – and once out she towel-dried her hair and put it in a loose bun before slipping on a vest and jogging bottoms.

She went back down into the kitchen and looked through the cupboards. Was it worth her trying to cook anything or would it be more considerate not to even attempt it? She found pasta – it was really hard to mess that up and so she put a pan of water on the hob and tipped the pack in once it was boiling. She looked through her emails while she waited for the food to cook, nothing from Gary. She heard steps on the stairs and Imogen felt a mixture of both excitement and dread, wondering what mood Adrian would be in today.

'Hello?' he called out apprehensively.

She poked her head out into the hallway to see him brandishing an old cricket bat he kept by the bed.

'I'm making dinner. Are you excited?' she said, smiling.

He leaned the bat against the wall and followed her into the kitchen, looking mildly irritated.

'You're home.'

'I am. I feel like I haven't seen you in ages.' She moved

towards him and put her arms around him. They kissed but she could feel him pulling away almost as soon as they'd started. The days when he could barely keep his hands off her were a distant memory.

'Tough day?' she said.

'Not really, quite boring on the whole, but I'm really tired after all that stakeout nonsense. I might just freshen up, if that's OK?'

'Of course it's OK,' she said.

And just like that he was gone again, back up the stairs. She heard the shower running. He seemed to be annoyed all the time these days, snappy and cold. She pushed her reservations aside like she always did and started to chop the garlic.

They sat opposite each other at the dining table, Imogen watching Adrian push the food around the plate as was usual. It was pasta with garlic and cheese, it wasn't anything special, but it was quite nice if she did say so herself.

'Did you find the boy?' he said, after several minutes' silence. It was unusual for him to actually ask about her day.

'No. We have a few more leads though . . . which is actually something I wanted to speak to you about.'

'Me?'

'Yes. Top secret of course, but when we were going through the father's financials we found he has regular payments going out to Shieldwall. I thought maybe you could find out what that was all about.'

'You know I signed an NDA when I started work there. I can't tell you anything. Just get a warrant and do it properly,' Adrian said, clearly annoyed.

'I'm worried it will tip him off that we're on to him.

That could put the boy in danger. If you can find anything then I can push through proper channels, but it might just be nothing, and I don't want to waste any time on it if it is.'

'Oh, right, and if I need anything for my job and ask you to get it for me then you'll do it, will you?'

'That's different and you know it. I'm trying to find a little boy before something terrible happens to him,' Imogen said, frustrated at Adrian and herself at the same time. She stood and took her plate out to the kitchen, opening the bin and sliding the food inside. Adrian appeared in the doorframe.

'I'll see what I can do,' he said with a resigned half-smile on his face.

'You think I'm a hypocrite, don't you?' Imogen said.

'I'll go in a bit early tomorrow and try and get to the files. They keep everything in hard copy in big metal cabinets. They're really paranoid about hackers and ransomware.'

'Is that something you can do?'

'Allison who works in the records office is pretty useless; she smokes like a chimney and is always off out on a cigarette break – so I'll see if I can look then.'

'There are no cameras in there?'

'Not in the records office. If I do this thing for you then you can't ask me to do anything else. This is a one-time-only deal.'

'Thank you. I really appreciate it.'

Adrian came over and put his arms around her waist before kissing her on the lips. She kissed him back and relished the moment while she could, before he took it away from her again. He didn't have the patience or passion he used to have and, as always, the interaction was on his terms.

Feeling so impossibly needy around him was starting to grate. It wasn't like she wanted him to be something he wasn't, she just wanted him to be *him* again. At first, she'd thought this shift in behaviour was a temporary thing, caused by the case they'd been working on, the fact that he'd left the police, Tom getting older, etc. She'd made so many excuses in her head, come up with so many theories about how he would be back to himself soon, but he still wasn't. If anything, the gulf between them was widening. Was this all she deserved? This tense and difficult relationship? Surely, she was worth more than that.

Was he ever going to change? And if he wasn't, could she live with that?

Chapter Thirty-Four

FOUR DAYS MISSING

Gabriel followed DS Grey's command and took DC Jarvis with him to look at the list of unoccupied properties managed by Dunn and Co. as, now that Peter Carlyle was in the frame, it made sense to look at any buildings he might have had access to. Gabriel got the impression from Ben Jarvis that he thought he was somehow better or more senior to him, probably because he had spent a couple of years as a PC locally, whereas Gabriel had done his uniformed training in Kent. There was something very aggressive about Jarvis – he had a school-bully vibe about him – and though it was unusual for Gabriel to take an instant dislike to someone, Jarvis had managed that feat.

They had eight properties to look through in total. Most had been vacant for several years, due to their owners being abroad and just using Dunn and Co. as a property management facility. Two of them were due to be destroyed soon, but certain legalities hadn't yet been finalised. He didn't know what they were looking for, but Gregory Dunn had handed over the keys to all of the properties in question. Gabriel couldn't tell if he was more motivated to find his grandson or to get his son-in-law put in prison. Why not both?

The first three properties had been relatively easy to

search – small, no hidden corners, nothing particularly sinister about them – and they were on their way to the fourth property on the list, an old factory that was due to be condemned soon. It had been standing empty for almost a decade and, according to Gregory Dunn, there had been some contention about who the proprietor was, which was stalling the demolition.

Standing at the entrance, Gabriel already felt uneasy – there was something wrong with this place and he thought he could smell coffee, which suggested someone else had been there recently. He looked over to DC Jarvis with wide eyes and then pressed himself against the wall, indicating to him that they needed to exercise caution. Gabriel felt he had honed his sixth sense for danger while in prison, and in that respect he had the edge over his colleague; he knew criminals in a way Jarvis probably never could.

Jarvis seemed confused at Gabriel's actions at first but then followed suit.

Gabriel's heart was thumping in his ears as they crept through the derelict building, where the floor wasn't cracked concrete it creaked underneath them. The whole structure looked unsafe and the tarpaulin-lined walls seemed to whisper as they walked past. He suddenly wasn't sure if they should be here on their own.

Gabriel couldn't tell what kind of factory this might have been as it was mostly empty with only the occasional pallet or pile of rubbish. An old mattress in one of the rooms made him very uneasy, although it looked like even that hadn't been touched in years, but still there was that recent, fresh smell of coffee. Finally, he saw a throwaway cup he recognised on a half-broken-down wall – Lava Java, one of the newer coffee shops in town. It had only been open a few months. That wasn't enough to consider calling for back-up though – they would be laughed out of the station for calling over a coffee cup – and so they carried on.

They went down the stairs into the basement and Gabriel got out his torch as the light was a little less than ideal down here. There was some sunlight pouring in through glass bricks but it was limited and the far corner of the basement was still in total darkness. There were blue plastic barrels against the wall, the smell of coffee replaced with a different smell now, an unpleasant and sweet odour. Gabriel looked over to Jarvis who was covering his mouth.

'Wait here,' Gabriel said quietly, shattering the silence, now confident the factory was actually empty.

He opened the first barrel: it was empty. The second one had some rubbish in it – wrappers and carrier bags, and a couple more coffee cups from Lava Java – and looked like it had been used as a bin. The third and final barrel was heavier than the other two. Gabriel held his breath as he spun the lid to release it and found it took all of his courage to keep spinning until he felt it detach. He pulled the lid to one side and had to look away when he saw the Hulk hat and the Spider-Man costume.

Jarvis started retching in the corner, contaminating the crime scene, and Gabriel yelled at him as he pulled out his phone.

'Go outside if you're going to do that!'

Jarvis didn't need to be told twice.

Gabriel looked back into the barrel, at the hat resting on the costume. Whatever was in that barrel, it wasn't big enough to be a child's body and the relief he felt was immense. He had expected to find a body. Thought he had. But it was just Marcus's clothes and whatever was weighing this barrel down, it wasn't a child. Maybe it was a dead animal of some kind, which would explain the sickly sweet smell in the air.

This was a significant lead. He knew everyone was working tirelessly to find the boy alive and with a couple of words he was about to give them all something to work with, something tangible, actual evidence. They knew Marcus had been here, so maybe they could figure out where the kidnappers had taken him.

Hopefully this crime scene would also give them more evidence against Peter Carlyle. Gabriel dialled DS Grey and listened breathlessly for the click.

'Hello, DC Webb. How did the property search go?'

'He's not here. Marcus. But he was. We found his clothes.'

'Stay put. I'll send the forensics team to bag everything and I think we'll get the canine unit down there as well, see if they can get any leads from his clothes. You and Jarvis secure the scene in the meantime and don't let anyone in or out of the property unless you know them.'

'Yes, ma'am.'

'Well done, Gabriel, great work.'

Chapter Thirty-Five

Today was the day Jason's mother and brother were both coming home. Jason had been so distracted by his father's appearance and all the problems he created that he'd forgotten about Luke's possible imminent release. He was so relieved when he got the call from Luke. Finally some good news.

After a night in hospital, Jean was being discharged, and Jason was eternally grateful that her wounds had only been superficial and that – despite what he'd thought he'd heard from under the bed – she hadn't been sexually assaulted. He didn't know how he would live with himself if she had.

As for Doug, he was still causing them drama even in death; Jason and his mother had been left with the funeral arrangements. The Black Lamb pub was putting on his wake and they'd found a few thousand in Doug's boot to cover the cost of a service. All in all, it was a better send-off than he would have had had he not turned up when he did. Jason was surprisingly unmoved by his father's death, and felt bad for not feeling bad, but their connection had been short and shallow and so there was nothing to mourn. Despite the whirlwind Doug had created when he breezed back into Jason's life, the impact was minimal and the memories were already fading. There was nothing left for Jason to feel, so he guessed the anger was gone. His dad hadn't left them because he had this big exciting better life, he'd left because he was unreliable and full of shit. Jason didn't need that in his life right now. Or ever.

Jason was standing outside the prison gates when Luke emerged and threw his arms around his brother in a way he hadn't been able to in months. Luke was more of a father to Jason than Doug had ever been and it was only now that Jason realised how much growing up Luke had had to do over the last few years. He had been fourteen when Doug left and immediately assumed the responsibilities of man of the house. The only way he knew how to provide was hustling and stealing, so prison was always inevitable for Luke. Jason wanted to make sure it wasn't inevitable for him, too.

When the brothers arrived at the hospital, Jean was ready and waiting. The swelling in her face had diminished to just an array of purple marks on her skin. She looked terrible but, at the same time, happy to see her boys. There was a man standing with her.

'These are my boys,' she said to him as they approached. He smiled at Jason and Luke.

'Your mum's been very excited to go home.'

'Christopher's been keeping me company this morning until you arrived.'

'Thanks, mate, we've got this now,' Luke said abruptly.

'Luke! Don't be rude,' Jean said, embarrassed.

'I'll drop by and see you in the week, Jean. Nice to meet you, boys. Look after your lovely mum there.'

The boys both nodded in unison at Christopher as he walked away. When he disappeared round the corner, Jason turned back to his mum, who was crying.

'I'm sorry,' she said to Luke, pulling him into her arms, wincing at the contact but still clinging on. This broke Jason's heart. He knew what she was apologising for –

for letting Doug back in when he was the snake Luke had always said he was. But with those two words a line was drawn under everything that had gone before and there was an unspoken agreement that they were going to be starting a new life.

Luke was forgiven for getting into a fight and ending up in prison.

Jean was forgiven for the years of hell she put the boys through by constantly allowing herself to be manipulated by Doug.

And Jason? There was only one thing he needed forgiveness for and he was going to fix it today.

'You ready to go, Mum?' Luke said.

'Can you bring those chocolates off the side?' Jean said. Jason wasn't sure – it was hard to tell with all the discolouration on her face – but he thought she was blushing a little. The chocolates were lavishly boxed, handmade chocolates from a chocolatier in town. Jason recognised the logo, although he had never been inside the shop.

'Where did you get these?' he asked.

'The lady from that bed over there, Barbara, sadly passed away last night. She was Christopher's mum – that's how we met – and Christopher popped in to say goodbye to me today as he knew I was leaving. He's been very sweet.' His mum smiled one of those coy smiles she sometimes got when she was starting to like someone. Jason had seen it too many times before. Whoever Christopher was, though, he couldn't be any worse than Jason's father. Things were already beginning to feel better. There was just one thing left for Jason to do.

'Are you two all right to get home? I've got a thing I have to take care of, but I'll be home a little later on,' he said, handing his mother the chocolates and backing out of the hospital room. Since Jason had seen the plea on television it felt like a matter of urgency to say something, like he couldn't go home with this weighing on him anymore, like he finally knew what to do to make things right.

Jason approached the police station with apprehension; he had always been brought up to avoid and fear the police, maybe even hate them. He had seen the news the night before, and the offer of a reward for any news about the young boy he had seen taken, the boy he could have saved. He wondered, had Doug not interfered, would the boy be home by now? He hadn't shown the picture on his phone to the police before, and he felt like maybe it was his desire to be absolutely nothing like his father that was driving him to making this decision now. He was walking into the lion's den, through choice.

The police had questioned him at his house when he'd called the ambulance for his mother, but they questioned him as a victim, and he only told them everything that had transpired that night – he never told them he knew the possible reason why his home had been invaded. Now, he was resigned to making a statement, even if that meant he would get in trouble. He wouldn't lie about any of it.

He hadn't told Luke what he was going to do because he knew what his brother would say. He would tell him to stay out of it, but the truth was he couldn't. He couldn't live with himself if a kid got hurt because of him. He had an actual photograph of the men who took the boy – that had to be useful. And if Jason wanted to be treated like an adult then he had to take responsibility for his own decisions. He knew – he *knew* – this was the right thing to do. He stepped forward and through the doors, approaching the front desk with caution.

'Can I help you?' The lady behind the counter smiled at him but he could see she was tired, maybe at the end of her shift, desperate to get home and go to bed. He knew that feeling.

'I need to speak to someone about that kid who was kidnapped. I have some information.'

Chapter Thirty-Six

Imogen sat across the table from the young man who had walked into the station claiming he had information about the Carlyle abduction. She could feel DC Jarvis shuffling nervously next to her and hoped he lept his mouth shut. He had a propensity to say the wrong thing. Jason Hitchin chewed his lip nervously and stared straight ahead, in her direction, but through her. He seemed really anxious, maybe even afraid. Was he just here for the reward money, to give them bogus information?

'I heard about what happened to your father. I'm really sorry,' Imogen said. News of a home invasion like that, especially with a fatality, spread through the station fast.

'Yeah,' he said, chewing his lip even harder than before.

'So, why have you come here today, Jason? What is it you think you know about what happened to Marcus Carlyle? You know you only get the reward money if it leads to the recovery of the boy.'

'I saw it happen. I saw them take him. I don't care about the reward. Keep it.'

Imogen sat forward. She could tell instantly that he was telling the truth.

'Were you the person who called the police? Were you in the house opposite?'

'Yeah. Why did no one come? Why wasn't it on the news?'

'Kidnapping is complicated; sometimes it's best if no one knows.'

'I guess.'

'What can you tell me about the people you saw take him?' Imogen asked.

'Two blokes, white, over forty, I reckon. White van. They had black face coverings like balaclavas.'

'Why didn't you come forward sooner?'

'I'm sorry. I thought I would get in trouble. I wasn't supposed to be in that house and I panicked. I'm really sorry.'

'So, Jason, tell me from the start what you saw.'

'I went round in the morning to my ex's house. I was angry for getting dumped and I knew she wasn't home as she'd posted online that they'd gone out on her dad's yacht for a couple of weeks. The kid was playing on his bike outside, and I helped him get it out of some wires before I went in the house. He was a sweet kid. Then this van pulled up. I looked out the window because I was worried it was Amanda and her family come back off holiday. I saw the men inside had a gun on the dashboard. They got out and pulled that boy into the van. Then they drove off.'

'Then what happened?'

'I called the police and I left.'

'Can you remember any distinguishing features about the men?'

Jason reached into his pocket and pulled out his phone. 'I took photos.'

Imogen took a deep breath and tried not to look annoyed. 'Next time, maybe start with that.'

He unlocked the phone and found the pictures, sliding the device across the table to her.

Imogen picked the phone up and looked through four

photos of the kidnapping. Only one had a clear image of one of the two men's face but it was so much more than they'd had up to this point. If only Jason had come forward sooner, maybe they could have found Marcus before he was moved.

'I'm sorry. I know I should have handed this in before.'

'Why didn't you?' she asked.

'I guess I wasn't sure it was real at first. I was scared. I could make a million excuses, but I really don't know.'

'What happened at your house . . . Was that anything to do with this?'

'My dad hasn't been around for the last seven years. He came home the day the kid was taken. I think that maybe messed my head up a bit. I showed him the photo and I think he figured out it was a kidnapping or something. He made us go back to Amanda's. We watched the house and we followed that lady with the suitcase to the bus station.'

'You took the money?'

'Not me, no. I didn't know what was going to happen. I didn't know . . . I swear. As soon as I figured out he was up to no good I bailed. I left my dad at the bus station and went home. When he came home later, he had a few grand and I realised what he had done.'

'Where's the money now?'

'I have no idea. He didn't tell me. He took me to a pub and was flashing it about a bit, bought some champagne in and stuff. I heard the guys who broke into our house mention the pub – The Black Lamb – so obviously they heard him talking about the money or someone who was there told them. He wasn't exactly discreet.'

'Were the men who came to your house the same guys you saw in the van?' Imogen said – she would make sure to pass on the name of the pub to officers dealing with the break-in and murder at Jason's house.

'I don't know, I didn't see them. I was hiding under the bed the whole time.' He looked embarrassed as he said it and wiped his eyes, even though he wasn't crying.

'It's OK. I can see how this was all very confusing for you.'

'I'm really sorry.'

'Officer Jarvis here is going to get you a hot drink of tea while I go and hand this phone off to my forensic tech guy. He will only take the photos and then I can get the phone back to you ASAP.'

'Am I in a lot of trouble?'

'I don't know yet. We need to recover that money so if you can give us any idea on that . . .'

'If I knew where he put it I would tell you. I don't want it.'

'OK. You relax here. I'll be back soon.'

Imogen left the interrogation room, happy to finally have a real lead on the kidnappers. If the men heard the information from someone at The Black Lamb then the chances were that someone there might know who they were. Now she had a photo as well. She might not have been able to get to Marcus Carlyle yet, but she was getting closer.

Chapter Thirty-Seven

Sara Carlyle could hear voices. It was her father, but she couldn't hear who he was talking to. From the tone of his voice, she guessed it was Peter. They had never got on; the two most important men in her life couldn't stand each other. Sara's arm was itching and she desperately wanted to scratch it but she couldn't move. Her throat felt strange too and she couldn't close her mouth – she was breathing but suffocating at the same time. She opened her eyes, struggling to focus on the room around her. She was in a hospital bed, surrounded by flowers. Her father was standing nearby, shouting something into his phone, although she couldn't really focus on his words. She felt like she was crawling out of a deep dark hole.

Her father turned and saw her, immediately throwing his phone on the chair and rushing to her aid, quickly pressing a red button by her bedside.

'Sara, darling, it's all right. Daddy's here,' he said in a soothing voice, reminding her of all the times when she'd woken up screaming in the middle of the night as a child and he'd come and sit by her bedside until she fell asleep again.

Two nurses rushed into the room and she felt scared as they pulled at the wires and tubes surrounding her.

'Can you hear me, Sara?' one of the nurses said. 'I'll get you more comfortable, just relax for a moment.'

Telling someone who didn't know what was going on to relax was an exercise in futility. Sara closed her eyes for a moment, desperately trying to remember what had brought her here. A panic set in as she remembered Marcus, leaving the money on the bus for the kidnappers, walking through the city and then being pulled into a small alley where she was attacked. She felt the pain in her side, itchy as the wounds were beginning to heal. She had survived, even though she remembered feeling certain as she fell on the cold hard ground and watched her blood ebb away from her that she was going to die.

She looked at her father's face, contorted with concern for her as the nurses pulled the tube from her throat, forcing her to close her eyes for a few seconds again. The manhandling stopped and she was just lying there. She could breathe now.

'Dad?' she said in a hoarse whisper. 'Where's Marcus? Did they get him back?'

'You just rest for now, darling,' Gregory said.

Why wasn't he answering her question? He was trying to spare her feelings. Where the hell was Marcus? The tears sprang from her eyes before she even had time to process her thoughts. She had so many questions. How had this happened? She did everything she was supposed to do.

'Where's Peter?'

'He's on his way. The police will want to speak to you about what happened, too,' Gregory said.

'I don't really remember anything.'

'Then you can tell them that. I'm here with you. I'm not going anywhere.' He leaned forward and kissed her on the forehead.

Where was her sweet baby now? The hurt was more than she could hold inside, she could feel the wave of

164

emotion pulling back inside her before the tsunami of grief hit. How on earth was she going to get through this? *Was* there any way through this? What if they never got their baby boy back? Who was she now if she wasn't Marcus's mother? She wasn't a mother at all. She was nothing.

'Is he dead?' she finally asked, unable to cope with the swirling thoughts in her head.

'No, no. The police don't think so.'

'So where the hell is he?'

'We'll find him, I promise,' her father said.

Chapter Thirty-Eight

Imogen stared at the photographs Jason had given them along with the images of the crime scene where they had found Marcus's clothes. Jason's photos were truly a gift, and it was so much more than they'd had yesterday. They hadn't been able to save Marcus yet, and she was damned if she was going to let those bastards get away with it. Statistically speaking, the odds of finding Marcus alive were decreasing by the second but Imogen refused to entertain the idea he might be dead. She wasn't giving up. It was hard not to be annoyed that she didn't have this information earlier, as it might have made all the difference, but still, better late than never.

The image of the white van was already providing a wealth of information. Though it had no distinctive markings, at least they now had a make and model, which allowed them to narrow their search even further. That's how these things worked: you start with an infinite amount of options and then narrow them down one by one until only a few possibilities remain. It was tedious work but it was almost always the way it happened. People didn't just walk in off the street and confess to things. If you were lucky, you got some idiot who committed a crime in front of a camera with a name badge on, or leave his DNA and fingerprints all over the place, but those cases were a million to one.

Gary was running the pictures through the facial recognition scanners.

So many threads connected to Peter Carlyle in some way but she still couldn't prove anything. Not at the moment. The fact that the property where they'd found Marcus's clothing was managed by Dunn and Co. wasn't conclusive evidence in itself of Carlyle's involvement. Several people worked in those offices so it could just as easily be a disgruntled employee.

She looked again at the picture of the barrel filled with rubbish Gabriel had found. They had managed to extract DNA from saliva on the coffee cup but it didn't match anyone in the database. There were individual photos of every wrapper in the bin – lots of sweets and crisps, the kind of things you buy to keep a kid quiet and distracted. There were some other scraps of paper, including a receipt. Paid in cash so not particularly useful. It was slightly crumpled in the photo and so she couldn't read the whole thing. She could see wrappers pertaining to most of the items on the list. The receipt also listed cigarettes – Mayfairs. She needed to get a look at the actual receipt and so she went down to Evidence.

She took the receipt out of the evidence bag to hold it up to the light. The ink was faded and the paper was crumpled. It had been marked incorrectly as being from the afternoon of the kidnapping, but actually it was from a few days before. She put the receipt back in the evidence bag before returning to her desk, grabbing the photos, and heading to the hospital.

Chapter Thirty-Nine

Adrian walked into the office about forty-five minutes before he was due to start work. He had told Mick to pick him up from HQ for tonight's surveillance instead of from home because he had to do some paperwork before they headed out. A different assignment meant a different schedule. He hoped Imogen didn't mind too much. Allison was in the office getting her cigarettes out of her handbag when he arrived. The amount she smoked, Adrian wasn't sure if there was anything else in her handbag but packets of Marlboro Gold.

'Hey, gorgeous,' she said. 'Is it that time already?'

'Almost, I'm a bit early.'

'We don't get overtime. Well, I don't. Maybe you do,' she said, smiling too widely.

'I've just got to check some things in the file room.' He put his backpack on the visitor's chair as she groaned, clearly annoyed her break might be delayed. 'I know where it is so I can grab it myself, don't worry.'

'Great! I've already been in there three times today.'

'Can you tell me if we keep a centralised list of Shieldwall employees?'

'Not here, we don't. In fact, I'm not even sure there is one in the building. It's certainly not something I've ever seen. Why do you ask?'

'Oh, I just wondered. Mick makes it all sound so mysterious and like it's a secret who our co-workers are.

I thought he was pulling my leg.' The way Mick had behaved in the Garvey house had made Adrian curious about what else went on here. What other jobs had Shieldwall crossed the line for? The urge to investigate was overwhelming so maybe he could scrape together some information. It was clear Mick wasn't being completely open.

'If you know an employee's name or number there will be a file on them in there, but a lot of the people they hire are freelance – sometimes just for one-off jobs – and as far as I can tell there are a fair few who don't want to be on any lists. I don't really know how it works, to be honest. I don't really deal with that side of things,' she said, suddenly clamming up, probably remembering she shouldn't be speaking about this stuff.

'Thanks, I was just curious,' Adrian said, trying to sound as unbothered as possible.

'Well, you crack on, I'll be outside if you need me.' She punched in the code to the file room and left the door open, which was not something she was supposed to do. Adrian felt bad that she trusted him, bad that he had lied to her. Still, he wanted to help Imogen. As if that could somehow make up for all the lies he had told her this last year. It was as if his whole life was a lie these days, so why not add this to the list? At least this lie was by choice.

The filing room smelled like a library, full of thou-sands of sheets of paper, dating back decades. Shieldwall preferred hard copies to digital and so their reports were mostly written up by hand and filed in this locked room. Allison was supposed to walk you to the file you needed, watch you read it and then put it back, then walk you back out and lock the room. No phones were allowed in the file room either, but Allison never checked. When Adrian joined the company she was not long back from her third maternity leave and he guessed her tolerance for the minutiae had gone out the window. It hadn't taken him long to figure out that she would do anything to get out of doing her actual job and, as there were no cameras in the filing room, if you knew how to get round Allison it wasn't hard to go digging for things you shouldn't. Luckily she had taken a shine to Adrian, probably because he had one of those trustworthy faces – he had been told as much many times in the past.

He still felt paranoid as he walked through the lines of filing cabinets, glancing behind him to check he was alone. He found the cabinet he needed and slid out the drawer, looking for the Carlyle file. He grabbed it and opened it to find there were seven sheets of paper inside: a receipt of payment, Carlyle's information and a referral number or something. Adrian pulled out his phone and photographed the sheets one by one, slipping his phone back in his pocket, opening the drawer again and putting the file back inside as soon as he was done. It took less than a minute.

A thought flitted through his mind, and as soon as it occurred to him it seemed like he had no other choice but to look for the name 'Corrigan' on one of the files. It wasn't in the drawer with 'Carlyle' – the last name there was 'Colman' – so he opened the drawer underneath and it was the first name he saw. It didn't necessarily mean anything that they had had dealings with him. They provided security for a variety of reasons.

There was too much in the Corrigan file for him to photograph before Allison returned, so he just grabbed the folder and slipped it in the back of his waistband, hoping his jacket would hide the bulk for long enough for him to get somewhere safe and put it in his backpack. He hadn't come here for this reason but, now he had seen it, there was no other choice. He was driven by something other than logic, though he wasn't sure if it was curiosity for the truth or just an obsession he couldn't let go of. It felt like the latter. Everything else was incidental until he knew who had attacked him. Until then, his mind would be consumed with finding out. He wondered what else he would think about when he finally knew, if that ever happened. It seemed like such a distant and intangible dream.

Allison popped her head into the room.

'You OK?' she said.

'Yeah,' he replied, straightening up.

'Did you get what you came for?'

'I was just checking I had the right address for a client. All done now. Thanks, Allison.'

He smiled and left the filing room with her following closely behind. He hoped he wasn't rustling the files as he moved. He grabbed his bag.

'Are you around Friday after work? A few of us are going for drinks in the Duke of York, if you want to join,' Allison said.

'I might be, I'll check. Thanks.'

The phone rang and he saw that as his cue to leave. Allison answered and he was in the car park before she had finished introducing herself. He had thirty-five minutes before he had to meet Mick for three hours' evening surveillance and, if he moved fast, he could ditch the papers at home and then get back in time. He walked past a bus stop and paused in front of a house. One of the good things about being ex-police is you tended to get adept at looking for CCTV and this was one area he knew there was none. He bent down as if to tie his shoe, swiftly removed the papers from his waistband and put them into his backpack. He slung the bag on his back and then started to sprint for home, propelled mostly by the anxiety that someone was going to catch him with the file.

Adrian got home and took the folder out of his backpack, hiding it inside the condiment cabinet in the kitchen. Imogen didn't cook from scratch so the likelihood of her finding it there was pretty slim. He desperately wanted to read through it but that would have to wait until later. He took out his phone and emailed the photos of the Carlyle file from his private email to Imogen, then deleted them from his phone, just in case anyone got hold of it. He had learned from Gary that it was best not to have an email app on your phone, and to just log in via a browser and not save any passwords. Losing phones was easy and commonplace, and a real easy way to give a stranger access to every part of your life.

He left the house as quickly as he had arrived, feeling an excited buzz for the first time in a long time. All the information he already had on Corrigan had come from the few bits he had printed off back when he was still a police officer. This stuff would all be new and there might be some names in there he wasn't familiar with.

He was out of breath when he reached Shieldwall for the second time, but still in time to see Mick pulling in. He waved a hello as his partner nodded for him to get in the car so they could go and watch their client's ex-wife's house – he was paying an exorbitant spousal maintenance fee and was sure she was cohabiting with someone, which would mean he could apply to decrease the monthly payments. It felt boring and pointless, especially as the man in question, Brian Harris, was absolutely loaded, but it was the job. Adrian smiled nervously at Mick as he pulled away. In a few hours, he would be able to look at that file again. In a few hours he might have another lead.

Chapter Forty

It felt wrong to be in Sara Carlyle's hospital room that afternoon – intrusive – so Imogen wasn't surprised when Gregory Dunn gave her the look she felt she deserved. He was still angry that the ransom drop had gone wrong. Well, so was Imogen.

Sara lay staring despondently at the ceiling, her eyes connecting with nothing, lost in her own thoughts, swallowed by grief. There was no sound, no tears, and yet her pain was deafening. Peter Carlyle was sitting in the chair in the corner, not saying anything, and he seemed to be avoiding Imogen's gaze, as though he knew she was on to him.

'I'm so sorry, Mrs Carlyle,' Imogen said, knowing it meant nothing, no matter her intentions.

'Now isn't really a good time,' Gregory Dunn said, still staring at Imogen like she was personally responsible for everything that had happened.

'Leave us alone for a minute, Dad,' Sara whispered.

Dunn sighed heavily and grabbed his jacket. 'I'll go pick up a coffee. Be gone when I get back,' he said to Imogen as he pushed past DC Jarvis and left the room.

Imogen stood next to the bed, but Sara didn't look at her.

'I don't remember much about my attack, if that's why you're here.'

'I wanted to show you a couple of photographs,' Imogen said.

'What photos?' Peter said angrily. He came over to the bedside and took his wife's hand.

'I don't want to see them.' Sara turned her head away from Imogen.

'It's just a couple of things we found at the scene. We still need to find out who did this to you, and we're doing everything we can to get Marcus back.'

Sara winced as she sat up in her bed. She glanced quickly at Imogen before holding her hand out. First, Imogen gave her the photos of the wrappers they'd found in the warehouse. As Sara looked through them her lips started to quiver and Imogen could see her holding her breath, desperate not to start crying.

'He loves those purple things, and Twizzlers; he loves Twizzlers.'

'They're American sweets, aren't they?' Imogen asked.

'Yeah, my best friend lives in New York and she sends him loads for Christmas.'

'Are all these sweets ones he liked particularly then?'

'Yes. Why?' Sara turned and looked at Imogen, her eyes glistening, ready to burst with tears.

'Just a little specialist, that's all – not just stuff you would grab off the shelf.'

'They must have asked him what he liked, I suppose. At least maybe that means they are being kind to him. Is there any evidence he was hurt? Was there blood?'

'The forensic team are still working through all the evidence, as it's a big area to cover, but our preliminary findings suggest he wasn't.'

Sara turned to the next photo and saw the hat and sweatshirt laid out.

'Why did they leave his clothes behind? Why is he not wearing his clothes?' she asked in a panic.

'Your father used your image of Marcus from the day

he disappeared at his press conference, so it's likely they realised we knew what he was wearing when he was taken. We found a receipt for a top and trousers amongst the rubbish.'

'Why did you want to know about the sweets?' Peter asked. Imogen locked eyes with him and saw he wasn't even trying to look upset.

'We just need as much information as possible at this time. There was a receipt for the food there, and the shop they came from may have CCTV. Whoever took him wasn't as smart as they think. We'll get them.'

'So you still have no idea who took our son or why?' Peter said.

'We have a few possible avenues of investigation thanks to your father-in-law's television stunt. We also managed to find the witness to your son's kidnapping,' Imogen said. Not that her team had had any part in it – if Jason hadn't walked into their station, they still wouldn't know who he was.

'Why didn't they come forward sooner?' Carlyle asked.

'We are looking into that.' Imogen took the photos from Sara and handed her a picture with a close-up of the face of one of the kidnappers. 'Do you have any idea who this is?'

Sara studied the image, but Imogen could see no hint of recognition.

Peter's face, on the other hand, was another story, and she saw his jaw working overtime as he suppressed the urge to rip the photo from his wife's hands.

'Sorry, no idea. Should I know who this is? Is this the witness?' Sara said.

'It's a photo taken by the witness, Jason Hitchin,' DC Jarvis said.

Imogen shot Jarvis a look, furious he'd revealed Jason's

name to the Carlyles. 'I had better go before your father gets back,' she said to Sara. 'I'll send someone to take an official statement about your attack as soon as you're ready, OK?' Imogen took the picture from her.

'I don't remember much,' Sara said.

'I know. But you never know what may help. I know this is no consolation whatsoever for what you're going through right now, but I am not going to stop until we've found Marcus and the person responsible for this is brought to justice.' Imogen glanced up and looked at Peter as she said it. She wanted him to know she was on to him.

'What possible justice is there for something like this?' Sara said before lying back and closing her eyes.

'Did you ever recover the money? What happened to that?' Carlyle said.

'The witness—' DC Jarvis started, but Imogen quickly cut him off.

'Thank you, Mr and Mrs Carlyle. We will let you know as soon as we have any new information.'

Imogen smiled reassuringly and then exited the room, tugging on DC Jarvis's arm.

As soon as they were out of earshot in the corridor she allowed the anger she'd been suppressing to explode.

'What?' Jarvis said.

'We don't just blurt out witness names in front of the victim's family. We need to find out what *they* know, not tell them what *we* know!'

'I thought it was a two-way street.'

'Not in a situation like this, for fuck's sake. If in doubt, keep your mouth shut and always defer to the senior ranking officer in an interview. From here on out you are to clear everything with me or Walsh before you say it – preferably before you even think it.'

'I think you're overreacting,' Jarvis said.

'Well, don't think anything unless I bloody tell you to. You can walk back to the station. I can't even look at you right now.'

'Jesus. No wonder Miles quit.'

She ignored his final remark and walked outside to her car, Jarvis following behind her. She was in the car when she saw him reach for the handle, so she put the car in reverse and pulled back. He started to shout something but she turned the radio on loud and just left him there. He had such a chip on his shoulder and she didn't feel comfortable around him. Yes, she was supposed to be training him, showing him how to do the job properly, but she wasn't sure if she had the patience for that and he certainly didn't seem to be cut out to be a Family Liaison Officer from what she had seen so far.

As the hospital disappeared from view, she started to cry, unsure where it was coming from or what it was about this particular moment that had sent her over the edge. She missed working with Adrian, having him beside her in moments like this.

She pulled the car over and looked at the pictures again. The sweets had been purchased a few days before Marcus was taken – so how did the kidnappers know what treats would keep him compliant? She would get DC Jarvis to visit the store and try and get an ID on the person who had bought the sweets. The advance knowledge of Marcus's favourite snacks solidified Peter Carlyle's guilt in her mind. He was behind this and she was going to get him and make him pay.

Chapter Forty-One

Adrian walked home with purpose, feeling bad because he hoped Imogen wasn't there yet. He wanted to look through the file he had taken from the office; he needed to get it back before anyone noticed it was missing. She seemed to be working later and later these days, no doubt in an effort to avoid him. Who could blame her? He was a mess. He couldn't get trapped in thinking about what a loser he was right now though – he needed to focus on figuring out if anything in those files was relevant to his assault.

He was thankful to find himself alone in the house and went straight for the cupboard, taking the file upstairs to Tom's room so he could spread the sheets of paper out. Imogen never went in there and Tom rarely visited since he got a girlfriend. It was barely even Tom's room anymore. At nineteen, Tom was already a man and he couldn't bring his girlfriend back to a single bed and the Spider-Man wallpaper Adrian had put up when Tom was about six. Adrian had promised to change the room for him and he made a mental note to ask Tom, before he left for his upcoming six-month trip to Australia, what colour walls he wanted.

The file was thick with papers dating back eight years. There were invoices for extra security for corporate Christmas events, or deliveries of sensitive items, and a few reports that seemed to be written in some kind of shorthand. Adrian noticed there were several reference numbers on the pages, similar to one he had seen in the Carlyle file he'd sent to Imogen. He knew he'd come across a number like that before and logged into his email to explore a hunch. He looked at his work correspondence and, sure enough, he had a reference number like the ones in the file. It was his staff number.

The numbers referred to people. That must be why it was rare to see employee names in any of the files, as they were all referenced by their number or initials instead, which was probably more helpful. Most of the reports Adrian had worked on so far had had actual names of the employees who were working on that particular case, but it looked like the numbers were used instead on reports that were more vaguely worded and light on details – like the Corrigan file.

There were so many pages to go through. He wished he could ask Gary to help him. Gary had an uncanny ability to see patterns where other people couldn't. He considered it for a moment, but then, how would he explain it to his friend? The weight of the constant lying was such a burden, and he'd found himself pulling away from friends, from Tom, from Imogen, just to get a break from it. He knew this couldn't be helping his healing process, hiding from the truth, but still, the alternative didn't feel like a life he wanted either. He could sense it trying to seep out of him though. It was on the tip of his tongue all the time. Another reason to pull away from people.

He reached under Tom's bed and drew the rest of his research out, to see if there were any correlating factors, anything he could see that crossed over. He still had the original list of names of people who'd been working at Corrigan Construction at the time of his attack, so he looked for any paperwork that pertained to that time period within the Shieldwall file. There was one file for the week leading up to the night of August 20th. The night he was raped . . .

As Adrian read the words a chill crept through him, and he was overcome with nausea. The report was of his own general movements throughout the week, from walking to the corner shop, to going to the pub, to the nights when Imogen came over, to every action he took while working the case, following him to interviews and even to lunch. It occurred to him that Corrigan could have hurt him by hurting Imogen, so he was grateful that they hadn't done that at least.

Everything he did had been detailed, right down to the way he usually walked home. Someone had been tailing him, just like he and Mick had been watching their client's ex-wife tonight. His job felt so wrong all of a sudden, so completely unacceptable. At the end of the report was a note saying the information had been passed on to SW at the request of RC.

Adrian looked at the list of ex-con employees he had obtained last year from Corrigan Construction to compare against the Shieldwall file and one name jumped out at him straight away. Shaun Wakefield. Maybe this man knew something about that night, or at least he might be able to point Adrian to someone who did.

At that exact moment he heard the front door slam and Imogen call out his name. He quickly gathered the files again and hid them under the bed. When Imogen was asleep, he would photograph the pages and return the file to work tomorrow. He needed to go into the file room again anyway, as he had a report from his surveillance earlier that day to log; he just had to make sure that Allison let him go in alone again. Then, after work, he would go and pay this Shaun Wakefield a visit.

Chapter Forty-Two

Imogen prodded at the food on her plate. She was too full of anger and sadness to be hungry. If only she had trusted her instincts about Peter Carlyle at the start then maybe they could have nailed him before Marcus had been moved, putting them back to square one. Adrian was also being his usual distant self, completely blind to her feelings. She was too tired tonight to deal with him.

Fed up, she got up and took her plate into the kitchen, throwing the contents away and then grabbing a beer from the fridge.

Adrian came in just moments later and silently did the same. What a waste.

'What are we doing?' she said as she watched him wash the plates in the sink without even looking at her.

'What do you mean?' he said, distracted.

'We just sat in silence for the last half an hour, neither one of us ate or said a fucking word to each other. What is this? What are we doing together?'

'Oh. No. Not tonight, please, Imogen. I had a rough day at work,' Adrian said.

'Did you lose a kidnapped child and find all his clothes in a barrel? Because that was my day at work,' Imogen snipped.

'I thought the new kid found them.'

'You know what I mean.'

'I'm sorry. How are you feeling?' Adrian turned around

and folded her into his arms, but the concern seemed feigned. She could tell it was disingenuous, that he was just saying what she wanted him to say so they could go back to their faux relationship.

'Don't pretend to care now that I have you backed into a corner,' she said. 'This is so lonely. I thought you just needed time, but the more time that goes by the further apart we get. There is no love here anymore.'

'Wow. OK. That's a pretty awful thing to say,' Adrian said, looking genuinely hurt, which made her feel like a bitch. Was this gaslighting? Was he making her think she was crazy for suggesting anything was wrong? Was she reading too much into things? The same thoughts swirled around in her head as they did every time they had a conversation.

Am I overreacting?

'You're a stranger to me. How can we keep doing this? I'm having the shittiest time at work and I don't have anyone to talk to about it.'

'You can talk to me,' Adrian said.

His eyes seemed glassier than usual; were her words finally getting through to him?

'You've made it clear you don't give a shit, Adrian.' She was hurting his feelings, she knew it, but still, she couldn't stop.

'Imogen, I love you, but I'm not doing this right now. I don't want to have this discussion.'

'Well, so what? I do. I can't stand this anymore.'

'Are we breaking up? Is that what this is? You're done?' Adrian said, his voice cracking a little as he spoke.

'No. I don't know,' she said, tears in her eyes. She could see that he was hurting too and it killed her but she was beyond the end of her rope, she couldn't live in this bizarre catatonic state anymore. A fight would be an improvement on this strange and sterile environment they had slipped into.

'I wish there was a way I could make this better. I wish this wasn't so hard,' Adrian said, his voice softening to a whisper. He looked like he was about to say something important but, before the words came out, the connection between them was gone again, and she watched him disappear inside himself.

'I need some air. I'll be back in a bit,' he said and then, before she had a chance to even think about what he had just said, he was gone, the front door closing behind him. What had she done?

Chapter Forty-Three

FIVE DAYS MISSING

Gabriel was sitting with DI Walsh outside the Carlyle house the next morning, ready to take over the next shift. He was happy to work all hours – it wasn't like he had anyone to go home to and so it made sense for him to be learning as much as he could. In truth, he had never been happier than he was right now. He finally felt as though he had found a purpose. Long gone were his aspirations of becoming a tattoo artist, although he did still like to draw at night instead of watching television.

Since Imogen had first raised her suspicions about Carlyle they had been sticking to Marcus's father like glue. The kidnappers had not been in contact since their threatening call to Peter three days ago. They seemed to have dropped off the radar completely. No workable information was coming through the tip lines, and though there had been lots of sightings, they'd turned out to be nothing. Lots of confessions. Lots of lies.

The door to the house opened and Jarvis beckoned them over very conspicuously.

'Any news?' DI Walsh said as they stepped inside.

'Nothing, no phone calls whatsoever. He went to the hospital for a bit to visit his wife. He's seemed quite agitated since,' Jarvis said.

'Where is he now?' Gabriel said, noting Carlyle's absence from the main living area.

'He went for a lie-down about half hour ago. Said he had a thundering headache and needed to sleep it off.'

'I'll go let him know we're here,' Walsh said before heading up the stairs.

Gabriel was standing face to face with Jarvis, who clearly didn't like him – no worries, the feeling was mutual. From what Gabriel had seen of Jarvis around the station, most people gave him a wide berth, and he seemed to actively speak only to the female members of staff. Gabriel knew his type; he had met them before. Jarvis saw every other man as competition or a threat, and probably didn't have any friends. Then again, neither did Gabriel. He wanted to speak, to say something. Maybe if they could get past this strange posturing they could become friends, but Gabriel couldn't think of a single thing they might have in common.

'I'll get out of your hair, then,' DC Jarvis finally said and went to grab his coat from the back of one of the dining chairs just as Walsh came rushing down the stairs.

'He's gone. Call DS Grey.'

Chapter Forty-Four

Imogen was standing outside the station smoking a cigarette she had taken from Denise the Duty Sergeant. They were barely into lunch time and her nerves were already shot. She was pissed off with everything so she was taking a ten-minute break.

It wasn't all on Adrian. When she took stock of her feelings, she also felt like she had failed Sara Carlyle. They had no leads on Carlyle after he'd disappeared from his home this morning but, as anxious as she was to get out of the station, she knew the answer to where he was would be in the paperwork, not trawling the streets. They were missing something, she knew that much.

She watched as the cars passed the station and wondered where they were going, wondered how many of them were good people, how many were bad. Was life ever that simple? She looked at her phone and the files Adrian had sent through to her before they had fallen out. She hadn't even thanked him, even though he'd risked his job to get them for her. She was a terrible girlfriend. Maybe he wasn't the only one at fault here.

She could see from the photos of the file that Carlyle had used Shieldwall to follow his wife a couple of times. The notes said he suspected she was in an extramarital relationship, but each time the team had followed her she had just met with her father. Carlyle had also used

Shieldwall to follow Gregory Dunn and take note of who he was meeting. It seemed like he was searching for some sort of leverage over his father-in-law. Maybe there was a business loophole he was trying to exploit? She would have to get Gary to look at the contract in the file to see if he could spot something she was missing; she couldn't think what possible reason Carlyle would have for following Dunn.

From what she knew about Shieldwall, the business had its regular paid staff, like Adrian, who did all the stuff that was above board – surveillance, searching public records, short-term security contracts like bouncing and nightwatchmen. But, invariably, companies like this also ran side gigs, things that were slightly less savoury. Imogen couldn't imagine they would be as stupid as to document things like that.

There was a breakdown of Gregory Dunn's finances in the Shieldwall file, and even with her basic under-standing she could see he would just about be able to pull together the exact ransom requested within a rela-tively short period of time. If it had been any more it would have taken him much longer. The fact that Carlyle had asked Shieldwall to gather this information spoke volumes and, while they couldn't use the information from this file, given how she'd acquired it, Imogen had a feeling Gregory Dunn would be more than willing to give them the same facts freely.

Checking her call history, she could see no missed calls from Adrian. Unsurprising really. She didn't know what the point of her confrontation with him last night had even been. She didn't want to break up, but she was so frustrated with his behaviour and sick of keeping her mouth shut. In retrospect, she wished she had.

She went back inside to find Gary sitting at her desk.

'So I have a possible ID on the suspect in the witness's photo,' he said. 'The angle made identification really tricky; I got a few possible hits back but, after factoring in the height as well, there was only one potential match left in the area.'

'Name?'

'Shaun Wakefield. I've already told Walsh and he's speaking to the DCI,' Gary said.

'Does he have any known connections to the Carlyles?'

'None that I've found so far. He works in construction, mostly. Did a couple of stints inside a few years back for selling stolen goods. A couple of minor traffic incidents since then, but nothing significant.'

'Now he's progressed to kidnapping.'

'Maybe even attempted murder,' Gary added. 'Also, he's got a white van registered in his name.'

'It gets better.'

'He's certainly ticking plenty of the boxes.'

'We need to get hold of Gregory Dunn's financials, see how easy it was for him to get the ransom money. That's a lot of money to have ready in such a short time. I wonder if the kidnappers knew exactly how much to ask for,' Imogen said.

'I'll get right on it.'

Walsh approached them both and nodded to Imogen. 'No news on Carlyle but we found the sweet shop where the sweets were purchased and they confirmed that the man in Jason's picture was the person who bought the sweets. Gary filled me in on the particulars. Wakefield paid cash but, when we showed them the photo, they recognised his face.'

'Ready to go and see this guy?' Imogen said.

'The DCI has signed off on the Armed Response Unit coming with us as Wakefield may be armed. There was a gun in the photo Jason Hitchin gave us. We just have to wait for them before we go in. However – the bad news is we're going to have to wait as they are currently on another deployment,' Walsh replied.

'What kind of deployment? We are looking for a missing child here. What's more important than that?'

'They are in the middle of an op. There's nothing we can do but wait. We can't go in without armed support. As soon as they are available they are coming to assist us.'

'Good. Finding Marcus has to be a priority over finding Peter Carlyle,' Imogen said.

'I'll keep digging and see if I can find anything else on this Wakefield guy. No harm in making the case against him ironclad. I might even find a connection somewhere between Wakefield and Carlyle,' Gary said before disappearing.

Chapter Forty-Five

After work, Adrian walked towards Shaun Wakefield's house on Starling Street. He had been down this street before; he remembered his old school friend, Gavin, had lived here and he would call for him sometimes. This time though, the pavement felt different – steeper, as though he were climbing up a hill. Every part of him wanted to turn back but the desire to find the truth was overwhelming. It had already ruined so much of his life and now his relationship with Imogen was hanging by a thread. He had to resist his primal instinct to run away.

As he drew nearer, he couldn't help but clench his fists, almost choking on fear, terrified of who he was going to find. His palms were sweaty and his fingers slightly numb. It was madness for him to have come alone. Why hadn't he told Imogen? What if both of those men were here? What if they hurt him again? But he knew he couldn't live like this any longer. He couldn't hold his breath every time he walked down the street or turned a corner, in case he heard that voice again. He had spent the last year wondering if the faces of the men he walked past belonged to the man he spent five hours with in the back of that van.

It was now or never.

He looked at the note crumpled in his hand to check the address. He didn't know why he had written the address down. He had stared at it for long enough that it was burned on his brain. He must have stood outside the house for almost ten minutes before knocking on the door. Moving in slow motion, he tapped on the glass, part of him hoping that no one would hear. The adrenaline coursed through him as he waited to see who would open the door. A shadow moved behind the frosted glass and Adrian held his breath as the door swung open.

The man standing in front of him was around the same height as him, with a beard and scruffy clothes. Adrian could smell beer on him.

He held his breath, waiting for the man to speak, to see if it was the same voice that made nightly appearances in his nightmares, always a low menacing whisper so close to his ear he could feel tiny droplets of saliva land on him.

'Can I help you?' the man said. That voice. Adrian felt his balled fists loosen a little as soon as he heard him. He recognised it: it was the other one.

Although it wasn't the man he'd most dreaded encountering, Shaun Wakefield was the one who'd been driving the van on the night he was raped. Adrian was relieved that he could identify the voice instantly, worried his mind had been so skewed that his memory couldn't be trusted. Worried that one day he would be standing face to face with his rapist and he wouldn't have a clue.

'I'm with the police,' Adrian lied, hoping Wakefield wouldn't ask to see ID. 'We have some CCTV footage that puts your Transit van outside the bookies on Sidwell Street at the time of a robbery that happened last week.'

'That's not possible.'

'You don't own a Mark Seven Transit van?'

'I do, but it's been parked behind the house for months. It's not roadworthy so I didn't bother getting the last

MOT done, just parked it out back until I got a chance to fix it.'

'Can you verify this?'

'I'll show you the van, if you want. It's got three flat tyres: it's not been anywhere.'

'If you don't mind?'

Shaun Wakefield walked round to the side of the house and opened a gate. Adrian followed him through to a garden that obviously had road access somewhere because the van was there. He checked to see if anyone had seen him enter the tall wooden side gate before closing it behind him. He studied the van for a moment, every hair on his body standing on end. The grass and weeds grew thickly underneath it; it clearly hadn't been anywhere in a long time . . . like fourteen months.

'See?' Wakefield said.

Adrian couldn't take his eyes off the van. He could tell it was the one, he could feel it. The nausea came over him with alarming speed and, before he had time to even think, he doubled over and threw up on the ground in front of him, jumping backwards to avoid the spray as the vomit hit the pale pink paving slabs violently in the shape of a chrysanthemum.

'Jesus, mate, are you all right?'

Adrian fought to regain his composure, but this was it, this was the break he had been looking for. A mixture of fear and relief enveloped him. He wasn't sure he ever expected to get this far.

The fact that Wakefield hadn't even recognised him yet confirmed he wasn't the brains of the operation – whoever that other man in the van was, he was the one Adrian needed to find – but for now, this would do.

Adrian straightened himself up and wiped his mouth on his sleeve. The hair on his arms bristled with a combination of fear and anger. Wakefield stood awkwardly, waiting for Adrian to right himself, and Adrian rushed at him and pinned him against the wall, jamming his forearm into his windpipe.

'You don't remember me, do you?'

'Never seen you before in my life, mate,' Wakefield said, genuinely surprised at this turn of events.

'We've met before. Well, sort of. You and one of your mates took me for a ride in your van over there. Take as long as you need. It'll come to you.'

Wakefield's confusion disappeared instantly and was replaced with panic. Maybe he didn't recognise Adrian, but he knew. Maybe they had done it to so many people that that was the only thing Adrian's sentence could mean.

'I didn't have nothing to do with any of that.' He whimpered and Adrian had to stop himself from pushing his forearm harder into his neck.

'Do you know who I am now?'

'You're that copper. We was just following orders. I didn't have nothing to do with what he did to you.'

'You knew though, right? You knew what he was doing, but you still kept driving.'

'I thought he was just roughing you up a bit. I'm really sorry about what happened to you, but I swear I got nothing to do with that. He weren't right in the head. I said to him after that night we picked you up that I weren't doing it no more. I haven't even got in this van since that night, I got home and parked up and there it's stayed. That was proper messed-up. I wouldn't have had anything to do with it if I had known before, like.'

'Who was he?'

'Who?'

'Your friend from the back of the van.'

'I can't tell you. He'll kill me. He's a fucking nutjob. I'm sorry.'

Adrian seized Wakefield by the collar and dragged him into the house through the open back door. He flung him into a dining chair, which almost toppled, and grabbed a dirty fork from the draining board before bringing it down into Shaun Wakefield's knee. Wakefield cried out in pain.

'I'm going to find him, one way or another. Why not make it easy for both of us and just tell me who he is. I'm not leaving here without a name.'

Wakefield's chest was heaving. Adrian was pleased that he was afraid. He didn't even know the meaning of the word yet.

'You're a copper, you can't just stab me!'

'I'm not police anymore, thanks to you and your friend. You ruined my fucking life,' Adrian hissed through gritted teeth. He had dreamed of this moment, being face to face with one of these bastards.

'I told you, none of that was my idea.'

Adrian ripped a charger cord out of the socket on Wakefield's kitchen wall, pulled Wakefield's hands behind his back and wrapped the cord multiple times around his wrists. Turning the dial on the stove until a blue flame appeared, he grabbed a slotted metal spoon from the draining board and held the spoon over the flame, waiting for the heat to turn it into a brand.

'How about going through the rest of your life with this pattern on your face, you piece of shit.'

'You're fucking crazy! Let me go!'

'You need to tell me who the other guy was. Did he work for Corrigan, too? How about Shieldwall? What do you know about them?'

'I can't. I won't. You don't know who you're messing with.'

'You don't think I know? I think I know better than most. Tell me his fucking name!'

'He's done much worse than what he done to you. He's wrong in the head.'

Adrian could feel the heat radiating from the utensil in his hand. He moved it towards Wakefield's cheek as Wakefield tried to lean away, his face glowing with sweat. He could see Wakefield's chest rising and falling quickly – he was terrified, eyes wide and glossy with tears.

Adrian lobbed the utensil across the room and yelled out in frustration. He couldn't do it; he didn't enjoy being the cause of so much fear. He had thought about this moment so many times, but he hadn't considered how it might make him feel to hold so much power in his hands. Now that he didn't have the rules of the police holding him back, or backing him up, it complicated things so much more. Sure, he could mess this guy up beyond recognition, but what would that achieve other than making Adrian feel even worse about himself? The man clearly wasn't going to talk and Adrian just didn't have it in him to force him. In a way, that felt good. In a different way, it made him feel weak and pathetic. He had been so close; so close to holding that burning hot metal against Wakefield's face until it was completely welded to his skin. That scared him – that he had even thought of something so awful.

Adrian opened a kitchen drawer and pulled out a sharp knife. Wakefield's eyes widened again but Adrian just reached behind him and cut the cord wrapped around his hands; he couldn't be bothered to undo the knot.

'You call me when you want to tell me what happened,' Adrian said, throwing a business card at Wakefield, who sat in the chair rubbing his wrists and sobbing, staring at the fork sticking out of his knee.

'That's it? You're not going to do anything else to me?'

'I'm better than that,' Adrian said.

He walked out.

Chapter Forty-Six

Shaun Wakefield dragged on his fifth cigarette since Adrian Miles left his house forty minutes ago. He couldn't stop shaking. First, his neighbour's dog was barking relentlessly so he went round and threatened to kill it, which went down like a lead balloon with the guy next door.

He knew all that stuff they did for Corrigan would come back to bite them in the arse when he was no longer around to protect them. Not that he would have protected them at all, protected himself, more like. He should call Smurf and tell him that the copper was looking for them. Wakefield hadn't been lying, Smurf was crazy and Shaun was terrified of him, but, at the same time, he knew if he was in trouble Smurf would come and help him out. Built like a brick shithouse and afraid of nothing, he was a man you wanted in your corner rather than against you.

There was a loud banging on the door, a closed fist pounding against the PVC frame. Wakefield threw his unfinished cigarette in the sink and ran the tap before going to answer the door. He could see the blurred silhouette of Peter Carlyle in the mottled glass and swore under his breath. He had enough on his plate without dealing with this right now.

'You absolute moron,' Carlyle said, bursting through the door the second Wakefield turned the handle.

'Hello to you, too.'

'Someone photographed you outside my bloody house.'

'Who? There was no one around, we checked,' Wakefield said.

'I saw the photo! Your face is clear as anything. You may as well be wearing a fucking name badge, you idiot. You've both messed this up. I thought you could handle it. Neither of them are dead and I don't have my money. Which means you don't get your money. Not to mention the fact that they now know who you are. You have no idea how much you have messed this up.'

'We got a lead on the money, but it didn't pan out. I sent you the details. The money wasn't there though.'

'Where is he now? Where is Marcus? The police can't find him.'

'Smurf's got him,' Wakefield said, trying to deflect Carlyle's anger. There was nothing in his voice that suggested concern for the child. That was what scared Wakefield about Peter Carlyle: if he could do this to his own son, what would he do to them?

'For God's sake, why?'

'Because, if there's no ransom money, he reckons he can get money another way.'

'What are you talking about? I told you to get rid of him if it went tits-up.'

'He's got a buyer. If you aren't going to pay us, Smurf's going to sell him.'

'Sell him to who?'

'I don't know. Someone who wants a kid.'

'This wasn't our arrangement. I need to talk to Smurf.'

'You don't want to talk to him right now, he's livid. Says this is all your fault. I tried to calm him down, but you know what he's like. I'd stay out of his way if I was you,' Wakefield said. They had known each other long enough to know that Smurf was someone you didn't want to get on the wrong side of.

'Call him. I tried but he's not answering. He'll answer for you though.'

'I don't know. It's not a good idea.'

Before Wakefield knew what was happening he was on the floor. Carlyle had swiped him across the face and he could taste the blood in his mouth, and feel a tingling in his lip as it began to swell.

'Call him,' Carlyle said, grabbing his phone from him. He opened it and started looking through the numbers.

'Hand it over then,' Wakefield said. Carlyle gave him the phone and he punched in Smurf's number from memory – he never kept it saved, too dangerous. He put it on speaker.

'What is it?' Smurf answered.

'It's me,' Carlyle said. 'Is he with you? Do you still have him?'

'For now, but it's too hot right now. I'm trying to arrange a handover with a buyer but the police presence around town is making them fidgety.'

'I want a cut of whatever you get for him,' Carlyle said.

'You'll be lucky. At this rate I'll be banged up before the day is out.'

'You'll be fine, they have no idea who you are – at least *you* had the good sense to keep your face covered. Get rid of him quickly. My money is all tied up and I just need a bit to tide me over. In a couple of months I'll be quids in again and I will see you right. I always do, don't I?'

'Fine. I'll go back to the house then.'

'Be careful,' Carlyle said before taking the phone from Wakefield's hand and ringing off.

'What about me? Don't I get a cut?' Wakefield protested.

Carlyle put Wakefield's phone in his pocket and grabbed a chair, smashing it against the wall. He picked up the chair leg and swung it at Wakefield's shin, the crack louder than Wakefield's subsequent scream.

'They know who you are, Shaun! It's only a matter of time before they find more out about me and figure out how long we've known each other. You just know too much about me for me to let you go. I should have known better than to trust you amateurs.'

'What kind of person wants their kid dead anyway?' Shaun said.

'No ransom, no dead wife, no dead kid means no insurance money. You pair have totally fucking ballsed this operation up. I thought you said this would be easy.'

'Yeah, well, we said no police. It would have gone smooth without the cops. Now we're all in the shit.'

'I'm sorry, Shaun. I can't let you live.'

Carlyle swung the chair leg again. This time it hit Wakefield on the side of the head. He heard a crunch, either his eye socket or his jaw, he wasn't sure which. His vision in his left eye started to cloud as he felt the blood pooling around his iris and he fell on his side, unable to speak, unable to protest anymore, unable to tell Carlyle what he wanted to hear.

He felt the wood come down on him again, the pain less this time. His eye was full of blood and he could feel it dripping from his nose. The chair leg coming down again and again. He could see blood on the kitchen floor now, a black puddle spreading beneath him, too much blood to get back. This was it. Shaun had always known he would die violently. If anything, he was a little embarrassed that it was at the hands of a toad like Carlyle, or whatever his name was this time. His life wasn't flashing before his eyes or anything, he could just sense a darkness reaching for him, the fingertips trying to get a grip and pull him backwards into the black. He felt Carlyle lift his head and wrap the phone cord around his throat. This was it, there was nothing more. Bye, then.

Chapter Forty-Seven

Adrian hovered across the road from the church, sipping on the remnants of a takeaway coffee he had bought to warm him. He ignored the vibration of the phone against his thigh. He had to concentrate on this for now so that he couldn't back out. Dr Hadley had given him the details of this group, as she'd promised; she said they met up weekly in this hall. He didn't imagine he would be able to talk to anyone about what had happened but, after what he had almost done today, he needed to at least try to find a way back to being the person he was before, if that was even possible.

He watched as three men went inside. He didn't recognise them, which was a bonus. He thought about Wakefield tied to that kitchen chair, about the anger that had surged through him as he held that searing-hot spoon next to Wakefield's face and knew he had to do something before he crossed a line. He tossed the empty coffee cup in a street bin and walked inside.

There was a man standing in the corridor pinning a leaflet to a communal noticeboard, the same leaflet Zoe Hadley had sent him a picture of.

'You OK there?' the man said before turning around to reveal a name badge. Tony.

'I, um, I was just passing and I thought maybe I could come and sit in.'

'First time in a group?'

'Is it that obvious?' Adrian shuffled uncomfortably, hating the idea anyone might be able to tell what had happened just by looking at him.

'Not obvious at all; I've just been doing this a long time.' Tony smiled.

'I'm not sure if I'm ready to come inside. I'm definitely not ready to talk.'

'There is no right time, you have to do what's best for you. Just remember we have all been there.'

'You too?'

'A long time ago now, but yes.'

'How long did it take you to recover?'

'It's different for everyone. I was lucky that I had a supportive partner to talk to at the time. He really helped me through it. Do you have someone?'

'I do, but I haven't told her.'

'She knows something's wrong though, right? Probably just thinks it's something else, probably thinks it's her fault. If you guys love each other then you should tell her. She can help you deal with this. It's hard to go through alone.'

'I just don't even know where to start.'

'Sometimes you just have to rip the plaster off and say it,' Tony said gently. 'You're welcome to sit out here on one of the chairs and just chill until you're ready if you don't want to come in just yet – I appreciate how hard it is. I have to go in now though, we are about to start.'

'Thank you.'

Adrian sat on the brown plastic chair and looked at the noticeboard as if he was interested in anything on there. There was a jumble sale on at the weekend followed by a craft fair. Brownies met on Friday evenings and Bear Cubs on Tuesday afternoons . . .

Adrian didn't break his stare from the noticeboard for

a second, just waited for Tony to go back inside the hall. Once he was alone, he watched through the slit of glass in the door as the men talked. He couldn't hear them, but he could see them having what would appear to anyone else to be a normal conversation. After about fifteen minutes he knew he wasn't planning on going inside and stood up, holding his hand up to signify to Tony that he was going to leave. Tony nodded a goodbye and Adrian walked out. Even though he hadn't actually spoken about what had happened, he felt better for even making this small step. The next step was clear. He was going to have to tell Imogen.

Ordinarily, when feeling anxious like this, Adrian would have gone to a pub alone to let off some steam. He didn't do that anymore though. Instead, he walked through the city, wondering if he would get any sleep tonight. He had found one of the men – at times it had felt like it might never happen. But it had. Now he knew he would find the other one, maybe not tomorrow, but they would meet again. Before today, he'd thought he might kill his attacker if he saw him again, but the incident at Wakefield's house made him worry that he didn't have what it took to defend himself. Was he too weak to fight for himself? His brain hurt just thinking about it.

He couldn't face Imogen tonight and so he walked to the Premier Inn and booked himself a double room. He didn't want to see her or talk to her right now. He needed to be completely alone. When he got in the room he lay on the bed and texted Imogen, telling her he was out with a friend and not to wait up. It was a thin lie, a pathetic one, and he knew she would see through it in a heartbeat. But he didn't have the energy for anything else, not tonight, at least. Tomorrow he would tell her; tonight he needed to rest.

Chapter Forty-Eight

The house on Starling Street was a little dishevelled, a little neglected. Wooden pallets rotting on the front lawn, if you could even call it that – a dry muddy square with the occasional green blade of grass fighting its way out of the cracks in the ground. There was a plastic bin in the corner full to the brim with empty cans, bottles and rainwater. Fireworks crackled and exploded across the city and overhead as the Bonfire Night celebrations got underway.

Imogen and Matt Walsh stood behind the armed police and waited for them to bust through the door. She was annoyed that they had to wait over five hours for the Armed Response Unit to assist on this assignment. Just because he *might* have a gun. These moments were always tense, even when there was no indication that anyone was even home and the house was completely still. Imogen imagined there was some kind of science behind the sixth sense you got when there was no one indoors, like sounds that were absent.

The armed police went in first, barely making any noise as they moved through the house with no resistance. Imogen held her breath, waiting for a shot to be fired or someone to be thrown through a window. She watched too much TV.

'Clear. In here. You're going to want to see this,' an officer called out.

Imogen and Matt walked into the kitchen to see Shaun Wakefield dead on the floor. He'd been badly beaten and a charging cable was tied around his neck. His face was purple and black, one eye bulging out of its socket and almost resting in the large slick puddle on the floor, which reminded Imogen of spilled nail polish. His other eye was on the side of impact and had disappeared inside his skull, along with half of his face. It was hard to tell he was the man in the photo.

'I guess we won't be asking him any questions,' Imogen said before turning to the armed officer. 'Any sign of Marcus Carlyle?'

'None; it's very sparsely furnished upstairs. Just a mattress on the floor in the bedroom, no sheets or anything.' The armed officer said.

'Let's get out and get forensics in here. You say you think Carlyle recognised Wakefield from the photos?' Walsh said to Imogen.

'I'm sure he knew who Shaun Wakefield was. It was written all over his face,' Imogen said.

'Well, he may well be our murderer. We need to get out of here as soon as to make sure we don't contaminate the scene just in case they did have Marcus here at some point,' Walsh said. 'Any sign of the van?' he asked the room in general.

'There's a van out back,' one of the armed police officers said.

'I'll go and check it out,' Walsh said, walking around to the back door carefully.

Imogen spotted something under the table, a business card. She bent over to see if she could see a name. There was blood on it, but there was something familiar about it, the spacing or the letters, the logo. She squinted to try and make any of it out. She could only distinguish the last four letters of the name. ILES. A cold chill ran up her spine as she realised why she knew the card.

It was Adrian's.

Walsh was outside and she was alone in the room. Before she even had time to think about what she was doing she picked up the card. Why was it here?

Walsh walked back in through the back door. 'Doesn't look like the van's been moved recently but it's got to be worth a forensic sweep. There must be a link between Wakefield and Carlyle, we just have to find it,' he said, as though it was a given they would.

'I suppose,' Imogen said absently as she slipped the card into her pocket. There had to be a logical explanation for this.

She had to get outside. By removing that business card she had tampered with a crime scene and stolen evidence. What else was in that house that she needed to worry about? The way Adrian had been behaving for the last year, she wasn't sure she even wanted to ask him; she wasn't sure she would even believe his answer. She stepped away from the scene and back out onto the street as they waited for forensics to arrive and do their job. It didn't matter though, she had already changed the crime scene. She felt sick with herself. This was not who she was. If anyone found out she could lose her job.

Chapter Forty-Nine

SIX DAYS MISSING

Tired and agitated, Imogen walked into the briefing room late the following morning, interrupting DCI Kapoor as she spoke to the team.

Imogen had stayed late at Wakefield's and she had gone back to her flat to sleep after getting Adrian's text that he was going to be out all night. This wasn't something he ever did. Where was he? Was it something to do with Wakefield? What had Adrian done? And why? She had not slept well after trying to call him several times and getting no answer, not willing to leave a message. Haunted by the fact that she had taken evidence from the crime scene.

'So, tell us what you found at the house. Any clues as to where Marcus might be?' DCI Kapoor asked as she turned to Imogen.

Imogen looked at Kapoor, trying to gauge whether the DCI knew what she had done at the crime scene. Maybe someone had seen her and told the boss. This was a perfectly normal question to ask at a briefing though and so Imogen pushed her paranoia aside.

'It was a bit of a shithole; Wakefield didn't seem to have money or means to pull off this kidnap on his own. The crime scene investigators are still gathering evidence and bringing it back to the lab, including his car and an abandoned van from the back yard. It looks similar to the one in the photo Jason Hitchin gave us but it doesn't look like it's been moved for months. From the house, we've recovered various implements that appear to have been used on Shaun Wakefield, including a fork and a spoon.'

'No knife?' Jarvis piped up with a smirk on his face, which was shut down immediately by DCI Kapoor's icy stare.

'He was strangled with a phone cord but he was beaten quite significantly before that so we aren't exactly sure of the cause of death, we're still waiting on confirmation. Whoever killed him wanted to make sure he was dead,' Imogen continued.

'What did the lab say on the forensics; how long?'

'They're still processing everything from the factory where they found Marcus's clothes so it's not going to be happening today,' Imogen said.

'*Any* new information on Marcus Carlyle's location?' DCI Kapoor asked.

'We couldn't find a phone or anything in Wakefield's house so there is not much to go on,' Walsh said.

'Why do you think he was killed?' Kapoor asked Imogen.

'I think the plan was always for Sara and Marcus to die. We know that Carlyle took out life insurance on both his wife and his son. The ransom drop fell through, they messed up the attack on Sara, and I suspect Carlyle was furious. Add to that the photo of Wakefield we obtained and it's not a stretch to assume that Carlyle might have been nervous that we were going to tie them together,' Imogen said, no longer holding back in accusing Carlyle. A day late and a dollar short.

'What did Sara Carlyle say about that?' Kapoor asked.

'I'll ask her; she seemed too fragile to interrogate properly when we spoke the other day. When I showed her the picture of Shaun Wakefield she had no idea who he was but I'm sure Carlyle recognised him. I'm sure that's why he's dead,' Imogen said.

'Any evidence Carlyle was there?' DCI Kapoor asked.

'Not yet, and we still haven't found him. He did have more than enough time to get to Wakefield's from when he disappeared from his home,' Imogen said.

'What exactly happened? How on earth did we lose him?'

'I've put a report in, ma'am,' DC Jarvis said, looking down.

'Hopefully forensics won't take too long to get to the Wakefield crime scene,' Imogen lied, terrified of what forensics would find at the scene.

'They're pretty swamped,' Gary added.

'Well, Marcus's crime scene has to take precedence here. The press are demanding answers. Since Dunn's plea they aren't talking about anything else. No one likes the idea of kidnappers going free and the cat is out of the bag about Marcus. Sad to say it, but no one is going to be crying over the death of an ex-con like Wakefield, so let's keep our focus on the evidence we found in the warehouse for now. I will need to release a statement to the press pretty soon and I would rather do it with some good news,' Kapoor said.

'Gregory Dunn, the grandfather, is pretty upset about the way we handled this. I wouldn't be surprised if he made another public statement. I know they want one from him,' Walsh said.

'I think he's more concerned with making sure his daughter is OK. They're very close,' Imogen said.

'Any other leads?' DCI Kapoor asked.

'Canine unit got nothing useful at the factory. Wherever they took Marcus, they took him by vehicle. No evidence of which type of vehicle though,' Walsh said. 'Also, we identified Wakefield as the person who purchased the sweets, a few days before the boy was kidnapped. We believe Carlyle gave them a shopping list before the kidnapping occurred.'

'I've got DC Webb looking into Carlyle's history. The fact that he has no family at all really bothers me,' Imogen said.

'What are you thinking?' DCI Kapoor said.

'Just that he is hiding his family from the Dunns, and now from us. How could he have absolutely no one? I don't buy it. Maybe there's something else in his past he is trying to hide.'

'Certainly wouldn't be the first time he's lied to us,' Walsh said.

'OK. So, we're going into Carlyle's past – we need to try and find a connection between him and Wakefield. Fingerprints would be nice. DC Jarvis, you go and ask Sara Carlyle if she knows about the life insurance policies her husband took out against both her and her son,' DCI Kapoor said.

'I can do that,' Imogen volunteered. She didn't trust Jarvis to handle the situation with the required amount of tact and sensitivity.

'Fine then, take Jarvis with you though. After that we need to go through everything with a fine-tooth comb again from the top. Having Wakefield's identity is a massive win, and if we can get to our third man before Carlyle does, then we have more of a shot of linking Carlyle to his son's kidnapping. We can't let this arsehole get away. Let's move,' Kapoor said and the room sprang into action.

213

Imogen stood up and signalled to Jarvis to join her.

'Just you and me then,' the DC said with a wink. Imogen resisted the urge to roll her eyes.

'Meet me out front in five minutes.'

He exited the room, leaving her alone. She pulled out her phone and dialled Adrian, out of habit as much as anything else. It felt strange spending any length of time away from him and, after what she'd found at the crime scene, her head was spinning. Where was he? Having not seen him the previous evening, she had to at least check that he'd made it home alright. She could deal with the rest later.

'Hello?' he said.

'You're alive then?' she said.

'Sorry, I didn't come back last night, fell asleep on the couch at my mate's house,' Adrian said.

'OK. Well, we've had another murder, I'm sure you've seen it on the news already. I don't know what time I am going to finish up today. My laptop's at yours so I'll need to swing by and pick it up after work. This Starling Street murder has complicated things a whole lot and so I might pull a late one going over the files.'

'Starling Street?' Adrian said quietly.

'You know it?'

'I had a friend who lived there when I was a kid.'

She couldn't tell if she was reading into his reaction, but there was definitely a pause, a hesitation.

'Yes, top secret obviously, but we think we may have traced one of the kidnappers. When we got to his place he had been murdered. Strangled with a phone cord. Because of the developments on the kidnapping case as well it's going to take forever to process both scenes and we need to connect the victim to our lead suspect.'

'He was one of the kidnappers?' Adrian said, surprised.

'Yes, we have a photo of him at the crime scene just before the child was taken.'

There was a long pause and she thought the phone had gone dead.

'Let me cook you dinner then; don't go home to an empty flat,' Adrian said in a flash of his former considerate self. Maybe her words had got through to him. Maybe she hadn't screwed everything up. Surely, he would have tried to dissuade her from coming over if he'd had anything to do with Wakefield's murder.

'Looking forward to it,' she said, allowing a nervous smile to materialise for a brief moment. Maybe there was a perfectly reasonable explanation for all of this.

Chapter Fifty

Jason had spoken to Amanda and explained the situation, what he did and why. He also told her what he saw and how he took pictures and gave them to the police. He returned all of the jewellery he took from the house, too. He was feeling much lighter for letting all of the guilt go and Amanda seemed almost flattered by the devastating impact their break-up had had on him. She'd even indicated she missed him and was sorry they'd broken up. He could tell she was enjoying the fact that she would have a story to tell about the jealous ex who broke into her house and witnessed *the* kidnapping from *her* bedroom window, as she had sadly been away at the time and missed it. While he had no intention of going out with her again, it at least made him feel less bad about the whole thing that she was taking it so well.

He lay on his bed, his mother downstairs cooking them a celebratory dinner while on the phone to her new friend Christopher, and his brother Luke in the lounge on the Xbox. Life was starting to feel a bit normal again, after the crazy week they'd had. It seemed wrong to think it but the fact that Doug was no longer 'out there' seemed to be having a calming effect on all of them. It was like a full stop on a bad story. They didn't have to worry about him cropping up anymore, and when people asked Jason about his dad, he wouldn't need to go into the embarrassing explanations full of holes and misinformation. He could just say he was dead, and then people would say they were sorry and the conversation could move on.

There was a gentle tap on his door and his brother peeked in.

'You decent?'

'It's good to have you home,' Jason said.

'Mate, you have no idea. Remind me never to go to prison again.'

'Never go to prison again.'

'So, we need to talk about what happened. Are you OK?' Luke said in his dad voice.

'Me? I'm the okayest person in this family right now.'

'Not saying much, mate. I know you got a bit close to Dad. How are you dealing with what happened?'

'You seem to be unfazed by the whole thing,' Jason said, deflecting.

'I knew it would end in a bad way for him. I just didn't think he would be here when it happened. Mum's hurting even though she's pretending she isn't, I can tell.'

'She watched him die.'

'What was it about, do you know?'

'Why would I know?'

'Because I know him. He would have tried to impress you with whatever little scheme he was working on, showing you how clever he was. That's what he did. I'm not sure Doug liked doing anything if he didn't have an audience of some kind. He knew his bullshit didn't work on me; you were fresh meat for him.'

'Dad stole some money from someone. A lot of money, I think.'

'And they came looking for it? Typical.'

'You know that kid on the news, the one they're looking

for? I think Dad stole the ransom they used to pay the kidnappers off. It's his fault that kid's still missing.'

'Do the police know this?' Luke said, shocked.

'Yes. I told them everything I knew.'

Luke rolled his eyes and leaned his head back until it thudded against the wall.

'Did they get the money back?'

'No. No one knows where it is. Dad hid it. I have no idea where. The police want to come and search the house.'

'You can't trust the cops. You need to remember that. They will fit you up if they get a chance. Me and you, we're nothing to them. We're the people that carry the can, the nobodies.'

Jason could see Luke really believed that and that made him sad. Luke had had to grow up early and he wasn't very good at it.

'I really missed you.' Jason smiled, pleased to have his brother's advice again, even if it was crap advice.

'Did the police say when they were coming?'

'Tomorrow. They spoke to Mum already; she told them they didn't need a warrant; they could just come and look but to let us have our family meal tonight.'

'And they went for that?'

'Apparently.'

Jason could see Luke's brain was working overtime on something. He stood up, distracted.

'They won't find his money here; he was stupid, but not in that way. How much money are we talking?'

'He reckoned nearly a million quid. Told everyone who would listen at the pub, that's why they came that night. I heard them say that his bragging was what got him found.'

'When the police are done, we are going to go look

for that money. I've got a couple of ideas of where it might be.'

'I don't want any part of that money. A little kid is missing because of what Dad did.'

'We can jump off that bridge when we get to it. We might not even find it. No harm looking,' Luke said in a way that reminded Jason of Doug. Even though Luke would hate to be compared to their father in any way, they were more alike than he would care to admit.

Jason still had the number for the police lady he'd spoken to, so if they did find the money then he would contact her directly. A part of him hoped they wouldn't. That way he could keep kidding himself about the part he'd played in this mess.

Chapter Fifty-One

Adrian finished washing the dinner plates and walked into the lounge. Since speaking to Imogen on the phone earlier, he felt a decision had been made for him. He watched the news and saw the report on the body found in Starling Street, knowing that his prints would be all over the house, knowing that there was no way to keep this from Imogen anymore. The thought that this was the only way to control how Imogen found out his secret was paramount in his mind. He couldn't let her just stumble across information that put him in Shaun Wakefield's van, then she would ask him questions when he wasn't ready to answer them. This was the moment he had thought about so many times, wondering what exactly he would say, how he would say it, how she might react, if she would even still love him.

'I need to talk to you,' Adrian finally said, sitting on the sofa, nervous energy bubbling inside him. Imogen was at the dining table with papers spread out in front of her. She was at the end of her rope, he could tell. He could feel the anger she didn't want to unleash. She wanted to know where he had been, what he had been doing, who he had been with. He couldn't tell her that without telling her this.

'What do you need to talk to me about? Can it wait?' Imogen said. He understood that he couldn't just demand attention after spending months being evasive about every single thing.

'I need to talk to you about the case, the case you're working on. I'm not sure it can wait.'

'Not really supposed to talk to you about it, you know?'

'I know. But if I don't do it now, it might be too late. Please?'

'Has it got anything to do with this?' She put something on the table and looked at him expectantly. She was tired, he could tell.

He glanced down at the table and saw his business card, covered in blood. A dull ache materialised in his stomach, pressing on his spine. There was no avoiding this conversation anymore.

Guilt consumed him in that moment, for what he was about to do to her. There was no way he could keep the secret any longer. The truth was rising to the surface, whether he wanted it to or not.

'You might want to get a drink before I start,' Adrian said.

'I'll be fine. Just spit it out.'

'You're going to have to be a little patient with me for a moment . . . this is difficult. You keep saying you want me to open up. Well, this is it,' he said.

He could feel the emotion coming to the surface, but he had to suppress it – if he started to cry, he wasn't sure he would be able to stop. He took a few deep breaths in the hopes of squashing any uninvited feelings. *Just say it.*

'Adrian? What's going on? What did you do?' Imogen said. She got up and sat next to him on the sofa, putting her hands on his, but he snatched them away. He didn't even mean to, it was just something he did now.

221

'Sorry,' she said.

'You have nothing to be sorry for. Not now and not ever.' His breathing was laboured. He was looking for the way to get the words out. *I can't do this.*

'Talk to me.'

'OK. I don't want to be having this conversation right now, but I have no other choice. Please just let me say what I have to say and you can ask me any questions at the end,' he said quickly, aware he was rambling.

'What's this about? What's it got to do with my case? Did you do something to Wakefield? Please tell me you didn't.'

Adrian took another deep breath before starting.

'I know you know I haven't been right for a while. I know I haven't been an easy person to be around and I've been trying, God knows I have. I've been so unfair to you and I really hope you can forgive me one day. I've been pushing you away, but it isn't because I don't love you, it's the opposite of that. I love you so much and I just don't want to ruin things between us. I hoped I would never have to talk about this but, as it happens, I think I do now.'

He looked up at Imogen, trying to memorise her face, her eyes, aware that in a few moments all of that was going to change. She might never look at him the same way again.

'That night during the Corrigan case, we had that big argument, remember? Our first real argument as I recall. I was an arse, as I usually am. Well, I went to the pub after and had a few drinks. The case was getting to me as they all seemed to. I had one too many and made my way home. I've done it a million times before.

'On the way home there was a van waiting for me on the street. The van you picked up today at the crime scene and sent for processing. I know that van. I've been inside it.'

She looked confused at what he had just said. He could tell she wanted to speak, to ask a question. Whatever that question was, he was about to answer it one way or another. He stood up. Maybe moving around would make this easier. How was he going to say the next part? How could he do this to her?

'When I was walking home, something happened. I've been trying really hard to put it behind me, but it's not been easy. If it hadn't been for you then I don't know if I would have made it. I'll spare you the details because, well, I don't know how much I actually remember. I had been drinking, as I said. I'm only telling you this now because of the van. When the report comes back there's a high chance there will be a DNA match to me. I was jumped and assaulted in the back of that van, on that night. I thought I was going to die, I *wanted* to die. You and Tom are the only reason I held on.' He looked at her, he could tell she wasn't understanding him. He had to make her understand. For the first time in a long time Adrian really wanted a drink.

'Why didn't you say anything at the time? You let me think you got yourself into a fight,' Imogen said, obviously assuming he was finished.

'I didn't want it to take over, you know? But it did anyway.'

'Who jumped you? Was it Wakefield? Why didn't you report it?'

The lump in Adrian's throat was starting to throb with pain. He could stop now, she hadn't made the connection. It wasn't too late to put this back in its box and leave it there. But then there was that bloody van.

'I didn't file a report because I didn't want to talk

223

about what happened.' He studied her face, watching for the moment when she understood what exactly it was he was trying to say to her. It hadn't happened yet.

Please don't make me say it.

Standing by the window, scanning the road where they had stopped the van and pushed him out half naked that night, he hadn't even noticed that he had balled his fists together so tight his knuckles were white and distended. He turned back to her. She still couldn't see it.

Congratulations on an acting job well done.

He had spent the last fourteen months since it happened terrified she would be able to just look at him and know. He stared into her eyes, trying to say it telepathically, trying to avoid speaking the actual words. It was getting harder to take in air as he waited for her to understand him. There was a shift in her countenance, something at the back of her mind maybe, something she was trying to ignore.

There it is.

She stood up, brow crinkled and mouth slightly open, a question hovering on her lips.

'What do you mean, Adrian? Why didn't you want to talk about it?' she said hesitantly. He could see the thought that was creeping up on her, the realisation. 'What are you saying?'

'I've wanted to tell you for a long time. But then I didn't want you to know. I just couldn't get my head round it, you know?' He felt the tears coming, he tried to keep them inside, but his eyes hurt as he strained to stop them falling. He blinked and felt the wetness on his cheeks. No going back now, his composure was lost.

Breathless, with an expression of complete disbelief. He could see her searching his face for something that would lead her away from the line of thought that just wouldn't let her go.

'Adrian, were you raped?'

He didn't speak but he knew that the look on his face was speaking for him. Answering with the smallest of nods, he finally exhaled. It was done.

She was at a loss for what to do or say.

'I'm sorry I lied to you. I just wanted to pretend it didn't happen at first, thought I would be OK. I know I've been impossible and you deserve so much more. I want you to know that I had an HIV test and it came back fine and everything. I never put you at risk, I promise,' he said, moving forward slowly, afraid of her reaction, desperate to hold her. He wasn't sure he could bear to be rejected right now.

'Jesus Christ,' she whispered. Charging forwards, she threw her arms around his neck and clutched him tightly. He welcomed the contact – some part of him had been worried she would leave. Her chest was heaving against his as she buried her face in his shoulder. He put his arms around her, a weight lifting from him as the wall he had constructed between them began to dissolve. Selfishly, it felt good to tell her the truth. As bad as he felt for doing it.

He held onto her for a few minutes. He had missed this, missed her.

'How could I have not seen this? The way you've been acting. It all makes sense now but I didn't see it. Why didn't I see it? Why didn't you tell me?' She spoke quickly, pulling away a little, her eyes darting from side to side as though she was still trying to piece something together.

'I couldn't. I really couldn't. I wouldn't even be telling you now if I didn't have to. I'm sorry but that's the truth.'

'Don't you trust me?' she said, stepping back.

'There are so many reasons why I didn't say anything.

Even saying it out loud right now feels so wrong, like it's going to go horribly wrong and I will lose you forever. I was scared in case you would think I was making it up or something. What if you didn't believe me?' Just admitting that out loud hurt. He wiped the tears that were falling freely with his sleeve.

'Oh Adrian, of course I believe you. I know you wouldn't make something like this up.'

'I wasn't thinking straight. Just the thought of you thinking I was lying was too much. I was so ashamed of myself. I still am. I didn't want it to become . . . *everything*. I wanted life outside of it, outside of me, especially you, to just be separate, to just carry on as it had before. I just wanted to forget it ever happened. To pretend nothing had changed.'

'I'm so sorry. I feel like I've let you down. I should have known.'

'This is not on you. I didn't want you to know.'

'I don't even know what to say. Why didn't you report what happened?'

'Imogen, I couldn't have. I didn't know anything about the attackers, I didn't see anything. I was drunk, I didn't fight back. There was no way it would have led to an arrest. There's so much I really don't remember at all. What I do remember I don't want to talk about. I hope you can understand.'

'Of course. I'm sorry, I didn't want to make you feel bad – worse.' She stopped for a moment, gathering her thoughts. 'So, Wakefield . . . he was the man who attacked you? And he just grabbed you off the street?'

'Him and someone else. By the railway bridge. I could feel there was someone there. But I guess I had a bit too much to drink. I know I can look after myself in a fight but what happened after . . . You just don't think like

226

that, you know? As a guy it's just not something I factor in. I got hit a few times and then put in the back of the van. Wakefield, he was up front driving and he never touched me. The other man was in the back with me. He wore a mask so I don't know what he looked like.

'I didn't know what he was going to do until just before he did it. I just thought they were going to take me somewhere and mess me up. Then he pulled my trousers down and I knew what was coming next. I couldn't fight back, I couldn't move,' Adrian said, taking a deep breath, unable to get enough air to keep going. It felt so wrong to be talking about it, as though he were spilling someone else's secret. But the floodgates had opened, and he had spent so long holding all of this inside him that now he couldn't stop it from coming out.

'Wakefield kept driving. I don't know if he knew what was happening in the back, he says no. I remember it starting but then it's like my mind is just a jumble of everything that came after. I remember small things like the smell, his voice, the way his fingers tasted when he shoved them in my mouth. I could feel him on me for days, sometimes I still do. It felt like it went on forever and then, like *that*, it ended. They knew who I was though because they stopped the van outside the house and dumped me on the street.'

The words that had been swimming in his mind for over a year tumbled out of his mouth with speed. Now that he had broken the seal on his secret it was hard to keep quiet, almost involuntary.

'How long were you in the van?'

'Five hours, I think.'

'And that whole time?' Imogen said, her voice cracking.

Adrian nodded before wiping his face on his sleeve again. He moved to the other side of the room.

'I don't remember all of it. There are certain moments that are so crystal clear but the rest of it is gone. I blocked it out completely. Even thinking about the things I do remember makes me want to disappear. It comes back to me all the time, a flashback I guess – a smell or a sound can throw me right back into that van. I remember being so angry with myself for not fighting back. I swear to God I couldn't though. I couldn't move.'

'I'm so sorry.'

'So many times I have wanted to tell you but I couldn't do that to you, to us. I thought we could work through it, that I might be OK eventually, but it's just there, all the time. There's not a second when I'm not thinking about it. I feel completely obsessed with it. I don't want to be, I'm exhausted by it, but it's not going away. I know this is a lot, and I know it has wider implications and I will completely understand if you need some time . . .'

'What do I need time for?' Imogen said, a flash of anger in her voice.

'To decide what to do. Whether you want to deal with this or not.'

'Adrian, I'm not going anywhere. Especially not now.'

'I don't need your pity.'

'Is it not clear that I love you? Would you leave me? If the roles were reversed, would you go?'

'Of course not.'

'Well then give me some bloody credit please. You're stuck with me.' He watched as she clenched her jaw; her shock had mutated into fury. 'What can I do?'

'There's nothing you can do really but if my DNA comes back on that van, I really don't want anyone to know about this. I can't have anyone knowing. The thought of the guys at the station finding out . . .' His voice cracked as he spoke, he was shaking just thinking about it.

'Did Wakefield say anything that could tell you who the other man was?' Imogen changed the subject.

'No, he seemed genuinely terrified of him. Although I don't remember much about the other man except his voice, the one in the back with me, I would know him, or at least I think I would. It was dark. He was big, much bigger than Wakefield. I think he was white. I remember staring at his wrist when my eyes were open; it was next to my face. I had my eyes closed for a lot of it. I tried to get Wakefield to talk about that night, but he wouldn't.'

'I wish you had told me before you went to see him.'

'I didn't know if it was him. He's not the first person I've been to see – I have been trying to figure out who it was for months. I printed out a list of possible suspects at the end of the case from the employment files Corrigan Construction sent over and have been working my way through them. It was an alphabetical list and he was the last one on it. Before you ask, he was alive when I left him, but my prints are going to be in his place, maybe even on the murder weapon. I touched a lot of things. Also, I threw up in his yard.'

Imogen puffed her cheeks out in exasperation. Adrian knew there was no way he could avoid becoming involved, and no way to explain his presence at the scene logically without going on the record about the rape.

'Did anyone see you? He was murdered, Adrian – if your prints or DNA come up in the investigation they will bring you in, I won't be able to stop that.'

'I'm not asking you to stop anything and I'm not asking for any favours. You have to do your job, I know that. This is the truth, nothing more. I didn't want you to find my prints or DNA there before I had a chance to explain. I couldn't have you putting this together on your own. I wouldn't want that. I did threaten Wakefield and I did hurt him a couple of times but then I let him go. I wonder if he contacted the other man from the van to warn him or something, maybe that's what got him killed. Maybe it was the guy who . . . you know.'

'I'm so sorry, Adrian. My God. Is this why you quit?'

'Partly. Mostly, I guess. I was no use to anyone. I mean, I was already pushing my luck on the Corrigan case as it was, but then the thing in the van happened and I just became so preoccupied and distracted. I was scared and angry all the time. I couldn't think straight. I couldn't live with myself if you got hurt because I wasn't doing my job properly.'

'You need to talk to someone about this. These things don't go away. We could go and see someone together, if you want. Have you spoken to anyone?'

'I saw a doctor, Zoe Hadley, to get a sick note. She checked my injuries and prescribed me some medicine, made me get an HIV test. She told me to talk to you. I also spoke to a priest. No one else. I did try to attend a group thing for survivors yesterday, but I ended up leaving because it was too much. I went there straight after I saw Wakefield, sat there for a while but couldn't go inside. I feel like the words have just been stuck in my throat since it happened, like I might blurt it out at any moment, but at the same time I feel like I'm choking on it, unable to say a word.'

'You went there straight from Wakefield's?'

'Yes.'

'What time did you arrive and did anyone see you?'

'I spoke to the group leader but I didn't go in. He saw

230

what time I got there and what time I left though. I left at around seven fifteen, I think.'

'This could be your alibi, Adrian.'

'I can't tell anyone else. I really can't,' he said, the tears falling as quickly as they were forming.

Imogen took Adrian's hand and led him over to the sofa; he could feel her fingers trembling as they sat down together.

'You've been dealing with this alone all this time and I have been so cross with you and feeling so sorry for myself. I thought you were cheating on me or something. I should have known.'

'I honestly don't know how you've put up with me. And I didn't want you to know, I worked very hard on keeping this from you. Please don't feel bad for not knowing. I'm glad I got to tell you on my terms.'

'Did you keep your clothes from the night of the attack?' she asked.

'I did, but I don't know why. I had no plans to report it. I just stuffed them in the back of the wardrobe in a black sack. I also had an anonymous rape kit done at the clinic on Sidwell Street.'

'Did they tell you why they did this to you? The men in the van?'

'They didn't say much of anything. I figured out it was Corrigan who was behind it, Wakefield confirmed that. It was a warning to back off. When you look into Wakefield further you'll see his ties to Corrigan Construction as well as Shieldwall Security. I've been trying to find out who it was on my own and it led me back to Wakefield. Then you found him dead. I believe Corrigan used sexual assault to control and undermine men that were in his way. He knows none of them would say anything about it to the police.'

'Have there been any attacks since? Do you know?' she said quietly. Adrian knew what she was implying, that he should have come forward, that he should have made sure whoever did it couldn't then go on and do it to anyone else.

'Wakefield said no. He said no one has touched that van since that night, said he got spooked because I was police and he refused to be a part of it anymore. He said he hadn't known what the other guy was going to do. Said they were just following orders.'

'Do you believe him?'

'I think he must have known. He was driving the whole time though. He didn't come across as particularly bright. Evidently, he just moved on to kidnapping kids. Anyway, it doesn't matter now, he's dead.'

'What happens when you find the man who raped you?'

'I don't know. I just have to know who he is. I can't spend my life wondering if it's everyone I meet. You can't even begin to understand how much it drives me crazy. I literally feel insane. I just need a name or a face . . . *something*. Like, I know it happened but without a name it all feels so unreal. I need him to be real. I need someone to blame.'

'You can't do anything to him though. I mean, I don't want you getting in trouble.'

'I'll worry about that when I get to it. For now, I'm just worried about the DNA in that van.'

'If you make a statement and explain . . .'

'No. I won't. I would rather get sent down for murder than have everyone know.'

'Why don't you want them to know? What do you think they will say? No one is going to think any less of you. I can't just let you take the heat for this, knowing what I know. I won't just stand by and do nothing. If you just let the DCI know . . .'

'You've seen the way rape victims are treated by people – the media, the internet, even some police. People think they can just look at a person and know what happened, which one of them is telling the truth. I've done it myself. People think there are circumstances where forcing yourself on someone is acceptable, like if the victim is drunk, which I was. Or that you might be doing it for some kind of pay-out, or fame, or God knows what else. A male police officer as a victim? They'll think I have some angle; they'll say things about me that I can't bear. I can't face that level of scrutiny. If you only knew how hard telling you has been, you wouldn't ask me to tell anyone else. Please don't tell anyone,' he said quickly, the panic rising, the fear that Imogen wouldn't let him deal with this his way.

'OK, OK. I wouldn't say anything without your permission. You know that,' she said, stroking his face, trying to calm him. 'Things are about to get messy, Adrian. I hope you're ready.'

'I am now.' He gripped her hand.

Chapter Fifty-Two

SEVEN DAYS MISSING

The rain was pelting thick and hard against the bonnet of the car. There was a storm forecast and a black cloud hovered over the rooftops like an invading force, the weather somehow matching Imogen's mood. She had been crying in here for the last twenty minutes, unsure what the hell she was meant to do. She knew she couldn't fall apart in front of Adrian and so she had left a little early this morning and just stayed in the car, waiting for this feeling of helplessness to pass.

She kept replaying the last year in her mind, seeing how she had twisted every scenario to mean something it hadn't. Now the veil was lifted, she wasn't sure how the hell she hadn't realised what was going on. The way he would tense when she touched him, the way he would just stare past the television whenever they watched anything. And when she remembered the very few times they had slept together over the last few months she felt like a complete monster for the things she had been thinking. She couldn't even bear to replay those moments in her mind and hoped that one day she could forgive herself for not knowing. She desperately wanted to talk to someone about it but there was no one. So, she gave herself permission to cry in the car for a bit. Whatever she was feeling didn't really matter at this point anyway;

she needed to be strong for Adrian. She closed her eyes for a moment and tried to centre herself, then checked the mirror to make sure it wasn't obvious she had been sobbing in the car.

Inside the station, she looked for Gary. She needed to get in front of this before the forensics came back and went directly to DI Walsh or, worse, DCI Kapoor.

She walked through to his office, which was the very definition of chaos, and found him sitting at his laptop studying photos of the Wakefield scene. The image of Shaun Wakefield's contorted and battered face looked different now she knew what he had done to Adrian. She couldn't help feeling pleased that the man was dead. Any sympathy she'd had was gone and the only reason she even gave a shit who had killed him was because she needed them to exonerate Adrian.

'Oh, hey,' Gary said, snapping her out of her introspection.

'Gary, any news on the forensics for the Wakefield house?'

'The lab is backed up at the moment. They're still going over the Carlyle kidnap site to look for any more crossovers with where they found Sara Carlyle. Wakefield's place is next on the list apparently, but they haven't even looked at it yet.'

'Anything on Marcus Carlyle's clothes that could tell us where he had been, or was going?'

'They rushed his clothing through first and there was nothing unexpected. The rest of the scene is still being processed. It's a mammoth job.'

'Is there any way a different lab could do the testing for the Wakefield case? Like, one that isn't ours?'

'I could make that happen. Why?'

'I'm just concerned about time for a start, so if someone else could get it done quicker that would be great.'

'And what else?' Gary said.

'Wouldn't it be better to get a different lab to do it anyway, to make sure there was no cross-contamination of the evidence? If we can prove a connection via different labs doesn't that make our case stronger?' she said, clutching at straws, aware Gary wasn't buying her shit. The truth was, the further away from her the evidence was, the better for her when this came out. There could be an argument that she'd had an opportunity to mess with the evidence and at least if it was processed off-site then there was no chance of anyone crying foul.

'I guess there could be an argument for that. Cross-contamination is not something that has happened in all the time I've been here though.'

'OK, well, I'm just concerned about the crime scene and there is a possibility that some of the information may be sensitive so I would like as few people from this district to know about it. It connects to a previous case and that's all I'm willing to say on the subject.'

'I'll get that sorted. Are you OK? You seem really on edge.'

'Don't ask me if I'm OK, Gary, surely you must know by now how much that winds me up.'

'You are so contrary, Imogen. I was just trying to be nice,' Gary said, raising his eyebrows.

'Sorry. I guess I didn't sleep well. Also, when you get the info I would really appreciate it if it could go through me first. Do you have anything new on the Carlyle case?'

'I'll come to the briefing room in a bit and tell everyone at the same time. There's nothing time-sensitive though.'

'Cheers, Gary.'

Imogen left his office feeling guilty, as if she was

breaking the law in some way, which she wasn't. It just felt wrong to have secrets from Gary. If only she could convince Adrian that he didn't need to be ashamed, then maybe they could all help him through this. She knew he had done the hardest part of recovery alone but now was the time to lean on friends. She wasn't sure if she could be the person he needed at the moment, she didn't know who that person was.

As she turned the corner, her mind elsewhere, she slammed into DC Webb. His torso was so solid she almost fell as she bounced off him. He grabbed hold of her shoulders to keep her from falling, letting go as soon as she was stable. He looked at her with concern, maybe something more than concern. *Shit.*

'Gabriel . . . I . . .'

'I'm sorry, I should have been looking where I was going.' He smiled; he had a killer smile.

'No, it's my fault. Got my head in the clouds today,' she said.

'I've got an address for an old cellie of Wakefield's, maybe he can shed some light on his activities before he died, if they were still in contact. He also might know who Wakefield was spending his time with these days.'

'I'll meet you at the car then.' She smiled and walked away.

All she could think was how grateful she was that nothing had happened between her and Gabriel Webb, though she wasn't patting herself on the back too much over it, disgusted that she had even entertained the idea while Adrian was struggling. Burying the part of her that felt guilty about what had happened was proving to be the biggest challenge she had faced. All she could think about was how she should have known. It was all there, all right in front of her. How stupid and how arrogant

Chapter Fifty-Three

On their way to speak to Shaun Wakefield's ex-cellmate, Imogen was desperately hoping they'd find something, anything, that might exonerate Adrian before his fingerprints were found all over the crime scene. It was only a matter of time.

The man they were looking for worked in a charity shop for the homeless in the centre of town. They walked in and a man behind the counter clocked them immediately. She already knew this was who they were there to talk to, she could tell by his shifty disposition. They let him finish serving the woman at the counter and waited for her to leave before Imogen pulled out her warrant card. The man nodded compliantly as he folded his arms.

'I'm DS Grey. This is my colleague, DC Webb. Are you Gavin Lomax?'

'I haven't violated my bail, I've just been working here all the time. They said that was OK.'

'We're not here to talk about you today. I wondered if you might tell us a bit about a former cellmate of yours – Shaun Wakefield.'

'I heard he died. Did you find who did it?'

'That's why we're here,' Imogen said.

'Well, I didn't do it!' he said defensively.

'No, I mean we wanted to ask you some questions about him.'

'Oh, right, nothing much to say about Shaun. Nice bloke, bit of a pushover.'

'How long did you two share a cell?' Imogen said.

'About eight months.'

'Can you remember anyone he particularly spent time with on the inside?'

'He spent time with everyone. He got used a lot, you know? That's how he got by inside.'

'What do you mean by "used a lot"?'

'Like, people took advantage of him. He wouldn't say no if you asked him for his lunch, or if you asked him to get you something from outside. People would get him to pay for their shit as well. He had a bit of a rep as being weak and a bit of a weasel. But he did make friends inside because of that so maybe he was on to something.'

A customer walked into the shop and Lomax shuffled uncomfortably.

Imogen lowered her voice before speaking again, aware Lomax didn't want the woman in the shop to know he was an ex-con. 'Who left first, you or him?'

'Him. He had already been inside for a while when I got there. Moaned a lot about how all his friends were on the outside now,' he said quietly.

'Like who?'

'Look, we weren't friends. I know he had a cellie before me but they fell out, which is how I got put in with him.'

'I don't suppose you know this cellie's name?'

'I do, he was a bit of a weirdo, to be honest. His name was Craig Murphy. Tattoos all up his neck and on his head. He's not inside anymore and we've crossed paths a few times. His whole family are wrong'uns though, so I steer clear of him. We have similar social circles, if you can call them that.'

'I don't suppose you know where he is now?'

'Probably where he's always been, up St James Close. Red-brick house with a green door.'

'You weren't friends, but you know where he lives?'

'He does some low-level pot dealing. I've never got any from him but he's where I would go if I wanted some. I'm trying to stay out of trouble. My girlfriend's pregnant and I don't want to go back inside.'

'I really appreciate your help, thank you,' Imogen said before nodding to Gabriel that it was time to leave. She could see Lomax relax as they moved away. She wondered how many times he had been inside, how conditioned he was to fear the police, to fear returning to prison again.

Seeing Lomax like that, she couldn't bear the thought of Adrian going to prison if she couldn't clear his name.

Chapter Fifty-Four

They pulled the car up in front of a red-brick house in St James Close. There was a man standing outside having a cigarette.

'That's him. That's Craig Murphy,' Webb said, looking at an image Walsh had sent across.

'Mr Murphy?' Imogen called as she opened the car door and stepped out. Webb did the same.

'What have I done now?' he said with a smile and a south London accent. She held up her warrant card and the smile stayed in place. She noted that he must have guessed she was police before she even held the card up. He had been here before. He was a big man with a shaved head and large spider tattoo on his neck, surrounded by smaller spiders that went up and under his beanie. She could see more tattoos poking out of his shirt. She leaned on the open car door, hoping this wouldn't take long. All she could think about was that ticking clock in the back of her mind.

'Nothing. We just want to talk to you about a former cellmate of yours. Shaun Wakefield.'

'There's a blast from the past.'

'Were you close with Mr Wakefield?'

'God, no. First chance I got I transferred out to a new cell. I was barely with him for a month. He was a right twat.'

'In what way?'

'You just couldn't trust him, you know? Always sneaking about, always whispering. Lots of little side deals on the go. Used to sell a bit of weed on the inside. Had lots of connections here there and everywhere. You never quite felt like he was being straight with you. I guess because he was a small fella and you do what you have to do to survive inside, and he is certainly a survivor. Why do you ask?'

'Unfortunately, Shaun Wakefield was killed two days ago. We are trying to get any leads on known associates.'

'And you found me? I'm not the person to give you any information on that little snake and I've got an alibi for two days ago. I just got back off a week-long welding course.'

'Where was that based?'

'BRIT training in Okehampton.'

'So, who should we speak to about Shaun Wakefield then? Can you remember anyone he used to spend time with?' Imogen said as she scribbled down his alibi in her notepad.

'He mostly hung out with these other two sneaks. Give me a second, their names will come back to me. It's been a few years and my brain ain't what it used to be,' he joked.

'Anything else you can remember about him? Did he have any regular visitors?'

'I really couldn't tell you that. Maybe you'll have better luck speaking to his crew. I remembered who they are now. It was Tez Harding – Terry – and Julian Crow.'

'Can I ask you if you know a Peter Carlyle?' Imogen said.

'Sorry, love, never heard that name.'

'You've been really helpful, thank you,' Imogen said.

'Anytime.' He smiled, adding a little wink before

stubbing his cigarette out on the pavement and heading back inside.

She got back in the car.

'Did you get those names?' she asked Webb as he got in next to her.

'Yep, I'll look into them, see if I can get a current location.'

She drove out of the close and headed back to the station. She didn't like being away from there at the moment. If the forensic report got to the DCI before Imogen had a chance to do any necessary damage control things could get out of hand and go very badly very quickly for Adrian. Tick, tick, tick. The clock kept moving forward relentlessly. She could feel the noose closing around Adrian's throat and she was powerless to stop it.

Chapter Fifty-Five

The kidnappers had not been in contact and Marcus was still out there. Until Imogen had proof that contradicted he was alive then she wouldn't accept that the worst had happened, no matter what the statistics said.

Imogen had checked with the airports; Peter Carlyle had not used his passport to travel outside the country. The hospitals she had contacted had no record of anyone matching his description being brought in. His cards hadn't been used, he had just dropped off the radar completely. That sort of thing was not easy to do, and she wondered if he had some experience in the art of disappearing.

The search at the Hitchin house had come back with no sign of the money and no evidence of any connection with Carlyle. Whatever possessions Douglas Hitchin had were in one holdall and there were no clues to where he had hidden the money. Everything had ground to a halt. The best lead they had was Wakefield's house and they were all waiting on the evidence gathered from that crime scene so they could crack on with something else. Every lead was either a dead end or led to something else they had to wait on. Even Murphy's alibi had checked out and so he was off the list. Now they were looking for Harding and Crow, the other men he mentioned that might have had a connection to Wakefield.

Imogen was sitting at her desk when she heard a strange hissing noise. She looked under the desk but there was nothing there. She heard it again and glanced around to see Gary peeking his head around the corner, trying to get her attention. He beckoned her to him. She took a deep breath and got up. She knew what was coming next. She had been bracing herself for this since she had spoken to Adrian the day before yesterday.

'Yes?'

'Come into the liaison room, I need to talk to you.'

He rushed on ahead and she followed closely behind.

'What's going on?'

'I got the DNA back on the Wakefield crime scene from the other day.'

'Right.' Imogen held her breath.

He looked at her for a moment, arms folded as he tried to read her face. Obviously she wasn't as blank a slate as she thought she was.

'You know what I am going to say, don't you?'

'Let's pretend I don't. Just tell me,' Imogen said.

'Is this why you wanted the report to go through you?'

'How bad is it?'

'It's bad. This is what we would refer to as a forensic slam dunk. Adrian's DNA is all over the Wakefield crime scene. Like, all over it. His fingerprints are on several things in the kitchen, including the door handle, a fork, a spoon and a cord that was apparently tied around the victim's throat and used to kill him, but also to bind his hands at some point. There were bruises and fingerprints on Wakefield's body that we still need to match, along with several DNA samples from the van out back and a load of vomit in the yard.'

'Have any prints or DNA from anyone other than Wakefield or Adrian been identified?' Imogen asked.

'You're taking this very well. What the hell is going on?'

'Was there anyone else there?' she said, looking for a shred of hope in this catastrophe.

'There was one other gloved person there – we found marks made by disposable Nitrile gloves but no other DNA. What do we do? You have to let Walsh and the DCI know. Fuck.' Gary looked panicked.

'Is there any way to trace the make of gloves?'

'Long story short: no.'

'What about the van? Did you get anything from that?' Imogen said, holding her breath in anticipation of Gary's answer.

'Wakefield's prints on the wheel.'

'What about the back?'

'There were traces of blood there, but the samples were tainted by heavy-duty chemicals. Looks like it had been cleaned thoroughly. It wasn't the one used in the Carlyle kidnapping though. It's been stationary for several months.'

Imogen sat down and took a few deep breaths to try to control her emotions. She had known this was coming but it didn't make it any easier. She didn't know what would happen next. Would she have to remove herself from the case? There was only one way to resolve this without arresting Adrian and that was to tell the truth about what happened to him and she knew she couldn't do that. She wanted to cry, then realised she was starting to. This was all so hard to handle – how the hell had Adrian been dealing with this alone for so long? She rested her head in her hands, staring at the carpet for a few moments to compose herself.

'What's happened? What's going on?' Gary asked.

'I'll go and speak to the DCI now. Does anyone else know?'

'No, I asked for the crime scene to be processed using

the Dorset lab after you told me it was a potentially sensitive issue. I didn't think you meant this, though. Why are his prints there, Imogen?'

'Not my story to tell, I'm afraid. Thank you for being discreet about this.' She wiped her eyes.

'That's it? I don't get any kind of explanation for all this?'

'I can't, Gary. If you ever trusted me, or Adrian for that matter, then you need to just accept that this really isn't what it looks like.'

'If I ask Adrian, will he tell me?' Gary pressed.

'I can't speak for him. But in all honesty, probably not. Not yet anyway.'

'OK. What do you want me to do? You know Adrian is going to be brought in for questioning over this. Is there anything else I should be looking at?'

'You didn't hear this from me, OK? Adrian maintains that Wakefield was alive when he left his house that night and I believe him.'

'The evidence suggests otherwise.'

'Then we need to find more evidence. Someone else was there. If Adrian did do it, why on earth would he leave his prints everywhere? He would know that we would investigate, right? You saw pictures of that crime scene, it was a mess. We need a complete analysis of Wakefield's life to find out who else might have been there after Adrian left. Check his phone records, social media if he had any. Someone else was there, and they killed him.'

'Does Adrian not have an alibi?' Gary said.

'Not one he is willing to share.'

'Do you know it?'

'Officially, no. But if he had told me then I wouldn't feel at liberty to divulge it,' Imogen said, really wishing she could tell Gary, but knowing it wasn't her place to say anything, knowing Adrian had to be the one in control of who found out and when. While betraying his trust might help him in the short term, it would do irrevocable damage to their relationship, and possibly damage his recovery too, so she wasn't willing to risk it.

'Hypothetically speaking, was what he was doing for this alibi legal?' Gary continued to probe.

'Absolutely one hundred per cent legal. Just private, that's all,' Imogen said, looking at Gary in a way that implored him not to ask any more questions. She was on the verge of saying something she would regret.

'Is he OK? Is it a medical thing? He's not ill, is he?'

'He's not ill. Please stop asking me. I desperately want to tell you and he would never forgive me if I did. Just know that he really needs us right now. We have to find the real killer.'

'I will pull Wakefield's life apart then,' Gary said, switching back to professional Gary.

'Thanks, Gary. There are people here who will be happy to think the worst of Adrian, but you just can't believe them. I'm going to go speak to the DCI now. She may well take me off the Wakefield case – I know I would – but if you could keep me in the loop I would really appreciate it.'

'Do you want me to come with?'

'No, I want you to do what you do best and find out what really happened. It's Adrian's only chance.'

Gary handed her the evidence folder and she opened it – just seeing Adrian's name in it made her feel nauseous. The easiest thing would be to tell the truth, but it wasn't her truth to tell. He would never forgive her if she did and so she had to let this play out the way Adrian wanted it to.

* * *

Imogen knocked on the glass of DCI Kapoor's office and she waved her in without even looking up from her computer. Imogen braced herself and walked into the lion's den.

'How did the search go at the Hitchin house yesterday?'

'The money wasn't there. They searched the place but there was barely a trace of Douglas Hitchin, let alone the missing ransom money.'

'That's not why you came to see me though, is it? What can I do for you, Imogen?'

'I've got the forensics back on the Wakefield crime scene. I thought you would want to see it.'

'Any nasty surprises?'

'You could say that, yes,' Imogen said.

DCI Kapoor looked up and nodded for Imogen to sit down, holding her hand out for the report, which Imogen kept a hold of.

'OK. You've got that look on your face that means you're about to tell me something I am not going to like. What's going on?'

'I don't even know how to communicate any of this but here goes. I think you need to remove me from the Wakefield murder investigation. Matt can take over for me. Some evidence has come to light which puts me in a compromising situation with regards to the crime scene and possibly the case as a whole. I can continue working on the Carlyle aspect of the case though, if you agree there's no conflict of interest.'

'What evidence is that? Do I get to see the report?'

'Of course, but I wanted to explain first.'

'Then explain.' DCI Kapoor took her glasses off and folded her arms. Imogen had her undivided attention.

'They found prints and DNA at the scene that belong to someone other than Shaun Wakefield.'

'Someone in the system? That's brilliant.'

'Not really. It's Adrian.'

'Adrian . . . Miles?'

'Correct.'

DCI Kapoor stood, an involuntary reaction it seemed, as she looked surprised to find herself on her feet, and immediately sat back down again, before holding out her hand for the report. Imogen passed it over. DCI Kapoor thumbed through the pages with an incredulous look on her face.

'Wow, you weren't joking, were you? He's all over this crime scene,' DCI Kapoor said, wide-eyed. 'Have you asked him about it?'

'I brought the report to you before I discussed it with anyone. Apart from Gary, of course.'

'You're right that you can't investigate this. Are you happy for Matt to speak to Adrian?'

'Yes. I think it's best if this all stays by the book. For everyone's sake.'

'Do you have any idea what Adrian's connection to Wakefield is?'

'It's not a name I remember him ever mentioning in the past. I just know he couldn't have killed him,' Imogen said; she wasn't lying, not really.

'You're taking this remarkably well, considering,' DCI Kapoor said with a raised eyebrow.

'Trying, ma'am.'

'We need to keep this quiet, for now at least. It would be a PR nightmare for us even though he has left the police, as we can't be seen to be protecting one of our own. Even if he is ex-police, the optics are bad. It could put him in danger as well. People have little enough respect for the police at the moment – if they think we are out killing people then we are in big

251

trouble. For now, I will let DI Walsh and DC Jarvis take hold of the investigation.'

'Could I make a request, ma'am?' Imogen said.

'Depends what it is.'

'DC Jarvis and Adrian have history; I would think DC Webb would be a better fit for this particular assignment.'

'Technically, DC Webb and Adrian also have history. You both put Webb in prison, remember?'

'I know, but I have been working closely with DC Webb on this case and his professionalism is above reproach. I don't know if I could say the same about DC Jarvis, Adrian did deck him once.'

'Hmm yes, you're right, I remember now. I'll take your words under advisement. Maybe you can both share Webb, and I'll just stick Jarvis on CCTV duty again,' DCI Kapoor said before softening a little and looking straight at Imogen. 'How are you with all this?'

'It's upsetting, but ultimately I just want justice to be done, ma'am.'

'Do you think you will be able to keep your distance from the Wakefield case?'

'As I strongly believe that this is all a mistake, I feel my involvement will only obstruct and confuse the investigation into Wakefield's murder. If I have no connection to any part of it, then my involvement can't be used against Adrian if this ever goes to court.'

'Were you ever alone at the scene?'

'No. Not even for a second. Walsh was with me the whole time and we were surrounded by tactical,' she lied.

'Very good. Do you think Carlyle might have killed Wakefield?'

'It's not my place to speculate, ma'am. I just feel like I have been doing so much work on Carlyle that it would take anyone else an age to catch up and we just don't know how much time Marcus has got left.' She didn't want to give DCI Kapoor a reason to take her off the Carlyle case, and directly implying Peter Carlyle might be involved in Wakefield's death could get her taken off the investigation.

'Yes, that's a good point. Fine, you stay on the Carlyles. Finding Marcus has to be our top priority at this point. You can take point on the Carlyle case and Matt can take Adrian.'

'I'll go through the evidence at the warehouse again.'

'Send Matt in, would you?' DCI said, sighing heavily.

'Would you like me to call Adrian and ask him to come in?' Imogen said, hoping to avert the humiliation of Adrian being brought in in a squad car. For his sake mostly, but also for hers. She wasn't sure how much more guilt she could handle.

'Do you think he would?'

'I do.'

'Then I will call him. Best if you keep your distance from the case from now on.'

'Thank you, ma'am.' Imogen left the office and went straight to her desk. She opened her bottom drawer, which was mostly full of chocolate bars, and dug out a half-empty carton of cigarettes she had confiscated from herself many months ago. There was a lighter stuffed inside the pack and so she went outside and lit up. She didn't know what was going to happen next, but she knew Adrian had no intention of giving up his alibi. To her mind the DCI would have no choice but to charge him if he couldn't offer up a plausible explanation as to why his fingerprints were all over the kitchen where Wakefield died. All her hopes lay with Gary right now. If anyone could get to the truth it was him.

Chapter Fifty-Six

Adrian stood on the pavement outside the station. This was it. He looked around and took in his surroundings, knowing full well he wasn't walking out of here today. He pulled out his phone and called his son, Tom.

'Dad?'

'Hey. Are you busy?'

'About to go out to the cinema but I've got a couple of minutes. Is everything OK?'

'I'm in a bit of trouble, and you might hear some things about me that aren't true. I just wanted to give you a heads-up so you aren't caught off guard.'

'What kind of trouble?' Tom asked.

'The kind that lands you in prison,' Adrian said, trying to sound more casual than he actually was.

'What?'

'Look, I didn't do it, that's all you need to know. It just might take a little while to clear this mess up. I don't want you to worry. I won't be in prison long. I've put some money in your account so you don't get caught short, but I will be out before you know it,' Adrian said with a lot more optimism than he felt.

'Where are you now? Can I come and see you?' Tom said in a panicked voice.

'No, I think that would make things harder. Just know that I love you, OK? And could you look after Imogen for me? I think she's going to try and be all superwoman but it's going to be difficult. Just give her a call once in a while.'

'How long do you think you'll be inside?'

'Depends on the investigation. Might take a week, might take a couple of months. Just don't lose heart. It's all going to be OK and I will be fine. Imogen is going to sort it out.'

'Can I visit you in prison? Is it Exeter?'

'I don't know. I don't want you in there. I'll call you instead. Will that be all right?' Adrian tried to sound like he wasn't crying. The thought of Tom seeing him in prison was too much to take.

'Always. I love you, Dad,' Tom said. Adrian could hear he was distraught. Was it fair of him to put his son through this just because he selfishly didn't want to disclose his secret? Every decision he made felt like the wrong one.

'I love you, too. Speak soon,' Adrian said and hung up.

Adrian composed himself and put his phone away before walking into the station to be greeted by DI Walsh who wore a bewildered but professional expression as he led him through to the interrogation room where DC Webb was waiting. To his credit, he did it very casually so as not to draw attention to them. A couple of familiar faces nodded their hellos to Adrian. He knew lots of people were confused about why he had left, and he had avoided a leaving party of any description, so for many of his colleagues he was just there one minute and gone the next. It was weird walking through as a suspect and he appreciated DI Walsh's discretion.

'For the purposes of the tape would you please state your name?' Matt Walsh said as he sat down.

'I am Adrian Miles. I waive my right to legal representation at the present time,' Adrian said, feeling strange to be on this side of the table, almost saying his rank by force of habit. His life was unrecognisable to him.

'Adrian, can you tell me if you were at Shaun Wakefield's property on the night of the fifth November?'

'No comment.'

DI Walsh looked up at Adrian. They both knew how this interview was going to go. Adrian would answer 'No comment' to every single question put to him. Adrian wasn't planning on telling the truth and he didn't want to lie and so this seemed like the only available option. No point paying a solicitor to sit there while he did that. He just had to hope Imogen would find out more information about what happened after he'd left Wakefield's house that night.

'Did you know Mr Wakefield?'

'No comment.'

'Did you and Mr Wakefield get into some kind of fight?'

'No comment.'

Walsh had to ask the questions, Adrian knew that much, and though it was evident he wasn't going to get any answers today, still they carried on, Adrian simply repeating the words over and over until Matt Walsh had run out of things to ask. DI Walsh sighed. DC Webb looked uncomfortable. Adrian remembered interrogating him and thought how strange it was that they should be in this position now, their roles reversed.

Gabriel Webb had been proven innocent thanks to Imogen's tenacity. Adrian only hoped she could do the same for him. There was only one way this day could go now and Adrian could see how reluctant DI Walsh was to do it. Adrian wondered if Imogen was watching in the next room. What a mess.

For the briefest of moments, he considered telling the truth, just pushing those words out of himself and out into the world, so they wouldn't have this hold over him anymore. Since the night it happened it had been looming in the background of every conversation. With every interaction he felt like a fraud and a liar because of the things he wanted to say but couldn't. Terrified that anyone might figure him out. But then he knew that confessing his connection to Shaun Wakefield at this point might even make him look more guilty.

The truth was that he didn't trust any of them with his secret. If he disclosed his alibi he would have no choice but to tell the whole story and on its own it would raise more questions than answers. As soon as the notion of telling came into his mind he pushed it out again. The thought of the fallout was too much. For now, at least, he just had to buy some time and this was the only way he could think of. He realised he had stopped listening to whatever Matt was saying and 'charging you with the murder of Shaun Wakefield' were the only words he heard.

Just trust Imogen, he thought to himself. She could fix this. She would get him out of this. She had to.

Chapter Fifty-Seven

Adrian looked at the inside of the holding cell. He'd thought he was prepared for this, but had felt the walls closing in on him before he'd even stepped inside.

'Did you do it?' DC Webb asked him.

'No comment,' Adrian replied with a raised eyebrow.

'If you didn't, then DS Grey will get you out. She won't stop until you're free. She saved my life, you know?'

'I remember. I was there.'

'Then you know,' Gabriel Webb said.

Adrian stepped inside and turned around.

'What's it like? In prison, I mean.'

'It's crap. The food sucks and it smells weird. Night times are hard and there are some real weapons-grade dickheads in there. But, really, just keep your head down.'

'Was it bad?'

'I never want to go there again,' Webb said, looking down, his composure gone for the briefest of moments.

'Is that why you joined the police?'

'Actually, you might think this is weird, but DS Grey is the reason I joined the police. My life was on a downward trajectory and because of her I got another chance. No one else was fighting for me, no one gave a shit, but she didn't stop. I want to be that guy, the one who doesn't stop till things are right. If it wasn't for her, I would still be in there.'

'That's good. I was worried you were here for revenge or something,' Adrian said.

'No. I want to be one of the good guys. I tried it the other way and I didn't care for it. Good luck in there, Adrian.' He smiled sombrely before leaving the room and closing the door.

Alone again, inside a holding cell this time. The past couple of hours had been a surreal nightmare and Adrian wavered between feeling numb and completely over-whelmed. Still, he knew it was within his power to stop this, to tell someone his alibi. He held onto that power, to the knowledge he could end this if he really wanted to. At least he was in control.

There was something else playing on his mind. Even though Imogen was convinced Peter Carlyle was the person who had killed Shaun Wakefield, there was another possibility. Supposing Wakefield had called the other man from the white van and told him Adrian was looking for him? Wakefield had seemed scared of him and with good reason. Adrian knew what he was capable of. There was a chance Imogen was wrong and his attacker was the one who had killed Wakefield, to stop Adrian from finding out who he was. He must have known Adrian would keep asking, keep pushing to discover his identity, and there would be nothing to find out if there was no one to ask.

He could hear the man in the cell opposite kicking the door relentlessly, obviously unaware you couldn't get through a steel door that way. The sound of the thumping steel mirrored the dull throb in Adrian's temple. He lay back on the bench and covered his face, trying to remain calm, to keep from falling apart. He had been through worse than this, that's all he had to keep reminding himself. This was nothing compared to the rape. At least here he was alone. He could get through this.

Chapter Fifty-Eight

The DCI had given Imogen five minutes to speak to Adrian before he was processed. She took a deep breath before entering his holding cell. Crying in front of him would be unfair, he didn't need to see that. She had to be the strong one right now, needed to focus on finding the evidence that would get him out of this situation. Carlyle and Wakefield were connected and as long as she worked the case from that angle then she might be able to keep a foot in the door.

When she opened the door, Adrian was lying on the bench with his eyes closed. The door clunked as it closed behind her after she slipped inside. For a few moments she just watched him, not knowing what to say, how to say it, what would be comforting right now. She just wanted to take him home and look after him. This was the hardest thing she had ever had to do. Especially knowing what she knew, knowing how much pain he was already in.

'I know it's my right as an ex-police officer, but I don't want to go into D wing. I can't be around rapists and paedophiles. I've given this a lot of thought and it's what I want,' Adrian said, obviously knowing it was Imogen without looking.

'The other option is that you go into B wing, which could be dangerous for you,' she said. 'What if someone recognises you? You've probably put a couple of those people inside in the past. You'll be out of harm's way on the vulnerable prisoner wing.'

'I can't, Imogen. It's not even an option. You know why.' He sat up, running his hands through his hair. He looked tired.

'Have you got a lawyer yet? Did you tell them? I can't believe you did the interview without one,' she said, not knowing what else to say.

'Yes, I got a lawyer, and yes, I told them, but I wanted to tell you as well. I don't want you to worry about me in there.'

'How can I not be worried? This is crazy. Are you sure you aren't ready to tell the DCI what happened? She would be understanding, I know she would. Even if you just did it privately, not on the record, it might change things. Please, will you just think about it?' she pleaded quietly.

'I'm not ready, Imogen. I feel sick with even just you knowing. I can't explain it. Please don't ask me again.'

'I'm so sorry. What can I do?'

'Your job. Find out what really happened. I swear on my life I did not do it,' Adrian said.

'I know you didn't. You don't have to keep telling me.'

'I phoned Tom and told him not to listen to anything he might hear about me. I don't want him visiting me in prison either. Please explain that to him.'

'You don't have to do any of this alone, Adrian, OK? Just trust me, trust the people who care about you. The DCI is going to work really hard to keep you out of the news and try and limit who knows you're in here, to keep you safer. I had better tell her you're planning on going into the main wing and not in the vulnerable prisoner wing. She won't be happy about that.'

'I will be fine. Please, just get me out. Find out who killed Wakefield.'

'I'm not working the Wakefield case anymore. I thought it best Walsh takes over to make sure if it goes to trial no one can say anything untoward happened. But I am sure Carlyle is linked and I'm still leading that case. Walsh will find out what happened at Wakefield's. We've got this.'

'I trust Walsh,' Adrian said.

'Me, too. He's as straight as they come. I don't want to leave you, but I better get back to my case. We still haven't found Marcus Carlyle and I'm starting to doubt we ever will. Add to that I don't want you spending a second longer than you need to in there.'

'You will find that boy. I know you will. You can do anything. Please, remember I love you. You know that, don't you? I'm sorry I'm putting you through all this,' Adrian said, finally cracking and letting the tears out. He wiped his eyes and Imogen rushed over. Kneeling in front of him, she took his hand.

'I've got your back, OK? It's my job to find out the truth and I will. You aren't putting me through anything. You're innocent. Remember that, please, and don't let the guilt consume you. Prison is going to be really tough and you have to trust that we will get you out of there. You need to stay mentally strong and not get inside your own head, OK?'

'OK,' he said, breathing out as though preparing for some kind of fight. In a way he was.

There was a knock on the door. It was time for her to go. Adrian looked up and Imogen could see the fear in his eyes. She didn't want to go but the best thing she could do for him now was find out everything she could about Carlyle and link him to Wakefield. She leaned forward and took Adrian's face in her hands. She kissed him on the lips. He didn't pull away but instead leaned into the kiss, holding on for as long as he could.

'I'll come visit you soon, OK? I love you,' Imogen whispered.

She backed up to the door and tapped on the steel without turning around. DCI Kapoor opened it from the other side. Imogen walked straight past her and out of the station. She wanted to stay with Adrian, to hold him, to make sure he knew she still loved him. She slipped to the side of the building and leaned against the wall, making sure she was alone before she allowed herself to cry.

Chapter Fifty-Nine

NINE DAYS MISSING

The following morning, Imogen had Shaun Wakefield's file spread out in front of her on her desk, noting any names or places she could investigate further with possible ties to Carlyle. She had been staring at it all night. She wasn't actively investigating Wakefield's murder, but there was no reason she couldn't read all the information that was available to her. She was certain it was where Wakefield and Carlyle crossed over that she needed to look to find Marcus. The pressure was immense.

Adrian was still in the holding cell and she knew they would be taking him away soon. It killed her not being able to sit with him. She was hoping for an 'Aha' moment, when something would just jump out at her and suddenly everything would make sense. What were the chances of that? The longer she stared the less sense it seemed to make. She knew this tied to Carlyle somehow and so she picked up his file again. The answers were here, she was sure they were.

'DC Webb?' Imogen said, not looking up.

'Yes, ma'am,' Gabriel said.

'What did we find out about Peter Carlyle's parents? There is no mention of them in the files. In fact, there is no mention of a family at all. There must be someone.'

'When questioned he said he was orphaned at a young age.'

'And we are just taking his word on that? I've been burned by that one before. Can you get a hold of his birth certificate and see if we can get death certificates for both the parents? I want to see their gravestones if possible. I don't believe a word that man says,' Imogen said.

'I'll see if I can find a living relative then.'

'At this point, I will settle for a distant cousin. There has to be someone who knows him from before he married Sara Dunn.'

'Anything else?'

'I don't know, really. Find out as much as you can. Check his phone records to see if you can find a mistress or something, someone he talks to regularly outside of the business. If we can connect him to Wakefield in any way then it's a bonus.'

'I got some info on two of the inmates Wakefield's former cellmate told us about. The person I spoke to said that Terry Harding moved abroad and is living as some kind of ex-pat in Spain, but I couldn't get a number or address for him; at this point it just seems to be a rumour. What little family he has haven't spoken to him since he came out of prison several years ago. Julian Crow also seems to have vanished off the face of the earth,' Webb said.

'What do you mean Crow has vanished, too?' Imogen said – people rarely just vanished.

'All his bank accounts got shut down and he disappeared in 2008.'

'What do we know about him?'

'Very little, really. He's from Plymouth originally, he was inside three times for theft and once for assault, as well as having some sealed youth offences. Seems like a career criminal from a young age.'

'Does Crow have any family we could speak to? Maybe they'll know where he is and we can find out more about Wakefield,' Imogen said.

'His mum's in a nursing home, paid for by the council, but she never has any visitors. I already spoke to the manager there and told her we would be popping by.'

'Where is it?'

'Here. In Exeter.'

'Let's go pay Mrs Crow a visit then. We'll stop off and get some flowers on the way. Let's keep looking for Harding, someone must know something.'

'I thought you were off the Wakefield case?'

'I won't tell if you don't,' she said.

Borrow Hill nursing home looked nice enough with a freshly painted yellow exterior, although Imogen couldn't shake the idea it was the 'last stop at the station', as her mother used to put it. Irene Grey had always instilled a deep mistrust of nursing and retirement homes in Imogen – although, in hindsight, Imogen knew it was so she would feel too guilty to put her in one, a decision she never even got the chance to make.

Webb had informed the manager they were on their way over to visit Lorelei Crow and, as they were led through the corridors to her room, Imogen glanced into the rooms; there was an overpowering feeling of loneliness and silence. Even though she could hear televisions and radios, there was a lifelessness to the building. They passed a room where the contents of the dresser were being emptied into a plain cardboard box, the bed stripped bare as it was prepared for a new occupant. The manager stopped at one of the doors and turned to them before reaching for the handle to let them in.

'I must warn you that Lori isn't always very lucid. She has dementia and so has good days and bad days. Been like that since she got here, and probably long before.'

'Thank you,' Imogen said. She really hoped this was a good day, as they needed to get some pertinent information from Lorelei Crow. Beyond her, Imogen didn't know what other leads they had.

They entered her room and were hit with the smell of lavender and talcum powder. Lorelei Crow was much older than Imogen had been expecting. She wasn't sure what exactly she had expected – and she felt intrusive being here. The room was well-lived-in; Lorelei had obviously been here for several years.

'Mrs Crow? I am DS Imogen Grey and this is my colleague, DC Gabriel Webb,' Imogen said softly, not wanting to startle the woman who was sitting watching *The Chase* at an impossibly low volume.

'Hello, dear. Call me Lori, I haven't been Mrs Crow in a long time. Not since my Aaron died,' Lorelei said. The door closed behind the manager, and Gabriel stood at the end of the bed, letting Imogen take the seat next to Lorelei Crow.

'Hi, Lori. I'm a police officer and I just wanted to ask you a few questions if that's OK? I brought you some flowers to cheer the place up. I gave them to the lady on the desk to find a vase for them.'

'Thank you. Are you here about Julian?'

'Why would you ask me that?' Imogen said.

'It's always about Julian. Especially since his father died. The apple didn't fall far from that tree, I tell you. I tried, I really did, but Julian was always a lost cause.'

'We'd like to speak to Julian, if possible. Do you know where he is?'

'Haven't heard hide nor hair of him for a long time. He was a troubled one, you know. I did my best but some people just turn out wrong, don't they? He turns up every few years looking for money, but I haven't got any now so there's no reason for him to stop by. He took it all already.'

'When was the last time you spoke to him?'

'I haven't got a clue, lovely. Ask at the desk when I moved in here, because I spoke to him just before that, a week or so before, when he told me he was selling the house from under me and I had to get out.'

'Was he allowed to do that?'

'Oh, he convinced me years before to sign it over into his name so he wouldn't have to pay inheritance tax if I died. Silly me, I listened to him. I always gave him too much credit and look at me now.'

'I'm sorry.'

'I expect he burned through that money faster than you can say jack rabbit and was destitute again in no time. He was always terrible with things like that. Took after his dad. Wanted to be all flashy, ideas above his station. He liked to give the illusion that he was better than he was.'

'Do you happen to know if he maintained contact with a man called Shaun Wakefield?'

'Sorry love, no. He doesn't get close to people, there's something wrong with him. That's how come he kept ending up in prison. Always trying to impress the wrong people. He never had any friends or girlfriends for that matter, just his wife Millie, but she died. She got run over and killed, it completely destroyed him. They lived with me in the house and I know she found him hard to deal with, they hadn't been married a year when she died. It was such a tragedy.'

'Where was the last place you saw him?'

'Funeral for his wife, Millie. He was devastated.'

'Do you have a photo of Julian?' DC Webb said.

'Pass me that red album over there,' Lorelei said, pointing to a large burgundy leather photo album on her dressing table. It was well-worn and Imogen could see it was important to her that she kept it close by. Whatever she said about her son, she still loved him.

Lorelei thumbed through the pages and then turned the album towards them. It was a wedding photo with the invitation stuck to the page just beneath it reading, 'You are invited to the wedding of Millie Barker and Julian Crow'. Except the picture wasn't Julian Crow at all. It was a much younger Peter Carlyle.

Imogen looked at Webb, who had clearly already figured that particular plot twist out.

'Do you have any childhood photos of Julian?'

Lorelei flicked further back in the book to a photo of a boy around ten years old. Imogen wasn't sure but there seemed to be a dimple in the centre of his chin. Peter Carlyle definitely didn't have a dimple now, and it wasn't something people grew out of.

How had Carlyle done this? Was he even really Julian Crow? What – and who – exactly were they dealing with here? How many identities beyond Crow and Carlyle did he have and which was the real one? This made things a lot more complicated. According to the woman on the desk, Lorelei had dementia before she came into the home. It was possible Carlyle had manipulated her into thinking he was her son.

'Thank you so much, Lori, this is really helpful. Do you mind if I take a photo of this picture?'

'Of course, please do. I'm sorry I couldn't be more help,' she said, patting Imogen's hand.

'You have been brilliant,' Imogen said.

They left Lorelei alone in the room, just as they had found her. Imogen felt a little bad about leaving her so soon and wondered if it would be OK for her to visit again – latent guilt for being a crap daughter while her mother had been alive, no doubt.

'How did you know to ask to see a photo?' Imogen said to Webb as they walked back to the car.

'I don't know. I think it was when she said about the wife dying. Coupled with the fact that he sold the house from under her. Sounds like he is driven by money and very little else. Perfect recipe for the kind of man who would take out life insurance on his own wife and kid and try to have them killed,' Webb said.

'Well, now we have a solid connection between Carlyle and Wakefield. A bit of a strange coincidence them being in prison together otherwise,' Imogen said.

'I'm not sure I believe in coincidences,' Gabriel said.

'We've got to hope he doesn't know we are on to him, although I have a feeling I made it pretty obvious I was gunning for him. Maybe I should have been smarter about it. I thought we were dealing with a common or garden shithead, but it turns out he's more of a black widow.'

'Let's get to the Carlyle house and see if there's any sign of him. Or maybe he's been to see his wife?' Webb said.

'Call Walsh. Let him know what's going on and ask him what we should be doing,' Imogen said.

They jumped in the car and pulled away. Maybe, if they could get to Carlyle, he would confess to the murder of Shaun Wakefield, or at least acknowledge their connection. Maybe he would admit to orchestrating this whole situation. So many maybes. The net was closing around Peter Carlyle, but he was obviously a smarter man than Imogen had given him credit for. Plus, they had to find him first. They couldn't count their chickens just yet.

Chapter Sixty

After a night in the holding cell at the station, Adrian was officially 'inside'. After the indignity of being searched, the stress of which he had not accounted for, he was glad to finally be alone in a cell. As he'd walked through the wing with the prison officer, he'd kept his head down, hoping he was going to be a single-cell occupant, and so, when the guard opened the door, he'd been relieved to see the cell was empty. The guard reeled off a set of rules he had obviously said hundreds of times before, but Adrian hadn't listened, just waiting for the door to shut so he could be alone.

Never in his life had he imagined being in a prison cell, not really, not even back when he'd bent the rules of an investigation or two. He'd thought he was smart enough to avoid going to prison. Had been so proud of himself for not being a complete fuck-up like his father. He remembered looking at his warrant card for the first time and was aware he was a better man than his dad. Sure, he was flawed, he knew that much – he had made mistakes and even broken a few laws himself, but never anything like this. Never murder. Still, he would rather be here than tell anyone the truth about what he had been through.

It didn't even make sense to him when he thought about it. Being in here was far more dangerous than uttering a few words, but it was the stigma of living the rest of his life as *that* person that he didn't want. He imagined what his former colleagues would say about him – some would say he was lying, some would say he was weak, others might pity him. Ultimately, this seemed like a smaller price to pay. He guessed he could change his mind at any time and tell them his alibi, but he wanted to give Imogen a chance before blowing the rest of his life to smithereens.

He stayed in his cell alone all morning, but he knew the door wouldn't remain closed forever. It wasn't long until lunch time and he would have to face the other prisoners at some point. He was getting hungry. He tried to think back to the last time he ate and realised it had been longer than a day, maybe two.

He heard the call for lunch and the clunk of the door as it opened. He got up and stepped outside onto the gallery. He felt dizzy. What was he thinking? He was in prison. Surely telling the truth had to be better than this? He noticed the eyes watching him as he stood there trying to regain his poise before making his way to the canteen.

The food was exactly as DC Webb had described it; Adrian knew he should eat but his appetite just wasn't there anymore. As he stood up from the table, he felt someone slam into him as they walked past.

'Watch it,' the man said.

Adrian looked him up and down, unsure of how to respond. He had always been a police officer when dealing with guys like this, but now he couldn't hide behind that. He was the same as every other guy in here. Stupid enough to get arrested.

'Sorry, I didn't mean to . . .' Adrian said, unsure what the best way to play this was.

'Just watch what you're doing,' the man hissed right into Adrian's face, spit landing on his cheek.

'Maybe you should watch it,' Adrian said, pressing his fork hard into the man's testicles. He didn't want to start a fight, but he knew he couldn't be seen to be weak. The look in the man's eye switched for a moment from excitement to fear, but then he was back again. Adrian removed the fork and stepped back. He could tell that a few of the inmates had seen the minor altercation and were whispering to each other. He had no idea what they were saying, though. He could feel everyone's eyes on them, hoping for something to happen, breaths held in anticipation. The man raised his fist and swung for Adrian's face, stopping just millimetres from impact. Adrian maintained eye contact; he had to let the man know he couldn't be intimidated. This was either a really smart move or really stupid.

'What's goin' on over here, Jeffo?' A guard approached and the man, Jeffo, stepped back with a slight smirk on his face. Adrian kept staring at him, making sure he knew that he wasn't backing down, that he wouldn't have a problem with this interaction continuing.

'Nothing at all, Johnson, mate,' Jeffo said. 'Just getting to know the new guy.'

The guard, Johnson, turned to Adrian. 'If you've finished, get out of here. I'll walk you back to your cell.'

Adrian didn't need to be told twice, and he wandered back to his cell with the guard following behind him. He was drawing plenty of attention as the latest addition to the prison and was doing his best to keep his head down, but also trying not to look scared. He still couldn't believe he was here, really actually here.

They arrived back at his cell and he went inside, relieved to be out of harm's way for the time being. The guard closed the door behind him.

'I know who you are,' Johnson said.

'Right, OK,' Adrian said, not really sure what the guard wanted him to say.

'Just keep your head down, OK? You'll be fine. I'll watch out for you.'

'Why would you do that?'

'Professional courtesy, innit?' Johnson said.

'I'm not on the job anymore.'

'Once a blue always a blue, that's what my dad used to say. He was a copper down in Plymouth.'

'Well, thank you. I appreciate it.'

'Just don't make any waves and you'll be fine,' Johnson said before leaving.

Adrian sat on his bunk appraising his room. The window was small and dirty, with a barely visible view to the street across the road. There was a small shelf-like table and a fairly comfortable-looking chair, although he could see stains and marks on the dusky blue fabric. He had been inside the prison before and had known it wouldn't be like a hotel room, but it was different when it was *your* room, *your* home for the foreseeable. It felt so much smaller. This was now his entire world until Imogen could get him out.

He scooched back on the mattress and put his back to the wall, bringing his knees up to his chest. He watched the door until the bell went again and they locked it for the afternoon, muttering a sigh of relief as soon as he was alone again. All those men out there, he hadn't even thought about how it would feel being in here with all these strangers. Strange *men*. It occurred to him that the man who assaulted him could just as easily be in here as outside. He wouldn't know either way. Helplessness crept over him as he deliberated what he should do next. How much longer could he sustain this?

Chapter Sixty-One

Imogen had already called through to Walsh to let him know that Carlyle and Crow were in fact the same person, although she wasn't sure which was his real identity at this point. Walsh was heading to the Carlyle house while Imogen and Gabriel were making their way to Wonford Hospital. As they pulled out of Barrack Road the phone rang, and she put it on speakerphone.

'Is he there? Has he been there?' Imogen said, exhausted, desperate for them to have uncovered anything, and aware the chances of them finding Marcus alive were next to gone.

'All still empty here. Really empty. We're getting a search warrant together for the place. Maybe Carlyle missed something,' Walsh replied.

'I'll go to the hospital and see if Sara Carlyle knows where he could have gone. If we can find him then maybe he can lead us to Marcus. If he did kill Wakefield then he killed our best lead as well. How do I tell her we haven't found her son yet?'

'Poor woman,' Walsh said.

'Might be worth checking the rest of the properties they have on the Dunn and Co. books again; Carlyle or whoever he's working with could be hiding Marcus at another one of those. So far Gregory Dunn has been more than helpful and I'm sure he would let us look,' DC Webb said.

'Good thinking,' Imogen said.

'I'll get in touch with him and see if he has any ideas,' Walsh said.

'Later,' Imogen said, but Walsh had already hung up.

She parked up the car and she and Webb jumped out and rushed towards the entrance. Peter Carlyle didn't exist, at least not as they knew him. They were dealing with an entirely different person to the one he had presented to them. A well-practised con man, he had fooled everyone, including his wife and father-in-law. Though Gregory Dunn didn't seem like the kind of man to suffer fools, Carlyle had well and truly pulled the wool over his eyes.

'Better let me do the talking when we get in there,' Imogen said to Webb as they walked through the hospital corridor.

'Whatever you say.'

'I've been really impressed with you so far, if you don't mind me saying. I'm not trying to patronise you or anything,' Imogen said.

'I appreciate you saying so, ma'am,' Gabriel said, looking a little embarrassed at the compliment.

'Please, just call me Imogen. "Ma'am" makes me feel old.'

'Well, thank you then, Imogen . . . and you're not old,' he said, his cheeks reddening even more.

Sara Carlyle was alone when they got to her room. She was looking out the window even though there was no discernible view.

'Sara?' Imogen said.

'Did you find him? Did you find Marcus?' she said with a slur, a side effect of the morphine.

'No, but we are still hopeful,' Imogen lied. 'We need to ask you a few difficult questions, I'm afraid.'

'Go ahead.'

'Have you spoken to your husband recently?' Imogen asked.

How do you tell someone their whole life is a lie?

'No. I think he's taken all of this really badly. We all have. I'm not sure he can bear to see me like this. He feels responsible. I think he's given up. He thinks we won't get Marcus back,' Sara said. 'He tends to disappear when things get on top of him.'

'Does he disappear often?'

'Maybe once or twice a year. I don't know. Just needs to get away from everything. I think he had a difficult childhood, not that he ever talks about it much.'

'Has he called you in the last four days?'

'No.'

'And where does he usually go when he disappears like this?'

'I learned early on not to ask,' Sara said.

Imogen might have found that strange a few months ago, but she had learned from her own relationship with Adrian that you make incremental allowances for behaviour until you accept things without question, because it's easier than pushing for answers. She tried not to think about that now, knowing she should have pushed harder.

'Can I ask where you met your husband?'

'Why would you need to know that?' Sara asked, confused.

'Just, maybe he's gone there or something. We really need to speak to him and we need to know places he might go.' Imogen's lie was barely convincing, but Sara really wasn't paying that much attention.

'I used to go to the theatre every day to pick up sandwiches for lunch. It's just down the road from our office and they have a lovely little café in there. I thought it would be a good way to support the place. Anyway, after a time I started bumping into him there, as he was always picking up lunch, too. We used to have the same sandwich. Prawn and mayo on granary with celery instead of lettuce. It just seemed like destiny. We hit it off straight away. We had a lot of the same interests. We were married six months later,' she said.

'Your father told us you signed a pre-nuptial agreement before the wedding.'

'Daddy insisted. He wanted to hand over the bulk of the business to me but he was concerned about the speed at which our relationship had progressed. Dad had cancer at the time. We didn't think he had long left, but he beat it, so Daddy retained a percentage because he wanted to keep some control, and he expressly wrote it into the contract that we couldn't sell our portion of the business without his permission. I know it sounds bad but he's just very protective.'

'How did Peter feel about the pre-nup?'

'He was a bit pissed off at first – he thought it spoiled the romance a bit and I was inclined to agree – but he signed it. He had his own money after all. I don't see how this is going to help you find Marcus,' she said suspiciously.

'You say he had his own money? He was well-off then?'

'On our third date he chartered a plane and took me to Venice for the weekend. He was always spoiling me with beautiful things. On our three-month anniversary he had two hundred red roses delivered to the office. He had a few properties he rented out on his own as well. I know money when I see it.'

'Did you ever meet his parents?'

'No, they died before he was born.'

'Do you know the name Julian Crow?'

'Sorry, no. What's all this about? Why do you need to know all that stuff about Peter? What's going on?'

'Did you know that Peter had taken out life insurance on both you and your son, for a significant amount of money?' Imogen said, feeling like an absolute bitch for doing this while Sara was still in her hospital bed.

'What are you saying?' Sara said.

'I know this is going to be hard to hear, but we have reason to believe that your husband was behind the kidnapping and what subsequently happened to you. What's more, we think he may be implicated in a murder as well. Maybe more than one.'

'What? No. You're wrong. Peter isn't capable of anything like that.'

'Do you remember that photograph I showed you the last time I came here? The picture of the man?' Imogen said.

'Yes.'

'He was photographed taking your son the morning of the kidnapping.'

'If you have the photo of the kidnapper why can't you find Marcus?'

'The photo had only just come into our possession. A witness only just came forward. Not having it from the start really set us back. When I showed you the photo it seemed to me as though your husband recognised the man. He managed to give the police officers we had stationed at the house the slip that night and a few hours later the man in the photo was found dead, and we still don't know where your husband is.'

The door burst open and Gregory Dunn blustered in, clearly annoyed.

'What's going on? Should you be talking to her alone? She's very fragile at the moment.'

Sara started to cry at the sight of her father and held her hand out to him. He moved forward immediately and took it.

'They think Peter had something to do with it,' Sara said. 'Tell them they're wrong! Make them go away.'

'Your husband is gone, Sara,' Imogen said. 'Knowing that your son has yet to be found, why would he disappear? We also have reason to believe he has been operating under an assumed identity. It's possible he already has a new identity on the go – he has to be getting money from somewhere and so far all of your accounts remain untouched,' she added.

'What do you mean?' Gregory Dunn said, softening a little.

'One of the suspects in your grandson's kidnapping was found dead in his home a little over twenty-four hours after we showed Sara and Peter his picture. The man was an ex-con, and while he was inside he was cellmates with a man called Julian Crow.'

'I told you I have never heard that name before,' Sara protested.

'We believe Julian Crow and your husband are the same person. We're going to look into the specifics but it's possible Peter met Julian in prison, as Julian seemed to spend a lot of time there. It might be that he found out about Julian's financial circumstances, and then after they were released he disposed of Julian in some way and took his identity. Julian Crow's mother has dementia, and we believe Peter targeted her in order to convince her to sign everything over to him. When the money started to run out, we think he assumed the identity of Peter Carlyle and moved on to his next target.'

'Peter's never been to prison . . .' Sara said, her voice trailing off.

'I'm afraid he has. We've just come from visiting Crow's mother. She showed us a photo of the man she knows as Julian from maybe ten years ago, but it wasn't her son – it was Peter. So whoever Peter is now, it's not who he was ten years ago.'

'I knew he was a wrong'un!' Gregory Dunn hissed, as if chastising himself.

'You're wrong, you must be wrong!' Sara said, sobbing openly now as her world crashed around her. Imogen couldn't help but feel sorry for her. Finding out your whole life was a lie had to be a complete nightmare.

Imogen pulled out her phone and called up the wedding photograph they got from Lorelei Crow and showed Sara and her father. Sara closed her eyes and looked away. Imogen could tell she didn't want to talk anymore. The problem was that Imogen still didn't know where Peter was – the theatre where he'd met Sara wasn't a strong enough lead – and so she had to keep pushing.

'You've never heard your husband mention the name Julian Crow? Or Shaun Wakefield?' Imogen said.

'No. I told you.'

'What about Terry Harding?' Gabriel interjected. The other cellmate Wakefield knew in prison.

'No.'

'Wait a minute,' Gregory Dunn said. 'I know that name. Terry Harding.'

'Terry Harding? Are you sure?' Imogen said.

'Absolutely. We sold a property to him a little over a year ago.'

'Can you remember what he looked like?'

'Oh, I never met him. It was all done through solic- itors. Proctor and Kaim, I think. Peter was handling it. I just remember seeing the paperwork. Beautiful property overlooking water, needed a total renovation though. He paid cash, no loans concerned.'

'Where was this property?' Imogen asked.

'Do you think he was involved? This Harding character?' Gregory Dunn said.

'We need to speak to him,' Imogen said before Gabriel had a chance to say anything. So far Gabriel had been on point about so many things, it wouldn't surprise her if he caught onto the same thing as her: that Terry Harding could very likely be Peter Carlyle's new alias. She didn't want Gregory Dunn to know that though.

'The property was in Warfleet, in Dartmouth. Lovely five-bedroom stone house on Weeke Hill, overlooking the water. As I recall they owned a local boating company. It was called Riverside Lodge, I think – something unimaginative like that. '

'They?'

'Harding and his wife.'

'Thank you, Mr Dunn. Again, I am so sorry, Sara. Please, if Peter does contact you just tell him we need to ask him a few questions. If you could not mention any other part of this discussion that would be appreciated.'

'Thank you, detectives,' Gregory Dunn said, still holding his daughter's hand.

Imogen felt terrible for tearing that woman's world apart – with everything Sara had already lost it just seemed so unfair. Peter Carlyle or Julian Crow – whatever his name was – seemed to be a veritable snake.

'Why did you bring up Harding?' Imogen said as they got back in the car.

'Just thought she might have heard his name. Anything is helpful at this point, right? Sorry if I overstepped.'

'You didn't, trust me. Your instincts were spot on. Considering what we know about how our man likes to take on new identities, it's important we track down this "Terry Harding". Peter Carlyle is not as smart as he thinks he is. He's going to lead us to Marcus.'

'You think Marcus is still alive?'

'I do. I really do. Until we find out otherwise then we operate as though he is,' Imogen said hopefully.

'What now then?'

'We have to get more information on the Hardings. We need to get to Dartmouth and find that house quickly; we have to find him before he disappears again – Marcus's life depends on it – and we need him to confess to the murder of Shaun Wakefield so that we can get Adrian out,' Imogen said, looking at her watch. They could get to Dartmouth in a couple of hours.

'Are you sure Carlyle did it?'

'A hundred per cent. Shaun Wakefield was our best chance at finding out who Carlyle used to be. As soon as I showed Sara the picture of Wakefield in the hospital Carlyle knew he had to get rid of him. He knew if we spoke to Wakefield he would have talked. He wasn't banking on us looking into Wakefield's past and finding a connection to this new identity he has assumed. We should get going now.'

'We don't have anything on the house or Harding. We should get as much as we can before we barrel in there, don't you think? Plus, it's a bit late,' Gabriel said.

'I know but I can't have Marcus out there another night. It's already been too long.'

'They didn't find Carlyle's prints at Wakefield's crime scene. How can you know he did it?'

'I just know. Gary said whoever else was there wore gloves. For now, we have enough to pay the Hardings a visit at least,' Imogen said.

'I just don't think it's a good idea to go right now. I know you want to get all this cleared up and get Adrian out but you need a break at some point, too.'

'Fine, but we should go back to the station now and look into Harding, find out whatever we can about the boat business, any family he might have, so that we aren't going in blind. I've got a visit with Adrian in the morning at the prison. We'll head to Dartmouth straight after,' Imogen said. This could be it, she could be getting closer to finding Marcus, to exonerating Adrian.

'When was the last time you slept?' Gabriel said.

'You know, I actually don't remember.' She wasn't lying.

'Look, we all want to find Marcus, but you've been hammering this for days; it's unsustainable. You need to go home and get some rest; I'll go back to the station and get the information together. I actually went home last night and slept, whereas I know you didn't.'

She was tired, there was no denying that. A couple of hours' sleep might help her get some perspective.

'I need to go back to the station and pick up my notes first, so I can run through them again.'

'As long as you promise to leave straight away.'

'I promise,' she said as she pushed down on the accelerator and headed towards the station. Still, in the back of her mind, she didn't want another night to pass without finding Marcus.

Chapter Sixty-Two

The door to Adrian's cell opened. Dinner. He wasn't sure if he could face going out there. This was a huge mistake. Longing to be back outside, annoyed with himself for not having the courage to just give up his alibi. But as tense as this situation made him, the idea of telling the world what happened to him filled him with a deeper dread than he could have imagined possible before that night.

There was a tap at the door and Adrian looked up to see one of the guards standing there. He had heard someone call him Ryman earlier.

The guard came through the cell door and sauntered towards the bed, a slight sneer on his face. Adrian could tell he was in for a confrontation of some kind. The other prisoners who walked past his door immediately averted their eyes when they saw Ryman in there. Adrian guessed he had a reputation of some kind. That's fine, Adrian had dealt with plenty of bullies in the past.

'Look at where you ended up. You lot think you're so much better than us,' Ryman said, as Adrian slid off the bed and stood.

'I don't think I'm better than anyone.'

Ryman cuffed Adrian around the face. 'Did I say you could talk?'

Adrian straightened up and looked directly at Ryman. There was no retaliating, he just had to take it, but that was fine because Adrian knew it wouldn't be long before he was out of this hellhole. Ryman was stuck in here for the foreseeable.

'I'll be keeping an eye on you. I could make life very difficult for you. Do you know what they do to your lot in here?'

Adrian shook his head, aware that it was a question, but also that he didn't fancy getting smacked in the face again.

'I might have some favours to ask from you. Nothing major, just roughing a couple of people up. You think you can handle that?'

'Sure,' Adrian said, not wanting to antagonise the man, but knowing he wouldn't be doing any favours for Ryman in here.

'Settle in, sunshine, this is the beginning of a beautiful friendship.' Ryman kissed at the air and then swaggered out of the cell looking pretty pleased with himself.

He shut the door behind him and Adrian climbed onto his bed and into the corner again. This was all like a surreal nightmare he couldn't quite get his head round, but then, life had been like that for over a year.

Maybe he died that night in that van.

Maybe this was hell.

Chapter Sixty-Three

Imogen had managed to stay in the station for about an hour before she started to nod off over her work and DC Webb forced her to go home. She couldn't face going back to her flat alone, so she went to Adrian's. It was the only way to feel close to him right now. She pulled up outside the house and looked at the darkened windows. Lifeless.

Inside the house was cold, even though it was warmer than your average November. The house was strangely vacant despite the fact Adrian had barely been gone forty-eight hours. The light in the fridge hurt Imogen's eyes as she opened it. She noticed the fridge was almost empty and freshly cleaned as she reached inside and grabbed a beer. The kitchen was spotless, too. Adrian had cleaned before he left, and for some reason that was all it took to set Imogen off tonight. She had been holding it together all day but all she could think about was the fact that Adrian was in prison.

Draining the first bottle of beer in record time, she reached for another before going into the lounge and sitting on the sofa. It felt hard and uncomfortable. Everything seemed to have harder edges without Adrian here. After flicking through the channels for less than a minute, Imogen turned the TV off and let the tears fall for a moment. Knowing she was alone made it easier to let go, get it out. Sobbing was strangely freeing when you weren't actively trying to stop it.

When she finally felt drained of emotion she wiped her sore puffy eyes on her sleeve and headed upstairs.

The bed was made, the bedding fresh. She put the beer on the bedside table and kicked her shoes off before lying on top of the covers. When she wasn't focused on the case all she could think of was how much of an idiot she had been these last few months. Why didn't she see how much pain he was in? Remembering moments here and there, cringing at the things she had been thinking, wishing she could go back and give herself a slap. She was a detective, for Christ's sake. Thinking back to that day, the day after – his bruises, the look on his face, the way he'd physically recoiled from her touch. It should have been enough to tip her off, but no, she was too self-absorbed to even think it might be about him and not her. What a bitch. In that moment, Adrian's words popped back into her thoughts.

The clothes. He had stuffed them in the back of the wardrobe in a black sack. She jumped off the bed and rushed over to the wardrobe. Falling to her knees she pushed past the shoes at the bottom and felt for the black plastic bag. Could she look? Should she? Without allowing herself to think for too long, she removed the bag. She reached into her pocket and felt for a pair of gloves. She usually had a few pairs on her person; force of habit. She put some on.

With the gloves now on she carefully opened the bag, not sure what she was so frightened of. After taking a deep, fortifying breath, she pulled out a shirt first. There were blood and alcohol stains on the collar and around the chest area, the pocket was ripped and the faint odour of Jack Daniel's and Coke emanated from the garment. She put the shirt back in the bag and grabbed Adrian's trousers next. They were dark blue and the blood had dried almost black in places, the fabric rigid and crumpled after being saturated and then stuffed in a bag. Not wanting to look too closely, she stuffed the trousers back into the bag and quickly closed it before shoving it to the back of the cupboard again.

She shouldn't have looked. It felt like a violation of privacy. Discarding the gloves, she shut the wardrobe doors. Edging backwards, she felt for the bed and climbed onto it. Grabbing Adrian's pillow she clung to it with her eyes clamped shut, wishing he was here.

At no point had she doubted Adrian's account of what happened, but this gave it more of a form in her mind. The thought of him alone and scared, terrified for his life . . . So much blood, so much pain. She had to get him out of prison, that was the very least she could do.

Part of her almost didn't want to visit Adrian in the morning – she couldn't bear the thought of seeing him like that – but none of this was about her or about what she wanted anymore. For right now, she didn't matter.

Closing her eyes, she prayed for the first time in decades – for Adrian, for Marcus, for everyone she had ever let down. God only knew how Adrian was doing inside the prison. Knowing him the way she did, she knew there was no way he would stay out of trouble. He would upset someone, say something stupid and end up dead. She was scared she might never see him again. In the morning she would renew her efforts, and this time she wouldn't give up until Adrian and Marcus were both safe at home with the people who loved them.

Chapter Sixty-Four

Adrian lay on his bunk and tried to sleep. His first night inside. A place he never thought he would be. The room smelled of stale sweat and some kind of industrial cleaner; it was a strange combination. There were other smells in the air, too, like the faint coppery scent of blood that he was desperately trying to ignore. It was quiet too, unbearably so.

Maybe the old Adrian could have handled being in here, but he wasn't that man anymore. Even with his eyes shut he felt the room closing in on him. There was nothing to think about except the van. He curled into a ball and made himself small as he tried to concentrate on the sound of his breath going in and out. He could almost feel the steel floor of the van underneath him, remembering the texture under his fingers as he lay there.

Think about something else, anything else.

He dreaded them opening the door again in the morning, knowing full well that he was a shit magnet. Knowing it wouldn't be long before he got into a scrape with someone, or the guard Ryman turned up looking for a 'favour', as he'd called it. Being in B wing was probably a stupid move. He knew some of the guards were aware he was ex-police and he couldn't rely on that information not filtering through to the inmates. You just didn't know who you could trust.

One day at a time, that's all he had to keep reminding

himself. He had managed to get through today without any major incidents and Imogen had already put in a request to visit him tomorrow, though he knew she would just pester him to tell the DCI about the rape he endured, knowing full well his alibi would get him out of there. He didn't know what he was so scared of, not when he broke it down. The DCI was a good person and, though he hated to admit it, confiding in a female felt like it might be easier. Still, it had taken him long enough to even tell Imogen, and he was still raw from that, still coming down. No, he would trust that she could get him out by finding out what really happened to Wakefield before he had to disclose to the DCI where he'd been.

The door opened and the guard from earlier – Johnson – was standing there.

This can't be good.

'Get your stuff together, you're moving,' Johnson said.

'What do you mean? Why? I don't want to go in D wing,' Adrian said, hoping this wasn't another guard looking to blackmail him. His eyes flicked to the clock; it was almost eleven. This wasn't official, whatever it was.

'Not D wing, someone on B wing has requested you as a cellie.'

'Now? Who? I don't want a cellmate.'

'I've just been told to come and get you. Come on. Chop, chop.'

'Can you do this? Don't I get a say in this?'

'Nope. Now move it.'

Adrian put his few items in a carrier bag and folded his blanket. As he stepped out of the cell the quiet hit him and he started to panic. Where was the guard taking him? Had someone recognised him? In the back of his mind one fear overshadowed all others: what if it was *him*, what if he was trapped in here with the man who raped him? A million scenarios ran through his mind as he walked away from his room. He felt very unsafe all of a sudden.

Why would anyone request to share a cell with him? He could feel his heart thumping as he followed Johnson down the length of the gallery until the guard stopped and motioned for Adrian to move forward. The cell door at the end was open.

'If this is some kind of set-up, you're going to regret it.'

'Just get in there,' Johnson said, nonplussed, folding his arms. 'And shut the door behind you.'

Adrian moved towards the cell, afraid of what he might find in there. He looked over his shoulder to see Johnson stepping back.

'Come in then,' a voice said from inside. There was something familiar about it though, something reassuring. He went towards the cell, part of him wanting to run the other way, knowing there was nowhere to run.

He walked into the room and there, sitting on the bunk, was none other than Dean Kinkaid, Imogen's ex-boyfriend and the last person Adrian had expected to see here.

The wave of relief that swept over Adrian was indescribable. Even though he didn't know Dean that well, he knew he could trust him, because the one thing Imogen had always stressed about Dean Kinkaid was that she trusted him unreservedly.

Adrian put his stuff on the chair and Dean stood up. He put his arms around Adrian and pulled him into a hug. It felt strange because he had never been that close to Dean.

'How did you know I was in here?' Adrian said.

'I saw your little kerfuffle in the cafeteria. You're not going to make many friends like that. How was your first day?'

'Just a bit on edge, you know? I recognise a few of the guys in here. It's only a matter of time before one of them recognises me.'

'Well, you're with me now, you won't get any random shit from now on at least.'

'Does Imogen know you're here?' Adrian said. He couldn't help but wonder if they kept in touch. Imogen never talked about Dean, but he knew they had burned hot and bright for the few months they'd been together and their break-up over two years ago had hit her hard. You don't just get over relationships like that.

'As far as I know, no. We don't really talk anymore. Anyway, I know it's impolite to ask but, seeing as we're old friends, what are you in here for? You here under-cover?' Dean said quietly.

'Not undercover, no. They think I killed someone.'

Dean raised his eyebrows and nodded, almost impressed at the severity of Adrian's crime. Adrian knew crimes carried currency in here.

'Why aren't you on D wing?'

'I refused. I didn't want to be among that lot. Everyone always assumes you're a nonce when you're in D wing.'

'You have bigger stones than I thought. If anyone finds out you're a copper, then even I can't save you.'

'I'm not police anymore, I quit last year. Anyway, someone already knows, how do you think I got this?' Adrian pointed to the purple mark under his eye.

'Who did that?'

'Guard, Ryman. Said he would blab if I didn't do him some favours.'

'Oh, don't worry about him, I'll have a word. Anything else I should know?'

'Me and Imogen, we're together,' Adrian said, assuming this would be news to Dean. He wanted to get it out in the open and the longer he left it the more awkward it would be to say.

'I always knew it was coming. I'm glad. She deserves someone a bit less . . . me.'

'Well, at the moment I'm not sure I'm the answer. Why are you in here?'

'This time? Gave someone a kicking. Don't worry, they deserved it,' Dean said. Adrian had no reason to doubt him.

'I'm going to lie down for a bit if that's OK. It's late,' Adrian said.

'Well, I've got your back now – so sleep. I'll get you up in the morning.'

Adrian climbed onto the lower bunk and pulled the blanket over him, feeling safer already. Imogen would probably be relieved to know that Dean was there, too. Like a guardian angel almost. He could feel his muscles relax and sleep beckoning. He embraced it, knowing that for now, at least, he wasn't alone in here anymore.

Chapter Sixty-Five

TEN DAYS MISSING

The coffee burned Imogen's lips as she drank it, but she needed it to wake herself up, it was the least she deserved, a burned tongue. Sleep had not come easy to her in the night, the absence of Adrian more overbearing than she could have imagined, and she needed to be on top form. They were going to get him out today, she was determined.

The wind had gone out of everyone's sails with regards to finding Marcus. No one wanted to admit that he might be dead, but they were all thinking it. Knowing his father was involved should have made things easier. The problem was that Carlyle was smart. He'd had contingencies in place. A way to disappear. He had obviously disappeared before.

'What do we have on the Carlyle case? Run me through it,' DCI Kapoor said once everyone was gathered in the briefing room.

Imogen sucked in a deep breath before starting. 'We have a lead on a possible new identity for Peter Carlyle. At the moment it's little more than a hunch, but it feels like it's enough to pursue.'

'What name do you think he's going by now?'

'Terry Harding. It's a name we've come across more than once now. Whoever the real Terry Harding was, he used to hang around with Wakefield and Crow in prison. I think, whoever Carlyle is really, he was in prison around the same time as the other three men. We're looking through the records for that time but obviously, with it being a remand prison, there's quite a lot of in and out, and we can't rule out the possibility he has changed his appearance significantly since he was inside.'

'I guess it's somewhere to start. What else?' the DCI said.

'Gregory Dunn, Marcus's grandfather, remembers selling a property in Dartmouth to a Terry Harding – he never met the man though, so it's possible it was Carlyle on the other end of the deal. We have the address and we're heading over there later on this morning. It may be where Peter has gone. We don't have a whole lot else,' Imogen said.

'Any of the tips from the tip line panning out?' DCI Kapoor turned to DC Jarvis and asked.

'No, lots of crazy theories and some genuinely unpleasant stuff. There was one lady who called in and said she saw the man in the house across the road from her pulling a child out of the boot of his car. We knocked on the door but it turned out she just hated the man who lived there and wanted us to harass him for her. She's filed a myriad complaints against him on all kinds of things,' Jarvis said.

'Brilliant. What about the property searches?' the DCI said.

'We've been through all the empty ones, nothing,' Jarvis said.

'Maybe they're not using an empty one,' Imogen said. 'Maybe it's one that's been rented out? Or maybe Carlyle faked a tenant to use the property for nefarious shit. I wouldn't put it past him.'

'Good thinking. Let's get every property they manage checked, and let's do it today. Knock on some doors, see if any alarm bells start ringing,' DCI Kapoor said.

'Can I ask how the Wakefield investigation is going?' Imogen said.

'We've narrowed down the time of death somewhat. Apparently, Wakefield had a huge fight with his neighbour at around half six on Bonfire Night for almost half an hour. Caused quite a ruckus in the street and there were multiple witnesses. So, we know he was killed after that,' Walsh said.

'What time did you enter the house that evening?' DCI Kapoor asked.

'Seven thirty,' Walsh said.

'That's good. That's nice and narrow. I don't suppose Adrian has given us an alibi for that time?' DCI Kapoor said.

Imogen was aware if she gave even the slightest clue that she knew anything at all the DCI would get the truth out of her. She didn't want to betray Adrian like that and so she had no choice but to lie to the DCI.

'Not one that I know.'

'Right. Let's keep pushing, Marcus is depending on us,' DCI Kapoor said.

As the room emptied, Imogen approached Webb who had been silent throughout the briefing. He looked exhausted; she wasn't even sure if he had gone home the night before.

'I've got a quick prison visit with Adrian but after that we can head straight off to Warfleet. Are you OK to sit in the car outside the prison?'

'Yes. I'm not going to freak out or anything, if that's what you're worried about.'

'No, I just don't want to put you in a difficult position.'

'I've already dealt with those demons. I don't have a problem with the prison. If I did I wouldn't have gone into this line of work. Anyway, I wasn't even inside that long, thanks to you.'

She wasn't sure if she was confusing Gabriel's gratitude for something else, but she felt guilty for ever having thought about him romantically – even for a second – back before she knew Adrian's awful secret. The only way she'd be able to stop that feeling was by clearing Adrian's name. She was going to find Carlyle and she would make him confess to everything he had done.

Chapter Sixty-Six

Imogen had been inside the prison as a visitor before this but it felt different now. Visiting Adrian inside was not something she'd ever thought would happen. The last time she'd come to see her now partner DC Webb. She had been working so hard at trying to get Adrian out that this was the first time she'd really thought about the reality of him being inside here. Walking through those gates had really driven it home. She was dreading seeing his face. What if he was hurt? What if he was angry with her for not getting him out already?

All she had been able to think about was what Adrian had told her. In her own mind there was nothing more damaging than rape. It was like killing someone without physically killing them, destroying something precious that could not be repaired. As a woman it was something she thought about often. Whenever she was walking home alone, in an underground car park, or a lift alone with a man she didn't know. Even for the briefest of moments it might pop into her mind that she wasn't safe, as though women were conditioned or resigned to the fact that it would probably happen one day. Another throwback to Irene's words of warning: 'Men only want what's between your legs.' And then of course there was the time she was sexually assaulted on the job when stationed in Plymouth, in front of Dean Kinkaid.

But this? What Adrian had been through, she couldn't

even imagine, it was the stuff of nightmares. She didn't even know much about what had happened, not having wanted to press him on the details, but she had seen with her own eyes the complete deconstruction of the man she loved. She had so many questions she wasn't sure anyone had the answers to, least of all Adrian. Worst of all, she couldn't fix it. It was unfixable. It was done.

She walked into the visitors' room after going through all the security checks and picked her table, looking round at all the wives and girlfriends, maybe one or two mothers. She could tell by their familiarity with the place, their complete ambivalence to their surroundings, that they had been here many times before. Did they all know each other? Were they friends? Did they meet up at the pub around the corner for drinks afterwards? Was this her life now – the partner of a con? The world was flipped on its head. She didn't recognise the life she was living.

A buzzer sounded and the doors opened. The men started to filter in, some excited to see loved ones, others looking more browbeaten and ashamed of their situation. Most likely first offenders as they lacked the hardness that came after the first stint inside. Imogen had witnessed it many times before in the job. Prison was just another aspect of some of these men's lives, completely accepted and sometimes even welcome. It offered a stability they couldn't keep a hold of on the outside.

She looked down at her hands. Being here was harder than she'd thought it would be. She twisted and pulled at the ring on her finger, another remnant from her mother and the only thing she had really kept of hers. It occurred to her that she wished she could go and see her mother, more than anyone, right now. She really wanted someone to talk to. She heard the scrape of the rubber foot on the chair opposite as it was pulled out. She had to keep reminding herself that her feelings in all of this were inconsequential. She was here for Adrian.

'Hello, Imogen,' Dean said.

She looked up.

It wasn't like she'd never expected to run into him again, but she certainly hadn't expected it here and now.

'What are you doing here? Where's Adrian?' Imogen said, looking towards the door, which was now closed.

'He wasn't feeling up to it. He seems pretty low, if I'm honest with you.'

'How are you here?'

'Do you really want to know?'

'I guess not. It's good to see you,' she said, not lying but not entirely sure how she was feeling about this. If anything, she was relieved not to have to speak to Adrian and she felt awful for that.

'So how come he's in here then? He won't say much about it. Just sleeps a lot,' Dean said as though they were talking about a shared pet.

'Are you sharing a cell?' Imogen said.

'I had him moved in with me last night after he almost got decked in the cafeteria. I'm pretty pally with a few of the guards. Adrian was just going to bail on you today and so I offered to take his place. Didn't want to leave you hanging. Getting visitors can be hard on some people, you know. Don't hold it against him.'

'I'm not going to lie, Dean, this feels really weird.'

'I know. I didn't do it to throw you, I promise. I want to help. If I can.'

'You know me and Adrian are together now?' she said nervously.

'I know, and I know he's not on the job anymore, and I know he's in for murder. Who did he kill?'

'I'm really not supposed to talk about this with you, of all people.'

'Come on. You know you can trust me,' he said, flashing the smile that launched a thousand ships. She was powerless against his charm. Nightmare.

'Do you know anyone called Shaun Wakefield? He's been inside once or twice. Adrian paid him a visit and he died rather brutally soon after. Unfortunately the crime scene was covered in Adrian's DNA and fingerprints.'

'Not familiar, no. Why is Adrian supposed to have killed this guy? I take it he didn't?'

'No, he didn't do it. That's what I'm trying to prove. We have a strong lead but still aren't there yet. We need to tie our lead suspect to Shaun Wakefield and prove he hired him then killed him to keep him quiet. It's complicated. The guy we are chasing is a chameleon, a ghost.'

'You'll get him out. Is there anything I can do?' Dean asked.

'Just keep him safe. He has a way about him, likes rubbing people up the wrong way. I don't want him to get hurt. He really does get into disagreements quicker than anyone I have ever known.'

'You're not going to tell me what this is about, are you?'

'I'm sorry, not my place to tell you. Ask Adrian, he might tell you something he won't tell me. I think he's afraid of upsetting me, trying to protect me maybe. See if you can get him to disclose his alibi to the boss, he won't listen to me.' Imogen wanted to tell Dean to pass on to Adrian that she loved him, but it felt inappropriate somehow.

'He's not very chatty, I must admit. I can see he's in a bad place,' Dean said, those green eyes of his boring right through her. 'You know, if he needs a lawyer, your father can help with that. You know he would want to help you.'

She was reminded of all those times she'd avoided visiting Dean in prison when he'd been inside before. She had thought today couldn't have been any weirder when she got up this morning. How wrong she was. Now, with this talk about her father, a father she had never had a relationship with, a father she had only known about for the last three years, whom she had only met a handful of times . . . This was all too much.

The way she felt about Dean would probably never change, as well as the knowledge that they could never be together. She felt bad for even entertaining those old uninvited feelings, but they came without warning. She would never do anything about it. She would never cheat on Adrian, and Dean came with a whole other subset of problems that she couldn't deal with. It was weird to think of Dean and Adrian in a cell together day and night, becoming friends. They knew each other but had always been separated by her. She was relieved though; the fact Dean was in there with Adrian made her relax a bit. Dean was more than capable of looking after himself, and she had no fear he would be able to make sure Adrian was safe too. And strangely she trusted Dean would make sure of that because he knew it was important to Imogen. She stood to leave.

'I had better get going.'

'It *was* good to see you,' he said softly.

She moved away before she even had a chance to respond. As if life wasn't complicated enough at the moment.

Chapter Sixty-Seven

Warfleet was beautiful, with a view of the inlet, little boats peppered across the surface of the deep turquoise water, the kind of place Imogen always imagined herself living eventually. The distant sound of gulls and the occasional whisper of laughter on the light breeze that gently tousled the leaves on the trees. They pulled into the driveway of a house on the hill, which looked down over the rooftops and through gaps in the trees to a breath-taking view of the inlet.

Imogen rang the doorbell, wondering if they should have waited for back-up. What if Carlyle himself answered the door? What if Marcus was there? Gabriel was standing beside her. She glanced down to see his fists clenched. He had his defences up. She had seen new DCs come in and go out just as quickly because they didn't have their wits about them, but so far Gabriel seemed to be adjusting to the position really well, showing initiative when he needed to, and more than once his open-mindedness had led to new information. There was nothing more dangerous than a police officer who had already made up their mind about what was happening in an investigation – things got missed, innocent people got hurt. She was hopeful things might work out for him. She rang the doorbell again when there was no answer.

The door was eventually opened by a heavily pregnant woman. She was young, attractive, quite petite and looked exhausted.

'Hello?' she said through pained breathlessness.

'Mrs Harding? I'm DS Grey and this is my partner, DC Webb,' Imogen said, pulling her warrant card out of her pocket and showing it to the woman.

'Oh. What's happened? Is Terry OK?' she said, worried.

'Is your husband not in?' Imogen said.

'No, he said he had some errands to run today, I've been trying to get hold of him but he isn't answering his phone,' she said, pushing her hands against the doorframe and burying her face in them. The muscles around the bump on her stomach were clearly hardening.

'Are you OK? Should we call a doctor?' Imogen said.

'Bloody Braxton Hicks again. I've had four false alarms this week. I'm not due for another fortnight.'

'Let's go inside. My colleague will make you a nice hot drink,' Imogen said, offering her hand to Mrs Harding, who took it immediately, digging her fingers in as they shuffled through to the lounge, where she grabbed hold of the back of the sofa instead. Gabriel disappeared into the kitchen and Imogen heard him clattering crockery as he attempted to make tea.

'Do you take sugar?' he called through.

'Two, please . . .' Mrs Harding responded, tailing off into a groan.

'Is there anything you need me to do to make you more comfortable, Mrs Harding?' Imogen asked.

'Miriam, please. Get this baby out of me. No one warns you what being heavily pregnant is going to be like. Swollen feet and sweaty creases.'

'Have you lived here long?'

'A few months,' she said, straightening up and blinking a few times before exhaling and then smiling. The pain had obviously subsided.

'It's a lovely location,' Imogen said.

'It is. So, why are you here? To see Terry, you said? Is something wrong?'

'This is going to sound strange, Mrs Harding, Miriam, but do you have a photograph of Terry that I could see? We had a report on someone matching his description and just want to check we aren't looking for the wrong person,' Imogen said.

'Our wedding photo is over there on the mantel. Everything else is still packed and in the garage. We've been meaning to sort it out but with the baby on the way it just didn't seem that important.'

'When was the last time you saw your husband?' Imogen said.

'This morning.'

Imogen walked across the room to the mantel. The photo was facing towards the back so she couldn't make out the face until she was up close. It was him.

It was Peter Carlyle.

'You both run a boating business?'

'Yes, well, Terry does now, he's just winding up his import/export business to take over the boating company full time. My father wants to retire.'

'How did you meet Terry?' Imogen said.

'I worked part time for my dad down at the boat rental shack. He came to ask about a boat and we hit it off straight away.'

Gabriel appeared from the kitchen as she spoke and placed a tea on the console table behind Miriam Harding. Imogen made the smallest nod with her head, indicating to him that they had found their man.

'Sorry, Mrs Harding. Can I use your toilet?' Gabriel said.

'There's one at the other end of the kitchen, just past the utility room, before the garage. So, Terry's the man you're looking for?' Miriam Harding said.

How could Imogen tell her the truth now?

'Your husband is wanted for questioning in a case we're working on. We have already spoken to him, but he was using a different name. We know him as Peter Carlyle. I'm sorry to have to be the one to tell you this, but he has another wife, in Exeter, she's currently in hospital after being stabbed. He also has a son who has been missing for over ten days now.'

'What are you talking about?' Miriam Harding said, her smile disappearing again as she bent forwards, gripping the sofa.

'Are you sure this is a false alarm?' Imogen said, rushing over to aid the woman, concerned, and really lacking any instincts for this kind of thing. Was she supposed to ask someone for hot towels?

'I didn't want to call an ambulance as they have sent me home twice already. I'm not ready for this. We haven't even built the cot yet,' she said, crumpling to the ground and getting into an all-fours position. Imogen noticed the floor was wet underneath her.

'DC Webb?' she called out.

'DS Grey?' Gabriel replied, rushing back into the lounge.

'Call an ambulance, please, I think Mrs Harding is going into labour.'

Chapter Sixty-Eight

ELEVEN DAYS MISSING

The leads were drying up as quickly as they found them. Their interview with Miriam had ended abruptly, and she was now in the care of the hospital staff, and they were no closer to tracking down their suspect. Carlyle had thought of everything. Imogen had read and reread every file, looked through every single tip they had received – and even they were drying up, none of them having amounted to anything. Everyone was just desperate for the thirty grand reward, not realising it was contingent on Marcus being found.

She marched over to Jarvis.

'How are you getting on with that property list?'

'I visited over half of them yesterday. Nothing suspicious as yet.'

'Any people of interest living in any of them?'

'No. Although a couple of them seem empty, like, unlived-in. Why would anyone pay rent on a place and not live in it?'

'See if you can get the keys off Dunn and check inside any properties like that.'

'Sorry I don't have any good news for you.'

'That's OK. This is the kind of stuff that takes the time, we can't help that. As long as we are meticulous then we can at least cross a few places off our lists.

Could you print me off a copy of those addresses and leave them on my desk? I'll cross-reference them later,' Imogen said, surprised at Jarvis' sensitivity. It seemed like he was actually trying to put the work in.

'I know you don't like me very much, Imogen – and I'm sorry if I've done anything to upset you. I do know what I'm doing though, I don't need you babysitting me, I can get through the list on my own. You need to start trusting me.'

'Clean slate as far as I'm concerned. Just pay attention and there is no problem. We need to find Marcus Carlyle, that's all we should be thinking about at the moment.'

'Is that really all you're thinking about?'

'Excuse me?'

'Well, it must be difficult, with Adrian inside. You must be quite distracted.'

'I don't know what you're implying, Jarvis, but I trust DI Walsh implicitly when it comes to uncovering what happened to Wakefield. My focus is on finding Marcus and the best way to do that is to find Carlyle.'

'If you say so.'

'You're a very difficult person to like,' she said, before leaving. It wasn't the first thing that popped into her mind but in the interest of diplomacy she opted for something a little less inflammatory. The dots of this all connected in some way, she just had to figure out how.

Chapter Sixty-Nine

Another day inside done. Adrian was coming to the end of his third day in prison and it was alarming how quickly he had acclimatised to it. Being told when to sleep, when to wake up, when to eat, when to be alone . . . It was alien and yet Adrian found it oddly comforting not to have to make those decisions for himself. He still wanted to be out, but he wasn't as terrified here as he thought he would be; he had Dean to thank for that. Still, with every passing moment Adrian felt like his cover was going to be blown and someone would stick a makeshift knife in him. Dean wasn't his babysitter, couldn't be with him every minute of every day, couldn't protect him from threats he didn't know about. Nonetheless, Adrian had never been more grateful for company.

'She looks good. Imogen,' Dean said as he leaned back in the one chair they had in their cell.

'I don't know if I'm comfortable talking about Imogen with you, Dean. No offence. I feel like she would be pissed off if we did.'

'Absolutely. I'm just glad she's OK. Glad she ended up with someone good, like you.'

'You see where we are, right? I'm in prison. I am literally your cellmate.'

'There are lots of good people in prison, detective.'

'Don't call me that,' Adrian said, still feeling undeserving of the title and concerned about who might overhear. He wasn't sure he even knew who he was anymore. It was only since leaving the police that he had realised how much his identity was tied up in being a police officer. It wasn't just a job for him, it was who he was. Without it, who was he now? He felt he had lost any definition. He looked over and saw Dean staring at him pensively.

'So, what happened to land you in here? What's the alibi you won't share? We know you didn't kill that man, so why accept the blame for it? Why accept this? Why not say where you were and get out? Are you covering for someone?'

'Just myself. My alibi is private.'

'Is it so private it's worth being in here?' Dean said leaning forward, scrutinising him.

'I think so.'

'I know I don't seem like the trustworthy type, but I've kept more secrets than you have had hot dinners. I'm not going to judge you. I'm not in a position to.'

'That I do believe,' Adrian said, smiling. He knew from a previous case he had worked on that Dean had suffered sexual abuse and worse as a child in the foster care system. Maybe he should trust him and say something. The urge to blurt it out was overwhelming, and in this setting, where he felt extra vulnerable, it was even harder to fight. He knew Imogen trusted this man and, as weird as it was, he trusted him, too. He didn't really have anyone else he could talk to about it, certainly not Imogen, not properly anyway. What was the worst thing that could happen? The inevitability of this discussion became apparent to Adrian. He should just say it now, get it over with. Then they could move on.

'How bad can it be?' Dean said.

'At the time of the murder I was at a meeting for male

survivors of sexual assault. During an investigation last summer I was abducted and raped.'

'And you don't want anyone to know that?' Dean said. His lack of reaction was comforting.

'I don't, no.'

'Why don't you want anyone to know?'

'Because I'm ashamed.'

'I've been there, and that takes a long time to go away. But even though you feel it, it's not on you. The shame doesn't belong to you, it belongs to the person who hurt you. Put it where it belongs.'

'You don't feel shame anymore?'

'Well now, I didn't say that.' Dean swigged from his coffee.

'What happened to the person who abused you?'

'I heard he passed away.' Dean smiled with a knowing glint in his eye. 'So, who is the guy they think you killed?'

'He was there that night, Wakefield, the guy I am supposed to have killed. He was driving the van while his friend assaulted me in the back. I was trying to find out who the other person was – the one who actually did it – and Wakefield was the only one who knew his identity.'

'Let me guess, he didn't tell you.'

'I had him pinned and I could have pushed him harder, but instead I bottled it and left. Someone else killed him, and now I'm back to square one,' Adrian said, allowing himself to feel defeated for a moment.

'I'm really sorry,' Dean said with a sigh. 'And Imogen knows all of this?'

'I told her after they found the body. I knew my prints were all over the scene and it would come back on me and I wanted her to hear the truth from me. Do you think I'm being stupid not saying anything?'

'No. Once it's out there you can't take it back. You

need to be ready when it is, or you don't stand a chance. You might never be ready, and that's OK too. I waited over twenty years before telling anyone what happened to me when I was in care. Some people never say a word. There is no one right way to deal with shit like this. The important thing to remember is that you are the victim. None of this is your fault, no matter how it went down. You can't turn someone into a rapist by your actions; they either are or they aren't.'

'I can see why Imogen likes you,' Adrian said. There was something reassuring about Dean. It felt like he had all the answers to all the questions, even the ones you didn't know to ask. There was also something very menacing about him, of course, and Adrian was glad he was on the right side of it.

'Imogen's going to get you out of here, you know,' Dean said.

'I know.'

'You just have to hold tight till she does,' Dean said, jumping up onto his bunk.

Adrian lay back on his bed, pulling his blanket into a ball and hugging it. It was hot in the cell, but he wanted the comfort of something in his arms. He couldn't explain it but, even though he was here in prison, he felt like he was on the right path, like he had made the right decision not to give his alibi. To give himself more time. But maybe that wasn't the right decision anymore. Maybe he did need to come clean to the DCI, if nothing else to make sure they weren't wasting police time and resources investigating him when they should be looking for someone else. Although he knew Imogen would make everything right and his secret would remain intact, maybe it wasn't fair to put her through this. She had already dealt with so much because of him.

The grip his secret had on him was loosening. Telling Dean hadn't been as hard as telling Imogen. Maybe it got easier each time, and he needed to take a chance and place his trust in other people. He had told four people now and the world hadn't ended. Being able to be real with someone for even a few minutes was a massive relief, better than the constant subterfuge of trying to appear 'normal'.

He would tell the DCI. He would help himself.

Chapter Seventy

TWELVE DAYS MISSING

Dean Kinkaid tapped on the glass of his cell gently when he saw the guard walking past. Johnson opened the door while rolling his eyes.

'What is it?' Johnson whispered.

'I need to go and have a chat with Danny Harris.'

'Now? It's five in the morning.'

'The early bird catches the worm.' Dean smiled. He knew Johnson wouldn't refuse him. The guard liked to play this game where he pretended he held the power, but they both knew the real dynamics of the relationship here. In another life, Dean imagined he might even be friends with Johnson. Even though he was easy to control he wasn't really a bad guy, and better than that he was trustworthy in his own way.

'How long are you going to be? I knock off at nine.'

'Well, I'm not going to take four sodding hours.'

'I've seen the way people come out after one of your chats. That takes more than five minutes. I really can't be arsed with the paperwork after, so promise me it's just a chat and I'll take you down there.'

'I swear. Just a friendly word or two.' Dean smiled his best reassuring smile, both knowing full well he was lying.

'Come on then.'

Dean looked back into the cell. Adrian was asleep.

316

What he didn't know couldn't hurt him. It felt good to have a purpose again. Being inside was fine for a while but it did get boring if you had nothing to occupy you. Dean usually had one or two side missions going on but he had put them to bed already. He was close to getting out. The truth was, he had been as happy to see Adrian as Adrian was to see him. For one, it meant he got to see Imogen again. He didn't think it would be so easy to see her in love with someone else, but it was, even though the strength of his feelings for her hadn't changed.

He had to wonder why he didn't feel jealousy like other people seemed to. He guessed he just thought if it was meant to be, it was meant to be. A very whimsical thought process for someone so rooted in pessimism and pragmatism. Maybe he'd always known Imogen was too good for him and so any time he had with her had been a bonus and he was grateful for it. Of everything he knew about life, the way he felt about her made the least sense to him; maybe that was part of it. All he knew was that his love for her was unconditional and did not depend on his possession of her. She loved Adrian and he respected that, so by looking after Adrian he was looking after Imogen.

Johnson unlocked Danny Harris's cell and let Dean inside.

'Don't be long, OK? I'll wait over there. If I hear any screaming then I'm coming in!' Johnson warned, although Dean knew it was an empty threat. He wouldn't come in. He never came in, no matter what he heard.

Dean stepped into Harris's cell. He was a single occupant, which was rare in this place, but judging by the smell someone had dodged a bullet. Harris's cell smelled of someone who spent far too much time masturbating.

'Wakey, wakey,' Dean said, lobbing a book from the window shelf onto Harris, hitting his shoulder and making him jump out of bed at an alarming speed. The bottom half of his body was naked but Dean kept his eyes trained on Harris's face.

'Kinkaid? What the fuck are you doing in here?'

'Well, this isn't a booty call so put some fucking pants on, man,' Dean said. Harris scrambled on the floor for a pair of trousers and pulled them on.

'I haven't got any weed, if that's what you're after. I ran out about a fortnight ago and can't get any more.'

'Just shut your hole and answer my questions. I don't want any bloody weed and, before you ask, I can't get you any either.'

'Can't or won't?'

'Let's just say both.'

'So what question could you possibly have for me?'

'What was the name of that cellmate you had in here last time, the scruffy one with the beard?'

'Shaun Wakefield.'

'You still friends?'

'We were never really friends, but yeah, I speak to him from time to time. He said he would hook me up with a job when I get out. He works for some kind of private firm that hires ex-cons and pays good wages for little jobs, the kind people who haven't been to prison might not want to do.'

'Well, I have bad news for you. He's dead.'

'What? Since when?' Harris said, more annoyed than upset, his job prospects suddenly looking a little bleaker.

'Did you spend much time with him on the outside?'

'A little. We weren't like best mates or anything, but he let me crash at his place sometimes. He was a good bloke. How did he die?'

'He was murdered,' Dean said, watching Harris's face for a reaction.

'Fuck,' Harris said, still annoyed. There was definitely no love lost there.

'Did you ever meet anyone else round at his place?'

'A couple of people, why? Why do you care about Shaun bloody Wakefield?'

'Do you remember any names?'

'Look, I don't want any trouble. I'm no grass.'

'I'm not asking you, mate. This is not optional. You need to tell me what you know.'

'Or what?'

Dean moved quickly and before Harris even had a chance to react he was pinned against the wall, Dean's hand clamped around his throat.

'It's pretty lonely in here, huh?' Dean said, his face less than an inch from Harris's.

'I'm straight. But I'll give you a blowjob if you want,' Harris sputtered nervously.

'Keep your knickers on, Harris, you're not my type.'

'Then I don't understand.'

Dean reached for Harris's right hand and pushed it into the wall.

'I'm guessing it's going to be difficult to knock one out if I break every one of your girlfriend's bones,' Dean said, sliding one hand over Danny Harris's mouth before swiftly twisting his thumb until it cracked with the other. Harris's eyes started to water, he struggled for breath as he began to cry, his nose swelling with snot. Dean grabbed another finger and Harris started to squeal under Dean's hand.

'OK. Fuck. I'll tell you. Stop doing that! Please,' he sobbed when Dean lifted his hand.

Dean let go and Harris relaxed. 'There. Isn't that easy?'

'Guard!' Harris shrieked. He took a deep breath to scream again but Dean swung at him, hitting him square on the jaw. He fell to the ground.

'Why did you have to go and make this unpleasant?' Dean grinned before bringing the full force of his heel down on Harris's hand. He grabbed the pillow from the bunk and covered the other man's face to muffle his screams before punching him hard in the left side, making sure he cracked a rib or two.

With his free hand, Harris grabbed hold of Dean's sleeve and tugged. He was ready to talk.

Chapter Seventy-One

Imogen was exhausted. She flopped in her chair, a strong urge to fold her hands on her desk and bury her face – maybe even catch a few minutes' sleep. She had been drinking coffee almost constantly since she woke that morning.

There was still no sign of Peter Carlyle – under any of his aliases – even though both of his wives were in hospital and being watched. He was a ghost.

What kind of a man could do the things he'd done? He had turfed an old lady out of her home, he had likely killed his first wife, attempted the murder of his second wife, and abandoned his pregnant third wife, and his son was missing, kidnapped, maybe even trafficked. God only knew how many other people Carlyle had left in his wake, how many other aliases he had. All he cared about was money.

She saw Walsh approaching and pulled her hair into a bun. Time to start working again.

'Do you have something?' she asked, hoping she didn't sound as tired as she felt.

'A picture of the real Julian Crow, taken a few days after he came out, not long before he returned home to his mother.'

Imogen looked at the picture. 'He must have taken his identity right after this. What's the date?'

'2008,' Walsh said.

'Lonely old woman, long-lost son comes back after a lengthy stint inside and promises to look after her. I wonder if deep down she knew it wasn't him. He worked her like he worked all those other women. Got her to sign over the house and then put her in a home, skipping off with the cash,' Imogen said.

'Have we had any luck finding out who else was in there with Crow, Harding and Wakefield at the same time?' Walsh said.

'That's going to take some time. There must have been thousands of people in and out over the course of their sentences. They spanned a four-year period.'

'We can exclude some by age and race before we dig out their photos. We know that much about him at least,' Walsh said.

'Got to be worth a shot. His real identity would definitely improve our chances of finding him, and hopefully Marcus.'

'Jarvis is on it.'

'We should go and speak to Lorelei Crow again.'

'We can't. She passed away,' Walsh said.

'How?' Imogen said, immediately suspicious.

'It looks like natural causes, but we have asked for an autopsy. There's no family to object so we should get the results soon enough.'

'This would be so much easier if we knew who the hell we were looking for,' Imogen said.

'He's covered his tracks impeccably well. Has just enough paperwork to be legit, but also enough to vanish without a trace. Gary went through and noticed he had been syphoning money out of the Hardings' business too.'

'What about the insurance pay-outs for Sara and Marcus?'

'That kid Jason showing up really screwed up his plans of a kidnapping gone wrong. It meant he had to think on his feet and I get the feeling his plans are not that adaptable. He must have decided it was better to lose that money than to get caught. There's an overlap in every case of identity theft – he sets one up just as he is about to let another one go. He may have three or four on the go at any one time. The man is a serious predator. We may never know the extent of the damage he has done. As far as we know, the other kidnapper still has Marcus Carlyle.'

'Maybe we need to look at how he chooses his victims?' Imogen said.

'Wealthy women with a limited family, by the looks of it. The question is where he's getting his information on his victims,' Walsh said.

'Shieldwall? We know he had them follow Sara for a while, and Gregory Dunn. Maybe he's used them before but with different aliases,' Imogen said.

'If that's the case then we're screwed. We can't just go on a fishing expedition at Shieldwall without a specific file to look for. We need to know the names,' Walsh said.

'Not even if it means a murderer is getting away?'

'He was with Sara for eight years and Miriam for two. He must have told some truths in that time, lies are easier to remember if they are close to the truth. Do you think they'll speak to us again?' Walsh asked.

'I'll go with Webb and see if Miriam Harding can remember anything more useful,' Imogen suggested.

'We're supposed to be training Jarvis and Webb equally,' Walsh said with a raised eyebrow, obviously noticing she was playing favourites.

'Then you take Jarvis and speak to Sara Carlyle. I'm sorry but he gets on my nerves.'

Chapter Seventy-Two

Jason stared out of the train window. He was a city boy and didn't like to travel much, never really having been very far out of the confines of Exeter. He had been to the coast a few times but he preferred being close to home. Luke had offered to take him out for the day as Jean's new friend Christopher was coming over to watch some *Columbo* with her. It had been his mum's favourite, apparently, and he didn't have much in the way of family and so Jean had invited him over for afternoon tea.

'This is our stop,' Luke said as the train pulled into Totnes Station.

'Where are we going?'

'Somewhere cool. Just stay close,' Luke said as he marched along, following a kind of map on his phone that someone had sent him.

It was a surprisingly warm day and Jason was over-dressed. He pulled his sweatshirt off and tied it around his waist as he struggled to keep up with Luke who was six inches taller with a much faster stride. His brother was moving with purpose as Jason dragged behind.

Leaving the station, they started to walk through a clearing and into a wooded area. Occasionally Luke would stop for a moment and adjust their trajectory before charging forwards. They made their way deeper into the woods and Jason wondered if Luke wasn't hiding something from him. Jason was getting hungry and tired of following his brother. He felt like a small child around Luke sometimes, more so than he had when Doug was around, but Luke had always been the substitute father Jason had never really had.

'Where are we? I'm knackered,' Jason moaned.

'Nearly there,' Luke said as they approached an abandoned Land Rover.

As they moved past the rusty car, they came upon another one, and then a massive amount of debris: corrugated roofing, rotten wood, fencing, unrecognisable plastics and fabrics. Up ahead, there was a building with a blue Land Rover parked out the front, though 'parked' was probably an overstretch of the word. The windows of the building had sheets of plywood resting against them, probably to protect against unwanted visitors.

'What is this place?'

'Doug brought me here once.'

'That's not an answer.'

'It's called Safari House. I don't know why. It's one of those semi-famous derelict places that those urban explorer types like to visit.'

'Who?'

'People who like derelict buildings.'

'And Dad brought you here? Why?'

'Looks a lot worse than I remember it. I reckon it's had a lot of visitors over the years. He brought me here because he wanted me to think he was cool. That was the only reason Doug ever did anything,' Luke said. Jason suspected Luke was more cut up about their father's death than he cared to admit. He had spent much more time with him, not like Jason, who had barely known the man.

'Why did you bring me here?'

'I reckon Dad left the money here. He always said this

was the perfect place to hide buried treasure. We're going to find it.'

'Are you serious?'

Luke didn't answer – he just charged forwards and pulled back one of the pieces of wood, sliding in through the gap it left. Jason followed him.

Inside, the house was so full it was hard to move, there were things everywhere. They moved through the rooms as carefully as they could, looking for places where Doug might have hidden the money. The sink was full of dishes still, even though the doors had fallen off the cupboards and the floor was damaged, and everything was covered in thick black dust and in some cases mould. Luke made his way into the kitchen and pulled the fridge open. Jason gagged at the smell, there was food in there – it seemed less than a few months old, but there was a solidified bottle of milk that had created a vacuum and looked ready to pop. He noticed the fridge was plugged in though, so the place couldn't be as derelict as it had first appeared.

'I'm not sure this place is abandoned,' Jason said.

'Well, we better hurry up then.'

'There's so much shit everywhere. Where do we even start?'

'Doug was a lazy shit, I doubt he did anything particularly ingenious with it.'

'How can you even be sure it's here?'

'I just know it. I know him. You check the kitchen cupboards. I'll check what used to be the lounge.'

Jason watched Luke disappear into the other room, heard the sound of furniture being moved and broken. He didn't want to touch anything in here, it looked toxic. The sun poured in through the tiny gaps in the plywood boards on the window and rays of thick dust clouds plumed every

327

time he moved. He covered his mouth as he coughed. There was only one cupboard with the door still on it and so he reached forward, terrified that some kind of rat king would be living in there. He remembered seeing a documentary on rat kings before and it had haunted him ever since. A nest of rats all connected by the tail to form one giant 'rat king'? No thanks. Jason held his breath and put his hand on the filthy brass cupboard handle.

'Jase! Come here. I've got it,' Luke called from the other room.

Jason backed away from the rat king cupboard, relieved he didn't have to open it.

In the other room there was a wood burner with a soiled cuddly toy on top of it. Luke had opened the cast-iron door and was pulling out stacks of money and laughing as he shoved it inside his backpack.

'We can't keep that money,' Jason said.

'Don't we deserve this?'

'Not really, no. Deserve it for what? What did *we* do to deserve it?'

'Come on, Jason, don't be such a killjoy.' Luke smiled at him.

'You know who you sound like right now? You sound like Dad, that's exactly what he would have said.'

Luke stopped laughing but carried on putting the money in his bag until he couldn't fit any more in, then he stuffed a few more stacks into his pockets before slinging his bag over his shoulder and standing up.

'You're not ruining this for us,' he said.

'We need to take it to the police. You think they won't notice us spending loads of money?'

'We can move away, go abroad, start a new life. This is a serious wodge of cash, Jason. Imagine the life we could give Mum,' Luke implored.

'Luke, it's not ours,' Jason said.

'Finders keepers.'

'A kid might die because Dad stole that money. I don't want any part of it.'

'Fuck's sake. Find your own fucking way home,' Luke said, storming off into the forest and leaving Jason behind to try to keep up. It was getting dark. He didn't want to get stuck here in the forest on his own. His brother had always been much quicker than Jason and so he struggled to keep up with him. He was well ahead of him now and Jason felt himself getting upset. What if he got lost here? He broke out into a run, drawing much closer to Luke, relieved when he could finally hear cars just beyond the treeline. He knew he would be able to get through to Luke. He just had to find the right words to convince him that turning the money over to the police was the right thing to do.

Chapter Seventy-Three

Miriam Harding was sitting up in bed when they arrived at the hospital and Imogen couldn't help but feel responsible for the forlorn look on her face. The baby was bundled up under a UV light next to her in a portable incubator.

Imogen handed over a box of chocolates she had bought in the gift shop, while Webb hung back.

'Congratulations. What did you have?'

'A little girl. Amy. She's a little jaundiced so they put her in this thing for twenty-four hours. After that we can go home,' she said, clearly exhausted and at the end of her rope, but with a smile.

'Have you heard from your husband?'

She shook her head. 'I've been trying to get my head round what you told me. Who is he? I don't see how he could have done the things you said. It doesn't make sense.'

'Was he ever absent for long periods of time?'

'He worked in import/export, so he had to travel a lot. I never questioned it really, he was always getting big bonuses and I assumed it was because of all the extra work he put in.'

'He took out life insurance on his other wife and son and tried to kill them both.'

'Not my Terry, he wouldn't do that. You must have the wrong guy,' Miriam said, but with an element of acceptance, as though she'd always known he was too good to be true. Imogen had been involved with con men before and almost without exception the people who fell prey to them often knew it was happening but still got conned. They would ignore their reservations and put it down to their own trust issues or something similar. Imogen could certainly relate to that.

Imogen pulled out her phone and showed Miriam the picture of Peter Carlyle with Sara and Marcus. There could be no denying the truth after that, then she scrolled to the wedding photo Lorelei Crow had shared with her. In each one Carlyle had that same smile, that same adoring look.

'I'm really sorry, Miriam.'

'That little boy is still missing? I saw it on the news. He did that? Is that what he had planned for us?'

'It's possible. We need to find him so that we can find his son, Marcus. We have to assume he has a contingency plan in place and maybe you know what that is.'

'I swear I don't. Why would I know?'

'Anything you can think of might give us a lead.'

'I'm sorry, there's nothing.'

'What are you going to do now? Are you going back to the house in Warfleet?' Imogen said.

'No, actually. I'm going to stay with my cousin in Norfolk. She's picking us up in the morning.'

'Good,' Imogen said.

'Are we in danger? Me and the baby?' Miriam asked.

'We don't think so. Carlyle seems to run a mile when the spotlight is on him. He works best under the radar. He must know by now that we've got to you, so you are no longer a viable asset to him, sorry to say. There is a police constable in the hallway just in case.'

DC Webb stepped forward. 'Mrs Harding, you told us you met when he asked you about a boat.'

'That's right.'

'What exactly was he asking you about?' Gabriel said.

'He wanted to buy a boat; we had a couple of our older ones for sale. He said he saw our advert online.'

'Did he buy a boat?'

'No, we didn't have what he was looking for,' Miriam said, but Imogen could see her mind working, trying to think back to something specific.

'What is it, Miriam?' Imogen said.

'I put him in touch with the company we buy our boats from. He might have bought one from there. He certainly never mentioned it to me again, which, given how keen he was on our first encounter, now seems a little odd. I remember him talking about spending a lot of time on his father's boat as a child. I don't think he was lying about that.'

'What's the name of that company you gave him the details for?' Gabriel said.

'The Big Blue. It's a company that operates out of Salcombe, further south.'

'Thank you. Are you going to be OK?' Gabriel asked Miriam.

'I don't know in all honesty. I haven't had time to really digest what's happening. The most important thing is that this little one is looked after. It's not her fault what's happening, is it? With what you've told me about the other things he's done, I consider myself quite lucky. Please get to him before he has a chance to hurt anyone else.'

'We will do our best,' Imogen said, meaning it wholeheartedly. She couldn't let this bastard get away with what he was doing.

* * *

Imogen was glad they'd reached Miriam Harding before Carlyle had hurt her or the baby. Now, they had to hope they got to him before he had time to get rid of Marcus. He must be getting desperate.

'We need to get a photo of Peter Carlyle over to The Big Blue, it's going to take an age to drive there and we just don't have the luxury of time at the moment. With every second he could be getting away and, if he goes, so does any chance of finding Marcus or getting Adrian out of prison,' Imogen said, for her own benefit as much as for Webb's.

She had to find this bastard and get her boyfriend back.

Chapter Seventy-Four

Walking through to the visitors' room in the prison was strange; Adrian felt like he was being herded. They had to stop at every door, and the guard would check they were all present and correct before the door was opened and they were allowed through, until they reached the next door and the process repeated again. With every new experience Adrian had inside, the more determined he was to survive through this, to get out. He knew he had the power, he just had to get in touch with the DCI when he was ready, he was almost there. A few more sideways glances from Ryman and he would definitely want out.

This was Adrian's first time in the visitors' room on this side of the table. Mick Roper smiled and tapped on the table nervously. A couple of the other prisoners gave Mick a little wave and a nod hello, which made Adrian feel a little less shitty. Mick obviously didn't have any qualms about being friends with cons.

'You didn't have to come.'

'I should thank you. They gave me the morning off to come say hi.'

'Why is that?'

'Well, they asked if you could get some information, actually. As far as they're concerned, you're still on the payroll, even in here.'

'What kind of information?' Adrian said, surprised to

hear that this hadn't gone against him. Maybe even a little concerned.

'Just who hangs out with a fella called James Redmond. That's all.'

'For what reason?'

'No idea. Just need to know any names of anyone he talks to. That would be grand.'

'I can do that.'

'Brilliant. How you holding up?'

'Good. Better than I thought,' Adrian said, and he wasn't lying. He hadn't thought he would make it this far, especially not after the cafeteria debacle on the first day. But here he was, growing strangely used to the atmosphere, not feeling as out of place as he probably should.

'If there's anything you need just let me know.'

'Thanks. I'm fine,' Adrian said, not sure exactly what he might need from Mick.

Mick told him of the boring surveillance tasks he had been doing on his own since Adrian had been inside. The fact that Adrian was inside didn't seem to matter at all to Mick, who was talking to him as though he were returning from a week's holiday. They weren't really friends anymore, that was something Adrian noticed more than anything. Mick had changed and the man Adrian had served with all those years ago no longer existed. He didn't fully trust Mick and he wasn't sure why.

'If you don't mind, I'm going to shoot off. Got just enough time to pop home and see my Nancy. She worked the night shift last night so I haven't actually seen her for about three days. Wouldn't mind spending a little quality time with her, if you know what I mean.'

'It was good to see you.'

'Later.'

Mick stood and left the room, and Adrian looked around for a guard to take him back to his cell. Ryman caught his eye and gave him a little wink before beckoning him over. Adrian could see he was getting off on the fact that he had power over Adrian, that he had information that could hurt him. If he told the other inmates Adrian was ex-police then he really would be up shit creek.

Adrian walked back to the cell with Ryman walking far too close behind him.

'I've got a little job for you,' Ryman whispered in his ear.

'What do you mean? What kind of job?'

'I'm going to slip something into your hand when we get back to your cell, and when next association comes round I need you to find an opportunity to take it into the cell opposite you, and hide it under the mattress on the top bunk.'

'Why would I do that?'

'Because I'm telling you to.'

They got back to the cell and Ryman checked it was empty before following Adrian inside. Out of his pocket he pulled a thin sheet of jagged metal with electrical tape wrapped around one end of it, a makeshift knife with a handle to grip. It was obviously made to look like it had been put together by one of the prisoners, except it hadn't. What was Ryman's game? Adrian knew if he did what he was told then there was a strong chance someone was going to get killed.

'I'm not touching that.'

'Don't make me ask you twice.'

'You can ask me fifty times if you want, mate. I'm not doing it. I'm not scared of you. Tell whoever you want about me,' Adrian said, staring Ryman straight in the eye. He could see Ryman wasn't used to being told no when he asked for things, but if there was one thing Adrian knew how to do it was front up to bullies. Most of the time, anyway. The thing most bullies had in common was their fragile egos. Well-rounded people didn't need to pull crap like this. He was calling his bluff, he just hoped it wouldn't backfire on him.

'You're making a huge mistake,' Ryman said with a smile.

'Do your worst,' Adrian said.

With that, Ryman launched himself face first into the wall, bouncing back and clutching at his face. Blood poured from his nose and his eyebrow had split. It took a few seconds before Adrian realised what he was doing.

Ryman smiled, reading his thoughts. 'Who is going to believe I did this to myself? You think it's tough on the wing? You're going to find out what it's like on your own for a few weeks. I can get to you anytime I want, remember that. A stint in seg will give you a chance to think about how you want the rest of your time in here to go.'

'That looks nasty,' Dean said, leaning comfortably against the doorframe as if leaning against a wall in a pub.

'Your new cellmate's got quite the temper,' Ryman said.

'Miles? He's a puppy dog. Are you trying to pull a fast one, Ryman? What's that in your hand?' Dean said, reaching down and taking the shard of metal from Ryman, who let it go with no resistance.

'Just stay out of this, Kinkaid. You don't understand the situation,' Ryman hissed, his tone softening as soon as Dean looked at him.

'So explain it to me,' Dean said, examining the make-shift knife in an exaggerated manner. Adrian wondered if he might be developing some kind of hero worship complex for Dean. He was like one of those effortlessly cool kids you went to school with who smoked pot in front of the teachers as they desperately sought his validation.

'He was threatening me because I know something about him. I said you deserved to know the truth but he told me to be quiet and then he nutted me.'

'That sounds pretty serious.' Dean smiled. 'What's the big secret?'

'He's police. Well, he was. He's probably in here undercover,' Ryman said with a triumphant smirk.

'Oh, that? I knew that.'

'You knew?' Ryman said, confused.

'I did. You see, me and Miles here are old friends. Good friends. We go back. Whatever power you think you have over my friend here, you don't. You're going to leave here now and forget what you know. If you tell anyone then I will reunite you with your shiny little friend here,' Dean said, holding up the 'knife'.

'You're friends?'

'You should probably piss off now,' Adrian said, feeling the need to have the last word.

Ryman looked confused and staggered out of the cell. Adrian didn't know how he was going to explain that injury to anyone.

One thing Adrian did know was he had been scared before Dean walked in, and he couldn't rely on Dean to be there every time he needed him, especially as he had already told Adrian he was coming to the end of his sentence.

Maybe it was time to rethink his plan. Prison was hard, an eye-opener. Certainly not the way he'd imagined it, not the way it got reported. You kind of expected all the external bullshit but what Adrian hadn't been prepared for was the way it messed with your head, the feeling that he deserved this, the feeling of worthlessness, that he would never be anything other than this. Thrown away, forgotten, forsaken. He needed to get out before it completely eroded any sense of self he had left.

Telling the DCI what had happened didn't seem as bad as some of the alternatives anymore, and that was a new feeling for him. He now saw the conversation with Mira Kapoor as inevitable. He would ask for her to come visit him. He would explain everything. He would get out of here.

Chapter Seventy-Five

Imogen and Webb were in the car park outside the hospital waiting for The Big Blue to get back to them. No point driving anywhere until they knew where they were going. The Big Blue had confirmed they knew Carlyle as a man called Clive Godwyn and that he had purchased a boat from them, and were trying to ascertain the location of the boat by ringing around local boatyards. The proprietor had been more than helpful and had offered to ring the owners' personal lines.

The phone rang.

'We think we've found it for you. He took it to be repainted at Fallow Creek Boatyard, it's just north of Dartmouth. I'll email you the address.'

'Thank you so much for all your help.'

'The boat he bought was called *Lady Luck*, but he's probably had it changed now. They predominantly do renovations at Fallow Creek but you're looking for a fifty-foot blue water cruiser, six-berth.'

'We should put you on the payroll. That was quick.'

'Happy to help.'

'Can you tell me if he ever had a child with him?' Imogen asked. 'A small boy.'

'I don't recall seeing a child with him, but once their boats are moored here there's no reason for our buyers to interact with us any further.'

'Thank you.'

Imogen started the engine and put her foot down.

She was beginning to lose hope that they would ever catch up to Carlyle, or whatever his name was now, and there had been no new leads on Marcus since they discovered his clothing. She couldn't admit to herself that hope of ever finding him was almost gone.

She didn't speak as she drove and Webb had the good manners not to interrupt her thoughts, the same thoughts that had been going through her mind over and over for days. How was Carlyle doing this? How was he getting away with it? How many people had he defrauded or killed so far? They might never find him. He had been smart enough to be several steps ahead of them before they even knew they were looking for him. It was like chasing someone through a building and turning a corner just in time to see them disappear round the corner in front of you. Never getting close enough, never catching up. She was terrified that he was too smart for her. What if he'd covered his tracks so well that there was no way for her to get Adrian out? She felt sick just thinking about it. She drove faster, harder.

'It's the next right,' Webb said finally as they drew nearer.

She had barely stopped the car before she got out and rushed towards the reception for the boatyard. There was no one there, but there was a bell that she pressed relentlessly until she saw an exasperated man rushing towards the reception cabin while wiping his hands clean.

'Yes, I heard you,' he snapped as he stepped inside the cabin from the other side and sat behind the glass screen, turning on his computer.

'I'm DS Imogen Grey. I'm looking for a boat.' She held up her warrant card, breathless, impatient.

'We have quite a few of those,' he said sarcastically.

'A blue water cruiser, used to be called *Lady Luck*.'

'Right. I know the one. She's called *Invicta* now.'

'You still have her?' Imogen said, relieved she didn't have to wrestle information out of this man. She was exhausted.

'She's moored upriver a bit, only a couple of minutes' walk down the walkway there.'

'Are boats always female?' DC Webb said.

'They are to me,' the man said with a smile. 'What's he done then? I thought he was shady; people don't pay in cash unless they're dodge.'

'Can we take a look at the boat?' Imogen said, unwilling to spend time on small talk.

'Actually, legally, as he hasn't paid this month's moorings fee, the boat reverts to our custodianship so I can let you on it, if you want. She's white with red and black detailing,' he said, rifling around in his drawer, then pushing some keys under the glass screen.

'Thank you,' Imogen said, snatching the keys and rushing out of the Portakabin. She didn't even realise she was running until she heard the heavy thump of Gabriel Webb's shoes on the wooden walkway behind her.

'Shouldn't you put gloves on?' Webb said as he clambered over the metal railing onto the boat behind her. She'd thought his height would have made things like this easy for him but she could see he was a little clumsy. She pulled a pair of gloves out of her pocket before unlocking the cabin door and walking down the steps.

Inside was all wooden with burgundy soft furnishings. It looked brand new, like a home. Moving from house to house without a permanent base of your own must get pretty tiring, even for a psychopath. Had Carlyle been planning on using this? No one currently lived here but she could see signs Carlyle had been here recently at least.

'Marcus! Call out if you're here. It's the police!' Imogen said, even though there was no sign a child had ever been here.

'Even if we do find anything how do we prove a connection?' he asked.

'I don't know, but something is better than nothing,' Imogen replied.

She opened every drawer, every cupboard, lifted every cushion. Gabriel went through to the inner cabins and did the same.

There was a watch in one of the kitchen cabinets. She had noticed Carlyle wearing it at the house; it had a distinctive emerald green face. On closer inspection it was a TAG Heuer Carrera, not a cheap watch and certainly not common. On the back of the face was an inscription '*Love from Sara*'.

Gabriel lifted one of the mattresses and saw a hinge, so he pulled the mattress to the side and stood it up against the side of the cabin, blocking off the light.

'Here!' he called out. He was scared of opening the hinged door on his own. It was the size of a double bed and so there was plenty of room for someone to be hiding in there. Imogen pulled her asp out of its holder and extended it full size, ready to swing in case there was someone inside.

Just boxes.

In the compartment under the mattress were lidded cardboard boxes, like the kind they used to store evidence in. Imogen pulled one out and looked through the paper-work inside. It was a comprehensive file on the Dunns – their net worth, the company, their holdings, right down to the colour of their bathroom tiles. Carlyle had done his homework on them before moving in.

Another box they found was information on Julian Crow – pictures of the actual Julian Crow, reams and reams of notes on his mother. It was clear Carlyle had spent time interrogating Crow and getting every last detail about his life so he could impersonate him after he was out of prison.

There were three more boxes. One on Miriam Walker, now Harding, and her family, one on Clive Godwyn – God only knew what had happened to the real Clive Godwyn – and the final box was on Shaun Wakefield. There wasn't as much information in that one but there were details of how Wakefield and Carlyle should contact one another, a shopping list of the foods Marcus liked, instructions on how to get Sara to comply with the kidnap demands. It was enough to connect Carlyle to Wakefield and the kidnapping and to prove Carlyle had a motive to permanently silence Wakefield.

Imogen couldn't help noticing that while this information was very helpful, it wasn't anything new. Not really. Why would Carlyle leave all of this here if he was planning on disappearing completely again? Had he figured out what they knew? He had given them just enough to close the case, just enough to – hopefully – exonerate Adrian. It was as though he was tying up loose ends. Did he somehow know that Imogen was driven by trying to free Adrian, and thought removing that motivation for her would give him more of a chance to get away?

She guessed Carlyle had never meant to implicate anyone else, didn't know about the other things Wakefield got up to. From what they'd discovered, Wakefield was a thug for hire, usually in a driving capacity. There was no mention of the other kidnapper in the files as far as she could see. Carlyle didn't have Marcus, she was sure of that now; if he had, he would have taken care of him and disappeared. That's what he was waiting for, why he hadn't left for good. There was still one more loose end for him to tie up.

There was a loud clunk as the exterior door slammed closed and the turn of a key in the lock. Imogen rushed out of the bedroom. As she ran through the central cabin she slipped; the floor was wet, there was water pouring in. She ran up the steps to get outside but the cabin door wouldn't budge and when Imogen spun around she noticed the gas on the stove was turned on and the knob broken off. He was going to kill them.

'Webb! We need to get off this boat!' she said as she started kicking the door. If the gas itself didn't kill them clearly the water filling the cabin was Carlyle's back-up plan. Although she wasn't sure how deep the water would need to be for the boat to start sinking, she wasn't willing to take the chance to find out.

Webb rushed over and began to kick with her. It was getting more difficult to breathe as the smell of gas filled the small unventilated area. Imogen started to cough. Gabriel pulled his shirt off and ripped it in two, tying one side around Imogen's face and the other around his own as a makeshift mask. It filtered out some of the smell but it wasn't going to give them much longer. The physical exertion was causing them both to inhale more air and Imogen was flagging. Gabriel continued to kick until finally the lock shifted. With a final laborious kick the catch released and the door swung open.

'I'm going back to get the file,' she shouted, her eyes burning from the gas.

'We've got to get out,' Gabriel said

'I have to get the Wakefield one at least,' she said.

Without waiting for her to say anything else he went back down into the cabin.

Imogen was nauseous and her vision was blurring. She felt sluggish and weak as she watched Gabriel trudge through the rising water.

'Got it!' she heard Gabriel call, then she felt his hand on her back, pushing her out of the cabin at what felt like a snail's pace, but it was the fastest she could go.

'You should have got out when I told you to,' she managed, grabbing the box from him.

'Not without you. We got the file,' Gabriel wheezed.

He followed behind her. Imogen threw the box onto the walkway and then jumped off the listing boat, collapsing on the wooden deck. She ripped the makeshift mask from her face and greedily gulped at the air.

'We need those other files on that boat,' she said, coughing.

'It's too risky to go back onboard with the gas still leaking and the boat leaning like that. I'll call it in.'

Imogen reached across to the box Gabriel had pulled from the boat and put her fingers on it. She sat up and looked around, eyes still stinging and her vision blurred.

'He must be here.' She scrambled to her feet, less steady than was ideal. 'Webb, you guard that box with your life.'

She started running. Carlyle couldn't have got far. She ignored the burning pain in her chest and pushed herself forward until she reached the car park and saw a black Mondeo pulling out. The man in the driver seat turned to her and saluted. It was Carlyle. As he accelerated, so did she. She was fast but she couldn't catch a car. There were no number plates but maybe there was something else about the car that was significant. She pulled out her phone and flicked to the camera. She quickly snapped a few running shots before doubling over and accepting defeat. She walked back down the hill to the car park just as a shirtless Webb emerged from the riverside carrying the box. She tried not to look at his tattoos.

'If you want to take this back to the station and log it I can wait here for the techs to come and do the boat stuff,' Webb said.

'Yes, please. Thanks for saving my life and all that. There are some T-shirts in the boot. One of them might fit you,' Imogen said, glad she kept spare clothes in the car for emergencies like this. Today it was a boating accident, tomorrow it might be a child vomiting on you. You never knew what the job was going to throw at you.

'Still no sign of Marcus.'

'I don't think he's got him,' Imogen said.

'What did you make of that boat?' Webb said as he placed the box in the boot and rifled through the bag of T-shirts.

'I think it was a trap. A lure. He seemed to be ready for us to find it and there was nothing in there that we hadn't suspected or confirmed already. There is no way those are his only aliases,' Imogen said.

'Do you think someone tipped him off?' Webb pulled a lilac retro Adidas T-shirt from the bag and pulled it on. It was too small for him and Imogen suppressed a smile. He seemed completely unfazed and she remembered that when they first met he had been wearing a leather corset. She guessed showing a bit of belly button was no big deal for him.

'It's possible. My money would be on his wife,' Imogen said.

'Which one?'

'Miriam. She seemed to be a bit too pragmatic about the whole thing.'

'Well, let's hope that doesn't bite her on the arse,' Webb said, shutting the boot.

'Sit tight. I'll go and log this. See you back at the station.'

She got in the car and headed back to the station. She really wanted to call Adrian and tell him the good news, but she guessed she had better wait and see what the DCI said about what they'd found.

She called Walsh instead. 'We found a boat with a load of paperwork Carlyle had put together on the various people whose identities he has stolen. There was a file that connects him to Wakefield. It might be enough to make him a viable suspect.'

'Brilliant. Give it to Gary. If there is a connection there, he'll find it.'

'Is the DCI around? I wanted to speak to her about Adrian.'

'Actually she's at the prison. Adrian requested she meet with him.'

'Did she say why?'

'Sorry, no.'

'Thanks, Walsh, I'll be back soon.'

Could she dare to hope that Adrian was telling the DCI what had happened and therefore his alibi?

Chapter Seventy-Six

'I was told you wanted to see me?' DCI Kapoor's face was rigid with indifference as she sat across from him in the empty visitors' room. She looked like she was very much 'sick of his shit'.

'I have some things to explain to you.'

'That's the understatement of the year.' She half-smiled.

'This is all connected.'

'Connected to what? Imogen showed me the results from the crime scene before. She says you didn't kill that man and she's going to prove it. Sad to say I trust her more than I trust you these days.'

'That's fair. Hopefully what I tell you will help make some sense of my actions over the past year.' He had never realised before how much he valued DCI Kapoor's approval.

'I agreed to meet you to hear your alibi. I don't know why you just couldn't tell me before we had to go through the whole rigmarole of arresting and charging you.'

'I guess I just need to rip the plaster off and say it.' He smiled half-heartedly, but she didn't seem amused.

'Please. I think we've wasted enough of each other's time on this. Be direct, we don't have a huge amount of time. You're in prison not a day spa.'

'Shaun Wakefield was connected to an investigation I was doing on my own. Nothing to do with your case. I went to visit him because I had a list of possible suspects

349

and he was on it. He wasn't the person I was looking for, but he knows them, whoever they are. I was trying to find out the name of his associate and I sought to pressure him into giving it to me.'

'Possible suspects for what? What do you mean, an investigation you were doing on your own? Is it for the company you work for now? Shieldwall?'

He leaned forward and lowered his voice. He could feel his tongue drying as he went to speak again, knowing he was getting closer to the truth. 'No. This was personal.'

'How personal?'

His mouth felt like cotton and he desperately wished he wasn't in this situation, but he was a grown-up. It was what it was. He needed to tell the truth. This secret was a festering malignance inside him.

'Last year, when I was working on the Corrigan case. On the night of the twentieth of August I was walking home from the pub, I was ambushed on the street and dragged into the back of Shaun Wakefield's van. The one they found in his garden, the one you took in for evidence. I found a link to Wakefield so I went to his house the other day to find out if he was one of the people who attacked me – he was – and I needed to find out who was with him. He wouldn't tell me, but when I left he was alive. I swear, I did not kill him.'

'He was very badly beaten. If you had anything to do with that . . .'

'I'll admit that some of that was me, I hit him maybe once or twice, but nothing that caused any significant damage. I saw the photo of his face, and I swear I didn't do that. I don't have that level of violence in me. He wasn't telling me what I needed to know and so I left before I went too far. I thought about it – I'd be lying if I say I didn't – but I walked away, I promise.'

'You have put me in such a difficult position. Your DNA at the crime scene means we had no choice but to follow the evidence. If you had just told Walsh this at the time of your interrogation I could have maybe helped you in some way. None of this explains why you opted for prison though. Why can't you just give me your alibi?'

Here it comes. He steeled himself, ready to say those words again.

Imogen was working hard to get him out, he should work just as hard to do the same.

'That's not everything. And at this point in time I would appreciate your discretion. I don't want anyone else to know what I am about to tell you.' Adrian cleared his throat; he could feel the vibration in his voice as he fought to keep his emotions in check. 'The man I am looking for, the other man from that night in August last year, he, um . . . he raped me. They drove me around for five hours, during which I was sexually assaulted multiple times, and then dumped me outside my house.

'I just needed to know his name. My alibi for the night of Wakefield's murder was that I attended a group for survivors of sexual assault – well, I sort of did. But I was nowhere near his house when Wakefield died and there is at least one witness who can attest to that.'

He felt DCI Kapoor's hand resting on his. Her hardened boss face had gone and she looked shaken.

'Is this why you no longer work for me? Did you leave the police because of the rape? You know we have confidential reporting procedures in place for incidents of this nature.'

'Yes. I couldn't face it. What we do as police takes the sort of courage I no longer have. I just needed time and space to get my head right. I only disclosed this information to Imogen just before I was charged,' he said, wiping his eyes, which he'd only just noticed were wet.

'Still, you have the right to counselling, have you seen anyone?'

'No. I didn't want to talk about it. Still don't. I went to that group after seeing Wakefield to try and talk about it, but I couldn't, and I left early. The group started at seven, and I was there from a quarter to to a quarter past. The coordinator saw me there, we chatted a little beforehand. He will be able to confirm this if I give him permission to talk to you. Telling you, telling anyone my alibi felt completely impossible.'

'I know this probably sounds a bit hollow even though it's not meant to be,' Kapoor began. 'A lot of people go through this, more than anyone really knows. Don't be afraid to ask for help. You shouldn't go through it alone. I take it as a personal failure that you did not feel secure enough to disclose the events of that evening to me personally. I strive to make our workplace inclusive and supportive. I am so sorry if we let you down. If there is anything I can do now then all you need to do is ask. You have a lot more friends than you know, Adrian. Many people were sad to see you leave. People can be more understanding than you think.'

'I'm not ready to go public with this – I just want to forget it ever happened – but with each passing day I realise that's a pretty unrealistic goal,' he said, using his sleeve this time to wipe his face. He felt embarrassed to be crying in front of DCI Kapoor.

'I'm here for you. I'll go and see the group coordinator myself and see what I can do to get you out of here.'

'Thank you, ma'am, but I am only telling you so that you know the truth. I would rather not make an official statement. I just wasn't comfortable with keeping this from you. I didn't like you thinking badly of me.'

'I completely understand. We have a long way to go on the stigma of rape – it's always two steps forwards and three steps back – but please consider how many people will be by your side should you want to come forward.'

'Maybe when I know who did it, I may feel more inclined to give a statement, but for now I don't see the point.'

'Adrian, now I know your reason for leaving I would like to extend an open invitation for you to come back. As long as I am DCI, there will be a place for you.' She gently squeezed his fingers.

Adrian felt the lump in his throat harden again. He hadn't expected this kindness – he wasn't sure what he had expected, but it wasn't this. Maybe he had underestimated the people around him. He wiped his nose with the back of his hand. Another weight lifted. So far, telling people hadn't been the complete nightmare he had been expecting. In fact, with every person he told he felt a little lighter.

Chapter Seventy-Seven

THIRTEEN DAYS MISSING

Copies of the files from the boxes they had retrieved from the boat sat at the table at the front of the briefing room. The boxes were darker from the centre line right down to the frayed corners at the bottom where the water had begun to infiltrate the cardboard. Gary had looked through them at breakneck speed, starting with the Wakefield files, desperate to find any clues to Marcus's whereabouts while trying to cobble together evidence to exonerate Adrian. Webb had already copied out any information that suggested Adrian wasn't the last person at the Wakefield murder scene, but without his alibi it would be difficult to prove.

In addition to what they'd seen while looking through the files on the boat, they'd found printed-out emails as well as a SIM card from which Gary had recovered text messages between Shaun Wakefield and Peter Carlyle detailing the Carlyles' home schedule, Marcus's allergies, the foods he liked. Lots of photos of Marcus and of Sara, instructions of when and how to dispose of them, including the instruction to keep Marcus alive until after the hand-off in case they were asked to provide proof of life again. Imogen got chills reading through Carlyle's communications – he barely seemed human, talking that way about another human being, let alone his own child.

Gary was still going through the rest of the files while Imogen waited to update the DCI and Walsh on her findings. Imogen hadn't seen the DCI since she'd got back from visiting Adrian yesterday and she still had no idea what they had talked about.

'Gary seems pretty determined to go through everything today, if that's even possible,' Webb said.

'He'll be there until next Christmas with all that info. There is an absolute mountain of stuff and some of it got wet so it will need to be dried and separated,' Imogen said.

'What did you get from the boat?' DCI Kapoor said as she walked into the room followed by Walsh.

'A lot is the short version. No leads on Marcus as yet. We did find evidence of surveillance on the Carlyle house as well as instructions on the schedules of all the occupants. These were sent via text on a pay-as-you-go phone but the SIM card was on the boat. We also found some blackmail texts. After the kidnapping went wrong and the money went missing it seems Wakefield and his associate didn't get the money they were promised. Wakefield's partner was threatening to sell the child on if Carlyle didn't get them more money. There was a definite familiarity there. There are a few texts that didn't make that much sense but Gary is working through them, too. We also have Wakefield's phone, which supports the theory that Carlyle killed him, as it was missing from the crime scene despite evidence it was used very close to his time of death. There were traces of blood on it, which are being tested now,' Imogen said hurriedly, desperate to get Adrian out as soon as humanly possible.

'Why would Carlyle leave all of that information on the boat? And who was Wakefield contacting just before he died?' Walsh asked.

'There was a text to Carlyle's phone saying Adrian Miles had been to visit him and if Carlyle didn't pay up then Wakefield was going to get back in touch with Miles and tell him everything. It seems even though Wakefield knew Miles was no longer police he didn't pass that information on to Carlyle. There was another text message to another phone – we're looking into the number – saying Wakefield had spoken to Carlyle and he was going to get in touch. From what we can ascertain from other text messages to this number, this was the accomplice in the kidnapping, the other man in the van. The tech team are trying to find any deleted texts on Wakefield's phone to see if there are any clues as to where they have taken Marcus,' Imogen said.

'Forensics have said the hose to the head – the toilet – was severed, which was why the boat flooded. The valves were left open, too. It wouldn't have gone under, the water was too shallow, but it certainly made things more difficult,' Webb said.

'Does this exonerate Adrian Miles?' DCI Kapoor asked.

'Gary checked the phones' locations at the time of death and the number for Carlyle's phone shows as being in or around Wakefield's house. Miles's phone shows him to be elsewhere. As for why Carlyle would leave the information there on the boat, my guess is that it's a way to power us down, make us a little less invested in looking for him, or too bogged down in evidence. Maybe he hoped to trap us in there and kill us. He is really clever, and so far has always been ahead of the game. There is evidence Carlyle knew Miles was ex-police after he was arrested. I'm guessing not much gets past him,' Imogen said.

'Why does it matter if he knew Adrian was police or not?'

'It matters because it meant we would keep chasing until we got Adrian out. Knowing he was one of ours must have put a different spin on it for Carlyle. He doesn't care about Adrian but he does want the heat off him. He needed to take away our motivation to find him. I think if he had Marcus he would have given him up by now just to get away. He's desperate,' Imogen said.

'He left us information we already knew, or would know soon enough, and all of the aliases he had used that were already burned. We think he was done with them and so he was throwing us a bone and trying to slow us down with information overload,' Webb said.

'And you had no indication he was capable of any of this when you met him?' Kapoor asked.

'I thought he was off from the start, to be honest. Lying, even. I suspected he might be trying to hide an affair or something, obviously I just wasn't thinking big enough,' Imogen said.

'How long has he been getting away with this?'

'At least twelve years as that's when Julian Crow got out of prison. He must have met him in there and then stolen his identity after he was released.'

'His prints weren't in the system?'

'We didn't take his prints and the bike had been wiped down completely so there were no prints to eliminate when we were investigating the kidnapping. Not even Marcus's. That Jason kid's prints should have been on the bike, too, but they weren't. Someone must have cleaned it before we got there on the morning of the kidnapping,' Imogen said.

'What do we know about his other victims?' DCI Kapoor asked.

'We know Millie, his first wife, died in suspicious circumstances and he collected on her life insurance. He had a firm alibi for the time of death, so he had an accomplice for that, too. As for other deaths he is behind . . . we may never know the real figure. I would wager there are more,' Imogen said.

'Not to mention what happened to the actual Julian Crow and Terry Harding: they were real people who don't seem to be around anymore. I guess we also need to assume there was once a real Peter Carlyle,' Webb added.

'Good point. If we get hold of him, we can ask him what happened to them.' Imogen agreed.

'Do we think Wakefield helped him get rid of his first wife, too then? Have they been working together for a long time?' Kapoor asked.

'We still have a lot of information to get through,' Jarvis said, not really adding anything to the conversation, but wanting to make his voice heard. Imogen could see he was annoyed that Webb was getting all the attention. Not everyone was cut out for CID.

'Right, OK. And we have no leads on where he might be right now?' DCI Kapoor said.

'We don't. He's good at disappearing,' Imogen repeated.

'Jarvis and Webb, I want you both going through all that paperwork with a fine-tooth comb. Find anything you can,' DCI Kapoor said.

'He must be absolutely cursing himself for losing that ransom money,' Walsh said.

'And cursing Jason Hitchin for calling the police – really Jason has been quite pivotal in us getting this far,' Imogen said.

'We've since spoken to Jason's ex-girlfriend's family now that they're back from holiday, but they don't want to press charges against Hitchin. And Sara Dunn – as she is now calling herself – is offering to pay for any damage Jason did to their property, and has asked to be put in touch with him. She wants to help him out for the part he played in identifying Marcus's kidnappers and I think it's taking her mind off her grief at the moment,' Walsh said.

'Good to know. OK, carry on going through those files. We might get lucky and find something Carlyle didn't think to hide. Imogen, can I see you privately?' DCI Kapoor said.

Imogen followed DCI Kapoor into her office, knowing this conversation was going to be about Adrian and wondering what he had said to her. Had Dean got through to him? Had Adrian told the DCI what happened to him? DCI Kapoor closed the office door and motioned Imogen towards a seat before sitting down on the edge of her own desk. Imogen had been trying to read her face in the briefing room, but she wasn't giving anything away.

'I spoke to Adrian. He told me his alibi, told me what happened to him,' the DCI said. Imogen could see she was shaken by it.

'Can we get him out now?' Imogen said, immediately starting to cry, surprised at how quickly the tears had come. She was so relieved not to have to lie about this to at least one person.

'It's probably not going to be tonight, but tomorrow definitely. Especially with all this new evidence. Good job on finding that boat. The fact that we now have the files from the boat as well as Wakefield's phone is a huge help to the case. There is footage from the argument with the neighbour, which is when Miles was the other side of town.' DCI Kapoor leaned forward and placed a hand on Imogen's shoulder.

'OK. Good. I don't want him in there. It must be killing him.'

'How are *you* doing? This must be hard for you.'

'My feelings don't matter at all. I'm such a selfish idiot. Over the last year I've had a million theories about his weird behaviour, but this wasn't one of them.'

'If Adrian's going to make it through this, he'll to need you to be strong, but being strong doesn't mean ignoring your own feelings and drowning in your own guilt.'

'It was so obvious. I'm supposed to be a detective, for Christ's sake. I was completely blind to his suffering. It didn't even occur to me. He's been going through that alone for months. I don't know if he will ever forgive me; I don't know if I can forgive myself. I should have seen it.'

'Would you like me to arrange for you to speak to a counsellor?'

'No. I'm fine. Really. I just want Adrian out and at home where he belongs.'

'He doesn't want to go on the record about his attack and so we need to get a watertight case together to prove without a doubt that Carlyle is Wakefield's killer.'

'We're working on it. We found a receipt for a coffee place just before the attack; Adrian used his bank card. I handed it over to Walsh; he's going to go and see if they remember him. I'm sure we have enough to get him out. Me and Gary are planning on pulling an all-nighter anyway. Getting Adrian out might seem like my personal primary concern right now but, in terms of this case, finding Marcus is still a priority.'

'Maybe it's time to put out a press release with Carlyle's face on it. He had his own child kidnapped by one, possibly two, violent ex-cons, which shows there are no limits to what this man will do. You get back to working on finding Marcus and I will issue a statement. I'll just have to check with the Dunns that they don't mind,' DCI Kapoor said.

'Thank you, ma'am.'

'Imogen, remember that I'm here if you need to talk. Don't bottle this up. You've both got a long road ahead of you. I feel I should also tell you that I have told Adrian he is welcome back here when he is ready.'

'You can do that?'

'I can.'

'Thank you.'

'I've got someone checking the CCTV at the various roads and intersections leading to the church around the time of Wakefield's murder. If we can get him on camera, he won't need to go on the record about his alibi. Keep the faith, we will get him out.'

'I'll speak to the Dunns and set up the press release,' Imogen said.

'Go on then,' DCI Kapoor said with a half-smile.

Imogen rushed back to Gary so they could sort and compile the evidence against Carlyle. Knowing that this time tomorrow she might have Adrian back and they could start to move forwards was a huge motivator. Imogen was tired but she didn't care. As soon as they found Marcus she would take some time off and sleep for a week if needs be. For now, she was happy to work all night to find Marcus and free Adrian.

Chapter Seventy-Eight

FOURTEEN DAYS MISSING

It was three a.m. Sleep was overrated anyway; Imogen didn't have time for that right now. Gary, Webb and Jarvis had all stayed late with her, looking equally despondent as they pored over the files and re-watched CCTV from any and all significant dates and locations, even though they had seen it all before.

Imogen had been staring at faces of people who had been in and out of the prison going back twelve years. Allowing for age and possible changes in appearance, so far she'd had no luck finding Carlyle. She'd seen some faces she recognised, people she had arrested, a couple whose deaths she had investigated, people she had questioned in connection with other crimes. After a while the images were all blurring into one homogenous blob with no distinguishing features or characteristics as she flipped through face after face after face.

That's when she saw him.

He was much thinner than the man she'd met, with a shaved head and a very angular face, all bones and hollows. It was him, though, the man they knew as Peter Carlyle. He looked rough around the edges, angry, hard. She read through his notes. Repeat offender, violence, theft, burglary, home invasion and lots of other petty offences going back to when he was eighteen, and he had a sealed juvenile record to boot. His real name was Jack Murphy.

'Webb, what was the name of that bloke we went to visit after Lomax? The one in St James Close?' she asked, knowing the answer already.

'Craig Murphy?'

'Lomax said the whole Murphy family were trouble, didn't he?'

'Wait a second,' Jarvis said, digging through a stack of his own handwritten notes.

'What is it?' Imogen said.

'That's the guy! The guy we had the tip about, the one with the kid in the boot of his car. Craig Murphy. I went to his house in St James Close.'

'Did you go inside the house?'

'No, but I spoke to him. He wasn't nervous at all; I didn't get any vibes off him.'

'Because he's a career criminal. I don't think he gets nervous around the police,' Imogen said, looking up Craig Murphy's file in the system. She had noted at the time she spoke to him his lack of reaction to her being police, but had ignored that niggle inside that it was an unusual response. 'In and out of prison and a jack of all trades by the look of it.'

'Why did you want to know about him?' Webb said.

'His cousin is a Jack Murphy. Look familiar?' she said, showing him and Jarvis the photo.

Webb's jaw dropped.

'That's Carlyle!' Jarvis exclaimed.

'Yes. I reckon that tip you got was legit. The neighbour *did* see him take a kid out of the boot of his car.'

'What do we do now?' Jarvis said, looking the most awake she had seen him in days.

Imogen pulled out her phone and hoped DI Walsh would forgive her for waking him up in the middle of the night.

'We get Marcus back.'

Chapter Seventy-Nine

The door forced off its hinges, Imogen followed the tactical unit as they barged inside Craig Murphy's house. She couldn't wait for them to clear the place. This felt like it, the last chance they had of ever finding Marcus.

He will be here.

It was as though she were trying to manifest him.

The house was messy, the décor feminine but dated. The smell of cannabis clung to every surface and the walls had thick, sticky nicotine streaks on top of the seventies wallpaper. The lounge had a coffee table littered with the paraphernalia that came with smoking pot – Rizlas, metal tins, bongs, pipes, the works – as well as a liberal sprinkling of tobacco, as though it had been used as confetti. There was no one home.

'There's a locked door up here,' a voice called out.

Imogen rushed up the stairs as they thumped the lock with the door ram. It sprang open.

Inside on the bed lay Marcus Carlyle. He was very pale, but seemed to be asleep.

'We need a medic,' Imogen said, afraid to touch him, worried she was wrong and she'd find he had no pulse.

'He's alive,' one of the officers said, after checking. Imogen reminded herself to breathe.

She rushed over and gently picked the boy up, and though he didn't wake he nuzzled into her.

'Looks like they gave him something to knock him

out,' the same officer said, pointing to a medicine bottle on the window sill.

'I'll get him down to the ambulance,' Imogen said, the officers parting and letting her through. 'Let's get you back to your mummy.'

He was dirty and pale, but he was alive. She didn't want to let him go now that she'd finally found him, but she handed him off to the paramedic who carefully placed him on a trolley and checked him over before nodding at Imogen. She hoped the nod meant he was going to be fine.

The adrenaline was the only thing keeping her going at the moment. In a daze of exhaustion, she entered the back of the ambulance and took a hold of Marcus's limp hand as he slept, wanting him to know he wasn't alone.

The sun was coming up as they arrived at the hospital. DCI Kapoor was waiting for them, looking immaculate as usual. There was never a hair out of place, a wrinkle or a crease. Imogen found it reassuring.

'Did you get Carlyle?' Kapoor asked.

'No, Marcus was alone, they'd dosed him up with something. Forensics are at the property now but there is no sign of him, or his cousin.'

'We've cut off a lot of his revenue streams. He's going to be looking for an easy mark. He will make a mistake. I know he will.'

'Now we have his real identity I'll go back and start looking into his real history, maybe that will give us something,' Imogen said.

'Not today you won't. You need to rest now. Marcus is safe. If you want to hang around until he is reunited with his mother then I completely understand, but you only have a few hours until Adrian gets out.'

'Really?'

'Yep. He gets out this morning. We can manage without you for a few hours.'

'You don't mind me bailing?'

'Give Adrian my regards,' DCI Kapoor said and rubbed Imogen on the arm.

Tired but full of nervous energy, Imogen didn't want to hang around. She just started to run.

She could hardly believe it. For days she had catastrophised Adrian's time in prison, certain he wouldn't get out of there alive and now it was really happening.

Just hold on a little longer. I'm coming.

Chapter Eighty

Adrian looked at the bed, glad he wouldn't be spending another night in here. Thankful that he had made it through without getting killed. He had been almost certain that if it was going to happen to anyone, it would be him. It had been difficult not to be fatalist about everything since the night he was attacked, as though he was destined for pain, misery and a brutal death.

He turned to Dean who was leaning against the wall, at ease as always. Their location didn't change the essence of who he was.

'I want to thank you for everything you've done for me in here,' Adrian said.

Dean smiled. 'I didn't do it for you.'

'You're a pretty amazing guy, Dean. I hope you know that. Maybe you don't consider me a friend, but I consider you one. I don't know how I would have got through this without you.'

'I don't really have friends,' Dean said, matter-of-factly.

'Well, you do now. I don't know if I can ever repay you, but if there is any way then let me know.'

'Stop now, you're making me blush,' Dean said, not blushing.

'At least let me buy you a beer when you get out.'

'Rather than a beer, maybe you could help get me a job. I hear the people you work for aren't averse to hiring people like me.'

'I could introduce you to Mick, he'll be able to get you an introduction.'

'I appreciate that.'

Johnson knocked on the door and then opened it. 'Time to go.'

Adrian followed Johnson in a daze. Was he really getting out? The charges against him had been dropped.

And so that was that. It was all like a bad dream that hadn't happened. Leaving the prison was much less of a bureaucratic process than coming in. He'd almost expected some kind of ceremony or going-away party but instead it just spat him out. He wasn't welcome anymore.

Imogen was waiting outside with her car. Her hair was wet and her skin glistened; she was not long out of the shower. She had clearly been crying and he felt responsible for that. He stood in front of her, unsure what to do, how to greet her. Unsure where they stood.

'I thought you would be at work. I was going to walk home,' he said, wanting to kiss her but desperate to get rid of his prison dirt first.

'I've been working all night, I go back in six hours. You can walk home if you want.' She smiled.

He opened the car door and got in the passenger side. He hadn't even been inside that long and yet sitting in the car felt so alien.

Imogen got in and drove them back to his house.

As they pulled round the corner into his street he was overcome with emotion, but he held back his feelings. There had been times when he wasn't sure if he was going to make it home at all. He could feel there was a lot on Imogen's mind – knew there was a lot they needed to talk about – but for now he just wanted to shower then go to sleep. He got out of the car and walked to the front door, glancing at the part of the road they had dumped him on that night. Would he ever be able to come home without thinking of that moment? So far he hadn't.

Inside, the house was almost exactly as he had left it. It felt strange being here again so much sooner than he'd anticipated, even though so much had happened since the last time he stood in this lounge. Once again, he was a completely different person.

'You OK?' Imogen asked.

'I'm going to shower. I need to before I can relax.'

'I can go back to my flat if you want to be alone.'

'I want you to stay. We can talk. I just need to get cleaned up first. I won't be long.'

'You hungry? I could make you something to eat, although come to think of it you've probably suffered enough.'

'I can't imagine anything better than one of your trademark burned and yet still somehow frozen pizzas right now.'

'Coming right up.' She smiled.

For the first time in a long time Adrian felt the shadow of optimism. He was hopeful that he could move forward. Knowing that Imogen was on his side had changed things. He didn't know why he'd thought she might not be. What happened had changed everything, and he'd thought it had broken him forever. But while it still drummed in the back of his mind, he found himself making space for more things. Looking forward more than looking back. He didn't feel the same level of self-loathing as he had before he told her. It wasn't until now that he realised how much of his energy he'd spent just thinking about telling her. It had been on the tip of his tongue for over a year, begging to be told, to be shared. But now that incessant noise in his mind had been silenced. The storm inside him had started to calm.

He came out of the shower and found Imogen was already lying on the bed with her eyes closed. He pulled on some clean clothes and settled down beside her, taking her hand in his. She nuzzled into him and he kissed her head.

'It's good to have you home,' Imogen said.

'It's good to be home. I missed you. Thank you, for getting me out.'

'It was a team effort,' Imogen said, but he knew the truth. He knew she had stopped at nothing to make sure he got out, just like DC Webb had said she would back when Adrian was in the holding cell.

He shuffled around onto his side to look at her. He felt peaceful, hopeful, with her next to him.

'Why don't you move in with me, like properly? You're here all the time anyway. I don't like it when you aren't here.'

'OK. But only on the condition that we get rid of your sofa, it's bloody horrible,' she said without hesitation, squeezing his hand.

'I'm sorry I lied to you, Imogen. I hope you can forgive me.'

'There is nothing to forgive. I'm just sorry you were dealing with this on your own for so long. I should have known. There is nothing we can do about the last year, but from now on it's important that you know I am with you. Together we *will* get through this.'

'Even with everything that's happened in the last few weeks, this is the most normal I have felt in months. It feels good to have you with me. I know it's not going to be exactly like it was before . . . you know . . . ever again, but I believe it can be good again. For the first time in a long time, I know I can get better.'

'Whatever you need,' she said looking up at him.

'Just you, that's all I need.'

The thought of lying here with Imogen like this was what had kept Adrian going when he was in the prison, and he was reminded how grateful he was for her.

He kissed her then, and even though they had kissed many times over the last year, this time there wasn't the constant thrumming of the voice in the back of his mind, telling him he wasn't good enough, telling him she deserved better, telling him he was disgusting for wanting this. For the first time in a long time he was in the moment and not trapped in his own mind. He kissed her deeper and pulled her towards him, sliding his hand under her T-shirt.

'We don't have to,' Imogen said.

'Yes, we do.'

Chapter Eighty-One

Jason was washing up after lunch. They had had a barbeque with Christopher, Jean's friend, who had brought over some steak and giant prawns. They had all eaten until they were bursting and they'd laughed and drunk fancy wine. Jason didn't remember seeing his mother happier than she was at the moment, but whether that was down to Christopher or the fact that Doug was no longer in the picture, he couldn't say. He would be lying if he said he wasn't relieved there was no chance his father would walk back through that door and screw their lives up all over again.

Even Luke was different, although Jason knew that was because of the stacks of cash they had found at Safari House. Jason had managed to convince Luke they shouldn't touch it until they had spoken to their mother about it. It wasn't like she wouldn't ask where the money had come from anyway and Jason didn't want to go through his life lying to the people he cared about.

From where he was standing at the sink, he could make out the sound of his mother laughing in the garden, where they were playing a game of cards. It was good to hear it. Luke was upstairs on the phone to a girl he had been seeing just before he got put away. Life was starting to look up. When Jason had finished clearing the kitchen – part of his promise to himself to be a better person than before – he grabbed a tub of chocolate ice cream and plonked himself on the sofa.

He turned on the TV; it always started up on the news channel. They were talking about the boy who had been kidnapped. He felt the pangs of guilt and, just as he was about to flick over, several pictures appeared on screen – three wedding photos, each with the bride's face pixelated out. It was an appeal for a man needed urgently to help with police questioning. The man was currently in Jason's back garden.

They were looking for Christopher.

Jason turned the TV off and went upstairs to find Luke. He could hear him on the phone in the bathroom so he banged on the door.

'Go away, dude,' Luke said.

'Luke, open the door,' Jason said, pounding even harder than before.

'Desperate, are you?' Christopher said from behind Jason.

Jason spun around and instinctively pressed himself against the door. Christopher's smile faltered for a moment and then readjusted. Jason could tell that he knew Jason knew something.

'Yeah. I'm going to shit myself if I don't get in there sharpish. I think it was the prawns,' he said, slapping his hand against the door urgently.

'Your mum mentioned it's her birthday soon. What do you think she might want?' Christopher said without cracking a smile. There was no warmth whatsoever in his gaze, just cold eyes that wouldn't let up for a second.

Jason felt himself fall backwards as the door opened. Luke thumped him in the back but, just as Jason tried to regain his footing he saw Christopher lunging forwards. Jason had barely enough time to slam the bathroom door and lock it with him and Luke inside.

'What the fuck?' Luke said.

'Christopher was just on the news, I saw it,' Jason whispered.

'What do you mean?'

'The police are looking for him in connection with that kidnapping, they were calling him Peter Carlyle, and other names. Have you got your phone? We need to call the cops.'

'Nah, it's dead; I was cut off. I was just about to put it on charge. Where's yours?'

'Mine's charging downstairs. Shit, shit, shit.'

There was a gentle knock on the door.

'Everything OK in there?' Christopher said.

'Out in a second,' Jason said.

'You can drop the pretence, boy. I know what you saw.'

'I didn't see anything,' Jason snapped.

'I had hoped I would be able to do this the nice way. Open the door.'

'We're not opening the door,' Luke said.

'I want that money you took.'

'I didn't take anything,' Jason said, the anxiety rising inside him. The fact was, they did have the money, although Luke hadn't told Jason where he had put it, as he knew Jason wanted to take it to the police.

'You've got five minutes. After that, I'm going to kill your mother.'

Chapter Eighty-Two

Imogen had left Adrian sleeping on the bed and come back into work. The relief of having him home was immense. The weight of their failing relationship was no longer crushing, and now she knew what the problem between them was, they could start moving forwards. She knew there would be more downs than ups, but at least she had a reason for him pulling away from her at every opportunity. As much as she wished it hadn't happened, she was at least glad that she knew about it now. Going through something like that alone must have been hell.

Gregory Dunn had lawyered up to the eyeballs and was already trying to limit their access to Marcus when he eventually woke up, claiming he would still be very distressed from his ordeal. He probably wasn't wrong. Getting Marcus back to his mother had been Imogen's primary concern and so it felt wrong to put him through anything else just so they could arrest his father. They would just have to find Jack Murphy, or Peter Carlyle as they knew him, another way.

Gabriel Webb clearly hadn't taken the break the DCI had offered them all. He squinted as he leafed through page after page of evidence, hunting for anything that might indicate where Carlyle had gone.

'Any luck?' Imogen said, grabbing a stack of papers from his desk and looking through them.

'I checked those already. Nothing.'

'I may as well give them a squiz as well.' She could feel the fatigue radiating from him; just being near him made her want to yawn. 'Why don't you go and grab some shut-eye, Webb?'

'I'm fine. I can do this.'

'We don't get paid overtime for this, you know?'

'I'd like to carry on.'

'Where's Jarvis?'

'Walsh sent him home about two hours ago. He was on CCTV duty. Couldn't find anything on that Mondeo you took pics of at the boatyard, unfortunately. If it was a rental then it was from somewhere out of town as none of the car hire places in the city have one rented out at the moment. It's also possible Carlyle just bought it for cash.'

She sat in her chair and continued reading through the paperwork. There were no lines to read between, there was nothing they didn't know already.

As if by magic, Gary appeared, looking excited. He walked straight into the DCI's office with his laptop open, raising his eyebrows at Imogen on the way. Imogen watched as they talked inside, trying to decipher what they were saying, although her lipreading must be off – she was sure she saw Gary say the word 'zebra'. DCI Kapoor caught her eye through the window and ushered her over.

'Gary's got something. Come on,' Imogen said to Webb, dropping the files on her desk and heading for the DCI's office, Webb following closely behind her.

'Have you ever heard of a thing called What Three Words?' Gary said excitedly.

Imogen shook her head.

'The postcode thing?' Gabriel said.

'Exactly!' Gary said with more excitement than Imogen had seen from him in a long time.

'Explain?' Imogen said.

'Basically, this company decided to revolutionise global location mapping by giving each three-metre square anywhere in the world its own location marker by using three random words. So every single three-metre square on a map, anywhere in the world, can be found using these three words.'

'And what's that got to do with us?' Imogen said, still confused.

'Oh shit, the texts?' Gabriel said.

'Yes!' Gary said again, clearly warming to Webb now.

'He discusses locations in the texts?' Imogen said.

'When Sara Dunn was in hospital after being stabbed, Carlyle received a text with three words: Yellow, Zebra and Lamp. We didn't know who the text was from or what it was about so it didn't really register as anything important. We thought maybe it was about a yellow zebra lamp which is, of course, ridiculous.'

'And that's a place, is it?' Once again, Imogen struggled with Gary's inability to get to the point without drip, drip, dripping out the information.

'I don't know why I hadn't thought of it before.'

'Where is it?'

'It's Jason Hitchin's home. It was sent just before the break-in and subsequent murder,' Gary said, looking almost relieved to have been forced to get to the point.

'Boss, if he thinks Jason still has that money, he will try to get it back. The home invaders ransacked the place and didn't find anything, but I wouldn't put it past Carlyle to try again. He sees that money as his and he not only wants it back, he might even need it to get away properly, with most of his other covers blown and his accounts frozen. We know he worms his way into people's lives and manipulates them. He could be there right now. It's the best lead we have had in days. The only lead.' Imogen shot an imploring look at the DCI. If Carlyle thought the Hitchins had the money he would do whatever it took to get it. They already knew he was capable of anything.

'Take Webb and go. Hurry. I'll send back-up.'

They both rushed out to the car. Jason Hitchin didn't live but three miles from the station; they would just have to floor it and hope they weren't too late.

Chapter Eighty-Three

Jason and Luke pressed against the bathroom door as Christopher pounded on it from the other side, trying to force his way in.

'You're running out of time,' Christopher said.

'If you touch one hair on my mother's head you will never find out where that money is,' Luke screamed.

'Keep your voice down. You don't want your mother to get suspicious. If she does, I will be forced to deal with her. You won't be able to stop me from in there. Anyway. Time's up. Remember. You both did this,' Christopher said before walking down the stairs. They heard the thunk of the latch on the back door opening. He was going back outside to their mother.

'What do we do? Do we call the cops?' Jason said.

'Then they will find out about the money and we'll lose it,' Luke said.

'Think about what you're saying. He is going to kill Mum.'

'Not if I kill him first,' Luke said before opening the door and rushing out. He bounded down the stairs and Jason raced straight into his mother's bedroom to use the phone. He picked it up but there was no dial tone. The line had been cut. He had to get to his phone downstairs. He pushed the anxiety that was bubbling to the surface deeper and hurried down the stairs. He could hear shouting coming from the garden, but he couldn't

380

think about that right now. He sped into the lounge to find his phone. It was on the table, but it had been smashed. It was unusable. Christopher had thought of everything.

He was starting to feel hopeless. When he went back into the hallway, he heard a tap on the front door. He opened it to find the police detective he had spoken to about the men he saw in the van. DS Grey.

'Please, you have to help us. That guy on the news, he's in the garden. He said he's going to kill my mum if we don't give him the ransom money that we stole.' He started to cry, he was so relieved to see her.

'Do you have the money?' DS Grey asked.

'Yes. But I didn't when I spoke to you. I didn't know where it was. Luke had an idea where it might be and we went and looked. We found it. We were going to give it back though. Please, stop him!'

'Is he armed?'

'I don't think so. Maybe with a knife. He was surprised that we figured it out. I think he thought he had longer.'

'Just wait in the lounge for a moment please, Jason. I know you probably want to help but it's better if you stay out of the way,' DS Grey said to him. She had a reassuring smile and he trusted her.

He stepped backwards into the lounge and she closed the door. For now all he could hear were muffled instructions through the door. He paced anxiously, clutching his hair. He couldn't lose his mother, too. That money was cursed and he wanted nothing to do with it. He just wanted his old life back, back when the biggest problem he had was Amanda snogging someone else. He sat on the sofa and buried his head in his arms, trying to block the world out until everything went back to normal.

Chapter Eighty-Four

This was it, the final stretch, make or break, do or die. Peter Carlyle – Jack Murphy – was in the garden and Imogen needed to get him into custody. He was as dangerous a man as they had ever dealt with, and as they might never know the extent of the damage he had done over the years, the least she could do was make sure he wasn't free to hurt anyone else.

'DC Webb, would you grab me a stab vest from the car? Then you look after Jason for me. I'll see what's going on outside.'

Webb slipped out the front door again. Imogen listened to the commotion in the back yard, the raised voices in the garden. Webb re-entered the house and handed her the stab vest.

'Will you be all right?'

'Peachy. Call and check on that back-up though, please, and make sure Jason is safe.'

Gabriel pulled out his phone and dialled as Imogen made her way to the back door, which was slightly ajar. She stayed pressed against the wall, hoping Carlyle was too preoccupied to notice her. She could hear Luke Hitchin screaming at his mother, telling her she had fucked up again, that she had brought someone worse than their father into their lives. Jean Hitchin sobbed as Carlyle told Luke he had bitten off more than he could chew.

As Imogen stepped outside, she saw Carlyle with a knife poised to drive into Jean Hitchin's ear, his arm locked around her throat as she sat in the garden chair.

'Carlyle,' Imogen said, 'put the knife down.'

'DS Grey?' He seemed surprised to see her there and it gave her some small satisfaction to know she hadn't walked straight into a trap.

'Put the knife down and we can talk, Carlyle.'

'I don't want to talk. I want my fucking money,' he said.

'I don't know what you're talking about,' Jean said.

'I told you. If you touch her you get nothing,' Luke said.

'Luke, is it?' Imogen said.

'I can deal with this,' Luke said through gritted teeth, holding a kitchen knife out in front of him.

'I need you to step away. I will deal with this situation. Let me talk to him. You just got out of prison, don't make things difficult for yourself. Your brother needs you here at home with him.'

Luke reluctantly stepped back just in time for DC Jarvis to appear outside. She wasn't sure she wanted him as back-up. He wasn't even wearing a stab vest. DC Webb followed after him.

'So, we know Carlyle isn't your real name. How long have you been doing this? Do you even remember your real name?'

'My real name doesn't matter.'

'How many people have you killed, Jack? How many children?'

'I told Sara I didn't want children. That was not my idea.'

'Worked out for you though, didn't it? Two lots of life insurance for half the work. Did you not care for Marcus at all?'

'He was an obstacle,' Carlyle said, closing his eyes tight. Trying to push any memories of Marcus out of his mind, she assumed.

'We found him. We found Marcus, he's safe, he's alive. Your little boy is safe,' she said, unsure whether she was trying to comfort him or piss him off.

Carlyle squeezed his eyes shut even tighter, as though trying to concentrate. 'If you had just stayed out of it I would be gone by now! I just want my money!'

'What was *your* father like? Did he love you?' she pushed.

'The only time I ever saw my father was in a prison visitors' room once a year. The rest of the time it was just me and my stupid mother. She made me realise that women will fall for anything. You should have seen the string of losers she brought through our house.'

'Is she still alive? Your mother?' Imogen asked.

'Oh no. You don't get to hear my sad story. I'm leaving now. I'm taking Jean with me and if anyone follows us, I will kill her.'

'I'm going to get you. I want you to know that's a promise. Even if you get away right now. I'm not going to stop until you're in prison.'

'I've been to prison before. Prison doesn't scare me,' he said, pulling Jean out of her chair and dragging her back towards the garden gate.

Luke Hitchin lunged forward and DC Jarvis tackled him to the ground.

When Imogen glanced down at them she saw blood. One of them was hurt.

'DC Jarvis, are you hurt?'

Imogen was conflicted about whether to chase after Carlyle and Jean Hitchin, or stay and look after DC Jarvis. DC Webb didn't seem to have the same reservation, taking off after Carlyle.

'It's not me. It's not my blood,' Jarvis said, scrabbling to stand up. 'The knife must have got him when he fell.'

'You should have secured that knife before you tackled him; call an ambulance and tend to the victim. Where is DI Walsh?'

'He's with the Jason kid. He kept trying to get out here.'

'Put pressure on the wound. Remember your training, Jarvis,' Imogen barked.

She rushed to the back gate and out into an alley that led to an adjacent road where she found Jean Hitchin heaped on the ground but – thankfully – in one piece. Imogen put a hand on her.

'Are you all right? Are you hurt? Where did they go?'

'That way,' Jean said as she pointed.

Imogen ran to the end of the road in the direction Jean had indicated. As she turned the corner she saw Webb halfway down the hill. He was tall and had a long stride – she wasn't sure if she could catch up to him. She raced back to where she'd parked the car by the Hitchin house and pulled out without checking, almost taking out a cyclist as she swung the car over to the wrong side of the road. She could see the cyclist shouting at her in the rear-view mirror but she just waved an apology. Catching up with Webb, she could see he was still too far away from Carlyle, but he was gaining on him. She remembered from the first time they met that Webb had asthma, but he didn't seem to be showing any signs of it now. She drove past Carlyle and pulled over, quickly calling in her location before jumping out of the car and turning to intercept him.

'Give it up, Carlyle! There's nowhere to go.'

He seemed shocked to see her there and slowed a little before turning down a side road that led to the riverside when he realised Webb was still hot on his heels. Imogen swore under her breath before slamming the car door and starting to run herself. Propelled by the pain and anguish this man had caused so many people, she increased her speed. Carlyle must be running out of steam by now, but he was a survivor by nature and she knew he would probably die rather than stop running. Part of her hoped she got to see that.

She could see the gap closing between Webb and Carlyle, heard the anguished groans as Carlyle pushed himself harder, faster. But then, like a leopard taking out a weak gazelle, Webb lunged forwards, sweeping Carlyle's feet out from under him. Within a few seconds Imogen was there too, with her knee pinning Carlyle's back as he struggled for breath. She secured his hands before Webb effortlessly pulled him to his feet.

'You OK?' she asked.

Webb nodded, but looked quite pale. She grabbed Carlyle's arm and started dragging him back towards the main road where she'd left the car, knowing full well Carlyle wasn't done trying to escape. She could almost hear him thinking about how to destabilise her and take off again, so she pushed him out in front of her so he had no way of knocking her off her feet. The sound of sirens got louder and closer and Imogen breathed a sigh of relief when she saw the uniformed officers running towards them. She didn't even want to process him at this point, she just wanted to get back to Adrian.

Back at the car, she watched the uniforms put Carlyle in the rear seat before turning to Webb.

'You did it, you got him,' Imogen said. Not even giving Carlyle a second thought; he didn't matter anymore, he'd been caught.

'*We* did it.'

'Just so you know, I'm going to be singing your praises to the DCI. Your tenacity in this case helped us get ahead of things. Carlyle was a bad guy. We got him off the streets, stopped him from hurting anyone else.'

'What happens now?'

'We get as much evidence as possible on him and pass it on; hopefully it will be enough to put him away for a long time. We still have a lot to do, but Marcus is safe and Carlyle is in custody. We can take the foot off the gas for a while. Get in the car, we'll go back to the station now and square things with DCI Kapoor.'

Gabriel got in the car next to Imogen. Whatever signals she thought she had been getting from him before seemed to be completely absent now, making her think maybe it had all been in her head, making her feel guilty as though it was something she was looking for, not something that was there. She had to stop beating herself up for what she thought was going on; it was more important that she focused on Adrian and his recovery than her own guilt. What was past was past, there was no changing that now. The future was all that mattered.

Chapter Eighty-Five

After finishing a quick debriefing at the station, Imogen headed over to the hospital where they had taken the Hitchins. She couldn't wait to be done with this case and to get back to Adrian, but she had to see it through. Adrian would understand.

Luke Hitchin had been admitted to hospital with what were – thankfully – just superficial injuries, and the missing ransom money was being recovered from its hiding place and would soon be returned to Gregory Dunn, minus the few thousand pounds that Doug had burned through before he was murdered.

Jason Hitchin was sitting outside his brother's ward biting his nails. His mother was inside at Luke's bedside. They were chatting and laughing but Imogen could see the pain behind their jovial facades. They were both putting a brave face on for each other.

'Hey, Jason,' Imogen said softly so as not to startle him.

'Hi, DS Grey. What's happened? Why are you here? Is there something wrong?'

'Everything's OK. Peter Carlyle is in custody; he's not getting out any time soon. I wanted to talk to your family. Will you come in with me?'

He nodded and stood up. She pushed through to the ward and saw both Luke and Jean's faces tense as they saw her.

'They've still got him. He's inside,' Jason said before anyone else had a chance to.

'What do you want then? Is this about the money?' Luke said, looking down, guilt all over his face.

'Actually, some good news.'

'Good news we could do with,' Jean said.

'To say thank you for returning the ransom and providing information that led to the boy's safe recovery, his grandfather wants to give you the thirty-thousand-pound reward. Jason handing in the photograph of the kidnappers led to us finding the people responsible for Marcus's kidnapping and ultimately to recovering Marcus.'

'Really?' Luke said, confused.

'That's not all. He heard about what happened today with Peter Carlyle, the man you knew as Christopher, and as he feels partially responsible for what happened, he would like to offer you a property to live in rent-free for the next year.'

Jean started to cry and Luke grabbed her hand and squeezed it.

'Why would he do that?' Luke said.

'I think he feels bad that he didn't know what a bad guy he was. Maybe this will make him feel a bit better about that. He knows Jason is the reason we found out how bad he was, and inadvertently Jason's information contributed to the safe return of Marcus Carlyle, the little boy. I think this is his way of saying thank you. He almost lost his grandson.'

'Can I thank him in person? I want to do something for him. I don't know what,' Jason said.

'I'll speak to him and find out.'

'Thank you, officer,' Jean said, smiling and teary, pulling her boys towards her into a hug.

* * *

Imogen walked out of the hospital feeling better than she had done in a long while. Even though Carlyle had got away with so much, there was nothing she could do but compile all the evidence and give it to CPS. Tomorrow they would go through everything. This wasn't his first rodeo, but she knew that once Gary started to do a deep dive on the man, Carlyle didn't stand a chance. Imogen would also send his photo out to various districts to see if they had any recollection of dealing with him.

There was something still bothering her though – they had never found the second kidnapper. They would question Carlyle about it but the chances of him being forthcoming were unlikely. All the evidence pointed towards it being Craig Murphy, as it was his house they'd found Marcus in and he was Carlyle's cousin. It seemed like a no-brainer. But no one had seen or heard from Craig Murphy since Imogen and Webb had spoken to him outside the house a week ago. When she was back in the office, she would put the case together and see if any leads emerged.

All of that could wait for now though. She was exhausted and she just wanted to get back to Adrian. She was excited to see him; she had forgotten how long it had been since she had felt this way. She got in the car and hurried home.

Chapter Eighty-Six

Imogen arrived at home to find Adrian had cooked a huge meal. It was far too much for the two of them but he seemed so pleased with himself so she ate more than she wanted to, until she had to undo her cords. He stared at her across the table, his eyes full of mischief. She had missed this side of him.

'What?' she finally said, smiling.

'I missed this. I missed us,' he said, tilting his head and sliding his hand across the table. She took it and he pulled her towards him until she had no choice but to sit on his lap. He kissed her.

'I missed it, too. It's good to have you back,' she said, trying not to look as sad as she felt.

'I'm not going to lie, Imogen. We're going to have good days and bad days.'

'Now, at least, we can go through them together.'

'What did I do to deserve you?' He looked up at her. Eye contact.

She focused on those beautiful big eyes, eyes that had been avoiding her for months. It was so good to be able to do this; it felt like home.

'Very bad things,' she said, kissing him, forcing him back into the chair rest, savouring this moment she had been unsure she would ever have with him again.

They stood up, abandoning the leftover food and moving over to the sofa.

'Let's go sofa-shopping at the weekend,' Adrian said.

'You sure? That's a big commitment. Who will get custody if we break up?' Imogen murmured.

'I'll take it for term times and you get it for holidays and either Easter or Christmas,' he said, kissing her again, pulling at her top.

'Sounds good to me,' she whispered breathlessly between kisses.

'Let's give this old girl a proper send-off then,' Adrian said into her ear, slow and low, all the hairs on her neck standing up on end, his breath against her skin more than welcome.

She leaned back to let him take control, unsure what she was allowed to do, still feeling guilty for everything she had thought for the last year. She was overthinking things, she knew she was.

Adrian stopped what he was doing and sat up.

'Why did you stop?' she said, folding her arms across her bare chest.

'You stopped first.'

'Sorry. Just distracted.'

'No, it's more than that. I thought we were going to try honesty?' he said, the sparkle in his eyes fading, replaced with something else – insecurity maybe.

'I just don't want you to think you have to pretend or do anything you don't want to do with me. I can wait as long as you need.'

'You think I'm faking it?' he said, eyebrows raised in incredulity.

'Not faking it, no. I just worry that you're rushing yourself to please me. I'm happy to just—'

'Have a sexless relationship,' he interrupted. 'How long do you think you would be happy with that, Imogen?' he said, definitely annoyed now.

'As long as it takes. I don't care about that.'

'I do. I care. This last year, not feeling able to be close to you has felt like torture. I know I can't go back and I know things are different, but I want to try to get back to what we had. They can't take that from me. I refuse to let them.'

'Then I won't let them either,' she said, leaning forward and undoing his trousers. They kissed again and sank into the leather sofa that Imogen hated so much. She could feel the cold leather on her back but she didn't care. Even arguing was better than the moratorium their relationship had been in for the last year. She followed his lead – knowing this was what he wanted made it easier. This felt like the beginning of a new chapter. Maybe they had a chance after all.

Chapter Eighty-Seven

Adrian got dressed for work with a smile on his face. Imogen had already left but things were starting to slot into place. He was taking back control. He could do this. Returning to Shieldwall felt strange after the last few weeks. Keeping him on the books hadn't even seemed to be a question. They'd accepted him back with open arms. A quick call to his line manager and that had been it. All had been forgiven. Welcome back. No officious hoops to jump through. He was a little less certain how he felt about them. The fact that Wakefield had done some freelance work for the company posed an interesting dilemma. Wakefield had surveilled him, and that had led to the assault. He wasn't sure how much Shieldwall knew about what their employees did on the side but he wanted to find out.

Adrian didn't want to make any assumptions, but still a nagging voice in the back of his head told him that the name of the man he was looking for, the man who had raped him, would also be in those Shieldwall employee files. Ignoring his first instinct to run a mile, he had quickly realised he was being presented with a unique opportunity. He was already on the inside – granted, he hadn't seen much – but he could play the game harder now that he knew what kind of game it was. As soon as he got a whiff of anything illegal, he would speak to Imogen about it; for now though, he was going to keep his suspicions to himself and take advantage of the access he had to the company.

Mick was waiting for him outside the house. He jumped in the car.

'Where are we going?' he asked Adrian.

'The prison.'

'Glutton for punishment you are.'

'There's someone I want you to meet,' Adrian said.

'Made friends in there, did you?'

'Just one.'

When Mick pulled up outside the prison, Dean was standing by the side of the road, waiting, looking just as cool as he always did. Adrian motioned for Dean to jump in the back of the car and he obliged.

'Adrian. Good to see you. Thanks for this,' Dean said.

'Dean, this is my friend, Mick Roper. Mick, this is my friend, Dean Kinkaid.'

Adrian wasn't sure but he could have sworn Mick reacted to Dean's name.

'Nice to meet you,' Mick said, staring in the rear-view mirror.

'Adrian tells me you're the guy to come to if I'm looking for a job.'

'Straight to the point. I like it,' Mick said.

'Yeah, I think it's about time I went straight and I heard your company doesn't mind hiring people with a chequered past.'

'Lots of situations arise that require a variety of skills. As long as you can prove yourself on the job then you're laughing.'

'I'm sure you won't be disappointed with me.' Dean smiled into the mirror, his eyes locked on Mick.

'I'll speak to our line manager and see what we can do.

I'm sure you'll get in though, mate. It's been a busy time for us, and we've lost a few people recently,' Mick said.

Adrian wondered if he was referring to Wakefield.

Adrian looked at Dean in the back seat. He was up to something and, though he didn't know what that something might be, it seemed like Mick had an inkling. The tension in the car was palpable. This was a side of Mick Adrian hadn't seen before, the scheming side. Adrian felt like a total gooseberry, the third wheel on a date he had gatecrashed without invitation.

They remained in silence for the rest of the journey, Mick and Dean occasionally glancing at each other in the mirror as though they were in some kind of stand-off.

Mick dropped Dean off at the Premier Inn and Adrian saw him watching the car until they were out of sight.

'Do you know Dean?' Adrian said.

'Nope. Never met him before. Why?'

'Just wondered, you two both seemed weird.'

'All in your head, mate. I'm always a bit wary about strangers I pick up from prison.'

'OK. What are we working on today?'

'The CEO of Channing Finance wants us to check on her dog.'

'You're kidding?'

'Nope. Nasty break-up, ex got the dog. She thinks he did it just to spite her and is mistreating it, so we have to go spend the next five days watching the house and seeing how often he takes the dog for a walk, among other things. She has a platinum account with Shieldwall so we couldn't say no.'

'I think I'd rather go back to prison,' Adrian joked. Really, a low-key dog-watching stakeout sounded like heaven right now.

Chapter Eighty-Eight

THREE WEEKS LATER

Dean Kinkaid had been working at Shieldwall Security for two weeks now. The stuff they were making him do he could manage in his sleep, so he was basically getting paid to sit on his arse all day. He wasn't really interested in getting a regular job, he wasn't interested in whatever the hell it was that Shieldwall were getting him to do. Their name had come up more than once during Dean's day-to-day dealings over the past few years.

Elias Papas, Dean's de facto boss and benefactor, had always steered clear of them and used Dean for any 'security' jobs instead. It looked like they worked in the same way he did, interpreting the law as merely a suggestion, often requiring a little creative interpretation, and, as their profile had been growing in the last few years, what was at first a minor inconvenience to Dean was becoming an obstacle.

Was there any low they wouldn't stoop to to get the job done? What he was interested in at the moment, however, was what had happened to Adrian and what involvement Shieldwall might have had in it. Dean was more than a little morally ambiguous, but one thing he couldn't leave unchallenged was rapists for hire.

Every morning, Dean would go in early and bring

Allison a coffee and a Belgian bun. She was so close to being completely smitten with him.

So smitten that she might let him into the file room.

So smitten that she might let him look at the employee file of one particular man who had done some freelance work for Shieldwall in the past.

A man called Craig Murphy.

The man who raped Adrian Miles.

THE END

Acknowledgements

As I write these acknowledgments, I am sitting in the attic self-isolating with COVID-19, which I caught on only my third meeting out to see friends in eighteen months. I waited until all restrictions were lifted, I wore the masks and sanitised regularly and followed all the rules – still unfortunately here I am. What I am thankful for is the massive privilege of living in a country where the vaccine that allowed me to feel safe enough to finally do those things is both accessible and free, without the vaccine I would undoubtedly be much sicker and/or in hospital.

Thank you to the people who read my books, I love receiving your messages of support, it really means a lot. I try to respond if I can. Also thank you to the members of the Facebook book group CRIME SUSPECT who are always wonderfully encouraging. If you aren't a member and love reading crime fiction, come join us.

Thank you to my family, especially in this last year when we have all had to work around each other in the house twenty-four hours a day.

Thank you to my agent Hannah, and Diane and everyone at Northbank Talent for your continued hard work on my behalf.

Thank you to Rachel, Helen and Cara at Avon for your amazing input and editorial support.

It's been a tough bunch of months, here's to the light at the end of the tunnel.

One summer. One stranger.
One killer . . .

The hottest thriller of the summer.

Available in paperback,
ebook and audiobook now.

Everything you think
you know is a lie . . .

The second Miles and Grey novel from
the Queen of Crime.

Available in paperback,
ebook and audiobook now.

Some things can't be forgiven . . .

'All hail the new Queen of Crime' *Heat*

The Angel

Some things can't be forgiven...

THE *SUNDAY TIMES* BESTSELLER
KATERINA DIAMOND

The third instalment in the Miles and Grey series.

Available in paperback,
ebook and audiobook now.

No one can protect
you from your past . . .

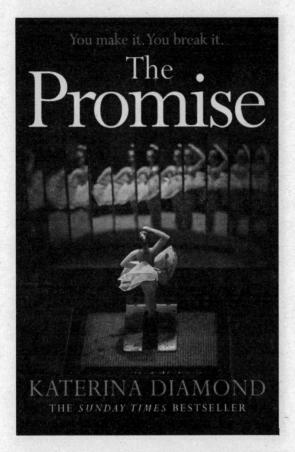

You make it. You break it.

The
Promise

KATERINA DIAMOND

THE *SUNDAY TIMES* BESTSELLER

The fourth in deliciously dark
Miles and Grey series.

Available in paperback,
ebook and audiobook now.

Their darkest secrets
won't stay buried forever . . .

The fifth explosive, twisty novel
in the Miles and Grey series.

Available in paperback,
ebook and audiobook now.

I'm alive. But I can't be saved . . .

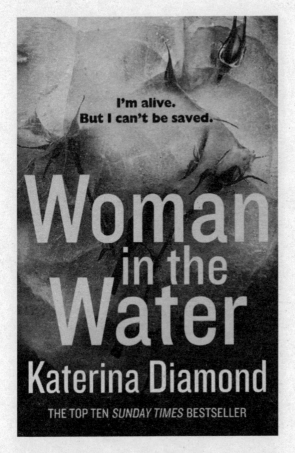

I'm alive.
But I can't be saved.

Woman
in the
Water

Katerina Diamond

THE TOP TEN *SUNDAY TIMES* BESTSELLER

The sixth in the Sunday Times
bestselling Miles and Grey series.

Available in paperback,
ebook and audiobook now.